CW00522317

**Stephen Baxter**

**Justina Robson**

**Eric Brown**

**Geoff Ryman**

**Jaine Fenn**

**Martin Sketchley**

**Peter F. Hamilton**

**Kari Sperring**

**Ian R. MacLeod**

**Adrian Tchaikovsky**

**Paul McAuley**

**Ian Whates**

**Juliet E. McKenna**

**Anne Nicholls**

**One of a Special Numbered Limited Edition Signed by the Authors**

**This is Number**

20

# Burning Brightly:
# 50 Years of Novacon

# Burning Brightly: 50 Years of Novacon

Edited by Ian Whates

NewCon Press
England

First edition, published in the UK, November 2021 by
NewCon Press

NCP 265 (hardback)
NCP 266 (softback)

10 9 8 7 6 5 4 3 2 1



"Chiron" by Stephen Baxter first appeared in Novacon Souvenir Booklet 1993
"The Spheres" by Iain M. Banks first appeared in Novacon Souvenir Booklet 2010
"Heatwave" by Anne Nicholls first appeared in Novacon Souvenir Booklet 2015
"Alien TV" by Paul McAuley first appeared in Novacon Souvenir Booklet 1998
"Softlight Sins" by Peter F. Hamilton first appeared in Novacon Souvenir Booklet 1997
"Erie Lackawanna Song" by Justina Robson first appeared in Novacon Souvenir Booklet 2009
Through the Veil by Juliet E. McKenna first appeared in Novacon Souvenir Booklet 2016
The Coming of Enkidu by Geoff Ryman first appeared in Novacon Souvenir Booklet 1989
"The Ships of Aleph" by Jaine Fenn first appeared in Novacon Souvenir Booklet 2012
"Acts of Defiance" by Eric Brown is original to this anthology
"Canary Girls" by Kari Sperring is original to this anthology
"Red Sky in the Morning" by Adrian Tchaikovsky is original to this anthology
"The God of Nothing" by Iain R. MacLeod is original to this anthology
"Bloodbirds" by Martin Sketchley is original to this anthology

ISBN: 978-1-914953-02-6 (hardback)
978-1-914953-03-3 (softback)

Cover art by David A. Hardy
Cover layout and typesetting by Ian Whates

Thanks to Teika Marija Smits for her editorial eye when too many plates were spinning

# CONTENTS:

# Burning Brightly: An Introduction

By Rog Peyton

I was chairman of Novacon 9 way back in 1979 when the very first Novacon Special was published. Guest of Honour was my good friend Christopher Priest and I'd asked Chris if he wanted to write something for the programme book thinking he might want to write a few words. He did but it wasn't a 'few'. He sent a 30-odd page manuscript entitled *The Making of 'The Lesbian Horse'*. The programme book was already fairly big and the inclusion of this would have been near-impossible. Should I reject it? No, this was not an option. Could we produce it as a separate item and charge a small fee? Possibly. Presenting this idea to the rest of the committee resulted in total agreement, though, as we were becoming the biggest Novacon to date, we were already showing what would be a good profit. So it was decided to actually 'give it away free'. Thank the rest of the committee for that – the bookseller in me shuddered at the thought but the fannish part of me agreed!

Of course, this was before home computers so the whole thing had to be retyped. A cover had to be designed, which I did with aid of Letraset – a laborious transfer system which some of the older among you may remember. Not recommended.

Novacon 10 followed – again, I was chairman and our Guest of Honour was Brian Aldiss. Explaining to Brian what had happened with the previous year's Novacon Special, I asked him if he had anything we could use – a long article or story – for free? This was Brian's turn to shudder but he then remembered he had a short piece, "A Romance of the Equator", that had only appeared in a newspaper a few weeks previously. Not first publication but would it suffice? Of course it would – and it duly became the second Novacon Special.

The committee of Novacon 11 managed to get a story from their Guest of Honour, Bob Shaw, by which point, it's fair to say, the Novacon Special had become a tradition. But there wasn't one for Novacon 12. I was chairman again and the GoH was Harry Harrison.

Harry provided a very short piece, just 3 or 4 pages – far too short in fact to produce a Special and unfortunately there wasn't time for Harry to write a longer piece.

Novacon 13 did provide a Special from their GoH Lisa Tuttle, and there has been one every year since. I produced every Special from 9-18 and designed the covers of all using Letraset. Anyone want a load of partially used sheets?

Over the years there have been suggestions of collecting all the Specials into hardcopy volumes but nothing has ever come of that idea. Until now. Obviously not all 40 of the Specials but just a select few. As I write this introduction, I have no idea how many or which pieces will be in the finished contents list but we owe a great thank you to every Guest who has, over the years, allowed one of their works, fiction or non-fiction, to be published for our entertainment. Thank you.

*Rog Peyton*
*Birmingham*
*August 2021*

# Chiron

Stephen Baxter

Her speed was immense.

Ahead of her, the radiation from the black hole's accretion disc was Doppler-shifted to a lethal sleet. Behind her the redshifted emptiness was broken only by the patient, glowering spark of the Squeem missile.

The semisentient missile had been pursuing her doggedly for years. With both of them travelling a whisker below lightspeed, it would chase her around the curve of the universe if it had to.

But she thought she had found a way to destroy it.

Gage let her enhanced awareness pan through the bulk of Chiron. Years of reaction-mass plundering had reduced the ice dwarf to a splinter, but it would survive to reach the lip of the black hole – and so would its precious cargo, the awareness of eighty humans downloaded into a heavily protected solid-state canister. The canister felt like a child, inside her womb of ice.

What happened to them all beyond the hole depended entirely on her skills as a pilot.

The black hole was only seconds away. She could make those seconds last a Virtual thousand years, if she wished.

In these last moments, she was assailed by doubt. Nobody had tried this manoeuvre before. Had she destroyed them all?

*Enough.*

She reduced her clock-speed to human perception. The black hole flew at her face –

When the Squeem conquered Earth, Anna Gage had been seventy-nine years old, thirty-eight physical. She was a GUTship pilot; for ten years she had carried bulk cargo – big, old GUTdrive freighters from the inner worlds to the new colonies clustered around Port Sol, among the ice moons of the trans-Plutonian Kuiper Belt.

She'd been half way through a year-long journey into Jove from Port Sol when the Squeem occupation laws had been announced.

The Squeem were aquatic group-mind multiple creatures. They crossed the stars using a hyperdrive system, which was still beyond human understanding. The Squeem had been the first extrasolar life forms encountered, and – except for the superfluid plant-animals found in the Kuiper Belt – the first non-human intelligence found anywhere.

Squeem ships had burst into the System in a shower of exotic particles and lurid publicity. Communication with the Squeem had been utterly unlike anything envisaged before their arrival. The Squeem didn't *count*, for instance. But eventually common ground had been found.

The Squeem had seemed friendly enough.

Then hyperdrive cannon-platforms had appeared over every major city, on all the inhabited worlds.

Human space travel was suspended. When the great GUTships landed they were broken up; the wormhole transit routes were collapsed. Humans were put to work on Squeem projects.

Anna Gage, alone, stranded between worlds, could scarcely believe it. Human resistance had imploded so *quickly*.

Still outside the orbit of Saturn, she dumped her freight and began a long deceleration.

She tried to work out what to do. Since she operated her ship on minimum overheads, her supplies were limited. She couldn't stay out here for long. But she couldn't return to an occupied Earth and let herself be grounded. She was psychologically incapable of that.

She came to a halt, with the Sun still little more than a spark ahead of her. She began probing the sky with message lasers. There had to be others out here, others like her, stranded above the occupied lands.

After a few days she got a reply.

*Chiron...*

She opened up her GUTdrive and skimmed around the orbit of Saturn.

Chiron was an obscure ice dwarf, a dirty snowball two hundred miles across. It looped between the orbits of Saturn and Uranus, following a highly elliptical orbit. One day the gravitational fields of the gas giants would hurl it out of the System altogether.

It had never been very interesting.

When Gage approached Chiron, she found a dozen GUTships drifting like spent matches around the limbs of the worldlet. The ships looked as if they were being dismantled, their components being hauled down into the interior of the worldlet.

A Virtual – of a man's head – rustled into existence in the middle of Gage's cabin. The disembodied head eyed Gage in her pilot's cocoon, and then swivelled and turned every which way, peering around the cabin. The man closed his eyes and the jostling pixels of his head enlarged, as if engorging with blood; Gage imagined his findings leaking from her tired ship down to the worldlet's surface.

The man smiled at Gage, but his eyes were wary. 'I'm Moro. You look clean.' He looked about forty physical, with a high forehead, jet black eyebrows, a weak chin.

'Thanks a lot.'

'You can approach. Message lasers only; no wideband transmission.'

'Of course -'

'I'm a semisentient Virtual. There are copies of me all around your GUTship. The slightest trouble and you will be discontinued.'

'I'm no trouble,' she said tiredly.

With Moro's pixel eyes on her, she brought the GUTship through a looping curve to the surface of the ice moon, and shut down its drive for the last time.

She climbed out of her ship and let Chiron's microgravity carry her down to the centre of a wide orange target painted crudely on the ice. When she landed, her boots crunched into ancient snow.

Moro met her in person.

'You're taller than you look on TV,' she said.

He raised a gun at her. He kept it there while her ship was checked over.

Then he lowered the gun and took her gloved hand. He smiled through his faceplate. 'You're welcome here.' He escorted her into the interior of Chiron.

Corridors had been dug through the ice and pressurised; the wall surface – Chiron ice sealed and insulated by a clear plastic – was smooth and hard under her hand. Moro cracked open his helmet and smiled at her again.

There was a large, oval chamber a mile below the surface, dug out by hand. The light, from huge strips buried in the translucent walls, had been mixed to feel like sunlight, and there was a smell of greenery, of oxygen. People were working here, building homes from the sealed-up ice, establishing gardens in synthesised soil plastered around the walls. The homes were boxes fixed to the ends of pillars of ice which sprouted from the walls like flower-stalks. It was like being inside a huge, gleaming egg. Gage, born in a tank on Mars, quailed from all this, but she recognised the wisdom of the design.

'Find somewhere to sleep. Later you can retrieve whatever you need from your ship. Tomorrow I'll find you a work unit; there's plenty to be done.'

*Work unit?*

'I'm not a colonist,' she growled. 'You think we'll be here that long?'

Moro looked sad. 'Don't you?'

She found a home, a crude cube of ice anchored by a long pillar to one wall. She moved her few personal belongings into the cube – Virtuals of her parents, book chips, a few clothes. Her things looked dowdy and old, out of place inside this gleaming ice chamber.

At night they turned the strip-lights down low. 'It's like living in a damn nursery,' Gage groused.

Dawn came with a brief flicker, a buzz as the lights warmed up, then a flood of illumination. Gage emerged from her cabin, nude; she stretched and stared down the length of her pillar at a field of cabbages growing in ice as old as the Solar System.

There were about a hundred people hiding in the worldlet. Fifty had come from a Mars-Saturn liner; the rest had followed in ones and twos aboard fugitive GUTship freighters, like Gage herself. (The cabbage seeds had come from ornamental gardens aboard the liner, she learned.) There were no children. Except for the liner passengers – mostly business types – the colonists of Chiron were remarkably similar. They were wiry-looking, AntiSenescence-preserved, wearing patched in-ship uniforms, and they bore expressions – uneasy, hunted – that Gage recognised. These were pilots. They feared – not discovery or death – but *grounding*.

Gage dug tunnels, tended vegetables, lugged equipment from GUTships of a dozen incompatible designs into the ice world and tried to build a city. The drives of some of the ships were dismounted and fixed to the surface, to provide power. The colonists improvised plants for air processing and circulation, for heating and for AS treatments. Crude distilleries were set up, with tubing and vessels cannibalised from GUTdrive motors.

It was hard work, but surprisingly satisfying. The ice cave had a feeling of roominess, of air; but Gage missed her tiny GUTship cabin.

She developed a relationship with Moro. They never became close – he had two other partners, who Gage became friendly with – but she did let herself get pregnant by him. The zygote was frozen, placed with a small store of others.

It was only after the storage of her zygote that Gage questioned her own motives in conceiving. How long was she expecting to be here?

Two years limped by. The Chiron colony remained undiscovered. It became self-sufficient, able to survive independently of the dwindling stores of the GUTships. The colonists monitored the news from the occupied worlds. There seemed to be no organised resistance; the Squeem's action had been too unexpected, too sudden and complete. As far as the colonists knew they were the only free humans, anywhere.

But they couldn't stay here forever.

They held a meeting, in an amphitheatre gouged out of the ice. The amphitheatre was a saucer-shaped depression with tiered seats; straps were provided to hold the occupants in place. As she sat there Gage felt a little of the cold of the worldlet, of two hundred miles of ice, seep through the insulation into the flesh of her legs.

Some proposed that the colony should become the base for a resistance movement. But if the massed weaponry of the inner planets hadn't been able to put up more than a token fight against the Squeem, what could one ad-hoc colony achieve? Others advocated doing nothing – staying here, and waiting until the Squeem occupation collapsed of its own accord.

'If it ever does,' Gage growled.

A woman called Maris Mackenzie released her belt and drifted up to the amphitheatre's focal point. She was another pilot, Gage saw; her uniform was faded but still recognisable.

Mackenzie had a different idea.

'Let's get out of this System and go to the stars,' she said.

There was a ripple of laughter.

'How?'

'One day Saturn or Uranus is going to throw this ice dwarf out of the System anyway,' Maris Mackenzie said. 'Let's help it along its way. We use the GUTdrive modules to nudge Chiron into a close encounter with one of the giants and slingshot out of the System. Then – when we already have escape velocity – we open up a bank of GUTdrives and push up to a quarter gee. We can use water ice as reaction mass. In three years we'll be close to lightspeed -'

'Yes, but where would we go?'

Mackenzie was tall, thin, bony; her scalp was bald, her skull large and delicate: quite beautiful, like an eggshell, Gage thought. 'That's easy,' Mackenzie said. 'Tau Ceti. We know there are iron-core planets there.'

'But not if they're habitable.'

Mackenzie spread her thin arms theatrically wide. 'We have more water, here in the bulk of Chiron, than in the Atlantic Ocean. We can *make* a world habitable.'

'The Squeem will detect us when we open up the drives. They can outrun us with hyperdrive.'

'Yes,' said Mackenzie patiently, 'but they won't spot us until after the slingshot. By then we'll already have escape velocity. The Squeem would have to match our velocity in normal space. We've no evidence they've anything more powerful than our GUTdrives, for normal space flight. So they couldn't outrun us; even if they bothered to pursue us they could never catch us.'

'How far is Tau Ceti? It will take years, despite time dilation -'

'We *have* years,' Mackenzie said softly.

A bank of cannibalised GUTdrive engines nudged Chiron out of orbit. It took three years for the ice dwarf to crawl to its encounter with Saturn.

The time went quickly for Gage. There was plenty of work to do. Sensors were ripped from the GUTships and erected in huge, irregular arrays over the ice-ship's surface, so they could watch for pursuit. Inside the ice cave, they had to take apart their fancy zero-gee homes on stalks. Even under a mere quarter-gee the suspended homes would have collapsed, embarrassingly. One side of the chamber was designated the floor, and was flattened out; squat igloos were erected across the newly levelled surface. The vegetable farms were re-established on the floor and on the lower slopes of the walls of the ice cave.

The colonists gathered on the surface to watch as Chiron sailed through its flyby past Saturn. Gage primed her helmet nipple with whisky from one of the better stills. She found a place away from the rest, dug a shallow trench in the ice, and lay in it comfortably.

Huge storms raged in the flat-infinite cloudscape of Saturn; the feathery surfaces of the clouds seemed close enough to touch. Saturn's gravitational field grabbed at Chiron, held it, then hurled it on, as if the two bodies were whirling skaters. Rings arched over Chiron like gaudy artifacts, unreasonably sharp, cutting perceptibly through the sky as Gage watched. It was like a slow ballet, beautiful, peaceful.

Chiron's path was deflected towards the Cetus constellation, out of the plane of the Solar System and roughly in the direction of the Andromeda Galaxy. The slingshot accelerated the worldlet to solar escape velocity. The encounter left the vast, brooding bulk of Saturn sailing a little more slowly around the remote Sun.

A week past the flyby the bank of GUTdrive engines was opened up.

Gage sank to the new floor of the ice cave. She looked up at the domed ceiling and sighed; it was going to be a lot of years before she felt the exhilarating freedom of freefall again.

A week after that, riding a matchspark of GUTdrive light, the Squeem missile came flaring out of the plane of the System.

Gage lay with Moro in the darkness of her igloo. She cradled him in the crook of her shoulder; his head felt light, delicate in the quarter-strength gravity. Moro had worked on the liner. He reminded Gage of herself – pragmatic, determined never to become Earthbound. His body was lean, his stomach flat.

'So we got two weeks' head start,' she said.

'Well, we'd hoped for longer -'

'A lot longer.'

'- but they were bound to detect the GUTdrive. It could have been worse.'

The Squeem had evidently been forced to concur with Mackenzie's argument, that pursuit with a hyperdrive ship was impossible; only another GUTdrive ship could chase Chiron, crawling after the rogue dwarf through normal space.

'The Squeem must have cannibalised a human ship, to launch so quickly,' Gage said. 'So the missile's drive has to be human-rated, limited to a one-gee thrust.'

The ice-world shuddered. Gage felt as if a huge hand were pressing down on her chest and legs; suddenly Moro's head was heavy, his hair prickly, and the ice floor was hard and lumpy under her bare back. The crown of her igloo groaned, and for a moment she wondered if it would collapse in on them.

The bank of GUTdrive pods had opened up, raising Chiron's acceleration to a full gee to match the missile. If Gage's analysis was correct, Chiron couldn't outrun the missile, and the missile couldn't overtake Chiron. It was a stalemate.

Gage stroked the muscles of Moro's chest. 'It's a neat solution by the Squeem,' she murmured. 'The pursuit will take years to play out, but the missile must catch us in the end. Although we may survive for years, the Squeem have destroyed us.'

Moro pushed himself away from her, rolled onto his front, and cupped her chin in his hands. 'You're too pessimistic. We're going to the stars.'

'No. Just realistic. What happens when we get to Tau Ceti? We won't be able to decelerate. We won't be able to stop.'

He wriggled on the floor, rubbing elbows which already looked sore from supporting his weight in the new thrust regime. He pulled at his lip, troubled.

Six months later the missile increased its acceleration to two gee. The Squeem had been smart, Gage decided; they'd given the missile the ability to redesign itself.

The colonists held another meeting to decide what to do. This time they sat around on the bare floor of their cave; their elegant zero-gee amphitheatre was suspended, uselessly, high on one wall of the cave.

Some wanted to stand and fight. But they had nothing to fight with. And Chiron, with its cargo of humanity, must be much more fragile than the hardened missile.

A few wanted to give up. They were still only fifty light-days from the Sun. Maybe they could surrender, and return to the occupied worlds.

But most couldn't stand the idea; it would be better to die. Anyway, a semisentient Squeem missile was unlikely to take prisoners.

They voted to run.

They had to rebuild their colony again. Drone robots crawled over the battered surface of the ice world, hauling water ice to the GUTdrive engines. Electromagnetic shields billowed wings of flux around the ice dwarf; at close to lightspeed, the thin stuff between the stars would hit Chiron like a wall.

The beautiful ice cave, with its sun-lights and vegetable gardens, was abandoned; it wouldn't be able to withstand the stress of two gravities. More tunnels were dug through the ice; new homes, made spherical for maximum strength, were hollowed out. They strung lights everywhere, but even so Gage found their new world gloomy, claustrophobic. She felt her spirits sinking.

The drives were ramped up to two gee in a day. It was like growing old, in twenty-four hours.

Only the strongest could walk around unaided. The rest needed sticks, or wheelchairs. Broken bones, failing knees and ankles, were commonplace. Those like Gage who'd grown up on low-gravity worlds, or in freefall, suffered the most. The improvised AS units were forced to cope with failing hearts and sluggish circulations.

Gage and Moro attempted sex, but it was impossible. Neither could support the weight of the other's body. Even lying side by side was unbearable after a few minutes. They touched each other tenderly, then lay on their backs in Moro's cavern, holding hands.

After three more months Maris Mackenzie came to see Gage. Mackenzie used a wheelchair; her large, fragile, beautiful bald head lolled against the back of the chair, as if the muscles in her neck had been cut.

'The missile is changing again,' Mackenzie said. 'It's still maintaining its two gee profile, but its drive is flaring spasmodically. We think it's redesigning the drive; it's going to move soon to higher accelerations still. Much higher.'

Gage lay on her pallet; she felt as if she could feel every wrinkle in the ice-world under her aching back. 'You can't be surprised. It was just a question of time.'

'No.' Mackenzie smiled weakly. 'I guess I've screwed us up. We could have just stayed in our quiet orbit between Saturn and Uranus, not bothering anybody, flying around in that beautiful freefall ice cavern.'

'The Squeem would have found us eventually.'

'We're using up so much of our water. It breaks my heart. My beautiful ocean, thrown away into space, wasted.'

Gage sighed. 'We've abandoned half our tunnels because of tiny gradients we didn't even notice under one gee. We're slowly dying under two gee, despite the AS units. We can't take any more. I guess this latest manoeuvre of the missile will be the end for us.'

'Not necessarily,' Mackenzie said. 'I have another idea.'

Gage turned her head slowly; she had to treat her skull as delicately as if it were a china vase. 'What?'

'Downloading.'

It wasn't a universally popular option. On the other hand, the alternative was death.

Some chose death. Eighty chose to survive, as best they could.

When her turn came Gage made her way, alone, to the modified AS machine at the heart of their warren of tunnels. The robot surgeon delicately implanted a sensor pad into her corpus callosum, the bridge of nervous tissue between the two hemispheres of her brain. It also, discreetly, pressed injection-pads against her upper arms.

Downloading a copy of her consciousness through the callosum sensor would take about eight hours. Gage returned to her cavern, lay on her back with a sigh, and fell asleep.

She opened her eyes.

She wasn't hurting any more. She was in zero gee. It felt delicious, like swimming in candy floss. She was in the ice cave – no, a Virtual reconstruction of the cave; the walls and house-stalks were just a little too smooth and regular. No doubt the realism of detail would return as their minds worked at this shared world.

Moro approached her; he'd resumed the crude disembodied-head Virtual form Gage had first encountered. 'Hi,' he grinned. 'Remember me?'

'I just died.'

Moro shrugged. 'Tell me about it. We're all stored inside the shelter now.' This was a hardened radiation shelter they'd built hurriedly into the heart of the ice world; it contained a solid-state datastore to support their new Virtual existence, their precious clutch of human zygotes, what was left of their vegetation. 'Our bodies have been pulped, the raw material stored in a tank inside the shelter.'

'You've a way with words.'

Maybe, when they got to Tau Ceti – or wherever the hell they ended up – Gage's awareness could be loaded back into some flesh-and-blood simulacrum of a human form. Or maybe not; maybe the role of Gage and the rest would simply be to oversee the construction of a new world fit for her child, and the other frozen zygotes.

'We're up to a thousand gee,' Moro said.

Gage's Virtual reflexes hadn't quite cut in, so she made her mouth drop open. 'A thousand?'

'That's what the missile is demanding of us.'

GUTdrive engines were well capable of such thrusts, Gage knew. In the heart of each drive Chiron-matter was compressed to conditions resembling the initial singularity – the Big Bang. The fundamental forces governing the structure of matter merged into a single, Grand-Unified-Theory superforce. When the matter was allowed to expand again, the phase energy of the decomposing superforce, released like heat from condensing steam, was used to expel more Chiron matter in a rocket action.

Once GUT energy had fuelled the expansion of the universe itself. The GUTdrives were able to extract more than the Einsteinian limit of energy from a given mass.

Moro smiled, but he looked sad. 'All our tunnels, and homes, have collapsed.'

'I never liked them anyway.'

'And the drones are having to strengthen the structure of Chiron itself; the thing wasn't built for this, and could fall apart, collapse under the stress.'

'That's it. Look on the bright side.' Gage rubbed Virtual hands over her Virtual arms. Her flesh felt rubbery, indistinct; it was like being mildly anaesthetized. 'Come on,' she said. 'Let's see what the food is like here.'

The chase settled down to stalemate again.

Their speed was already so close to that of light that time was passing a thousand times as quickly inside Chiron as beyond it. (By common consent the clock-speed of their Virtual cave had been set to human normal.) Everyone Gage knew in the Solar System must be long dead, despite AS treatment. She wondered if the Squeem occupation still endured. Maybe not. Maybe humans had hyperdrive ships of their own by now. This solitary drama might be the last, meaningless act of a historical tragedy, yet to play to its conclusion.

Gage sat under (a Virtual image of) the sky, watching starlight bend itself into a bow around the ship. It was a beautiful sight; it reminded her of Saturn's rings.

Problems were looming, she thought.

She sought out Maris Mackenzie.

'We're going bloody fast,' she said.

'I know.' Maris Mackenzie looked lively, interested. 'This is the way to travel between the stars, isn't it? Carrying live, fragile humans through normal space across interstellar distances was always a pipedream. Humans are bags of water, unreasonably fragile. And they crap inordinate amounts, endless mountains of -'

'Yes,' said Gage patiently, 'but where are we going? Tau Ceti is long behind us. And we're heading out of the plane of the ecliptic, remember; we're soon going to pass out of the Galaxy altogether.'

'Um.' Mackenzie looked thoughtful. 'The Squeem missile can't catch us.'

'No, but we still can't stop.'

'What do you suggest?'

'I was a good pilot,' Gage said. 'I'll bet I'm a better pilot than the Squeem missile. Let me pilot Chiron. Maybe I can find a way to shake off the missile.'

Mackenzie laughed, but she let the laugh die. 'Outsmart it. Why not? I don't see how, but maybe it's worth a try.'

Gage set up a simulation of her old one-woman freighter cabin; for subjective days she revelled in the Virtual chamber, home again.

But she got impatient. Her control and speed of reaction was limited. She dismissed the cabin and found ways to interface directly with the sensors of Chiron, internal and external.

The GUTdrive felt like a fire in her belly; the sensor banks, fore and aft, were her eyes. It was odd and at first she ached, over all her imaginary body; but gradually she grew accustomed to her new form.

Sometimes it felt strange to return to a standard-human configuration. She found herself staring at Moro or Mackenzie, still seeing arrays of stars, the single, implacable spark of GUT-light superimposed on their faces.

She searched ahead, through the thinning star-fields at the edge of the Galaxy. She had to find something, some opportunity to trick the Squeem missile, before they left the main disc.

The black hole and its companion star lay, fortuitously, almost directly in the path of Chiron.

The hole was four miles across, with about the mass of the Sun. Its companion was a red giant, vast and cool, its outer layers so rarefied Gage could see stars beyond its bulk.

The hole raised tides of light in the giant. Material snaked out of the giant in a huge, unlikely vortex which marched around the giant's equator. The vortex fuelled an accretion disc around the hole, a glowing plane of rubble that spanned more than Earth's orbit around its Sun.

Some of the giant's matter fell directly into the hole. The infall was providing the hole with angular momentum – making it spin faster. Because of the infall the hole was rotating unusually fast, thirty times a second.

Gage thought this over.

She summoned Maris Mackenzie. A pale Virtual of Mackenzie's disembodied head floated over an image of the hole and its companion.

'Hear me out,' Gage said.

'Go on.'

'If a black hole isn't spinning – and it's uncharged – then it has a spherical event horizon.'

'Right. That's the Schwarzschild solution to Einstein's equations. Spherically symmetric –'

'But if you spin the hole, things get more complicated.' It was called the Kerr-Newman solution. 'The event horizon retreats in, a little way. And outside the event horizon there is another region, called the *ergosphere.*'

The ergosphere cloaked the event horizon. It touched the spherical horizon at its poles, but bulged out at the equator, forming a flattened spheroid.

'The greater the spin, the wider the ergosphere,' Gage said. 'The hole ahead is four miles across. It's spinning so fast that the depth of the ergosphere at the equator is a hundred and forty metres.'

Mackenzie looked thoughtful. 'So?'

'We can't enter the event horizon. But we could enter the ergosphere, or clip it, and get away safely.'

'Hm. Inside the ergosphere we would be constrained to rotate with the hole.'

'That's okay. I want that. I want to flyby, clipping the ergosphere, and slingshot off the black hole.'

Mackenzie whistled. 'It could be done. But we would have a margin of error measured in metres. It would require damn fine piloting.'

'I'm a damn fine pilot.'

'Why do you want to do this?'

'Because,' Gage said, 'the missile will follow me through the ergosphere. But after we've passed through, the hole will have changed. The missile won't be able to work out how…'

Slowly, Mackenzie smiled.

The drones tunnelled through the interior of Chiron, reshaping the little world to prepare it for the black hole tides to come.

For Gage's scheme to work, the speed of Chiron would have to be raised much higher. When Chiron flew by the hole it would need an angular momentum comparable to that of the hole itself. So the drones ravaged Mackenzie's frozen ocean, hurling the stuff of Chiron into the GUTdrives.

Of course Chiron couldn't exceed lightspeed; all the GUTdrives could do was shave a little more off the ice dwarf's asymptotic approach to the final barrier. But the kinetic energy they provided poured into Chiron's increased effective mass. As the hole approached,

Chiron's effective mass was about a tenth of the Sun's. For every second passing in its interior, a hundred years wore away outside.

Ahead of her, the radiation from the black hole's accretion disc was Doppler-shifted to a lethal sleet. Behind her the redshifted emptiness was broken only by the patient, glowering spark of the Squeem missile.

Massive particles from the accretion disc tore through the neural nets which comprised her awareness. She felt the nets reconfigure, healing themselves; it was painful and complex, like bone knitting.

The black hole was only seconds away. She could make those seconds last a Virtual thousand years, if she wished.

In these last moments, she was assailed by doubt. Nobody had tried this manoeuvre before. Had she destroyed them all?

*Enough.*

She reduced her clock-speed to human perception. The black hole flew at her face –

The misty giant ballooned over Gage's head, its thin gases battering at her. The fabric of Chiron cracked; ice from the Solar System flaked into this black hole, here on the edge of the Galaxy, flaring x-radiation as it was crushed.

Chiron's lower belly dipped fifty yards into the ergosphere. The gravitational pull of the hole gripped her. It felt like pliers in her gut. She was hurled around; she was a helpless child in the grip of some too-strong adult.

Then the gravity grip released. The hole system was behind her, receding. The pit dug in spacetime by the hole's mass felt like a distant, fading ache.

She watched the patient GUTspark of the Squeem missile as it approached the hole. It matched her path almost exactly, she saw with grudging admiration.

The missile grazed the lip of the hole. There was a flare of x-radiation.

The GUTspark was gone. After all these years, the GUTspark was gone.

*It's worked. By Lethe, it's worked.*

Suddenly Gage felt utterly human. She wanted to cry, to sleep, to be held.

Gage met Moro and Mackenzie on a simulated Mars surface. Gage wasn't nostalgic, usually, but since the hole flyby she had felt the need to retreat into the scenes and motifs of her childhood.

'It was simple,' she said.

Mackenzie smiled.

Moro growled, 'You've told us.'

Gage told them again. 'Any slingshot flyby extracts some spin from the target body. Chiron even slowed down Saturn, a little.

'We took so much spin from the black hole that we almost stopped it rotating altogether. It became a Schwarzschild hole. Without spin, its event horizon expanded, filling up the equatorial belt where the ergosphere had been.'

Chiron had clipped the ergosphere safely. The missile,

following Chiron's trajectory exactly, had fallen straight into the expanded event horizon.

The long chase was over.

'I guess the missile wasn't an expert on relativistic dynamics after all,' Mackenzie said.

'But we're not so smart,' Moro said sourly. 'After all we're still falling out of the Galaxy – even faster than before the hole encounter, in fact. And two hundred million years pass for every month we spend in here; we might be the only humans left alive, anywhere.' He looked down at his arms, made the pixels swell absurdly. 'If you can call this life. *And* we don't have enough reaction mass left to slow down. Well, space pilot Gage, where are we heading now?'

Gage thought about it. They could probably never return to their home Galaxy. But there were places beyond the Galaxy, massive stars and black holes that a pilot could use to decelerate, if she was good enough.

She smiled. 'At this speed, we'll be there in a subjective day.'

'Where?'

'Andromeda…'

# THE SPHERES

Iain M. Banks

INTRODUCTION:

"The Spheres" was included in the original draft of *Transition*, when the plot involved the central character, Temudjin Oh, discovering that he was originally a Neanderthal. The publishers seemed happy enough with this idea, but between the first and second drafts I decided it was an unnecessary complication in an already complicated book. So out it came. Meant some revision of a later chapter, too. I didn't think the initial chapter was quite independent or strong enough to work as a short story, so it would just have remained forgotten and abandoned on the hard disk and various backup media had the iPhone app people not asked for exactly this sort of stuff for the app equivalent of DVD extras. And then Novacon 40, of course. (Shame this has prevented me presenting you with my extensive early works of what is basically Vogon poetry, but there you go. Something for Novacon 50, perhaps.)

*– Iain M. Banks*

## THE SPHERES

Dorming Lake is an extensive but shallow body of water resting on a vast pitch lake in the Slate Desert. The city of Last Resort lies on the western shore of the Lake beneath high, banded sandstone cliffs. The city is renowned for the views out over the great Lake – proportionally the largest body of shallow water in the world, the far shore lying nearly ninety kilometres over the horizon yet the waters' depth a near perfect uniform one point one metres – and for the presence of the Spheres, a phenomenon associated with the locality for some two hundred years at least and manifesting as glowing balls of light which float over the surface of the lake, amongst the buildings of the city and occasionally out over the nearby desert.

The size of the Spheres varies between approximately twelve centimetres and two metres in diameter and individual Spheres have been reliably observed to alter in size by a factor of two. Their overall colour is usually described as being like that of a setting sun, varying between orange-yellow and deep red, and they cast a light of about similar intensity to an unobstructed sunset, producing a light by which it is perfectly possible to read a newspaper on the rare occasions when a Sphere is observed during the hours of darkness. Some vehicle drivers have claimed that they were able, when seemingly accompanied by one of the Spheres moving parallel to the road they were driving on, to turn off their driving lights entirely even during the most profound depths of the night, navigating solely and allegedly quite safely purely by the luminescence cast by one or more of the Spheres.

The amount of heat given off by the Spheres is far more variable than their light. At its least it is no more than that one would associate with the light being given off by a Sphere at any particular moment – that is to say, a Sphere glowing as brightly as they are ever observed to, its body yellow, would radiate the same degree of warmth as one would expect to experience from the sun when it is the same colour and perceived size in the sky, the exact amount of warmth differing there after only according to the size of the Sphere concerned, a small one naturally radiating less heat than a larger one of the same shade. It is also noticeable that when Spheres come into contact with water or paper they normally appear to produce no steam or charring, respectively.

However, on occasion the Spheres produce a great deal of heat and can easily induce paper or cardboard to quickly char and burst into flame from more than a metre away. Dry wood, too, has been observed to burst into flame on contact with a Sphere so energised. By all accounts many a wooden building in Last Resort met a fiery fate due to the Spheres, though the instances may be less than is at first apparent due to the effect of opportunistic individuals blaming a fire on the Spheres when in fact its cause was of a more mundane and materialistically and financially inspired nature. Many of our nation's finest insurance investigators and loss adjusters hail from Last Resort.

The Spheres are most commonly observed, however, during the hours of daylight, especially around dawn and dusk. They have been seen to emerge from the Lake itself, though they occasionally descend from the upper reaches of the atmosphere, and some witnesses hold that they have seen them emerge from the wastes of the desert, particularly from the lee side of tall slate dunes.

They are generally quite silent, though there are many reports of them making a variety of usually quiet sounds including hissing, fizzing, creaking and light popping. A smell similar to that of the ocean spray is often associated with the Spheres, as well as odours not dissimilar to those emanating from hot springs and minor volcanic phenomena. Smells of burning are commonly observed when Spheres are present too, though these are thought to be only indirectly caused by them, resulting from them coming into contact with flammable materials whilst in that state of excitement which causes them to radiate great heat.

It is noticeable that the Spheres often float at about head height on an average human being, especially when in the company of a group of people, and there are reports, most reliably from school teachers that when in the presence of a large number of children of a similar age they will float at the height of the youngsters present.

They appear to be able to float right through both wood, brick and stone buildings without causing any damage to the materials concerned or to themselves, emerging from the far side of a wall in exactly the same form as they entered. Generally, however, they tend, when within the limits of the city itself, to conform to the town plan, progressing down streets, lanes and alleys individually or in small groups, their velocity varying between that of a human strolling and that of a horse trotting. They appear even to observe the rules of the road, pausing to let traffic pass when they do not simply rise and float above such obstructions.

They frequently seem to follow particular individuals or small groups of people and show what can only be described as great interest in automobiles, boats – especially steam ships – clocks, printing presses, machinery in general, trams, steam locomotives, railway rolling stock and all the infrastructure and general paraphernalia associated with rail and tramways.

When they enter buildings they usually do so either through open doors or through glass windows, in the latter case again without fuss or damage. They have been known to follow individuals from the quayside or railway terminus through the city streets and into a succession of building and rooms within said buildings, exhibiting no qualms about entering even into toilet stalls, to the distress of many a lady newly arrived in town and even to men not normally prone to hysteria. (Locals, who will have grown up with the Spheres from toddler-hood, seem scarcely to notice them at all, unless they be tourist guides or directly involved in some other aspect of the commercial exploitation of the Spheres as a phenomenon attractive to outsiders.)

To the touch, the Spheres are as insubstantial as gossamer or gas, but cannot be batted or pushed away, and repeated attempts to do so seemingly increase the likelihood of them becoming hot and therefore potentially destructive. People involved in intimate acts such as osculation appear to be no less fascinating to them as those asleep or sitting quietly reading a book.

Individuals have been burned and even disfigured by a blast of heat emanating from a Sphere, though these are mercifully very rare occurrences. No deaths as a direct results of contact with a Sphere have been reported, though people have died in building fires apparently caused by them and there are reports of people distracted by Spheres falling off cliffs or suffering fatal rail or road traffic accidents.

Natural philosophers speculate that the Spheres may be akin to ball lightning, though cynics claim this conclusion is only arrived at because the two phenomena appear superficially similar and are equally difficult to study under laboratory conditions; ball lightning because it has yet to be created within a laboratory and the Spheres because one has yet to be successfully confined within one. The Spheres have proved of enduring if frustrating interest to those of a scientistic persuasion and entire libraries of papers written about them exist both within Last Resort itself and the regional capital.

It is as abundantly clear to our friends the natural philosophers as it is to any lay person that the Spheres exhibit all the characteristics of awareness and possibly even intelligence, however there are no corroborated accounts of any meaningful communication with them, despite the best efforts of at least two generations of scientific researchers and the claims of certain individuals and religious orders, of which Last Resort has a fascinating and ever changing variety.

The Spheres appear to be confined to the immediate area surrounding Last Resort, being but rarely observed further than twenty kilometres from it, either out across the Lake or in the desert. Whether this is due to some special property of the city's location or not is hard to say. Aboriginal reports, to the extent they can be deciphered or believed, hint only that the phenomenon may go back many hundreds or even thousands of years. Recent reports of Spheres being observed further away, for example in the regional capital, may confidently be dismissed as mere shim-sham and filli-faddle, the result of the spreading fame of the Spheres producing hysterical reactions and even envy in the weak-minded and the commercially unscrupulous.

The Spheres of Last Resort remain a fascinating attraction unique to the area and are sure to entice, entrance and attract generations of tourists yet to come!

The young natural philosopher in the fashionable frock coat snorted as he finished reading the information sheet. He crumpled it in both hands – appropriately into a ball, he observed – and threw it across the carriage. It bounced off the naked shins of a sleeping holy man, almost waking him, and disappeared under a seat. The night train rattled over some points, swaying and then settling.

On the seat beside the young man sat a large square wooden box. He tested the padlock securing it, absently patting a pocket in his waistcoat as he did so, then became aware that in doing so, he was advertising to any thief present where to find the key. He looked round the night-light dim carriage, but he seemed to be the only person awake. He checked his pocket watch; three hours to dawn, five until arrival. He patted the top of the stout box, placed one arm over it, brought his hat down over his eyes and sat back to sleep.

Pachan Knertosk, a personable young journalist-adventurer of the respected Trabuhn tribe recently arrived in our fair city, reports that he has devised a new method by which to attempt communication with the Spheres. Mr Pachan, who gave up promising studies at the renowned medical college in the regional capital to pursue his new quest regarding the famed Spheres, reports that he places high hopes in a collection of specially treated glass lenses which he has brought with him.

The precise manner in which these lenses differ from ordinary glass lenses has not been revealed to your reporter, though she was permitted the apparently rare privilege of inspecting them in the presence of their owner in the *Enquirer*'s office and is able to confirm that they are darkly shaded, of a mostly uniform brown or blue tint and about the size of the circular front-pieces found on the running lights of a tram or trade motor vehicle.

The only clue your reporter is able to offer to the nature of these special properties Mr Pachan is investing such hope in is that she was able to observe that, as their owner packed them away, one lens partially occluded the view of another, and, as it was rotated, the better to pack it into its specially constructed travelling case, the view through the consecutively placed lenses did not merely dim by the sum of their apparent shade, but rather seemed multiplied, to the extent the view through the two of them disappeared entirely, being replaced rather by a perfect darkness!

Kner sat in his small hotel room, eyes widening, the angle his back described against the bed-head gradually increasing as he sat up. His grip on the two-sheet newspaper tightened as he read the words after 'occluded' with mounting horror.

He had started reading the article with a feeling of some satisfaction. It might not have been on the *Enquirer*'s front page, but it was of reasonable length and accompanied by a small engraving of his face, completed in the newspaper's office by its sketcher while he had been talking about the lenses to the very attractive young reporter.

He might have been, just a little, trying to impress her, he supposed. He had shown her more of his lenses and their associated equipment than he might have shown a male reporter, both because he would not have been hoping to secure a luncheon date with a male reporter, and also because he would not have expected a mere girl to notice very much that he had not specifically pointed out to her.

But she had spotted the interference effect produced when two of the polarised lenses sat with their planes of shading set at right angles to each other! Damn the girl! As smart – or at least as observant – as she was comely, indeed, but why did she have to provide the evidence for such attractive brains by jeopardizing his whole enterprise?

He threw the paper aside, sprang out of bed, pulled on his hose, boots and top coat, grabbed his hat and prepared to sally forth. This changed everything. He has been hoping to conduct proper scientific studies into the Spheres using the polarised lenses – the only such articles south of the Capital, he was sure – and create a sensation that would both make his name as a natural philosopher and, with any luck, secure him a not inconsiderable income from those willing to view the Spheres through the lenses, seeing things in them – features, differences, purposeful changes and the like – which nobody had ever glimpsed before.

To this end, to increase interest and wet appetites both here in Last Resort and with luck beyond, he had spent much more time going around talking to people and telling them that he had a new technique with which to observe the Spheres in heretofore unparalleled detail than he had actually trying to track down any Spheres to investigate. He had taken the opportunity – just the day he'd arrived on the train, as it happened – to view two of the entities which were leaving the town, heading out across the calm surface of Dorming Lake, and had been encouraged by the view he had had of them, but on that occasion he had simply been holding one of the lenses in front of one eye, which meant that he alone had seen any hint of detail in the glowing orbs. To convince others he would need to take photographs, and that meant setting up his tripod and camera plates and arranging at least one polarised lens within the specially constructed cradle in front of the camera's main lens. That would all take time.

Just finding a spot where the Spheres might hold still long enough for a suitably long exposure might well prove problematic; he had wanted much longer to work out where the Spheres were most likely to be seen and where they tarried. He had thought to do this work himself, partly through pride, partly because he was already thinking of the scientific paper he had already imagined himself presenting to the Natural Philosophical Society in the Capital, and partly because it would save money doing it all himself. Now, regrettably, he would be best advised to take up the offer of one of the many Sphere Guides or Trackers who preyed upon rich tourist at the railways station and, for a fee to the hoteliers, in the salons and lounges of the town's lodging establishments.

Well, he had no choice. The secret was out. He could not take the risk that another investigator of the Spheres – charlatans and mountebanks to a man though they undoubtedly were – might read of his lenses in the *Enquirer*, work out that they were polarised and somehow obtain an example or examples from the Capital, so removing the advantage he was so confident of and relying so heavily on.

The time for carefully considered preparation and build-up was over. He had to leap into action, decisively and without delay, or suffer ignominious defeat!

Further to our account in the last issue regarding the dashing young journalist-adventurer Mr Pachan Knertosk and his quest to probe the properties of Last Resort's world-famed Spheres using secret and heretofore unavailable impedimenta in the shape of specially formulated glass lenses, we are now able exclusively to report that the aforesaid young gentleman has lost no time in launching himself into his investigations and has revealed a hitherto undisclosed further ambition of unprecedented audacity.

Your reporter was privileged to be present at the inaugural unveiling of Mr Pachan's several apparatuses for the purposes of viewing said Spheres in, quite literally, a new light. In the presence of several other interested parties, Mr Pachan set up his instruments near the well-known focus of Sphere attentions at the junction and switching house for the South Shore Tramway Terminus on Trade Street. There we were serially fortunate enough to observe several Spheres on the given evening as they hovered, ever mysteriously, about the cabling boxes.

Not the least interesting spectacle this reporter has been witness to regarding the Spheres (in whose presence she has, in common with all the inhabitants of our good city, grown up) was then revealed through the medium of a specially converted camera designed, adapted and utilised by the resourceful Mr Pachan. This threw an inverted image of the spheres onto a translucent glass plate temporarily situated at the rear of the device where in the normal course of events a photographic plate would reside.

Thus far, nothing of any great or unusual novelty had been evinced, however with his next alteration to the delicate and unique appliance through which we were observing the two Spheres, Mr Pachan was able to so adjust the controls of his apparatus that it was immediately and most clearly shown that both glowing objects had patterns upon their surfaces which, as far as this reporter has been able to glean through widespread and assiduous investigation both amongst the acknowledged experts on the Spheres here in our sweet city and by telegraphic communication in the regional capital and the Capital of our great nation itself, had never been seen before!

The patterns concerned were in basis stripe- or chevron-like in nature, and seemed entirely to envelop the bodies of the two Spheres under immediate investigation. These stripings were then at time observed to be dotted with triangle shapes, rhomboid shapes like squares tipped on their corners, hexagonal shapes and other geometrical forms familiar to all school children beyond a certain age. These shapes appeared to slide or revolve around the surface of the Spheres, as though carried by the underlying framework of aforesaid bands or chevrons.

Moreover, as though this unprecedented revelation were not enough, it most certainly appeared to almost all of those present at this unrivalled and extraordinary display that the patterns so exhibited altered not simply by chance or in any kind of random manner, but rather in a fashion which entirely suggested (this impression proposing itself independently to five of the seven or so people present without any hint of persuasion coming from any one of those there), that some form of communication might be passing between the Spheres. For it was seen quite plainly that one pattern of stripes, triangles, tipped squares and the like, would be displayed on one Sphere only for the same pattern, usually somewhat altered in its detail, to be repeated or indeed nearly mirrored on the other a few moments later.

In all due solemnity, and with the benefit of over a full day during which to recover from any temporary over-excitement, however warranted by the extraordinary sights so witnessed, your reporter has no choice but to affirm that this was the single most uncanny experience, regarding the Spheres or anything else, that she has ever witnessed. Only the subsequent revelation by a highly energised and excited Mr Pachan – for the demonstration had as entirely surpassed his own expectations as it had those of the others present – that simply observing such patterns on Spheres was but the first part of his mission amongst us, and that he had still greater plans, was able to overleap said experience in the subsequent reckoning of the evening's astonishing events.

For, as the *Enquirer* can exclusively report, the young gentleman fully intends to study these patterns with great and methodical diligence from this point on with an aim to deciphering what information these curiously quivering stripes and strange geometrical shapes might contain – for it is his supposition, shared by many recognised and scholarly authorities well versed in the behaviour of the Spheres, that these unique orbs are indeed possessed of a form of intelligence, or at the very least a highly detailed awareness of their surroundings.

That having been accomplished, as he is most persuasively convinced will happen, and in relatively short order, he then intends, with the aid of some light-based signalling equipment for which he has yet to conceive the precise design but is eloquently convinced will prove relatively trivial in its ease of construction and operation, to attempt to communicate with the Spheres using formulations of light-based patterns based on those already observed on the Spheres themselves as detailed above.

Given how much Mr Pachan has achieved in so short a period already, we can only speculate what revelatory wonders might await us in the weeks ahead!

The object of this page-filling paean of breathless if sometimes confusingly overcomplicated praise sat up in his bed and wanted both to shout for joy and to tear his hair out. It was perfectly obvious the darling girl reporter was falling in love with him, from her prose as well as her admiring glances, but she'd done it again! She'd telegraphed the regional capital and the national capital, the Capital itself, talking to experts there! What was she thinking of? Why hadn't he thought to ask her not to? Sweet fool! Beautiful, exasperating idiot!

Once again, he would have to move things on even faster than he had thought or expected to.

Still; exciting, he supposed.

He threw the paper aside and once again dressed as quickly as possible.

Clushetre Xin Lo, youngest, most dynamic and by far the prettiest of the two-strong reporting team of the *Last Resort Enquirer*, had to try to calm herself as she settled into her little camp seat near the lantern equipment Kner had set up near the South Shore Tramway Terminus on Trade Street. They had tried other locations (or rather *he*, Kner – that is, Mr Pachan – had tried other locations, for her editor, who made up the final part of the three-strong journalism team the *Enquirer* was able to boast had had some stern words to say to her regarding journalistic integrity and professional objectivity) but they… he had returned here, to the scene of his first triumph – so ably reported! – for the next great step in the whole thrilling process.

Finally Kner was ready to attempt to communicate with the Spheres. Half the town had turned out to watch. His fame and that of his experiments and goals had spread, in part because of her and her reporting. Regarding Mr Pachan and his trick lenses, the town had gone from weary seen-it-all-before indifference to impolite scepticism to reluctant but still wary interest (the town had seen too many hoaxers: swindlers and fakers over the years to relax its collective guard easily when it came to seemingly fascinating and always pocket-emptying new developments concerning the Spheres) to, eventually, something close to genuinely excited enthusiasm.

Many people had had a chance to see the patterns on the surfaces of the globes for themselves, through Mr Pachan's converted camera, and it helped that he charged only a modest sum for adults and nothing for children. Others had seen the photographs Pachan had eventually taken of the patterns (it had proved more difficult than he'd thought), published in a special supplement of the *Enquirer*. Either way, that something attestedly new and apparently important had been discovered about the Spheres for the first time in decades seemed incontrovertible.

Then, after some weeks of frantic effort on the part of Mr Pachan, Miss Clushetre and Mr Pachan's two principle local assistants (there were many others, mostly earnest young men, desperate to help, once the provenance of the undertaking became clear to all), the dashing if rather tired-looking young journalist-adventurer-cum-natural philosopher announced that, whilst there was still some long way to go to comprehend all that would one day be known of the Spheres' language (for so he termed it), he now had enough of its symbols and their associate meanings worked out to make an attempt at communication with the Spheres with some hope of the enterprise succeeding.

That time had come. A windy, dusty day gave way to a still, balmy evening with a beautiful red and gold sunset and a quiet, ruddy light that seemed to rub itself into the faces of the many hundreds of people crowding round the small stage where Mr Pachan would conduct his first experiment in communication. A bank of seats for local dignitaries had been arranged at municipal insistence and expense immediately behind the stage, but hundreds more people milled about the tracks of the Terminus, some carrying their own seats and benches, some just determined to stand and crowd as close as possible to the action, whatever that might turn out to be.

Xin Lo had been of some small help at the beginning, in the heat of the afternoon, before too many people arrived, but now she thought she ought to take her place and ready her notebook. The good journalist, her editor had intoned, should not be part of the story.

It took some time. People all had to get settled, Kner had some problems getting the pattern-throwing lantern focused to his satisfaction, and then there was, of course, always the possibility that the Spheres would not show up. They usually did, most evenings around this time, and often before and often afterwards too, but there were no guarantees. The most trustworthy of the Sphere Guides and self-proclaimed Sphere experts declared that the chances of no Spheres appearing at this location on any given evening was approximately one in eleven, however they also held that – given the numbers of people suddenly showing up – all bets on the matter were off. Sometimes Spheres appeared attracted by large gatherings of folk, sometimes they positively avoided them. It was impossible to predict. As of now, judged not least by the amount of muttering going on in the crowd, the Spheres were late.

Xin Lo took some deep breaths, re-folded her notebook, checked the end of her pencil for sharpness once more, patted her waist bag where the spare pencils and notebook lay, patted herself on the upper chest through the fabric of her best dress, and tried to get her heart to behave. How awful it would be if no Spheres turned up! Not the end, not even a material setback, really, but embarrassing for Pachan. He had – at last! – declared his admiration for her just the day before, and she had reciprocated. Then they had embraced, and kissed, quite passionately – she blushed at the memory. He had also informed her that he was currently too impecunious – and far too busy – to marry, but that he hoped both circumstances would change before too long, and it would be a great honour and delight for him if she were at his side. She had then informed him that she would pursue her chosen career for as long as she could, subject only to the unavoidable responsibilities and duties related to children, should they be blessed with any.

He had blinked, then smiled. So sensible and progressive a young woman, so far from the Capital!

The sun had fully set now. A select few of the Terminus' overhead lights hissed and glared to compete against the gaudy remnants of light left strewn across the western horizon.

A group of four Spheres appeared from the direction of the Lake and floated – seemingly unconcerned and oblivious – over the heads of the crowd assembled to watch them. Xin Lo let out a deep breath. Thank goodness! The air was still, the assembled people quiet. Even the trams were absent, turned back a stop further down the line just for this one special evening.

Pachan made a last few adjustments to his lantern apparatus. The light ought to be near perfect for the apparatus and its transmissible patterns.

The four glowing orbs, each about a forearm-length in diameter and orange-red in colour, drifted over the Terminus' telegraph hut, lingered above the Main Line transformers and then settled gradually through the warm air towards the junction and switching house, the gable end wall of which had been given a fresh coat of whitewash the better to act as a screen for the lantern's projected image.

Pachan let the Spheres settle for some minutes; they floated slowly to and fro about the otherwise plain and unprepossessing building. Then he turned the lantern on and gradually increased the brilliance of the beam. The white circle being thrown on the pale gable end of the junction and switching house caused no alteration to the Spheres' behaviour.

Pachan set the specially prepared filter matrix in place, in front of the lantern's projecting lens. He adjusted the focus minutely, and started to rotate the lenses.

It swiftly became clear that the Spheres found this part of the display very interesting indeed. They stopped in their casual, drifting motions and seemed fixed in the air, as if staring transfixed at the slowly rotating image. Then they went quickly towards it, casting shadows across its surface, then they darted out of the way – two vertically and two horizontally – to leave the image without blemish.

How exciting it all was! How vindicated Kner must feel!

Suddenly, one of the Spheres came rushing towards the lantern itself, so fast that Xin Lo, almost in line with its precipitous approach, felt herself shrink back. She was aware that everybody else around her had done the same thing.

The Sphere bobbed round and over the lantern. Kner, she was relieved to see, had stepped back from the machine and the seemingly inquisitive Sphere, which had increased in size and brightness as well as in speed of mobility. Pachan stood about a metre back and to the side of the lantern while the Sphere dipped and bobbled and darted back and forth, all around it, even underneath, between the legs of the stout table supporting it, all without causing any obvious damage or disturbance.

The Sphere then gave every impression of losing interest. Its movements slowed, it decreased in brightness, shrank a little and it started to drift back towards the three other Spheres, still hovering near the now static image on the wall.

Kner stepped forward, touching the lantern to set its lenses in motion once again.

The Sphere leapt on him in an instant. There was a collective gasp from the watching crowd as the glowing orb seemed to jump onto

Pachan's shoulders, swallowing up his head in its incandescent mass. Xin Lo felt her eyes widen and her breath catch in her throat. Initially unable to move, she started to choke, unable to shout out or scream, unable to believe what she was seeing. The Sphere stayed attached to her beloved's shoulders. He stood still, one hand outstretched towards the lantern, his arms and upper body brightly lit by the Sphere engulfing his head. Some people started to shout and scream.

The noises increased in number and volume as Kner sank very slowly to his knees and then fell forward onto the decking of the stage as the Sphere finally released him and raced up through the air and curved away, heading for the Lake, swiftly joined by the other three shrinking Spheres. They disappeared over the rooftops. Kner lay still on the boards.

Xin Lo moved at last, rushing forward to leap onto the small stage and kneel by her fallen love, cradling Kner's head in her hands, sobbing when he offered no movement or response. More people thundered onto the stage now, pressing round her. She heard a couple of doctors demanding to be let through, and the suddenly formed crowd parted for them.

In the few moments before she had to let him go, before first his care and then he himself was taken away from her, she had the chance, even in that tumult of people, to look into his eyes and see that he was still alive, that his eyes were not closed and were not staring drily ahead like those of the dead, and that indeed they still blinked, albeit slowly… but also that they now betrayed no hint, no slightest sign whatever of animation, recognition or intelligence.

No wonder I always lost track of myself. I'm sitting at a little café a short way from the railway station, back to the wall, nursing an Americano and watching the boats stream up and down the Grand Canal. Just along the broad quayside, a line of tourists stand with their luggage waiting to pick up water taxis. At the next table two Australian guys are arguing about whether it's espresso or expresso.

'Look, for Christ's sake, it's there in black and white.'

'That could be a misprint, man, like Chinese instructions. You don't know.'

I am still toying with my new-found senses. Sensibilities, even. I have done no more leaping into other people's brains, whether

Concern or civilian. I do seem to have a sort of vague spotter sense, which is quite useful. I can sense that the baffled, disordered, demoralised intervention team is still milling about the Palazzo Chirezzia, its members collecting themselves, tending to their wounded, making their excuses to each other and themselves, still not entirely able to understand what really happened, and waiting for back-up and assistance to arrive.

This is all happening just a few hundred metres away from where I'm sitting. I am ready to move quickly away if I need to, but for now I'm happy that I can see them without them seeing me. Another sense; they give the impression of deaf people talking loudly amongst themselves and not realising that they are doing so, while I am sitting here quite silent. I would be nervous about putting it to the test, however I'm oddly but perfectly confident that a spotter could pass me by right here, a metre or two away, and have no idea that somebody capable of transitioning was sitting watching them. And of course they have no idea what I look like now.

I have been able to take more control of this glass-walls, future paths sense. At the moment it is telling me that nothing especially threatening is imminent. Looking backwards is possible too, though. It's like I can see down corridors in my head, in my memory, and as though there is a near infinite series of doors angled to partially face me as I look down from one end of any particular corridor, so that by looking closely and then zooming in on each one, I can see what happened during different transitions I once made. There is an uncanny impression that this is at once one corridor and many, that it leads off in an explosion of different directions scattered vertically and horizontally and in dimensions I would struggle to put a name to, but, despite this, my mind seems able to cope with the experience.

Here is the time just passed when I bamboozled the whole of not just one conventionally-configured but high skill-and-experience level Concern intervention team, but two (and more like three, if you count the people watching the perimeter), all at the Palazzo Chirezzia, barely an hour ago.

Here is the time I blew that musician's brains out while he sat in his preposterously blinged half-track.

Here is the time I sat in a room with somebody I thought I loved and her hand moved through a candle flame like silk.

This is me chasing two fucked up kids through a Parisian sink estate and watching them die. And again, except differently.

Look, here I am saving a young man from certain death.

And this is me with my pals walking down a street and stopping by a fat old geezer sunbathing in his postage-stamp size front garden, one sunny day.

I sit, indulging myself in my own quaint slide show, amused as all hell.

The clarity this far back is amazing. I'm still not all that near the end, though, surprisingly. Look how much more there is to go!

There is another corridor, one I can see down only dimly, as though there is a pane of smoky glass in the way. A whole new twist to this corridor, too, as though it has been rotated by some dimension I am only vaguely aware of, though I still seem to be able to see right down it. And a different character to the light, the smell, the fragre, the everything about this part of my memories. Trying to move down this strange corridor, it is as if I bump up against a glass door, as though the smoky glass I imagined obscuring its view has been made – within this patently virtual context – solid. I peer in, nose metaphorically against the glass like a poor kid at an old-fashioned sweet shop. I push at this door but it gives only part way, resisting.

I get an impression of a train carriage full of rather squat and ugly people, a dusty town lying beneath an escarpment on the shore of a calm sea. That's all. But the fragre, the feel and look and smell of the place…

Can this be me? It doesn't really feel like it. So, am I looking into somebody else's life? That shouldn't be possible, should it? But then who knows what is possible with my still increasing suite of senses? I pull back, check down the single corridor that is lots of corridors. There is this strange discontinuity only here, behind the hazy barrier that manifests itself as smoked glass. Very odd. Clearly, further research is required.

I've let my Americano grow cold. The Grand Canal still froths with boats passing to and fro. The arguing Aussies are gone. Confusion tempered by affronted professional pride still reigns at the Palazzo Chirezzia. And there is a little fear there, too, because their back-up has started to arrive at last and they've heard Madame d'Ortolan is also on her way, with questions.

A warm wind scented with tobacco smoke and diesel exhaust stirs me from my reverie, back to the present and the insistent reality of the here and now.

Indeed; all this historical stuff is highly intriguing, but there is the small matter of my being hunted with pretty much every resource the Concern is able to bring to bear. That needs attending to. Beyond that, the coup Madame d'Ortolan would appear to be trying to mount is either proceeding or not. I have already done what I can in that regard. I can only hope that my attempts to alert Mrs M to the targets I'd been sent after worked, and they have been warned, and put themselves safe.

My present embodiment came complete with a mobile phone. I tried calling my new friend Ade, on his way here with a cunningly worked container full of septus, but his mobile telephone is switched off and his office tells me he is away, expected back tomorrow some time. I look at the timepiece wrapped round my wrist. The smaller but more important hand points to the two parallel lines just off the vertical, to the left. Eleven. Adrian said that he should be here by four in the afternoon.

We are to meet at the Quadri on the Piazza San Marco, safely surrounded by the tourist throng.

It seems I have to wait.

I pay and go for a walk, crossing the Grand Canal by the Scalzi bridge and coming back the same way half an hour later – an elegantly curved new one is only a week or two from being opened. I wander into the station, sit down in the café and order another Americano, the better to sip slowly. I have a faint desire to count how many platforms there are in the station, but it is residual, easily ignored. The phone rings a few times and its screen shows me the faces of the people calling: Annata, Claudio, Ehno. I don't answer.

I take several more walks around the western end of Cannaregio and the nearer parts of Santa Croce and sit in several more cafés, none too far from the Palazzo Chirezzia, keeping the vague hubbub in internal view at all times. I sit quietly, seemingly watching people, actually probing further into my own pasts and returning again and again to the quite different fragre concealed, as though behind shaded, smoky glass, at the end of the corridor that seems to twist.

I am sitting in a little tourist café on the Fondamenta Venier near the Ponte Guglie when I am recognised. I prepare for the worst, but it is just somebody who knows this body, this face, inquiring why I'm not at work this afternoon. I look furtive and embarrassed and stick to vague generalities, mostly keeping my head down. The man nods, winks and taps me on the shoulder before he walks off. He thinks I am waiting on my lover. I drain my lemon tea and leave. I've had enough coffee.

I walk to another café, on the Rio Tera De La Madalena. A spritz this time, and some pasta. I keep seeing that strange twisted corridor in my mind's eye, keep venturing down it to peer down and push at the hazy barrier separating it from me. I feel certain that, like the other corridors, it contains memories which belong to me, but I also have the equally strong but quite uncanny feeling that it stretches back beyond my birth. But how can that be?

The barrier keeping me out of the corridor seems to give a little more each time I attempt to negotiate it. Through it I keep glimpsing the same train carriage full of the same ugly, hairy people. It has become almost familiar by now. There is a particular ugly, hairy person at one end, guarding a solid looking box on the seat beside him. Is this some sort of translated vision of Adrian on his way here with the box of septus? That doesn't feel right. The fragre is quite different.

The ugly young fellow wears a wide-brimmed hat, currently pulled down over his eyes – to let him sleep, I suppose. He jerks, as one does when one falls but does not fall asleep, and I do the same, back in my seat in the tourist café on the Rio Tera De La Madalena (it's been a long day, and I've just eaten). He stirs, stretches, and I find myself doing the same. Exactly the same. I can practically feel my mirror neurons firing.

He is me.

And suddenly I'm through, and there.

A carriage – a train carriage, I'm guessing – full of strangely dumpy, coarse featured, extravagantly hairy people, almost all asleep. Dear fuck, some of these brutes are females! They are all fat looking, all swelling out at the bottom of their rib cages, where their clothing allows me to see such physiological detail.

Their faces, though, those thunderous brows, the noses, all squashed. And here is the young male towards the front of the carriage, sitting with his hat over his eyes with a stout wooden box by his side that he seems to be protecting. I feel drawn to him. I really think I might be him, though I can't understand how and I have no memory of this, none at all. Could that really be me? But he looks so ugly! So squat, so fat. Powerful looking and with a big head, room for plenty of brains there, but – good grief! – so coarse-featured, so plug ugly!

At the end of the rail line – I can distantly see – there is a great city, full of more of these dumpy, midriff-spreading people amongst whom he is – relatively – tall, handsome and fair of face. His life winds out into the conventional past there. Youth, childhood, parents, friends, toddler-hood, babyhood, birth; it all just peters out, as you'd expect. Unremarkable. And nothing beyond. His time line through the many worlds, starting in this one, stops here, originates here, like a crack in a great pane of glass stops somewhere.

And shifts – here, right at this point a couple of weeks further into the future from this scene in the train carriage – into something quite different, into a whole entirely other deck of worlds, into all we've ever known, all because he has the spiffing idea that maybe the one way nobody has ever looked at these strange Spheres is through recently invented polarised glass.

The Spheres were more and less than strange. Just another long-taken-for-granted feature of the locality in Last Resort itself, they were seen as exaggerations of some natural phenomena by most people in the regional capital, including many who'd seen them personally, while by the time you got to the Capital they were knowingly regarded as part of a definitively unlikely wide-eyed country-hick mythology.

And then he tries to talk to them and they try to talk back, and before he knows it he's been plonked down in another existence altogether, reborn – literally reborn, genuinely reborn – though this time in a human not a Neanderthal body (because that's what people here would call the people who inhabited the world that contained Last Resort and Dorming Lake and the mysterious, blatantly alien Spheres; Neanderthal).

I was born a Neanderthal!

Before I was human I was not human, and – as if that's not enough – I once talked with something either not of this world or so outlandish and exotic it might as well have been alien. To the best of my knowledge – as ever, with the Concern you can never be sure, but, equally certainly, there would surely be rumours – we have encountered no worlds at this stage of development or anything like it where the Neanderthal species is anything other than a long-extinct throwback, something less than a memory, and this applies no matter how far afield we have tried to cast either our transitioning or envisioning.

Which means that I come from further away than even the most hazily distant vision ever glimpsed by the most insanely gifted envisionary whom the Transitionary Office has ever persuaded to throw caution and potentially sanity to the winds, in the hope of seeing something profoundly different. They saw nothing so removed from us, nothing so profoundly *other*.

I look back at my human self from the perspective of the young Neanderthal man I once was, and see myself as any of that species would see any example of Homo sapiens; as a walking skeleton. To them we would appear as cruel, small-brained, cadaverously elongated wraiths in fleshly form. Too tall, too spindly, too unbalanced, our general appearance would be as repellent and difficult to look on to them as the emaciation of those near death through anorexia or starvation is to us. The waist; too narrow, too unsupported somehow, as wrong looking as that of a wasp or an ant seen in close up. The head; too long, too small and narrow. The legs; too stretched and friable seeming, and the whole; just wrong, a sort of perversion.

Even an obese human would look wrong to them, crudely inflated rather than properly proportioned, a mere waddling record of all the fats they'd chosen to consume. They would still sense the misproportioned skeleton beneath.

No wonder I always lost track of myself.

I snap out of it when the waiter nudges my seat – deliberately, probably – waking me from my dream.

# Acts of Defiance

Eric Brown

A storm lashed the island during the night, and in the morning a dense mist concealed the view of the bay from my cottage. It was raining for the fifth consecutive day. The weather was conducive to nothing more than staying inside before the fire, reading and warming oneself with a dram or two.

I worked all morning on my portable typewriter, and towards lunchtime replaced it beneath the floorboards of my study. Old habits died hard, even though I was no longer on the mainland where the government might swoop unannounced at any time. I had moved to Shapinsay after the death of my wife, fleeing painful memories and the Party both. None of us were free these days, though paradoxically I did feel a little less imprisoned on the island which measured just five miles by four.

A little after one o'clock I put the kettle on and made myself a cheese sandwich. Through the window and the mist I watched the post van; the tiny red vehicle was a hundred yards away and negotiating the rutted lane with care. I wondered if the delivery would be for myself or for Manning, my neighbour. I hoped the latter: the post seldom delivered good news these days.

I took the coffee and sandwich back to my study, sat in the armchair overlooking the bay, and waited.

In due course I heard the van's engine. It would cut out if the delivery was for me, continue onwards if it was for Manning.

It stopped. All I could hear now was the soughing of the wind in the eaves and the patter of rain on the window.

The letterbox rattled. I remained in my seat, picked up the sandwich and took a bite. The engine started up again as the van continued on to Manning's croft.

Few people bother to contact me these days. My daughter comes to see me once a month from Kirkwall, and occasionally I hear from my old publisher – but increasingly less so as all my books are now out of print.

I finished my sandwich and moved into the hallway. My heart set up a frantic knocking when I saw the distinctive envelope on the doormat. Buff brown, edged in red: an official communiqué from the Party.

I picked up the letter, took it to the study and sat for a moment or two in silence. Then I slipped a thumb under the flap and ripped open the envelope.

*Dear Mr Roberts,*

*According to our records, you are in possession of…*

I read on, sickened. The letter listed half a dozen novels which the government had decreed were subversive and therefore would be impounded. Amongst them was one of my favourite books: *Acts of Defiance* by George Houghton, first published in 1930.

A representative of the Party would arrive on the island to impound the books within the week.

The letter was signed, *F. C. Iqbal-Smith.*

I set the letter aside, aware of my shaking hand, and crossed the room to a bookshelf. I pulled down the Houghton and read a few lines.

I removed the remaining five volumes from the shelves, novels by Gordimer, Isherwood, Lessing, Nabokov and Walker.

I heard the post van as it passed my cottage on its way back to rendezvous with the ferry. I wondered what delivery Manning might have received.

I put the novels on the desk and regarded the shelves. Rather than rearrange the rows of books so that they abutted each other, cover to cover, it had come to me a couple of years ago to allow the absences to speak for themselves, in mute testimony.

There had been times when I had counted the gaps, but no longer. The exercise was too depressing, as each gap represented more than just the absence of a book. All across the country, volumes that had been read and loved for decades, sometimes even centuries, were no more. They had ceased to exist, just as if their authors had never expended the effort of committing their considered words to paper.

*Ceased to exist…*

The notion brought me close to tears.

I stared through the window at the drifting mist, then picked up the letter, stuffed it into the pocket of my jacket, and left the cottage.

I pulled up my hood and leaned into the wind. The icy easterly bit into my bones. I walked along the coast, taking the clifftop path above the bay, a shortcut to Manning's croft. I walked fast, but slowed down when I came to the more treacherous sections of the path. I was fuelled by anger, impotent though that emotion was.

Manning's company would be some succour.

A dram or two, a rant with a like-minded soul…

It would make the pain a little easier to bear.

I thought of Emily as I walked, and how her early death had spared her. She had been fifty-five when she passed away, just a year after the Party had come to power. She too had loved books. It would have destroyed her, what they were doing now in the name of ideology.

The low, turf-roofed croft loomed into view through the grey mist. A welcoming light shone in the window of the front room. I imagined Manning in there, snug in his armchair before the open fire, absorbed in the past. A retired professor of medieval English literature now in his eighties, he dwelled in the long lost worlds of Langland, Chaucer and Gower.

He opened the door before I had the opportunity to knock.

"I thought you'd be along. A drink, Ed?"

I followed him into the front room, little more than a cave packed with five thousand musty volumes. Ten years ago it had taken the government assessors more than a week to catalogue his holdings, with Manning cursing them every minute of their stay.

He poured me a peg of Scotch, bought from one of the many illicit stills that had begun production shortly after the Party's proscription of all forms of alcohol. I pulled the envelope from my pocket and passed it to him. He scanned the letter over his half-moon glasses, his eyes when they lifted to regard me full of silent pity. "And your beloved Houghton."

He gestured to the coffee table beside the fire, where I saw a familiar buff-coloured, red-edged envelope.

"You too," I said.

We dropped into the armchairs, warmed by the flames. He passed me the government communiqué.

The Party had selected ten volumes to confiscate, to be destroyed, all of them by the greatest writers of the previous century.

"Oh, Christ," I managed at last. "There's neither rhyme nor reason, James."

He lifted his glass to his lips and drank, watching me. "But there is. Thought *and* feeling. Not content with proscribing works which make us think, as in the early days, now they don't want us to feel, either. They've finished with the philosophers. Now they're targeting the finest novelists."

I took a soothing mouthful of Scotch, resting my head on the back of the chair.

"I've just heard from Raymond's wife," Manning said. "They took him in for questioning last week. She hasn't seen him since."

"They discovered the press?"

He nodded. "They took it away to destroy."

I sat in silence for a time, looking into the metaphorical abyss as I stared at the flames of the open fire.

I indicated the letter on the coffee table. "'Iqbal-Smith'. Do you think he really exists?"

Manning smiled. "I doubt it. The name's a signifier for their unholy alliance."

"Is there any hope?" I asked.

"Of course, Ed. There's always hope."

"What, with the Party destroying books and executing dissidents? With the press discovered and Raymond arrested?"

"There'll be other presses, other Raymonds. There will always be people who resist, who'll find new ways to communicate now that the internet is so heavily censored."

I stared at the books that surrounded us on shelves, or were piled around the room in tottering columns. Every one of them was tagged, logged by the authorities.

"It's only a matter of time before they come for everything," I said. "Soon, children will get out of the habit of reading, or being able to envisage a wider world and different mind-sets."

I sat in silence, watching the flames.

Manning was staring at me.

"What?" I said.

He seemed to be considering his words. "There's always hope, Ed." He hesitated. "I want to show you something."

I sighed. A paper he was working on? A treatise he was preparing for a daring small press somewhere? And where might this tiny act of defiance lead? How many people might actually read his wise words? I would have said he was preaching to the converted, but the religious analogy stuck in my craw.

He set his glass aside and climbed to his feet, stooping as he trudged away from the fire. "This way." He led me into the kitchen.

He opened the door to the larder and knelt, removing a square of linoleum from the floor to reveal a trapdoor. He lifted a metal ring and pulled, then reached down and turned on a light switch.

In the dim light I made out a flight of wooden steps and a whitewashed wall. "My predecessor had this dug out twenty years ago, just after the Party came to power."

"What on earth for?"

"He foresaw the future." Manning smiled over his shoulder. "He had a still down here and made his own whisky."

He moved carefully down the steps, and I allowed him to get ahead of me before following.

"Well," he said when we were standing in the cellar, perhaps ten feet by ten, "what do you think?"

I stared about me in wonder, aware of my heartbeat. "My word."

I calculated that there were about five hundred books down here, ranked on shelves around the walls. I reached out and pulled one down: Dickens's *Hard Times*, appropriately enough.

I opened the book and stared at the top left corner of the boards.

"No," he said. "It isn't tagged. And none of the others are, either. The authorities don't know about any of them. I've collected them over the years, many donated by like-minded souls."

Excited, but at the same time apprehensive, I ran my eye along the serried titles: works by the European greats, Dostoyevsky, Chekov, Tolstoy, Balzac, Zola, Thackeray, Elliot, the Brontës… The list went on; authors long deemed verboten by the Party.

"There must be more than five hundred," I said.

"Six hundred and eleven," Manning said, smiling.

I swallowed, feeling a little sick. "If the bastards ever found out…"

"What have I got to lose? I'm an old man. This is my last gesture of resistance."

I caressed the ranked volumes, my heart swelling.

"I've been keeping these to myself for years, but it's time to share them. I'm loaning the odd volume out to people I trust, here and on the mainland. Choose one to take with you."

I stared at him. "I can?"

"Be my guest."

Where to start? Dickens had always been one of my favourites. Over the years, the Party had confiscated my entire collection of his novels. I could start with his first book, and reread his entire oeuvre. I selected *Pickwick Papers*, admired the embossed cover, the interior illustrations by Hablot Knight Browne. Then I returned it to the shelf.

"Not today," I said. "They'll be coming in a day or two for the Houghton and the others. If I had *Pickwick Papers* in the house… I think I'd be so nervous I'd give the game away. When they've gone, I'll be back for it."

"I'll put it aside for you."

We left the cellar, and Manning turned off the light and lowered the trapdoor. When we were back before the fire, with our whiskies replenished, I said, "Will you be all right, when the government man comes?"

"Ed, they've been before and haven't searched the place. I admit, though, that the old heart starts hammering a bit." He smiled. "But they've no reason to suspect anything."

"Be very careful who you loan them out to."

"Only the trusted," he assured me.

I felt blessed to be considered amongst their number.

Before I left, an hour later, he said, "Did you hear the explosion last night?"

"An explosion? I didn't hear a thing, but then I'm a heavy sleeper."

"Around two. I wondered if it was the freedom fighters, bombing the refinery at Gairsay again, or the church or the mosque at Kirkwall."

"Good luck to them," I said.

It was almost four o'clock when I left Manning and made my way back to my cottage.

The rain had ceased, but twilight had fallen and the wind had not let up. It roared in from the east, buffeting me. I had set off to see Manning with the letter in my pocket a couple of hours ago, full of despair. Now the letter no longer had the same power to disturb. Manning's hoarded treasure trove warmed me.

I was rounding the bay to the headland and my cottage when I saw something through the mist, fifty yards away on the beach. At first I thought it was a seal, common on this side of the island. As I moved closer, though, I realised I was mistaken.

I stepped off the path, cut through the dunes and waded through the thick, retarding sand. I was panting hard when I came to the body. A girl, I saw – well, a young woman, blonde, perhaps in her twenties. I assumed she was dead, but when I knelt beside her, her head turned suddenly, surprising me. Her eyes fluttered open and regarded me – something shocking in their mute appeal.

I realised, now the time had come to think straight, that I was a little drunk.

"I'll… there's a doctor along the road. I'll fetch him –"

She reached out, gripped my arm. "No!"

I stared at her. She wore jeans and an anorak, soaked with sea water. I said, "What happened?"

"Just…" she said, "help me."

I attempted to lift her, scoop her up in my arms forklift fashion as if I were a man of twenty. I staggered, almost fell on top of her. So instead of picking her up, I assisted her to her feet and walked her along the beach – her limping all the way – through the dunes to my cottage.

Once inside, I half-carried her to the bedroom and lay her on the bed. She stared up at me, shivering uncontrollably.

"You need to get warm. I'll draw a bath. Are you injured?"

"Bruised," she said. "Exhausted. I don't think anything's broken." Her accent was southern English, not Orcadian.

I made for the door, then paused. "What happened? Who are you?"

She shook her head minimally. "My boat capsized last night. Out in the straight."

"You came from mainland Orkney?"

She closed her eyes.

"I'll draw that bath."

I filled the tub with hot water, then helped her into the bathroom. "You'll be hungry. I have bread and soup."

I left her and found some clothing – a pair of old trousers, a shirt and a baggy cardigan. I opened the bathroom door a couple of inches and squeezed them through the gap.

Later, she joined me in my study before the fire, seeming tiny in my cast-offs. She was small and blonde and smiled when I introduced myself; she told me that her name was Penny. I gave her a bowl of soup and a slice of bread, and poured two mugs of coffee. We ate in the armchairs before the fire.

"You said your boat capsized," I said, watching her.

The authorities didn't allow just anyone to own boats these days: you had to be registered with the local government, or be Party member.

She nodded, spooning soup.

"Was it yours?"

She shook her head, not to be drawn.

"Were you alone?"

She nodded

I ate my soup.

She said, "You live here by yourself?"

"I've been on the island for years. I didn't like the atmosphere on the mainland – Scotland, that is. The…" I watched her, then chanced it, "the repression."

She nodded, gave me a tense smile. "You don't belong to the Party?"

I gestured to the gap-toothed bookshelves. "They're taking my favourite books," I said.

"Bastards!"

I recalled Manning's mention of an explosion in the night, but thought it wise to say nothing.

We finished the meal. "Would you like a drink? Whisky?"

"I'm tired. Would it be okay if I…?" She gestured towards the bedroom.

"Yes, of course. I'll sleep on the sofa-bed in here."

She limped from the room. "Edward," she said as she paused at the door, "can I trust you not to tell anyone I'm here?"

"I won't tell a soul," I said.

I dried her clothes before the fire. I went through the pockets, of course, but as expected found nothing that might confirm her identity.

Later, as midnight came and went and I could not sleep, I took my copy of *Acts of Defiance* from the shelf and began reading it for the very last time.

*

In the morning I made toast and coffee and we ate breakfast before the open fire. Dressed in her own clothes, with her hair dried and brushed, she looked presentable, even pretty to my old eyes.

"I'll leave here at twelve," she said, "walk down to the quay and catch the ferry to Kirkwall at two."

"It won't take two hours to reach the quay," I said.

"It'll be for the best if I'm away from here."

"Will they be looking for you?"

She hesitated, then shrugged. "Maybe, but I'll be fine."

"If there's anything I can do to help…"

She smiled, and I tried to recall the last time a young woman had smiled at me in such a way. "You've already helped me more than you can imagine, Edward."

She saw the books piled on desk, reached out and picked up the Houghton. She read a line here and there.

I said, "They're coming to take them away."

"Where will it stop?"

"It won't," I said. "It never does with such regimes. It can't stop. You see, the internal logic of repression is that the latest diktat must be more draconian than the last. That way they keep us in a constant state of fear."

She shook her head. "It *will* come to an end, one day."

I smiled at her naivety, but said nothing.

I was startled, minutes later, by a loud knocking at the door.

Penny jumped up. "Who–?"

"Maybe Manning, my neighbour. Don't worry. But perhaps you should slip into the bedroom."

She nodded, thought to pick up the second cup and plate, and hurried from the study.

I moved down the hall, wondering what Manning might want at this early hour. He never normally got out of bed before ten o'clock.

The knock sounded again. I opened the door and stared, open-mouthed.

A stranger stood on the threshold, a well-dressed middle-aged man whose suit shouted bureaucracy and whose lean, unsmiling face was like a thousand others from the Party's rank and file.

I found my voice. "But… but the ferry isn't till one," I said.

"I came to the island yesterday, Mr Roberts."

I looked past him, searching for a vehicle.

"And my colleague dropped me at the end of the lane."

I nodded, stepped aside and let him in. I showed him to the study, where he stood in silence and gazed around at the books on every wall.

Once, a few years ago, when a Party representative came to confiscate a selection of my books, he brought with him a search warrant and went through the cottage from top to bottom. If this one were to do this now, I wondered how I might explain Penny's presence.

"You received the official communiqué from head office?"

I pointed to the letter on the coffee table.

"And the books in question?"

I indicated the pile on the desk. He sat down in the chair and pulled a softscreen from his valise.

Without looking at me, he reached out his hand, palm up, and moved his fingers – *Give*, he semaphored.

I passed him the book from the top of the pile, the Houghton.

He activated the softscreen, then opened the book and pressed the silver tag within its covers against the screen. As I watched, a line of text appeared: *Acts of Defiance* by George Houghton, Collins, 1930, first edition. He scrolled down the screen, and blocks of text showed, one after the other. He paused it on page 101, then opened the copy of my book to the same page and compared the text. Satisfied that this was indeed the book his Party had proscribed – and I hadn't removed the original and substituted it with some innocuous text – he nodded his satisfaction.

He went through the process with the remaining five books, then rolled his softscreen and replaced it in his valise, along with the proscribed novels.

"What will happen to them?" I asked.

"I'll take them away with me."

"I know that," I said. "But after that – what will your *Party* do with them?"

He looked at me with emotionless eyes. "They will be immolated, along with all the other proscribed texts collected this week."

*Immolated...*

He paused in the process of rising from the armchair, then sat back down and gestured at the shelves. "Why, Mr Roberts?"

The question staggered me.

"Why what?"

He gestured again, his bafflement unfeigned. "Why keep all these?"

I sat down across from him and said, "To read, to re-read –"

"*Novels*" – he said the word with contempt – "made up stories."

"Do you read?"

"I read the only two books that matter."

I sat in silence for a while, staring at him. "You asked me *why*," I said. I gestured at the shelved books. "I read to keep me in touch with my humanity, and with the humanity of others. Literature – the *novels* you so obviously despise – allow me to share the visions, the thoughts, the ideas of others beside myself. They show me that I am not the centre of the universe, that my psyche is not the only one that matters: it bestows," I finished, my voice shaking, "the gift of empathy."

But that, I thought, is something that you would never understand.

He was staring at me now with frank incomprehension. "The ideas of others do not matter, Mr Roberts," he said at last.

I bit back my desire to reply.

He rose to his feet, and I tried not to show my relief that he was leaving.

"If you don't mind, I'll have a quick look around."

My stomach turned. "Do you have a search warrant?"

"My, my," he said, "you are behind the times. The Party no longer needs a warrant these days."

He moved from the study. I sat and listened to him in the kitchen, and then in the sitting room. I leaned forward, held my head in my hands. How would I explain Penny? It was only a matter of time before he entered the bedroom and found the girl…

I heard his footsteps in the hallway and looked up to see him opening the bedroom door. He stepped inside and passed from view. I closed my eyes. My heart hammered and my mouth was suddenly, awfully dry.

I heard him moving about in the room, but that was all, no exclamations, no sounds of interrogation.

I heard the bedroom door close, and his footsteps as he returned to the study.

I looked up, my heart hammering.

"I'll see myself out," he said, then paused. "Oh – Mr Manning? Mr James Manning?"

I stared at him, still incredulous at the fact of my reprieve. "I beg your pardon?"

"Mr James Manning, The Croft? Should I take the lane?"

"You'd be quicker taking the clifftop path," I said. "Turn left as you leave the cottage."

He thanked me, then said, "God be with you, Mr Roberts."

I stared at him, expressionless.

He moved from sight. I heard the front door open and close.

I waited a minute, two… After five minutes, my heart knocking, I stood and moved to the bedroom door, opened it an inch and said, "You can come out now, Penny. He's gone."

There was no reply.

I pushed open the door and stared around the room, expecting the girl to emerge from her hiding place, grinning at the close call.

There was no one in the room.

I moved to the window. It was open a couple of inches. I stared out into the mist. There was no sign of Penny, nor of the Party man on the clifftop path.

I returned to my study and poured myself a whisky, my hand trembling. I waited for a sound to indicate that the girl was returning from wherever she had concealed herself out there.

Twenty minutes passed, then half an hour. Unable to wait any longer, I stepped outside and walked around the cottage, calling her name.

The wind raged and the rain fell ceaselessly. There was no sign of her.

I returned inside, paced back and forth. I waited an hour – trying to read but unable to concentrate – until I was sure that the Party man had had time to visit Manning and confiscate the books.

I pulled on my coat and left the cottage. I needed to talk, to tell my friend about Penny – and my suspicions about the girl.

I took the path along the edge of the cliff, careful on the more treacherous stretches, rounded the bay and approached Manning's croft through the mist.

I knocked on the door – and just as he had yesterday, Manning opened it and said, "I thought you'd be along."

"He's been and gone?"

He made no reply. I followed him into his book-filled front room. He moved to the fire and stood hunched with his back to me, staring down at the flames.

"I don't know where to start," I said. "On my way back, yesterday… down on the beach. A girl. I thought she was dead. I… The long and the short of it is that she wasn't – so I took her back to my place. And… look, the explosion you mentioned – I suspect she had a part in it."

Manning turned and stared at me, and I fell silent at the expression on his face. I wondered if he'd heard anything I had said. He looked ashen, shocked.

"James…?" I said.

He moved past me without a word and stood just inside the door to the kitchen, staring. I joined him on the threshold.

"Oh, Christ," I said.

The Party man lay on the floor before the larder, the hair on the back of his head matted with blood.

"He's dead," Manning said. "I hit him with a poker when he moved towards the larder door."

I swore again, feeling dizzy now.

"I couldn't let him go down there," he murmured.

I nodded, assessing the situation.

I said, "What are you going to do?"

He stood staring at the body. "I… I really don't know."

I came to a decision. "He told me he had a colleague on the island who'd dropped him off. We don't have much time –"

"To do what?"

"We'll take him to the cliff, throw him over." I moved to the front room window and stared out. "We'll walk across the gravel, then across the heather – the tussocks won't take our footprints – right to the cliff edge. Are you up to that?"

He stared at me, gestured helplessly.

"James," I said, "will you help me with this?"

Belatedly, still in shock, he nodded.

We returned to the kitchen. I thought to place a plastic bag over the Party man's head to prevent any telltale dripping of blood. I took his valise and placed it over his shoulder. Then between us we carried the corpse from the croft, crossed the gravel and then the springy heather, and came to the edge of the cliff – the easterly limit of the land where the path was at its most treacherous.

The wind raged, howling, and the rain fell in sheets. I removed the plastic bag from the Party man's head, and we picked up the corpse again. Taking the arms and legs between us, we swung the body back and forth to gain momentum and, on the count of three, pitched it over the cliff. The body seemed to take an age to fall the fifty feet to the rocks below, where it hit with a sickening crunch of bone.

I stared down, but veils of mist concealed our handiwork.

"When his colleague turns up," I shouted against the wind as we made our way back to the croft, "I'll tell him that he called on me, took the books he came for, then left for yours – taking the clifftop path. He'll have no reason to suspect a thing."

Manning nodded. "Very well."

He opened the door and we passed inside, out of the raging wind.

He crossed to the fire and warmed his hands. After a short time, he said, "It wasn't the books I was protecting, Ed."

I looked at him, mystified. "It wasn't?"

"Before he asked for the books, he said he'd like to look around. He stepped into the kitchen and approached the larder."

"He *knew* what was in the cellar?"

Manning shook his head. "He heard a sound down there."

I was slow. I shook my head. "A sound?"

"Jasmine is hiding in the cellar."

I repeated the name, dazed.

"My granddaughter, Ed.

"Your granddaughter? But I never knew –"

"The raid on the refinery went to plan, but her boat capsized in the storm before she could put in at the quay beyond the headland. The idea was that she'd spend the night with me, then leave by ferry today. Then she'd hide up in Kirkwall for a while."

"Good God."

"Jasmine told me how you helped her, Ed, and how she hid when the Party man arrived."

"When he entered the bedroom…" I shook my head. "Can you imagine how I felt?"

He smiled, grimly. "I think I can."

I indicated the kitchen door. "Is she still down there?"

He nodded, moved from the fire and entered the kitchen. He looked at me. "She doesn't know what happened to the Party man, and I don't want her to find out. When I let her out, please don't tell her what I did, what we did."

"Of course," I said.

"I killed a man," Manning murmured, and shook his head as if in disbelief.

I wondered how I might have acted, faced with the choice of either killing a man or allowing a loved one to be arrested.

He opened the larder door and lifted the trapdoor. "It's okay, Jasmine. You can come out now."

She crept timidly from the cellar, glancing from Manning to me. "Edward…" she said.

She followed us into the front room and huddled before the fire. Manning poured her a Scotch and passed it to her.

He could hardly bring himself to look her in the eye.

Her hand shook as she sipped the whisky.

"Ed knows all about the raid," Manning told her.

She gave me an uncertain smile. "Thank you for helping me, Edward."

"It was the least I could do," I murmured.

She looked from me to Manning, forcing a bright smile. "Apart from the last bit, it was a success. We blew the pumping station – and we didn't harm a soul." She nodded to herself, lips pursed, resolute. "That's important, you see. It's the Party who kills, not us. That way, we can claim the moral high ground."

I looked at Manning. He winced, stony-faced.

I could no longer stand the atmosphere in the tiny room, and made my excuses.

I left them seated before the fire, staring into the flames, and made my way home through the wind and the rain.

At nine o'clock the following morning, as I sat reading in my study, a prolonged knocking sounded at the door.

I laid my book aside, stood up, and prepared myself to confront the Party man's colleague.

# HEATWAVE

## Anne Nicholls

*On the way to the past, 2091*

Yan Yan clutched the armrests as the jayplane shuddered and veered. She wasn't rich so she'd never flown before. Below, the cork-oaks of Spain were afire for a hundred kilometres in either direction. Thick smoke roared up to the sky in turbulent swirls that tossed the plane like a plastic bottle in the ocean. She shrieked. The plane banked further and suddenly she could see the necklace of scarlet flames stretching over the hills. Yan Yan Harper, post-grad anthropology researcher, closed her eyes and tried not to think of the many ways she might die before she even got to the project in Gibraltar.

When she'd left England, Oxford had been hip-deep in floods. France wasn't too bad but from the Pyrenees south there'd been nothing but drought. Fields or forests, it was all the same: yellow, brown, veiled in drifting dust. The only patches of green snaked beside irrigation channels.

As the jayplane came in to land, she saw tractors scraping huge firebreaks above La Línea. They swept below her, then the undercarriage bounced on the runway. She stifled a gasp of relief when the plane rolled to a halt.

A skinny, harried woman met her at the gate. 'Ms Harper, I presume?' Her rapid-fire words held a Yankee accent. 'Pleased to meet you. I'm Lucy, Max's PA here in good old 2091, but he'll be with you every step of the way. Welcome to the $H_20$ Project. Dr D'Oliveira and the geology woman are in the Executive Lounge. Let me take you to them while we wait for the engineers to finish loading.'

All Yan Yan wanted to do was sleep. The inoculations had left her groggy but they couldn't infect the fragile population of the past. Then her nai-nai had kept her up half the night, warned by the ancestors that Yan Yan should stay at home in Manchester like a good girl 'or you'll be swallowed by fire-dragons.' But every time the rest of the family had calmed the old woman down enough to get her to bed, she'd crept back into the room Yan Yan shared with Aunty Karen and pleaded 'Don't go!' in her croaky Mandarin.

Lucy introduced her to a pompous little man the shape of a bowling-pin. She couldn't slide a word between the tides of his pontification. She wondered if his students found him this boring as Doctor D'Oliveira lectured on. 'Climatology's the only thing that can save us now,' he concluded. 'But sadly' – he prodded her arm to wrest back her attention – 'some idiots are too greedy to see that. Thank goodness for Reznik International!'

Luckily, a tall, weather-beaten young man came up and interrupted, eyes crinkled in a barely-suppressed smile. 'Dolly, you don't have to sermonise. Global warming, rising sea-levels and all that. We're all with the programme here. That's what this jaunt into history's about, remember? Finding solutions.'

The doctor sputtered, 'Don't call me Dolly!' but the tall man ignored him. 'Max Sandford, Ms Harper.' He shook her hand with the crude vigour of an American. They always seemed to be trying to prove their masculinity. The Chinese found it ill-mannered. 'Or may I call you Yan Yan?"

'You may, so long as *I* may have my hand back.' She withdrew it, pretending to blow on her mashed fingers, and smiled up at him. 'Thank you.'

Max grinned, unabashed. Did he know how sexy he was? He added, 'And just coming in with his girls and matching goons is our patron, Mr Reznik. Make nice to the money, now.'

*Earlier that day*

Oleg Rezhnikov watched as his butler ushered out the Chinese delegation. Permitting himself a wolfish smile, he sauntered to his terrace, dropping his clothes behind him. Anya and Kyoko welcomed him to the hot tub with the fabulous views over the Black Sea far below. Naked now, he grabbed brandy and a Havana from the bar. He didn't relax completely until the security array showed the gates closing firmly behind the helicars. The power magnates were safely on their way back to Beijing. What they didn't know wouldn't hurt them.

Which was that their 3D tour of the gas-fields had been carefully edited. Up in Siberia, the melting of the permafrost released vast clouds of methane. Rezhnikov Inc was a good citizen of the world, carefully harvesting the stuff that would otherwise wreck the ozone layer. Rezhnikov was doing it for the good of all mankind. And secretly to sell off unregistered quantities of gas to the power-hungry triads for rather a lot of cash. Except it obviously wasn't as secret as he would have liked.

Oleg snapped a command. Voice-activated, the display now changed to show the riot dying on the marshy tundra. His private army were hauling the last of the protesters into trucks. Most of them were still walking, sort of, but the unconscious ones were harder to shift. Dead weights. Half of the stupid do-gooders hadn't even thought to bring oxygen masks. What the hell did they think $CH_4$ was? He smiled at the savings on knock-out gas. Naturally his jammers had blanked their phones but Rezhnikov Inc had old-fashioned cable so Oleg could enjoy the show. Some quite pretty girls – they'd be useful for export too. The rougher-looking men would be more profitable as spare parts. All in all, a good day.

And, once he'd changed to his American persona – Ollie Reznik, darling of Washington, chairman of eco-charity $H_2O$ – he was off on the holiday of a lifetime.

*Gibraltar airport, 2091*

Yan Yan had never been in a VIP lounge before, nor among so many VIPs: the botanist, the zoologist, the palaeontologist and a lot of other world-renowned 'ists'. At only 29, she was the youngest by at least a decade. She sat in a corner, practising pranayama breathing, but her eyes were busy. Her eleven companions were schmoozing, bragging, talking to one person while looking past them for someone more influential. She'd never felt more dumpy, more moon-faced. More invisible.

And who was that lean and rangy giant with the dreadlocks and the panther's walk? He stepped aside and a burst of chatter erupted as everyone turned to the door. Yan Yan had to stand on the sofa to peer between the heads at their patron.

At first glance Ollie Reznik, methane millionaire, impressed her. Tall, 3D-star good looks; suit of fine silk; radiant white teeth under a trendy moustache; gold-mirrored sunlenses over his pupils; even the casing on his armtab was gold. That and the two glittering ladies hanging on his arms. And that demigod of a thug.

These were her first impressions. First visual impressions. Then Reznik came closer. A wave of fear ploughed through her gut. Despite his glinting smile, the man radiated not so much menace as an icy indifference to others. His mask of charm hid a hungry ghost.

*Perhaps*, thought Yan Yan, *my grandmother's spirit-tales are real after all.*

*On the road to* $H_2O$, *2091*

The feeling stayed with her through all the formalities of sorting luggage and matériel to the correct parts of the road-train. There must have been a dozen great long shuttles with the Reznik logo. Cranes swung above them; swarms of men in the cobalt and white of his companies heaved and carried and stacked. The din was indescribable. Sweat and the smell of hot metal wavered in the dazzling sunbeams that pierced the high, dim roof of the station. Yan Yan stuck even closer to Lucy, who was following Mr Reznik, his strutting concubines and a phalanx of bodyguards. Max Sandford cursed and rushed back to where a load had crushed a worker's foot.

Reznik and retinue boarded the fancy shuttle at the front. Yan Yan caught one glimpse of his gold eyes and ducked, afraid he might somehow feel her glance. She made to follow but a muscular steward blocked her. 'You don't want to attend a dreary board meeting, ladies and gentlemen,' he said in a soft, Southern drawl. He stretched an arm towards the rear of the shuttle. 'This way. Mr Reznik's laid on refreshments for you.'

'How kind,' said D'Oliveira, shoving his way past and glaring at Yan Yan for daring to get in front of him. Another minion handed him a strawberry daiquiri. D'Oliveira closed his eyes and sighed with pleasure. Around him, the rest of the dozen specialists were already chattering in the luxurious lounge.

'Hi, Dolly, remember me? Maryam.' The tall Berber woman chuckled at the way his outrage died on seeing her beauty. She latched her arm through his. 'Only another twelve hours, Dolly, then it's off we go to Wonderland. I was sat on the jay behind little Yan Yan here. It's so funny when plebs cringe at the whoosh of anti-grav, don't you think?' she added with a malicious smirk. 'Bet the temporal transition will be even worse.'

Yan Yan faded quietly into a corner. Sun Tzu, author of *The Art of War,* counselled observation before action.

As the shuttles got underway, Yan Yan sat back, wondering quite why there were cocktails and caviar when she could see, through tinted windows, shanty towns with starving migrants from the north. The wetlands of France wouldn't take them. They were condemned to struggle for survival in the deserts of Spain, Italy and Africa.

The road-train ran along a dyke. On one side, the rising Mediterranean battered the concrete; on the other, people in tower blocks gazed enviously into the train. Then, beyond the city walls, smog gave way and sun burned down on the parched landscape. Ragged palms and scrub petered out into barren hills.

Around a bend she saw an aqueduct. There were figures on it! People! People spraying lightning! And no one in the shuttle was doing anything about it.

Yan Yan clapped her hands to her lips. Outside the window, actinic bolts writhed across refugees raiding the pipeline. Migrants writhed and blackened and died in their turn. A child, couldn't have been more than ten, grabbed the pickaxe someone dropped, and managed to get in one smash on the concrete before the soldiers mowed her down. Water fountained scarlet through her body.

A clang echoed through the shuttlecar. Yan Yan whirled round. A metal tray clattered in circles on the floor, drinks shattering in arcs of crimson and glass. The waiter pounded up the aisle, a gun in his hand. Everyone scrambled out of his way.

Before he reached the door, a melodic chime prefaced an announcement in a soft Japanese accent. 'No need to worry. They cannot get past our security.'

Swiftly, the waiter hid his gun under his jacket. 'Sorry about that, folks,' he said with a smile. 'Help yourselves to another drink while I mop this mess up. Don't want these pretty li'l rugs to get stained, do we? And wouldn't you know it? We're coming up to $H_20$ right now.'

Maryam pretended indifference but Yan Yan turned to peer at the project's perimeter. The wall, of course, was aflicker with holo-ads, kilometre on kilometre of them. The one she saw most often was EdF, Eau de France, with sun-sparkled springs in the Alps. The fact the glaciers were neither white-painted nor dammed like they actually were spoke of a lost and glorious past. *Rub the refugees' noses in it, why don't you?*

thought Yan Yan. Outside the windows, drones whirled through the smoke, bringing seawater to douse distant flames.

Yet the minute the shuttle passed in through the gates Yan Yan felt as though they were driving under a green roof. Cathedral-like aisles of trees led to a huge open space backed by a circle of verdant cliffs. Squinting against the dazzling sun, she realised the walls weren't rocks but buildings. Each ledge was a terrace of pumpkins or corn, each vine a cascade of beans. Of course her own Archaeology Department at Oxford was roofed with vegetables but it was nothing compared to this.

Rapt in the miracle of $H_20$, Yan Yan barely realised they'd rolled to a stop until the doors hissed open. A scent of greenery wafted moistly inside. She stepped down into its embrace. Here, under the vast dome that ran on solar power, $H_20$ boasted a heat exchanger and cooling plant, a moisture-farm that collected every drop of water from human exhalation and excretion – that went to irrigate the plants that gave food and air and cycled the moisture back again – and a dozen other marvels Yan Yan couldn't even name. This was the healthy heart of the biosphere that was supposed to be leading humankind safely into the future.

And the key to Yan Yan's Neanderthal dreams.

*Farewell Dinner,* $H_2O$ *Project, 2091*

Yan Yan, uncomfortable in her one and only brocaded tunic, had the miserable feeling that the heat was melting her make-up. Twilight fell over the Mediterranean and from up here in the cliff-top hall, she could see the thousands of lights climbing the hills and pooling along the shore. Campfires and the mansions of the rich. She jumped as her copy of the seating-plan was beamed to her arm-tab, then smoothed her hair and tried to look poised instead of self-conscious and more excited than she'd ever been in her life.

She was sat between the palaeontologist, and Maryam, the fashion-plate geologist who seemed to have been tailing her from Gatwick. Foods from every cuisine confused her senses, and the babble of egos and eagerness made it hard to hear when Dr Bell, specialist in Cro-Magnon culture, introduced himself. Round-faced and nerdy in a cute way, he was rather sweet. 'Of course I ex-expect you'll be just as interested in the N-n-neanderthals as we are, Maryam,' he said, not in the least abashed by his occasional stammer.

'Totally,' Maryam answered, deadpan. 'What I wouldn't give to swap beauty tips with a troglodyte who speaks "Ug".'

Bell, mildly drunk, hadn't entirely followed this. He winked at Yan Yan, then beamed owlishly at Maryam. 'Ah-ah-ah. No swapping anything. 500 metres and no closer, that's the rule. Don't want to cause a time-paradox or anything, do we?'

'I doubt we'd do that anyway,' retorted Maryam. 'Isn't that why the *Explorer*'s moored on those pontoons in the bay? I mean, if we drop a scanner of anything, it'll just get washed away on the bottom of the Med when the thaw floods the plain. And the trogs aren't exactly going to print it in *The Times.*'

Yan Yan blurted, 'Think they'll hold up to the transfer? The pontoons, I mean.'

'Not nervous, are you?' Maryam asked, knowing full well that she was.

'Be fair!' said Bell, when he saw Yan Yan wasn't going to answer. 'This isn't like a Heinrich Event, Yan Yan. Quite see why you'd be w-worried if it w-was. Sea got too hot, the Laurentide Ice Sheet crashed into the s-s-sea, three hundred metre waves smashing right over Denmark. Poseidon got c-c-cross.'

Maryam rolled her eyes. 'Yes, but we're not going to *be* in a Heinrich Event. We're there thousands of years between Heinrich Events. It's just going to be like in a helicar coming down to land at the Plaza. You don't just go through 30,000 years in a heartbeat, do you?'

*Don't you mean 40,000?* Yan Yan wondered, but Bell distracted her by patting her hand. 'Don't worry, Yan Yan. Maryam's right. We'll just drift back through the centuries with the *Explorer* sinking gradually onto the plain under today's M-med until we land all nice and flat on our gy-gyros.'

The anthropologist pulled a face. 'Yes, but it's still two hundred metres down.'

Maryam tutted in disgust and turned away.

'Don't mind her,' said Bell. 'I d-didn't think much of flying either. Sick as a d-dog, I was, but that might have been the saké I had to stop my knees shaking. Never mind that. Transition'll be nice and slow. Just think! When we get up in the morning we'll be able to watch how your

Neanderthals got through the Ice Age. Think what a help th-that'll be when we get back to now. These are the smart ones, the ones who c-came s-south away from the snow. You'll be able to get DNA samples and all sorts. Fresh, steaming c-coprolites without all that annoying f-fossilization.'

She winced and grinned, but she wasn't persuaded. Glancing at her worried frown, he tried even harder to reassure her. 'Anyway, we've found pollen from trees that don't grow if it ever drops below 14 degrees.' He nudged her and gave a lop-sided grin. 'I s'pect we'll get a nice tan. Besides, we're only going to be there a month. The chances of a Heinrich Event hitting in one little month are inf –ifn –ifinen – not going to happen.'

Then one of the glitter girls ting'd her champagne flute and the speeches began. 'Pioneering expedition to save our planet'; 'Private finance for research into surviving natural disasters'; 'NGO co-operation with the Disasters Emergency Committee… Reznik's charity gives Europe the privilege of leading the world into a safer future…'

*It's not a speech, it's a hagiography,* thought Yan Yan, clapping like everyone else as she wondered what Reznik's real purpose was. She didn't like the way his thoughts were hidden behind his gold-covered eyes.

*The Explorer, Bay of Gibraltar, Transition*

Yan Yan, wired on caffeine, backed up a step as Max squeezed into the specialists' cabin. 'Everything OK, folks?' he asked, catching her when she tripped over Maryam's feet. Yan Yan closed her eyes, blushed and pulled away. Bell was cute but she wouldn't turn Max away if she found him in her New Year's money. She swallowed. If *The Explorer* bounced across the waves like this, what would it be like when it sank through the years?

He was answered by a chorus of 'Yes' and 'Get on with it'.

'Check your armtabs, folks,' he said. 'Thirty-seven minutes until –'

The door slammed behind him. Everyone saw the locking-wheel spin to settle on red. Max hit the override. Nothing happened. He stabbed the button again, then punched it. More nothing. He wrenched at the wheel in frustration, then spoke to his headset. 'Lucy, what's happening?'

The PA sounded desperate. 'They've locked me out of the control room, Max. Said there's a temporal leak or something. They've already started the countdown. Ten seconds –' Static overrode her voice.

'Who authorised this? Why didn't anybody tell –'

His final *me* stretched into a roar like a jayplane taking off. Yan Yan felt herself falling, dropping into a void, ultra-fast vibrations trembling through her every organ as though she were about to break apart. Spears of coloured light lanced through a weird sort of darkness, leaving it blacker than before. Her own scream visibly shook the air around her. Up and down lost all meaning. Her heart beat so hard it threatened to burst out of her chest.

And suddenly it didn't matter any more. Some kind of euphoric poured through the cabin's vents. People near the walls began to cackle in slow, horrible motion, those at the back laughing higher and faster than they should. 'Einstein doesn't work in time!' giggled a physicist, thinking the champagne in his glass disproved relativity. Yan Yan knew she should be scared but it was too much trouble. She settled back to enjoy the ride.

Something startled Yan Yan awake. Heat shot through her, stemming from that warm patch where her cheek rested on Max's thigh. Nostrils full of a scent of soap and masculinity, she sat up, then reeled over, clutching her head. Only the fact she was already on the floor stopped her falling. Endless darkness enfolded her. Suddenly afraid, she tried to feel if her arms and legs were… still there. *I'm real! We didn't die.*

Safety-lights sprang on, bright enough to dazzle her.

A chemist – she couldn't remember his name – moved his hand oh so slowly to grasp hers. 'Where's the bloody analgesic?' he moaned. 'It's supposed to come on in forty minutes.'

Amidst groans, several people lit up the screens on their armtabs. 'It's only been thirty,' slurred Becky, the doctor. 'We shouldn't have landed yet.'

'A minute for a thousand years, that's what the temporo-phys guys told me.' Max tried to stand up but couldn't even make it to his knees.

'I make it thirty minutes too.'

'And me.'

'I feel sick.'

'Is the door still jammed?' asked Yan Yan.

'Good question,' Max replied. 'I'll tell you when one of us can move.' His fingers flickered over the face of his armtab. 'Lucy? Are you there? Lucy?' But his PA, still in 2091, didn't answer.

Eventually, Becky succeeded in reaching her shoulder-bag. With enormous dedication she extracted a narrow tube. 'Stim,' she mumbled, stabbing it into her bicep. In minutes her face had more colour. She wriggled her fingers, then rose to her knees. 'Hang on. I'll – '

Ribbons began to stream in a gentle breeze from the vents. 'Forty minutes. Right on time,' Max said thoughtfully, turning to inhale the fresh fragrance of dayglow drops. 'Even if we did set off early.'

Yan Yan watched him, making sure it was plain old-fashioned dayglow drops before she breathed it deep into her lungs. Animation returned. Only then did she think of his words.

*The Explorer, 28,000 BCE. Oops.*

As soon as the waiter pushed himself from his sprawl, Max seized his elbow and spun him round. Yan Yan jerked the man's jacket backwards so the neck-hole pinned his arms. With all the speed of martial tai chi she ripped the gun from his holster and kicked his legs from under him, jumping onto his back to pin him down. He tried to buck her off but screamed when she twisted his wrist. The waiter subsided and she slackened her hold, though it was still painful enough to immobilise him. Putting her foot on his cheek, she bent to press the muzzle of the gun to his skull. 'Who sent you?' she hissed, just as Max said, 'How'd you get that gun through the scanners?'

'Excuse me, *sir,*' panted the waiter, his one visible eye sparkling with a rage he could barely contain. 'I was about to see if we had any stowaways in your locker. Mr Reznik sent me to see to your personal security. Wait-staff is my cover.'

Yan Yan and Max met each other's gaze. Was the man telling the truth?

'Look,' the waiter said, 'we don't exactly know what we're going to run into out there, do we? OK, it's not dinosaurs 'n' stuff but what about mammoths and lions and hairy guys with spears? Reznik has a lot invested in you boffins. I'm here to keep you safe.'

'Not sure you're doing a bang-up job so far,' snapped D'Oliveira.

The waiter/guard shot him a poisonous glance. It was wasted as three loud clunks hurled daylight in through the suddenly-open door.

One of Reznik's men leaned in, saying, 'Thank God! We've been calling you but –'A chorus of 'What's going on?' broke on a wave of armtabs trilling. Even Yan Yan's creaky old model pinged up its holoscreen. Reznik International's flame-and-water yin-yang logo encircled $H_2O$'s globe, then Reznik himself came on the screen. Every screen in the shuttle. Two dozen copies of him said in perfect synchronicity, 'I cannot apologise enough, my friends. Do not worry. We are perfectly safe. A coupling started to give way so we've had to set down earlier or we'd have lost the bio and marine labs. Earlier in our trip, I mean. I'm sorry to disappoint but we never reached the 40,000 mark. We're twelve thousand years later, in 28,000 BCE or thereabouts, but at least it's warmer.'

A babble of 'You mean we won't see the Neanderthals at all?' and 'How can we get back to the right time?' drowned his words. When next Yan Yan could hear, the methane magnate was saying with an apologetic smile, 'I've got the temporo-phys people on it. We'll have all you pioneers back safely right on time. Meantime our wait-staff will break out some goodies. You stay in here and have yourselves a lunch while my scouts do their job. And I hope you'll join me tonight to celebrate under the stars of a long-gone age.'

The waiter held out his hand for the gun. And the door was locked again. For their safety.

Yan Yan took her cabin-bag to the ladies'. Lipstick, check. Pepper-spray, check. Jewelled hair-comb with steel blades, check.

The buffet was sumptuous but it couldn't stop Yan Yan's impatience to explore the world outside the shuttlecar. She shared her frustrations with the oceanographer, one Diego Montoya. Tall, olive-skinned and lightly bearded, he fizzed with enthusiasm. 'I'm lucky, then. Haloclines, that's my job. You know, how salty the currents are and what that does to the temperature and circulation. If we're lucky, this data could really help us protect the Gulf Stream.'

'At least you can still do your job.' Yan Yan pulled a face. 'My specialism's the Neanderthals and if we're stuck in 28,000 BCE they've gone extinct.'

'There might be some relics or something,' Diego said. She wondered if his attempt at consolation was a way into flirting, but why would a hunk like him bother flirting with her?

'I suppose.' Yan Yan sipped her drink. 'And I'll be free to give Bell a hand with his Cro-Magnons. They're cool too.'

Maryam tottered over, wide-eyed, lipstick askew. She spoke urgently. 'Dolly's saying we might not be able to get back to the present. Our present.'

Max glided up to hiss in Maryam's ear. 'Can the hysterics! Things are tense enough without you starting a panic.'

Diego slid an arm around the beauty's shoulders. He glared at Max, and cooed, 'It will be all right, Maryam.' He gave her a squeeze. 'You are the best in our field, are you not? As I am in mine. So Reznik will have the brightest minds at the helm. They'll be taking us back any moment, you'll see.'

Yan Yan jerked her head at Max, inviting him to bend so he could hear her whisper, 'But if we're going back, or going on, why are they scouting here?'

'Good question.' Max pondered. 'Maybe it's just a chance to get as much data as they can.'

'Yes, but I just hate being trapped in this benighted shuttle when there's a whole world out there. I want to *see!* Smell air that's never known diesel or coal fires. Why won't they just unpolarise the windows so we can at least look out?'

'Don't want to divert any power from the computers, probably.' Max sounded bitter. 'Or the forge, or whatever the hell they're doing up there in the engines.'

Yan Yan didn't ask why the project manager was being kept in the dark, nor why all the experts were being contained instead of leading a safe exploration. When a loud clang gonged through the walls, Diego had less empathy. 'Well you're supposed to be the head honcho. Why aren't you up there finding out?'

Max looked down at the Puerto Rican and smiled thinly. 'They're playing with radiation and I forgot my lead suit.' He stepped closer, backing Diego against the wall. 'Would you like to pop along and give us your sailor's opinion?' he grated.

Diego put up his hands. 'Hey, man, it's cool. Can't a guy ask a question around here?'

Max half-closed his eyes. 'Only if he's real polite about it.'

But then the question was settled by an announcement. This time it was Reznik's gemologist Kyoko, copied on a dozen tablets, saying in eerie chorus, 'Mr Reznik and his engineers have isolated the problem. It will take at least eight days to replicate the part but regrettably we cannot go further into the past. Therefore we shall be carrying out our studies here and now. Lucky plenty of climate-data is still available to us, and that's always been our priority at Reznik International: here to save the world.'

Reznik's drones didn't come back until late afternoon, but their clear reports meant the windows could be unpolarised. No thundering herds of mammoths, nothing overtly dangerous. Finally the stranded scientists gazed out at lands no one had seen since the melting of the last Ice Age had flooded them. The Mediterranean Plain was savannah, with parklands dotting the rolling hills. A drone coming in across the salt-marsh startled geese into flight, and scores of black-headed gulls. High above, eagles circled. Yan Yan felt trapped and frustrated. Surely if the drones said it was okay, it was okay?

Finally the door opened. The professors and PhDs spilled out, babbling excitedly, pointing armtab scanners and recording the racket of nesting birds. Yan Yan and Bell followed Max to watch his shouting-match with the chief of Reznik's security.

Calmed by the man's apologetic reassurance, Max looked down at Yan Yan plucking his sleeve. 'Can we use the hover-scooters now?' she asked.

'Sure. Pairs, remember. Stick with your buddy and be home before sunset.'

Thrilled, Yan Yan flew her hover out into the wide land. Diego looked round for Maryam but she'd disappeared, so he rode drag with Bell beside him. At thirty klicks an hour they'd soon rounded the Rock. Beneath them rodents and small deer fled from their swift shadows. Off to their left was Africa, blue with distance. And ahead was the shimmering Atlantic.

Seals barked as the trio flew over them. 'Must be young ones who got left behind,' said Diego over their armtabs.

'Never mind that!' squealed Yan Yan. 'Look! Hunters!'

'500 metres,' warned Diego as she swerved towards them, but he needn't have worried. She and Bell hovered at a wary distance, keeping behind a tumble of rocks on the shore. Yan Yan zoomed her scanner to maximum magnification. She could hardly believe her eyes.

'They *are* Neanderthals!' Thousands of years after they were supposed to have died out, the beings had short legs, barrel chests, backward-sloping faces streaked with clay. There was no doubt about it. She was ecstatic.

'You're in luck,' Bell told her softly. 'Looks like those so-called contaminated samples weren't contaminated after all.'

'I never did trust those datings,' she replied, beaming. 'Which means they're co-existing with Cro-Magnons.' She stared from the holo-images on her armtab to the tiny figures in the distance. Half a dozen hunters clubbed baby seals. Blood spattered. Yan Yan swallowed. But was this any worse than factory farming? At least it was for the Neanderthals' survival.

'Sun's going down,' Diego said.

So they headed back to the *Explorer*, the sea turning red behind them.

*Still 28,000 years ago, but a week later*

When the cooks brought out a gateau as dessert, Yan Yan knew it heralded bad news. Their picnic tables were arranged on a meadow in the last of the evening sunshine: two tables for the 'ists', as Max had taken to calling them, and three long ones for Reznik Security. Oddly enough the techs dined on the *Explorer*'s deck. The camouflaged plastiglass of the portadomes made it hard to see where the labs were. Yan Yan found it strange that the biodome was the biggest of the lot, and the first to be erected. Surely it should be Dolly's or Diego's? Weren't the rest of them just kind of along for the ride?

Beside her, the Puerto Rican stood, shading his eyes as he peered this way and that. Max came over and slapped him on the back. 'If you're looking for Maryam, Reznik's invited her to join him and his arm-candy.' He pointed with his chin to a fancy table on the foredeck of the *Explorer*. There was Maryam, throat glittering in the candlelight as she tossed her head back in a ringing laugh.

Diego slumped in his chair. 'Diamonds are a girl's best friend, no?'

'Well hers, obviously.' Yan Yan patted his arm while Bell poured him a glass of wine.

Max slid into the seat Diego had been saving. 'If you gotta pay for it, pal, it ain't worth having. Pass the cream.'

Picking up on his tension, Yan Yan asked him, 'They're still not letting you into the cockpit, are they?'

'No, nor the biolab. And the way we went over the figures, the *Explorer* should have had more than enough energy to shift the loads we calculated without wrecking the couplings. I reckon Reznik brought over a lot more than he said.'

Bell leaned forward. 'Where is it then?'

'I don't know. Hovers don't leave tracks and somehow the geo people are too busy to let me use their drones.'

'What d'you think they're up to?'

Max looked them over with his level grey gaze. 'Got a pretty good notion.' He jerked his chin over to where Reznik stood. 'Let's see what the big guy's story is.'

Everyone's armtabs chimed. In the screens the low sun slanted off gold metallic eyes. 'We are very sorry, people.' Reznik sounded too sincere. 'We are unable as yet to fix our transport problem. Looks like we'll be here for the full month.' The mogul raised his voice over the hubbub. 'No need for alarm. We'll have you back home right on schedule. Anyway, this is a much better climate. Meantime this is your chance for a detailed survey. What you learn now could save the world.' He raised his glass. 'To you, time crusaders, and to success.'

*28,000 years ago, dawn, day ten*

'Don't let 'em see the spare batteries,' Max whispered, as Yan Yan, Bell, Diego and he loaded up their hovers. The zoologist had put his name down for one but he'd get over it. He had more than enough lizards here to keep him happy.

Yan Yan kept her eyes on her hands but Bell jerked his head round like an owl. Max elbowed him. 'Don't look so guilty,' he hissed.

It was a useful warning. Somehow Reznik's forces were there every time anyone turned round. She too had tried to get a peek inside the biodome but the woman in cobalt blue wouldn't even unlock the door. The guardswoman was pleasant, chatty even, but even Diego's flirting couldn't change her mind.

The four flew off through the pearly dawn. Rabbits and red deer scampered out of their way, leaving dark tracks through the dew.

Cicadas sang the sun into being. It rose, bringing blue to the sky and green to the land. Trees were alight with blossom. Dandelions glowed against the new grass of spring. Butterflies danced on the tangy breeze.

Just short of the hovers' limit, the twenty-first century quartet landed in a clump of willows. It was hot and still under there, except for the whine of insects. Yan Yan took off her jacket, knowing the mosquito repellent would keep her safe. They swapped out the batteries, Max checking the connections. 'Right, we're fifty k north of the Explorer,' he said. 'We can cover another twenty-five k before we have to turn back. Keep your eyes peeled for technology. Yan Yan, you're with Bell. Diego, come with me.'

'Why can't *I* go with her?' the Puerto Rican snapped.

'One fighter in each pair,' Max said flatly. 'You guys, northwest. We'll swing along the shoreline. Stick with your partner. Check in every hour.'

'That's not fair! I can fight.' Diego glared at their retreating backs. Wordlessly the others swung aboard their hovers and raced off. Diego's anger faded to unease as he realised he was alone. Hastily he raced after Max.

Yan Yan and Bell rode within eyesight of each other, closing up only when they passed through dense pine forest. In one sunlit valley she spotted a group of Cro-Magnons, the women and children gathering edible buds or digging up roots while the men scouted a herd of horses. She veered away, sorry she couldn't stop to record them, but finding out what Reznik was up to took priority.

'We'll get another chance,' Bell whispered. It came out crackly since they were so far from the transmitter they had to use old-fashioned radio. 'Whoa! Max, you gotta see this!'

Soon all four were crouching in the shadow of an enormous oak. It hung over a river where men in jeans were panning for gold. Even as she watched, a rifle cracked. The miners dropped their pans and scattered.

A body splashed into the river: a Neanderthal, rolling as the current pulled him out of sight. Five more burst out, yelling, waving clubs and spears. They raced towards the guard, not understanding the dumdum bullets that tore through them.

'That all?' called someone from a shuttle.

'Yep.'

'Well get back to work then! Reznik's not paying you to lollygag.'

Sullenly the miners came out from their hiding-places. Yan Yan was close enough to hear one complain, 'I didn't come here to shift corpses.' Another replied, 'Quit whining. Better us hauling bodies so the bluecoats can guard our asses.'

Max crawled backwards, the others following. They regrouped in the rocks where they'd hidden their hovers. He passed round a canteen. Even here in the shade it was so hot a tortoise was worming his way into the long grass. Overhead, birds warbled a cheery requiem.

'So that's one part of Reznik's plan,' Max said.

'What do you mean, one part?' asked Diego, dark eyes wide with fear.

Yan Yan said, 'I want to know what's in the biodome.'

Max said, 'I want to know I can get you all out safely.'

She cocked her head. 'He's obviously planning to go back to our time. He can hardly spend gold here, can he?'

'Yeah. But is he planning on taking us with him?'

Yan Yan followed Bell, the last pair to head back to the transport bay. Nobody stopped them. Nobody was waiting inside. Sighing with relief, she headed across to her lab.

The door slammed shut behind her. Anya leant casually against it, looking somehow larger than before. Reznik, perched on the lab stool, tossed aside a flint scraper and aimed his blank golden eyes at Yan Yan. 'So kind of you to join us. Would you care to see what our drones picked up this afternoon?'

Yan Yan felt the blood draining from her face.

'Ah, you've guessed.' At Reznik's command Yan Yan's armtab spewed out its holoscreen. From on high, tiny dots rode across the landscape. The image swooped dizzily into a close-up of her. Of her friends. From the willows on, not a moment of their adventure went unnoticed. It zipped through on high speed, except when they spoke. Every word they'd whispered rang clear. Yan Yan locked her trembling knees.

The film stopped. 'You may remember,' Reznik said, a hint of a Russian accent creeping through, 'that Clause 34 of the contract you signed expressly forbids industrial espionage. Clause 27, of course, was an oath of secrecy. Don't worry. You may still carry out you research. You will be returning to the twenty-first century. So long as you behave, you will be returning with all your limbs intact. I think you'll be impressed by what you see after dinner.'

The 'ists' were delighted by the strawberry meringues and champagne but Yan Yan felt uneasy. The level of chatter over the picnic tables rose, the slanting Mediterranean light making a perfect evening for romance. If she ever got any. Bell seemed oblivious. Post-borers were so far away they were no louder than the crickets.

Kyoko tinkled a spoon against her glass as Reznik stood. Once again all the armtabs chorused his speech. 'My friends, I have an announcement from our future. Please save your questions until after the bulletin.'

An anchorman couldn't keep the grief out of his voice. Each of the 'ists' heard it in their own language. But it was the images which shocked. A wall of water two hundred metres high slammed through New York. Oslo. London. Amsterdam. Every low-lying town around the Atlantic was drowned. Hovercars, trash and bodies swirled along the flooded streets, crashing through the windows of shops and offices and homes. A liner smashed into the Statue of Liberty, both of them torn and sinking in a shriek of tortured metal. Starlings screeled homeless above wrecked buildings. The tidal wave swept down through Philadelphia, heading for Miami and Belize. Every part of the Eastern Seaboard was gridlocked with people trying to escape, or awash with flotsam, and sharks feasting on corpses.

Screams and sobs broke out from the specialists. Yan Yan cried out, 'Mama? Nai-nai!' and wept as she realised everybody she knew in England was lost.

Reznik turned up the volume and spoke. 'A Heinrich Event. The very catastrophe we came here to avert. We are too late. Rising seas in our time have undercut the Arctic ice sheets. Diego, as our oceanographer, can you tell us what will happen next?'

'Snowball Earth,' he gulped. 'The new Ice Age.'

'Anya, our representative from the Disasters Emergency Committee?'

'Starvation,' said the blonde vixen flatly. 'Plague from millions of human and animal corpses. No infrastructure. Masses dying as they migrate in a quest for shelter. Looting and fighting for food. It will be at least five years before it's safe to return.'

'But we are here,' continued Reznik. 'We have the perfect chance to thrive and create aid.'

Dolly's chair clattered as he leaped up. 'If you can get a message through, why can't we get back?'

'$H_2O$ has more power than we do,' Reznik said suavely, 'but they'll need it all to help the survivors. We've decided between us that for the next five years it's in everyone's best interests if we stay here. We *will* get back, but not until we've accumulated enough power of our own. We have all this wonderful sunshine. Our technicians can create more solar batteries. We can grow food and medicines that'll be needed up ahead. We know there's no Heinrich Event threatening us in this time.'

Max shouted, 'Why can't we go back to before it happens and warn everybody?'

Reznik shook his head. 'Max. Max. It's the Cassandra Curse. For the whole of the twenty-first century brave souls have warned us what global warming would do but did society listen? No, my friends, tonight is for mourning. Tomorrow we start our new battle for humankind's survival.'

'Where did Reznik *get* all these plants?' Bell murmured as he and Yan Yan weeded their way along a row of seedlings. The sun was a mere handspan above the horizon but heat shimmered in the air.

'Biolab,' she panted. 'That snotty bitch Kyoko must've been anticipating this. How come Max didn't spot a tonne of machinery being brought through his scanners? D'you think he's in on it?'

'He didn't know about the waiter's gun. Besides, he was as surprised as we were when we found the goldminers.'

'So he's stupid, then?' she asked. 'Or just a good actor?'

'I think he didn't expect his employer to be playing a double game. Notice how they keep the tech guys away from us?'

Yan Yan shrugged and uprooted some twitchgrass. 'I thought it was just the usual soft science/hard science divide until I clocked the guards. D'you think they'll kill the locals to keep 'em off our crops?'

Bell jerked his chin to where the men in blue were stringing electric fences. 'They won't need to. Deer and boar, my arse. It's not the wildlife they're shutting out. It's our ancestors.'

'They've still got eyes, though. What if they start farming twenty thousand years too soon? What'll that do to the timelines?' Tears ran down her cheeks as she thought of her drowned relatives. 'Remember when I said Nai-nai warned me to watch out for the fire dragon? She got it wrong. A water-dragon washed her away.'

'What *is* this stuff anyway?' Bell asked to distract her from her grief. 'It's nothing I've ever eaten.'

She poked at a blue-green thistle, snapping off a leaf with her gloved hands and bringing it up to sniff. White sap beaded stickily, smelling caustic. 'Medicine, I suppose. There's an awful lot of it. Wouldn't you think we'd do carrots or turnips or something edible first?'

Bell shrugged in his turn. 'That's probably what Max and the others are planting.'

'Yeah.' Her voice was bitter. 'Everyone except Reznik and his glitter girls.'

'And the temporo-techs.'

'Let's see if we can catch one during siesta.'

That was easier said than done. Day after day the men in blue stayed aloof. New wire fences were erected around the *Explorer*. Reznik said it was because the Cro-Magnons were getting too nosy. Armed guards patrolled between the lab domes that the 'ists' now called home. Only Dolly really believed it was for their safety – because he was surely too important to risk.

At least after lunch the specialists were free. Some weeks later, Yan Yan was gearing up for another sweaty afternoon filming a pretty Neanderthal mother when Diego invited her to go fishing with Bell and Max. They launched the dinghy off the Atlantic coast. It was a baking hot day in early summer. Yan Yan enjoyed the fresh breeze as they bounced over the sun-sparkled ocean. She was as excited as any of them when their net pulled in hake and octopus. On their way back they spotted one of the techs line-fishing off the rocks. His rod dipped. A huge tail splashed out of the water and the man was almost pulled in. 'Gi's a hand!' he yelled in a Cockney accent.

They moored close by, Max and Bell jumping ashore. It took all three of them to land the monkfish, which fought such a battle it amazed Yan Yan the rod didn't snap. 'Where's your minder?' Max asked as the tech clubbed the fish with his gaff. The brute must have been at least a metre and a half in length, hell to get into the fridge on the tech's hoversled.

'He's off after seal-skins,' the tech-man panted. 'Some of this season's pups got left behind. I don't mind fishing but I'm buggered if I'm going to bash babies to death. Take a picture?' the mixed-race Cockney asked, posing with one foot on his catch.

Max clicked his armtab. 'There you go.' After introductions he asked, 'So, Charlie, is it right that we can't get back?'

'Nah.' Charlie chuckled. 'It's a load of old bollocks to keep you boffins quiet. It's just that the longer we stay here the more we get paid.'

'Did you lose anybody in the flood?' asked Yan Yan.

'What flood?'

'What d'you mean, what flood?' she yelled as Max barked, '*The* flood! The one that drowned Earth.'

'Don't tell me you fell for that?' the man snorted. 'One o' them disaster films, wa'n't it? Nah, everthing was all right last time we heard.' The man's ruddy face twitched. 'Bugger! We're not s'posed to tell you that.'

Max loomed over him. 'In case we run amok?'

'Well yeah. He reckons the threat of plague will keep you here all nice and quiet.'

'So my dad's not dead?' growled Bell.

'Wouldn'a thought so.'

'Can we get in touch with our folks?' Yan Yan asked eagerly.

Charlie scratched his stubbly chin. 'Well no. We ain't got enough juice yet. 'Least, that's what they *say*. All them solar cells, you'd've thought so. Look' – he laid a meaty hand on Max's arm – 'you won't let on, will yer? Lose me me bonus, that would. Anyroad up, me and the temporo-phys whatsits and the guards, we all signed on for five years in the sun, but it's time travel, innit? We'll be back wiv a fortune right after we left. *Right* after we *left*, geddit?' He was the only one who laughed at his pun. 'Look, clear orf, will yer? He ain't too bad for a bluecoat but I don't want the bastard to catch me fraternisin'.'

The four all began to speak at once but Charlie's face hardened. ''E's got a gun. One o' them with the pottery bullets what break up the minute they 'it you. Lotsa little bits that tear you to ribbons so you die in slow agony.' He boarded his hoversled and roared into the distance, the stink of fish-guts trailing in his wake.

'I guess he doesn't want us breezing up to him at the next soirée,' Bell said thoughtfully.

Puzzlement morphed into rage and planning. 'Know their strengths and their weaknesses,' Yan Yan said. They looked at her. 'What? It's in the *Art of War*. Know ours too and we'll know how to use them. Diego, see what info you can charm out of the lady guards.'

'Right up my street,' the Puerto Rican said with a grin. Bell rolled his eyes.

Days passed, each of the four listening, watching, taking notes. By now summer was at its zenith. Three storage sheds appeared from the locked shuttles, just in time for the first harvests. Carrots, beet, early peas – Yan Yan and her friends scarcely saw each other they were so busy gathering and storing.

And the blue-green thistles came into blossom. Branching stalks held hundreds of flowers in every shade from pink to mauve. They wafted a sense-turning perfume. As she sat down to dinner Yan Yan found herself smiling serenely.

So did everyone around her. It was Max who said dreamily, 'Pinchbowl.'

'Huh?'

'You know, pauper's marching powder? Hibifana? Makes you feel all happy and full of beans even if you're thin as a line of credit.' Each of the quartet looked at the other. Diego glanced furtively round and whispered, 'Reznik's a drug-dealer.'

Their armtabs chimed. 'The secret's out,' blared Reznik from every screen, flashing clips of their conversation to everyone else. 'You, my dear scientists, have a choice. Work with me and you go back with one percent of the profits of this little vacation.' Sculpted lips twisted in glee as he waited.

Sure enough, Diego squared his shoulders belligerently. 'What about if we don't, huh?'

'Then,' Reznik chorused, 'let's just say your work may be published a trifle… posthumously.'

Yan Yan drew her friends' attention, beckoning them close enough to hear her whisper, 'Ssh. Let the enemy think we are weak where we are strong.'

Dolly put up his hand, quavering, 'How much is one percent likely to be?'

'A couple of tens – with four zeros on the end.' The mogul cocked his chin derisively. 'Two hundred thousand big ones, for those of you who can't count. And you have the satisfaction of knowing your nearest and dearest will be happy in your arms. If they survived, that is.'

Kyoko glided towards Diego, who froze as two guards seized him from behind. Paradrops on their gauntlets jabbed into his bloodstream. He would have sagged to the ground if the guards hadn't been holding him up. The female bent to run her tongue over his face while Kyoko smiled and held up a syringe. 'So let's all take the loyalty oath, shall we? Because only *we* have the antidote. If you talk about this when we're up in the future we can kill you with a' – she drew speech marks in the air – 'phone call.'

The scars from the implants healed. All too soon the equinox brought torrential rain. Rivers overflowed. As the marsh spread, geese and waders honked and squawked. Great flocks of swallows paused on their journey south. A couple of the techs and a guard started up a black market in sealskin waterproofs. Only the hardiest of souls ventured far.

One night after dinner Yan Yan invited her co-conspirators to her dome for a planning session. Once the other 'ists' had realised they were free to plot at this hour, the mutiny was made of seven: zoologist, topographer and scanmistress in addition to the original four. Dusk had given way to a thunderstorm. They ran from the mess tent, glad to throw off their wet coats when they reached the anthrolab were Yan Yan lived. They huddled close to the wood-burning stove, swigging hot crab-apple wine. All of a sudden the lights went out.

'Not again!' Max got up with a sigh but Diego said, 'No point, Max. You're not an electrician.'

In the soft glow of the fire Yan Yan patted his leg. 'Stop feeling so damn' guilty, Max. It's not you. It's the weather. Or that gangster up there.'

Zoology said, 'We all fell for it. How's the Tomorrow plan coming?'

Everyone flinched as the door wrenched open. The black Cockney slid in, rain dripping off his sealskins. He swivelled, holding out some kind of stick that blazed white in a dazzling flash of lightning. Max and Diego climbed to their feet but the tech pulled a crude sign from under his coat: 'Clear of drones. Don't talk. Take your armtabs off.'

Yan Yan felt naked without hers. She missed its warmth, its companionship. It wasn't alive but through it the world could talk to her. She watched it fade in the heap on the table, bereft when its lightpulse dimmed and died.

'I ain't falling for Reznik's propaganda no more,' Charlie said. The red of the fire burned in his hooded eyes. 'He's gonna plant bombs in the Arctic and Antarctic. He says why wait on the whims of the inevitable? I heard him talking. Well, I hacked his armtab, the slimy bastard. He's gonna cause a new ice age and stay here till the plague's burnt out. He wants to go back and conquer an empire. My son's up there in the future. I don't want him getting no Black Death.'

'A plague? He's planning a plague?' Diego squeaked. ''Course he is,' he answered, scratching the site of Kyoko's injection. 'Up there as well as back here. Bastard bastard.'

Max spread out a map of the camp, which made Charlie boggle. 'So it's not just about getting home. We have to stop him. Welcome aboard.'

'Anybody else with us?' Yan Yan asked. 'And who's on the other side?'

Charlie thought about it. 'Of the four temporo-techs, two definitely wanna derail 'is plans. Dunno 'bout the others. They're loners so they ain't got nuffink to lose. That Anya's got my mate 'andy 'Arry hopping or he'd be here too.'

Diego winked. 'I've got a couple of… friends… in the guard. Natalya's the quartermaster-cum-armourer. Tasha's – well, let's just say she's good in a clinch.'

'Yeah.' Charlie nodded vigorously. 'Didja see her chuck that Cro-Magnon guy over her shoulder when he got too close to the fence?'

'She's not the only one ignoring the five hundred metre rule,' Yan Yan said indignantly. 'This afternoon when I was watching Nelly and her baby – '

'Who?'

'The Neanderthal mother I'm studying. You know, the smiley one with the baby boy and the spiral tattoos on her cheeks. I was hiding up a tree and Reznik and that creepy goon of his, that dude who oozes about like a tiger, they were stalking her. I screeched like a lynx. She looked up and the moment she saw them she went pale like she'd seen them before. She started running before either of 'em could get close. Good job they never saw me.'

'How are you g-getting on with Nelly's clan?' interrupted Bell.

'Great! I've even started picking up bits of their language. She keeps smiling at me and KalKal likes the shiny pebble I left for him.' Max growled. Yan Yan blushed. 'Well I might never get a chance to interact with them again! And don't think Bell hasn't cosied up to those Cro-Magnons with the strings of claws around their necks.' She returned the anthropologist's glare. 'Sorry, Bell, but we're not the only ones. Right, the Tomorrow plan. What resources have we got? I want to win this war before they know they're in it. Diego, how's your charm offensive on Maryam?'

'In these shoes?' Maryam eyed the Puerto Rican Casanova over her glass of champagne. 'I'm not going anywhere. But don't worry, lover boy. We can be as private as you like down in my cabin.'

Diego followed her swaying backside into the bowels of the *Explorer.* She might have been a mere 'ist' but she amused Reznik enough for him to give her a room aboard. A room with air-vents. Handy 'Arry had knocked up a neat little aerosol.

The Latin lounge lizard, being who he was, couldn't help a little pre-sabotage fun. Then the alarm vibrated against his wrist.

Maryam disentangled her lips from his. 'What's that, honey?'

'Just someone with poor timing. They can wait.' He forced a smile, pretending to smother exasperation. 'But I really, really have to go to the john. Don't start anything without me.'

*I'd have put a scanner in this chica's bathroom,* Diego thought as he closed the door behind him. Which is why he turned the shower on until the place filled with steam. Hurriedly he squirted the pinchbowl into the air-duct – except for one last small puff that he shared with Maryam before inserting his nose-plugs. She didn't notice. She was adrift in a balloon of dreams.

Elsewhere in the *Explorer,* security staff hardly noticed their mood shift from boredom to pleasant release. The gas drifted towards Reznik's inner sanctum, potent but invisible.

In his suite, Reznik yelled into his armtab. 'Answer me, damn you! What the hell, Kyoko, get your butt up here pronto.' A pause. 'Could be fun.' Suddenly he sounded cringingly coy even to his own ears. 'Yoohoo, darling, where are you? What the fuck? Security!'

He slapped a command on his armtab. Nothing happened. The panic-room doors didn't crash protectively around him. But the ordinary doors clicked and he knew he was locked in. It was uproariously funny. He collapsed on the couch, giggling.

Meantime, Tasha straightened her uniform and went on with her daily patrol. As usual she found the temporo guards on the roof of the shuttle they guarded. They were sprawled shirtless, catching some rays in the evening air. 'Want a drink, guys?' she called softly, slipping up the ladder.

Patrolling at the perimeter, Jason Eckvald squinted into the golden horizon. He was thinking about that red-headed siren of a cavegirl who kept sneaking away to see him. She was practically a mermaid; he just liked collecting shellfish for dinner. Malis, she was called, but her sweet nature made the name a lie. Maybe he wouldn't go back to the twenty-first century. Now he'd shot down painted savages armed only with spears Jason didn't have the stomach for building an empire on death. Maybe he could learn the language and move in with the tribe. But out loud he kept to the company line.

Which was unfortunate. A paradrop pellet stung his neck. As advertised by arms dealers, in seconds he was paralysed. Apart from his lungs and bladder. That was humiliating. But not as humiliating as waking up handcuffed with a bunch of furious mercenaries.

Out at Gold Mine Creek, Max parked his hover-scooter. He and his passenger, Natalya, were both dressed in Reznik blue. Caps low as if to ward off the sun, they stretched and strolled over to the captain, who asked, 'Anything exciting back at base?'

'Nah. Just thought you might like to share some brandy. And we were curious about our one percent of the goldmine.'

'Want to join us for dinner? No, I suppose you'd better get back.' The captain checked his pickets were where they were supposed to be. Very conscientious, he was. Then he took a glug from Natalya's hip-flask. 'Here's gold-dust in your eye.'

The quartermaster slipped a little something in the guards' coffee. They were going to need an awful lot of soft leaves over the next forty-eight hours.

It was Max who spoke to the miners. 'We're ditching Reznik and his vultures. We're heading back to our own time. Your share's just got a whole lot bigger. You with us?'

The dozen miners muttered amongst themselves. Natalya stepped forward, hands on hips. 'You know me, boys. I'm the one you come to when you want a new pair of pantyhose.'

Feeble chuckles.

'Think Reznik really wants to share?' she asked.

'Oh come on!' snarled a miner. 'He knows we're not going to blab. He made us have those exploding oath implants.'

She laughed. 'Come on yourselves. Do you honestly think those implants can actually tell what you're saying? He doesn't need to cart your asses back to the twenty-first century. You're dead weight, just a sad footnote to archaeology.'

'I n-never thought it would be this easy.' Bell clinked Yan Yan's glass with his. Around them a victory party had broken out. Handy 'Arry had bodged up some fireworks. He and his pals on the security team had stripped the Reznik contingent, bound them head to foot in polycling and left them lying like a bunch of cocoons, all their gadgets out of reach. Apart, of course, from Reznik's golden eyes. A constant subharmonic disrupted their signals. As a bonus, it made the gangster's head ache.

Yan Yan tapped her temple. 'A war is won before the first battle is fought.'

'Sun Tzu again?' asked Max. Diego had one arm round Tasha's waist, the other around Natalya's.

'Yes. But if we do get back to our time, we'll be facing Reznik's pals at $H_2O$. And stopping his murderous minions in the Arctic. This was the easy bit.'

Max took a swallow of crab-apple cider. 'I just hope I can get Lucy out alive.'

Neither of them pointed out that his PA might already be dead.

Tomorrow Day dawned grey and humid. They'd loaded the last of the kit aboard the *Explorer,* all apart from Diego's. And the prisoners. Reznik's glitter girls, Maryam and the rest of his gang still wriggled helplessly in their cocoons. Most of the 'ists' were hanging around impatiently or saying a last farewell to the past. The shuttle from the mine had been delayed by a river in spate but it was here now and techs were finalising the linkage. All the domes had been dismantled, the drug crop destroyed. Everything else was ready but not even Charlie dared interfere with Diego's delicate instruments.

'Damn the man!' snapped Max. 'And you guys over there, you get that shuttle linked up PDQ.'

Yan Yan put a hand on his chest. 'I'll get our annoying oceanographer. You've got enough on your plate.'

She found Diego on his knees in front of a box on a folding chair. It stood isolated on a patch of flattened yellow grass. 'Get your skates on, bonehead! Everybody's waiting – '

He flung up a hand and shushed her. Jagged lines scrolled across an oscillator. 'Run!' he shouted, scrabbling to his feet. 'Run for your lives!' he gasped into his armtab. 'Get the *Explorer* fired up quick!'

Caught in his anxiety, Yan Yan lurched into a trot. She fell as the ground rumbled beneath her. Diego didn't even notice. He pelted past Max and up the gangplank. All around them birds screeched into flight.

Bell pointed at the writhing human bundles. 'We can't leave them to die!'

'But they haven't got the mine-shuttle hooked on,' shrilled Dolly. 'There's no room for them.'

A roar came towards them from the south. Again the ground shook and birds swirled squawking in alarm. 'Cut 'em loose,' snapped Max. 'They'll have to take their chances.'

Sprays of solvent began to slick through the tough plastic cocoons. Yan Yan cast a glance over her shoulder. A blue line broadened on the horizon. Close at hand the sea slurped away, leaving fish flapping dazedly on the mud. Her hand flung out. 'Tsunami!'

Yan Yan scrambled aboard, then pressed against a window to see if her little family of Neanderthals had managed to get to safety. The doors slammed shut and the shuttle began to thrum. She manoeuvred her armtab, desperately scanning on widescreen. The engines whined up to a growl. 'There she is!' Yan Yan screamed. 'Go *on*, Nelly!'

Closer at hand, if the anthropologist had cared to look, Reznik's bunch of crims were squirming out of their carapaces. Yan Yan jerked back as a head jumped outside the window. Reznik! He screamed impotently to the sky then took off at a run.

A hundred metres away Nelly was scrambling up a cliff. Her baby clung to her hair, jouncing up and down on her back, but they had a long way to go. She risked a glance at the wave. Huge and dark with debris, the crest towered across the treetops. It was rushing towards her. And towards the *Explorer*, quick as a cannonball. The engines howled. Yan Yan's nails dug in as she clenched her hands in anguish. Would Nelly make it? And the poor little baby?

'L-look!' Bell pointed out the window. A low mound had slackened the force of the sea but the truncated wave was still as tall as a towerblock. 'M-maryam. Anya.' Just as the two women raced round a hairpin, Kyoko and Reznik zoomed past them on an overloaded hover. They too were speeding towards the cliffs. Nelly was halfway up now, and her mate was starting down to help her. The roaring wave had spouted around the Rock and tumbled closer.

The baby slipped – Yan Yan's heart pounded – but Nelly gripped him tightly in one arm, scrambling up the steep bluff.

A pebble turned under Anya's foot and broke her ankle. She fainted with the pain. Reznik was slaloming up the tumbled base of the cliff. Maryam was pounding up its lowest slope.

Someone in the shuttle was praying in Hebrew, someone else in Italian. Diego shouted above the thrumming. 'It's Mount Teide erupting in Tenerife. It's not a full-blown eruption but the tremors have set off an underwater avalanche.' His lips moved again but Yan Yan couldn't hear him above the engine noise. The *Explorer* was shaking loose but gravity was fighting back. Her engines were game, though. Their pitch screamed higher until Yan Yan's nose started bleeding. Nelly wasn't going to make it –

And she'd seen who was flying beneath her as though he were a bird. The pretty mother's face suddenly looked very young and very scared. Yan Yan and Bell had never told anybody, of course, but they'd been close enough to her Neanderthals that she could have reached across the narrow stream and clasped Nelly's hands. They'd tossed her a bar of chocolate and mimed eating it. Nelly nibbled a corner but soon spat it out. Presumably the sugar hurt her teeth. They'd given her a ball of string. Yan Yan realised, *I made her trust us enough for Reznik to get hold of her.*

Now Nelly scrabbled desperately, loose scree sliding beneath her. Baby KalKal was crying. Her mate was still too far above to help. The whine of the engines seemed to slice into her head. She had one last glimpse of paradise. Emotion had Yan Yan split in two.

With the roaring deluge still thundering closer.

Yan Yan tore her gaze away to look for Reznik. The gangster mogul was struggling to throw Kyoko off his hover. He was halfway up the cliff. Her weight swung the scooter off balance. Kyoko cartwheeled into the rocks and dropped into the rising maelstrom. Reznik slammed face forwards into the precipice but managed to cling on. The hover tumbled after Kyoko, lost in the thundering waters.

Nelly was less than fifty metres below her mate, but panting with exhaustion and fear. Reznik was maybe no more than ten behind the glorious redhead and gaining fast. The caveman was uncoiling a rope but it wasn't long enough to get Nelly past the overhang. And there was only one rope.

Glancing down in terror, Nelly traversed by clinging on with fingers and toes. She reached for the twisted coil and leaped upwards. Her mate strained to heave her and the baby up.

Reznik grabbed for her. Nelly shot her heel out, tumbling him into the flood. She grasped the rope. Yan Yan watched him fall to the curse of the fire-dragon. *Must thank Nai-nai when I'm back home.*

And that was the last Yan Yan saw as the *Explorer* sprinted through time.

*Europe, 2091*

Oh, parades and heroes and lecture-tours. It turned out simple enough to decommission the polar bombs. What a boon the armtab is, recording crimes as evidence. As if the ones the 'ists' had taken hadn't been enough, Lucy had quite a lot of dirt on $H_2O$ as well. She hadn't needed rescuing once the pinchbowl was out of her system. She and

Max were between projects, which was code for honeymooning in Hawaii.

In the green room after their first conference in England, Yan Yan had organised a tiny banquet. The only guests were Mama and Baba, Auntie Karen and Nai-nai, and of course Bell. She passed him a fried locust and said, 'Bit of an anti-climax, this, isn't it, sweetie? No desperate dash across the Atlantic, no fighting pen-pushers to get to generals.'

Bell kissed her nose. 'Yep, it's th-that all right. N-no ice age.'

Unseen in Diego's lab a seismograph jiggled. The sensors in Greenland, then Scandinavia and Iceland, were sending messages. Atlantic buoys lofted. Diego snuggled with a friendly barmaid as Nature did what Reznik had failed to do.

Icebergs headed for the flooded fields of Oxford.

# Alien TV

Paul McAuley

Before Alan Smith could get into the convention, he had to endure a few minutes of low farce at the registration desk. Howard had promised to arrange a day membership, but the woman behind the desk, wearing an ExoCon 8 T-shirt, with a soft toy of an alien fastened to her shoulder like a pirate's parrot, couldn't locate Alan's badge. She called over a colleague and they riffled through a printout and searched the boxes under the desk with an increasingly harried air. At last, the woman found him listed as 'Friend of Howard Hutton', misspelled his name in purple Magic Marker on a blank badge, told him to wear it at all times, and, before he could protest, pushed the pin through the lapel of his brand new Cerruti jacket.

So Alan was feeling more than slightly pissed-off as he went around the desk and display boards at the top of the broad flight of stairs, but then he saw the sports-bar-sized screen at the far end of the big lounge and it was as if eleven years had dropped away. The screen was tuned to alien TV, of course. Not the compilation channel which played on cable, which flipped from one video stream to the next every thirty seconds, but the real, live, uncensored thing.

It was one of the panoramic views, looking out over a valley wooded with parasol trees towards low, eroded mountains, the mountains blue against the indigo sky, the crowded caps of the parasol trees (reminding Alan of the umbrellas of shoppers jostling through the city centre in the cold Easter rain) dark violet mottled with glittering cyans and purples. Ruins of a tower stood salt-white in the middle distance; half a dozen aliens were dipping and weaving above its jagged top.

Alan had seen the first decoded clips released by NASA when he and Howard had been engineering freshers and best friends at Cambridge, both of them science bugs from provincial city comprehensives, intimidated by the gilded arts students and the ancient rituals of the university. Alan, a sci-fi fan, had been more interested than most because here was the wondrous reality that his beloved science fiction novels, with their gaudy covers, clumsy prose and stagy melodrama, had only approximated. Aliens living on a desert world half the size of Earth with a moon as big as Mars, twin planets really, only fifty light years away. Aliens simultaneously transmitting a thousand different TV programmes, saying hello to their neighbours. But it had been Howard who had dropped out of engineering to take astronomy and biology instead, Howard who had systematically collected and digested recordings and NASA press releases and scientific papers, who had submitted articles about the aliens to popular magazines, who had, just before graduation, struck gold, and published a three-page piece in the colour supplement of one of the Sunday papers. After university, Alan had joined an international company specialising in mass transit systems, married, and started a family. His sci-fi collection had been sealed in a carton which moved with him unopened through various postings until it was lost somewhere between Bangkok and Munich. Meanwhile, Howard had drifted into the freelance journalist scene in London. He had come to Alan's wedding and had once visited Alan in Paris, his first posting, but gradually they had lost touch. Then, a month ago, Alan had found one of Howard's books in an airport bookshop. Howard's email address was printed at the end of the brief preface, and on a whim Alan had sent him a message. Howard's response mentioned that he was going to be a guest at a convention in Liverpool; Alan had a meeting with the city council that same weekend. The coincidence was irresistible; they had arranged to meet.

Alan had stayed in this hotel two years ago, during a corporate hospitality jaunt to Aintree, and had been amazed by the brazenness with which the city's unofficial hostesses, with their bleached hair and artificial tans, had mingled with the race goers in the big lounge which, with its chandeliers and tall gilt mirrors, was a replica of one of the Titanic's passenger lounges. But there was no sign of that cheerful rowdiness now, although there were plenty of people sitting on banquettes around tables or in circles on the carpet. The lights in the big chandeliers were on, even though it was the middle of the afternoon, and the room had the dowdy, exhausted look of twenty-four-hour fast food joint. Alan walked slowly down its length towards the big screen and its strange alien panorama, but saw no sign of

Howard. Most of the conference delegates were men tending towards forty or older, a sizable percentage with beards and straggly hair, most wearing T-shirts or denim jackets and baggy jeans or sweat pants: the uniform of students twenty years ago. They talked animatedly or hunched together over laptops or palmtops; no one was watching the screen. There was a comradely buzz of conversation, a stale smell of beer and cigarettes. The ashtrays were overflowing; the tables were cluttered with empty glasses and bottles. It was like a cross between a computer fair, a science convention and an all-night party.

Howard wasn't in the bar to one side of the lounge either, or in the 'real ale bar' to the rear. Alan felt a mixture of amusement and frustration. It was so like Howard, famously absent-minded and always late for lectures, to have invited him and then to have forgotten all about it. Alan looked at the pocket programme he had been given along with his badge. A panel on starship design, another on alien behaviour, a third on possible translations of alien glyphs. Howard was giving a talk later in the evening, on the timeline of the aliens' history, but it was scheduled to start after Alan's flight was due to leave. Alan stood in the back of the room where the current programme item was being held, someone showing slides and speculating about caste relationships in one of the non-flying species domesticated by the aliens and used as both labourers and a food source, but he couldn't spot Howard amongst the rows of intent people and slipped out.

And saw Howard coming down the stairs on the far side of the lounge, talking with a heavily made-up woman in a business suit and followed by a man with a professional video camera up on his shoulder. Howard was better dressed than Alan had expected, in suit, tie, and polished brogues, his wiry hair short and neat, a bit of a paunch stretching the front of his shirt, but otherwise Howard, the same square white face, the same gold-rimmed spectacles, the same grin when he saw Alan coming towards him as he said goodbye to the TV people.

They caught up over gassy pints of beer in the bar. Howard still had the same braying laugh, the habit of adjusting his spectacles by pinching their bridge between thumb and forefinger. Their frames had marked his damp white skin. He still bit his nails, Alan saw, but his fingers were no longer inkstained. Screens banked along one side of the bar were showing various channels of alien TV. Howard kept glancing at them, their light sliding over the lenses of his spectacles. He had brought a paperback copy of one of his books, and signed it with a cramped yet fastidious hand.

'I still remember what you said when the first clips were shown,' he told Alan.

'I remember how pissed we all were.'

NASA had released the clips at six o'clock Eastern Standard Time, eleven at night in Cambridge, pub closing time. The TV lounge of the college had been crowded with raucous undergraduates drinking from cans of lager or beer.

Howard said, 'And we were drinking coffee.'

'So we were. God, yes. The only sober people in the room. And that woman, what was her name? The mature postgraduate.'

'Eileen O'Neil.'

'Right. She said that it was like the first moon landing.'

'It was more important than that,' Howard said.

'Well, it was a long time ago, anyway. Eleven years. Jesus.'

'It's still important,' Howard said.

There was an awkward silence. Alan asked about the publishing business, genuinely interested in how Howard managed to scratch a living.

'I get by,' Howard said, with an evasiveness that might be mistaken for modesty if you didn't know him better. He had never liked talking about himself; Alan had known him for two years before he realised that his parents were divorced. He still stooped, as if mortified by the presence his height lent him.

'It's amazing,' Alan said. 'I mean, that you can make money with this.'

'It was the biggest thing in a thousand years,' Howard said. 'The public interest didn't last, but there are still plenty of people all over the world studying the aliens. Your company keeps track, I bet. Most big companies do. And the people here keep track too.'

The response was so smooth that Alan wondered if it was the kind of soundbite Howard gave to TV people. He said, 'Of course we keep track. We'd be foolish not to.'

All the big discoveries had been made years ago, of course, but, like its competitors, his company still monitored the alien TV broadcasts, using AIs to sift out anything potentially interesting. Otherwise, people watched alien TV about as much as they watched, say, QVC. A few watched all day; some watched for a few minutes with the same kind of inert fascination (how long *can* that guy talk about car wax? Just *what* is that freak thing doing?); most, like Alan, caught a few seconds while flicking past late at night, in the usual hunt to confirm that, yes, there was nothing worth watching on any of the two hundred cable channels.

Howard said, 'There's a lot more to it than stealing their technology. Exobiology, behavioural studies, language, history, just to begin with.'

He ticked them off on his fingers, hunched forward in his chair so that his knees brushed Alan's. Alan pulled his chair back a little, but Howard didn't notice.

He said, 'The aliens have been civilised for at least a million years. They want us to know all about them, and the amount of information in their broadcasts is phenomenal. Of course, companies like yours look for stuff to steal, and universities have research programmes, but alien TV is like astronomy. Most comets and novas are still spotted by amateurs, and there's plenty of room for amateurs to make valid discoveries by watching alien TV. We pick up the stuff no one else bothers to watch. AIs are programmed to sift data in a limited number of ways, but the human mind is infinitely flexible.'

Alan laughed. The same old Howard, earnestly pedantic, hoping to win any argument by sheer weight of words. He said, 'You don't have to convert me. I used to watch that stuff as much as you.'

'It's still just as much fun,' Howard said, glancing at the screens as he leaned forward to pick up his pint. 'We could watch a thousand years and still have things to learn.'

Alan laughed again. 'You sound… evangelical.'

'It's what I do,' Howard said. 'You might think that I don't have a proper job, but this is it. I'm off to the States later this year. They hold a big convention every year, over the Labour Day weekend. Five thousand people from all over the world.'

'And do they find anything? Anything important, I mean.'

'If you mean commercially important, no. But that's not the point. It's the sense of wonder, like your old science fiction books. One of the other GOHs here used to be a science fiction writer, in fact.'

'GOH?'

Howard grinned and said, as if confiding a clue to a secret code, 'Guest of Honour. It's great for egoboo, but it's also nice to meet your readers.'

They had another drink, and Howard insisted on showing Alan around the dealer's room. There was a stand for a company selling the satellite dishes and decoders needed to access the raw alien TV broadcasts that were relayed from the joint NASA-ESA radio telescope. Trestle tables were loaded with racks of data needles containing thousands of stills and hours of edited video sequences, magazines, self-published theses as thick as bibles, computer programmes for image capture and analysis, models and sculptures of aliens and alien buildings, maps, field guides to the flora and fauna of the alien planet and its moon, exquisitely detailed dioramas of landscapes, even a table of tattered sci-fi paperbacks.

Howard chatted knowledgeably to the dealers, signed copies of his book proffered by deferential fans. This was his element – more important than alien TV to these people was the culture they had created around it. Howard had never really grown up, Alan realised – still the same fascination with trivia, the same selfish irresponsibility. He wanted Alan to stay around for his panel, and said that afterwards the convention committee would take them out for a meal in this really great Greek restaurant, but Alan made his excuses. In truth, he felt a touch of claustrophobia, surrounded as he was by the products of tens of thousands of hours squandered on simulated scholarship no one would ever read. The last thing he needed was to be trapped in a taverna with a bunch of obsessives.

'We should keep in touch,' Howard said. 'I've always said companies like yours could learn a lot from us.'

'It's not really my field,' Alan said carefully.

'But it affects everything. You know,' Howard said earnestly, 'I still remember what you said when we saw the first broadcast, that nothing will ever be the same again. You were right. Alien TV changed us, and it's still changing us.'

'I said that?' Alan felt now that he was being manipulated, that Howard wasn't interested in him because of their old friendship, but because of his connections. He said, knowing how feeble it sounded, 'Listen, Howard, it was terrific to meet up again, but I really do have to go and get ready for my flight. Don't let me hold you up.'

But Howard followed Alan out through the revolving doors into the rain, and was still talking about the importance of his work as Alan got into a taxi. 'The beauty of their world,' Howard said. 'And ethics, and philosophies we can't even dream of. The intangible that stands behind the tangible. By using their technology without understanding them, we're changing ourselves in ways we can't predict!'

He had to shout the last, because Alan had shut the door and the taxi was pulling away.

Alan went back to his own hotel and packed and called his wife, then took the elevated train (a subsidiary of his company ran it) out to the airport. He sat in the bar until his flight was called, chatting with a couple structural engineers whose company also had a share in the construction of the space elevator. The feeling that he had escaped from some suffocating dream slowly left him; after the second drink the whole unfortunate episode began to take on a comic aspect, and before he left he managed to make a couple of jokes about it to his new companions.

Nairobi was only an hour away by scramjet. Alan looked out of the port (every seat was a window seat in business class) and drank a gin-and-tonic and ate chilly peanuts while the blue-white curve of the Earth turned below. His wife was there to meet him in the crowds at the airport, and she drove him through the dusty streets out to the compound where they lived. It was evening here, still very hot. The elevator stood against thunderclouds to the northwest, limned by blinking warning lights, vanishing into the bruised sky like a *Land Of The Giants* version of the Indian Rope Trick. Alan's firm had just won the contract to build and service the huge elevator cars – each as big as a ten-storey office building – that would shuttle between the Earth's surface and the terminal in geostationary orbit.

Later, after he had given his son and daughter their presents and helped the nanny with their bathtime, and picked over an unwanted dinner, Alan sat in his big leather chair in his den, sipping a gin-and-tonic, restlessly flicking through the channels on his screen. And there was the alien TV compilation channel, one of them facing the camera or whatever they used, gesticulating with half a dozen limbs, including the bright red thing that looked like a long spiny penis, then *flip*, an aerial shot of one of their roosts, hundreds of tall thin spiky towers studded with openings and platforms and ledges that reared up out of scrubby desert with tens of thousands of aliens swooping and gliding at all levels, *flip*, a view across the rolling green grassland of the alien's big moon, with the alien's planet a blue-white chip stuck in the dark sky, *flip*, aliens clustered around some huge half-dismantled machine under a tented roof of gauzy material, *flip*, hundreds of ape-like creatures working in a flooded field, *flip*, a wide canal running across a red desert, *flip*, *flip*, *flip* . . .

What did it matter exactly how old their civilisation was; whether or not they were on their way here to eat us or conquer us or sell us the squidgy things they sometimes rubbed over their bodies; whether the formal battles they fought, hand-to-hand aerial combat above the vast natural amphitheatre of a shield volcano, were over religion or whether red- or blue-banded squidgy things were best? They were aliens. What they did was inexplicable. Only the few streams which featured the universal language of physics and mathematics were comprehensible, and only what human minds and hands did with the knowledge gleaned from those broadcasts was important. The space elevator, the use of artificial photosynthesis to end world hunger, the extension of human lifespan, pinch fusion, the ceramics used in scramjet motors, monomolecular films: all developed from clues gathered from watching alien TV, but developed by people.

Alan had been lucky enough to live through those few months when everything in the world had changed utterly and forever. But it was not possible to recreate the excitement of the first months after alien TV had started, the banner headlines, the thousands of hours of speculation on TV, the T-shirts and dolls and instant books, the bombing of a NASA ground station by Catholic extremists who claimed alien TV was a conspiracy by an alliance of Zionists and atheists. Briefly, it had been something everyone had to have an opinion on, but then the media had moved on to the next thing which had caught the fickle public imagination. The world had moved on, leaving alien TV to the research and development laboratories, university academics, and obsessives like Howard and his T-shirted friends.

So why, with the screen flickering through a series of otherworldly images, did Alan feel as if he had lost something? Why did he feel a spurt of envy at the thought that Howard was still possessed by a secret which had once possessed him, but which he no longer possessed?

He sipped his gin-and-tonic and watched alien TV until his wife called to him. He flicked off the screen and dutifully went up.

# Canary Girls

Kari Sperring

"O sisters too, how may we do
For to preserve this day
This pore yongling for whom we do singe
By, lully, lullay?"

– *The Coventry Carol*

High, high above the city, the great dirigibles hang serenely, rose gold against the scarlet sky. Broken images flicker across their skins, transmitted from the wolves hunting below. Rags of memory, here a glimpse of a family meal; there a snatched kiss; there an agonising instant before death. The wolves cull them all, as they nullify the panic in the streets. Block by block, cell by cell, mind by mind, the population are caught, checked, and reset to obedience.

There must not be alarm. There must not be emotion or individual action. The factories must run and their flesh components must work, and that was the whole of the law. The city serves, the wolves patrol and the people… the people know service and punishment.

A city of women, this, reaching back long years, though the wolves do not know it and the people do not remember. A city built by women, built *on* women, pragmatic to the core. It had its outward beauties, once – still has them, had the wolves eyes to see them. But its truest beauty has always lain in the worn hands of the women, who watched and worked and served down through all those years.

Under that sky, deep down into the bowels of the city, a skinny girl child huddles in the shadows by the arcade, skin alert for the hint of any wolf. Her gaze turns here and there, returning always to the broken statue and, beyond it, the great dark tower of Osburh's finger, reaching up and up beyond the dirigibles. Kings and dictators, masons and mobs have tried to bring that finger down, but the stone resisted them all, its roots sunk deep into all that was the city, impervious. It is the promise

Osburh made at the holy stream, back before the city was born. As the girl's gaze falls on the tower, brightness flashes across the floating screens…

*Here's Osburh, slight in torn linen gown, on her knees amidst the ruins of the fort. Her head is bowed: the ragged ends of her short hair fall forward to hide her face. Her bare feet are bleeding. Through the rents in the linen, her scars show red on her tanned skin. Her hands dig into the sandy loam at the river's edge. The men watch from a safe distance, unwilling to come any closer to this place of haunts and goblins. Osburh's fingers close on a lump of cool stone: when she lifts it free from the soil it fits perfectly in the nest of her palm. From its pale surface, the Holy Lady smiles serenely, haloed in waves. This place, Osburh whispers to the Lady, to the stone. This place for the women who need shelter, the women who serve, the women who protect. This place is ours and always will be.*

Human memory is fragile. Not so the memory of stone. It is whispered in the factories and dormitories, under the pounding of the machines, that the stones of the tower shelter all the memories the wolves stole, all the memories that are forbidden. It is said that anyone who lays a hand on that stone at the right time will fall heir to them all. No one knows if this is true. The tower, and the tumbled ruin of the minster about it, are off-limits to the flesh population, closed off behind walls of steel and stinging electricity. The girl draws in long, shaky breaths, eyes fixed on the tower, and makes a dash for the statue. A siren wails: a long beam of light reaches down from the closest dirigible, drawn by the motion. Further down the precinct, a wolf raises its eyeless head and sniffs. The girl bites down on a shriek and makes a grab for the plinth as the wolf pitter-clatters on steel claws across the paving. Half-forgotten words tumble from the girl's lips as she clings and climbs and, above her, bronze becomes flesh on the skin of the dirigible.

*Godgifu rides tall and proud in wool and linen and gold, her brown hair unbound under her veil. Her horse steps high across the Lady Ford as she journeys to the war-stained shell of Osburh's shrine. The handful of nuns wait for her outside their wooden huts, faces taut with hope they do not dare express. She smiles at them and from her hands spill perpetual rights over land and river, silver to pay for rebuilding, and grace in the face of the king and his earls.*

*Such, then, the seed of the city. Sown by women, it rooted by the Lady's stream, spread concentric roots out through the loam to grow gardens and homes and craft workshops. And, where the women built, the men followed, bringing walls and courtrooms and halls. Here, the women carded wool and spun thread for the household looms. There, the men raised guild houses and called each other sir. The looms wove gold from cloth and, stone by stone, Osburh's shrine grew, to the glory of the wealth and work of the city.*

*Here, then, the first taste of fire.*

Somehow, the girl finds herself atop the plinth, curled in between the legs of the horse. A cool bronze hand holds hers: she looks up into eyes the colour of autumn pools. Below, the wolf's claws scrabble and slide, finding no purchase on the smooth stone. The woman – the woman of bronze – raises her other hand and points. Out beyond the wolf, beyond the searchlight, silent over the paving walks a goodwife in a dirty cream shift, cradling in her arms a heavy load of kindling. Where she steps, her footprints are traced in ash. The girl shivers, but the bronze hand does not release its grip. The bronze woman speaks without sound, and at once flames leap upwards, ringing statue and girl and goodwife against the claws and teeth of the wolf. *Follow,* says the statue, all without noise. Under the girl, the plinth shimmers and fades. Arms wrapped tight about her, she follows the ashy footsteps down through the aisle of fire.

*She holds her head high, Goodwife Joy, as she proceeds to her execution. The bundle of kindling she carries is meant to shame her, but the feeling passes her by. What she does, what she has done, is for the poor of the city, and she will not repine. Men must always build hierarchies, between man and man, man and woman, man and god. But she, she will not concede. When the renegade priest came, preaching freedom from Latin words and laws, she listened and believed. When the prior's soldiers followed, she granted the priest passage out under the walls and stood firm. She will be free: in her worship, in her words, in herself, and for that she will burn.*

*She does not cry out when the flames taste her skin. She has her freedom, and no one shall hold her more.*

The ash clings to the soles of the girl's feet, silencing her tread. The goodwife leads her out of the precinct, towards the tumbled remains of the priory. The priors ruled this city once, making rules for trade and worship, work and marriage, custom and behaviour. Now, in their stead, are the dirigibles and the wolves. On the screen overhead the Goodwife smiles as she burns. The girl steps on to the last ashen footprint and finds herself at one end of the narrow lane. Here the marks of fire are plain, charred black runnels in the soft sandstone. The wolf quickens its pace and she shudders, seeking a place to hide.

Overhead, cannon thunder and let fly. She presses into a doorway, trying not to breathe as the wolf paces forward. The dirigibles bounce and sway as the cannonballs pass. One drops at the mouth of the lane, sending chips and shards of cobble stones spinning. A fragment lands at her feet, glistening grey-brown as a new memory is set free.

*Here's Christian, high on the leads of her home. Built against the wall, this house, and thus eyeless on one side. She can hear the voices of men singing somewhere out in the twilight meadows outside the city. "Then we will sing, boys, God bless the King, boys, Cast up our caps and cry Vive le Roi!" The royalist army is a seething mass, men and horses and guns all comingled. The devil prince is somewhere among them: through the song she hears the howling of his great white demon dog. "Send word to the militia," she calls down through the trapdoor, and little Bet the maid goes rushing into the streets. Out in the grey, a match flickers; the evening breeze brings the scent of gunpowder and sweat. She turns to go, and, turning, does not see the cannonball that arcs to strike her home.*

The girl is terrified now, legs weak, tears seeping from the corners of her eyes. Musket balls whistle by her; she clings to the stone of the door-arch. Dust and ash block her view of the tower. She is trapped here, she is lost, and the wolf clicks ever closer. She closes her hands into fists, feeling her nails score the palms, and tries to remember. There was more, she is certain there was more. The wolf rounds the corner and a gasp escapes her chapped lips. The eyeless head swings towards her; she can hear the deep mechanical drone of its breath. The images swirl faster now, one piled upon another across the screens.

*The women file out into the Great Park, carrying baskets laden with rubbish of every kind to fill the quarries against enemy use. Christian's house gapes empty behind them… Now, they bind wounds left by bullet and shell, wash the blood from the cobbles. The mayor's wife weeps, as the city walls fall at the order of a new and vengeful king.*

*Another shift. The weavers, man and woman side by side batter their way inside the mill to tear down the hated, thieving, power looms. The rich would leave their hands and bellies empty, stealing work away for personal profit. The factory owners summon the militia, but the women, the city, are not quelled. In back rooms and attics, small feminine fingers weave ribbons and decorate watch cases, while the men build new and better machines. Wool floats away down the river, to be replaced by steel and spring and gears.*

The wolf is almost on her. The girl gulps, coiling in on herself. Behind her, the door suddenly gives way and she falls, back into darkness. Beneath her is the softness of carpet; the air tastes of lavender and paper. She blinks and her sight clears. No wolf, shut out by the stout wooden door. Instead, a parlour, all polish and comfort. Books are piled high on every surface; beside the fire three women sit, heads bent together as they talk.

*Rosehill women: Cara and Sara and Mary Ann. Their fingers are ink-stained. There's no time in this circle for tatting and gossip. Their minds are bent on change, on raising up the poor. They write of free schools and workers' unions and suffrage for women. They are radicals, all three, nurtured here in the shadow of Osburh's minister. They call no man master: they hold full mastery of themselves, and they are loved. The city knows their worth, told in their legacies in stone.*

The wolf howls outside the door, siren once again summoning the lights of the dirigibles. One of the women looks up and meets the eyes of the girl. She raises a finger to her lips, then holds out a key. "Up," she whispers, "you must go up. She is waiting."

On the other side of the parlour, a half-open door leading to a stair. The girl climbs, the key clutched in one hand. The searchlights flash behind the curtained windows; further voices join that of the first wolf. She unlocks the door at the top of the stair and steps out onto a shallow tiled roof. To her right, the tower looms, across the rooftops and the lane. She takes a step towards it, and reaches out her hands. The air is cool and water-scented. The beam from a searchlight strikes the roof, and there she is, the winged woman, holding out her arms.

*Viola has done this so many times before. She balances on the end of the balloon basket, gazing at the crowds down below. The parachute is snug against her back, tucked into its shell. She is impatient to jump and be gone. Her aeroplane awaits her, her true wings, somewhere beyond tomorrow. She nods to her pilot and steps out onto air.*

The girl is swept up in a rush of canvas and wind. A beat of wings, another, and they are soaring above the roofs. The wolves snarl and wail in the lane below. Overhead, the dirigibles sail on. The winged woman laughs as they fly, as they dance and swirl up here in the golden night. The girl can see them all, now, the women of this city, remembered in sharp colours on the great floating screens. Here, the canary girls on their way to the factory where the shells they make dye their skins bright yellow. There, Osburh's nuns, singing as they tend their garden. Here's Alice, the first woman to wear the mayoral chain, fighting for the rights of her working people. Women baking and brewing, sewing and building, reading and writing and creating and upholding each other, each one a stone in this ancient city. On the roof of the hospital, Bess watches for fires, ready with her tin hat and bucket of sand to dowse as many as she may. Hilda is in the street kitchen, doling out hot soup to those who lost their homes, their loved ones, to the blitz. Florrie runs calculations for the engineers, to keep the aircraft flying. Tomorrow, they will walk eleven miles over the fields to find beds for themselves, but tonight they serve. The women march on; here are the factory hands, striking for fair play; there, Meto delivers her maiden speech in council. And somewhere, Pauline is singing.

The winged woman circles the minster spire, once, twice, before setting the girl down on its edge, where Osburh waits to welcome her home.

**Author's Note**

I was born in Coventry, in the same year that the New Cathedral was officially opened, and while we moved away when I was seven, the city remains special to me. I'm one of many children of women who migrated there in the 19th and 20th centuries from all over the world – India, Italy, Ireland, North Africa, and, in my case, Wales. My memories of the city centre on women: not just my mother but her sisters, my cousins, my teachers and neighbours. Coventry owes its origins to a woman and interesting women – often radical – are spread through its history.

All the women in this story are real, save one, the nameless girl. I have adapted and embroidered their stories in places, and, in one case, given a name. But, if you are interested, they are:

**Osburh** – an Anglo-Saxon saint who founded a convent on a site that became Coventry. That's about all we know about her – even the century in which she lived is under debate. I've elected here to set her at the earlier end of the possible range.

**Godgifu** – wife of the earl of Mercia, Leofric, and a wealthy and effective woman in her own right. She and Leofric endowed a monastery in Coventry and are closely associated with the area. She's also the earliest known element of the connection to Wales – her son Earl Aelfgar was a close ally of the North Welsh king, Gruffudd ap Llywelyn, and Gruffudd married her granddaughter.

**"Goodwife Joy"** – in 1432, a woman known only as 'a mayor's wife' was burned at the stake in Coventry for Lollardy – a form of early Protestantism that believed religious books and services should be available in the language of everyday people, and not Latin, and which opposed other aspects of Catholicism. The movement began about 14 miles from Coventry, in Lutterworth, and Coventry was an early stronghold of radical and freethinking. Beyond how she died and her husband's rank, we know nothing nothing else of this woman. I have used the surname of Richard Joy, who was mayor in 1425, as it has a good resonance.

**Christian** – otherwise known as Lady Hales of Whitefriars. The Hales family were minor aristocracy and known radicals involved in the promulgation of Protestantism. Coventry was a parliamentarian stronghold in the English Civil War: Lady Hales really did live in a house built against the wall and was killed by cannonball fire when the city was assaulted.

**Cara** and **Sara** and **Mary Ann** – The Rosehill circle was a group of social reformers and freethinkers that grew up around the house of ribbon manufacturer Charles Bray and his wife Cara. Women were very influential in this group, headed by Cara, her sister Sara, who was a suffragette, and their close friend Mary Ann, better known as the writer George Eliot.

**Viola** – real name Edith Maud Cook. Born in Suffolk, she was a balloonist, parachutist and Britain's first female aircraft pilot. She made her living via fairs and stunt work, under the name Viola Spencer and Viola Spencer Kavanagh. Sadly, she died in Coventry in 1910 when a parachute jump went wrong. But she deserves far more recognition that she gets for her place in aviation history, and Coventry was an early centre for the manufacture of aircraft.

**Bess, Hilda** and **Florrie** – my Jones aunts, all of whom were living and working in Coventry during the blitz. Bess was a nurse, Hilda a ward aide and Florrie a comptometer operator. I grew up with Bess and Hilda; sadly, Florrie lost her life as a consequence of the firebombing of Coventry. My mother says she was splendid.

**Alice** – Alice Arnold, the first female mayor of Coventry and leading trade unionist. Born in the workhouse.

**Meto** – Meto Lakha, Coventry's first female British Asian councillor and a significant community leader.

**Pauline** – Pauline Black, of course!

# Softlight Sins

Peter F. Hamilton

Ghosts drifted through Douglas McEwan's mind as he drove down the long road towards the execution. There were four spectres, the family of Adrian Reynolds: his mother, his abominable father, and his two lovely young sisters. The forensic team's *in situ* video had shown them in their beds, captured in a frozen pose that feigned sleep: eyes closed, lips relaxed, fingers splayed like albino starfish. In each case their throats had been slit open, black yawning gashes that had sprayed thick jets of blood across the sheets.

The phosphene mirage was broken when Douglas's police escort switched on their lights and sirens. The five-car convoy was motoring along a thin ribbon of road that cut through the heavily wooded Ling common to the north of King's Lynn. Tall pines and slim silver birch trees stood sentinel duty on either side, their small yellowed leaves swirling through the air like a rusty snowstorm, settling on the grass verges where they formed a soggy mantle. Twin lines of parked press vehicles were backed up a hundred metres from the entrance of the Clinical Rehabilitation Institute.

A dense knot of people was blocking the road ahead. The media circus. And to Douglas's eyes they did look like clowns, dressed in their bulky garishly coloured parkas, noses and cheeks raw from the chill morning air. A double rank of police in blue-grey riot tunics had linked arms, creating a barrier to hold them back from the road.

A hundred shouted questions merged into a single unintelligible bawl as Douglas drove past. Cameras zoomed in.

Protesters had taken up the prime sites on either side of the Institute's gate, their stamping feet pounding the mown grass strips into rucked quagmires. The police were three deep here, forming a funnel down to the gate, both lines visibly wavering from the pressure of the protesters' bodies.

On Douglas's right was the LIFE! group, opposing any form of capital punishment. From what he could see a majority of them were women. They held hundreds of white candles aloft, ranging from small nightlights to elaborately carved half-metre columns of wax. A ragged chorus of defiant voices sang Abide With Me.

Gobs of mud pelted the car. Douglas switched his wipers on, smearing the windscreen with brown streaks. It was the TRUE JUSTICE group on the other side launching the deluge. Trim young men in the main; hair cut close to the skull, wearing olive-green military-style sweaters, a red crucifix stitched on the breast. And so much hatred leaking from their hard young faces. They were carrying a forest of placards; obscene demands for Adrian Reynolds to be hung, fried, shot, gassed, guillotined, poisoned... The gallows erected next to the Institute fence had a straw-stuffed effigy of Adrian dangling in a noose. As soon as Douglas's car swept through the gates someone put a torch to the wooden structure. A well-planned optical bite for the cameras.

Then he was through, the gate closing behind him. Something about the savagery of the protesters bolstered his own determination.

And what an irony that is. Me, the man who prides himself on his liberalism, having to find refuge in the stiff upper lip tradition the minute adversity strikes.

The Institute building was only three years old, paid for by the European Federal Criminal Psychology Bureau. A four storey cube, with green-tinted mirror glass that bounced the forest trees back at him, their bare autumn-ravaged trunks long and wavery.

It was part secure hospital, part research facility. The Bureau had originally hoped the doctors could use laser imprinted subliminal commands to insert new behaviour patterns into the more stubborn social recidivists. A technique that would produce, if not model citizens, at least reasonably honest ones. That research was still continuing, but for the last year the Institute had concentrated on developing Softlight.

It had been the idea of Doctor Michael Elliot, a neurologist who had been studying memory retention to see how long the rectification commands would last.

What his research uncovered was the amnesia mechanism, the method by which grey cells discard the unwanted memories of each day's events, preventing the brain from being cluttered up with a billion irrelevant details. Elliot isolated the governing neurological code and managed to adapt the laser imprint technique to transmit the sequence throughout the brain. Softlight: the total erasure of memory and behaviour patterns. Personality death.

Anyone committing a capital crime could be mentally executed, leaving behind a perfectly viable body; an adult infant ready to be named, educated, and returned to the world as a fully functional member of society. Capital punishment without death. For the PC politicians of the Brussels Federal Assembly it was a dream solution.

Adrian Reynolds was about to become the first subject.

Barbara Johnson was standing in the Institute's reception area, her long face taut with agitation. Douglas had met her on several occasions – she was Dr Elliot's deputy.

She led him to an interview room on the third floor where Adrian Reynolds was waiting. A couple of muscular-looking male orderlies stood patiently outside.

"Ten minutes, Douglas, please," she said, apparently embarrassed at rushing him. "No more than fifteen. The judge is already here."

"Sure," he said, and walked into the interview room.

Most Court Defence Officers tended to develop a sense of responsibility for their clients. But Douglas had taken it to an extreme, always refusing prosecution cases. The price he paid for his quirk came in the form of people like Adrian Reynolds. Twenty years old, with a father who had abused him from the age of eight – sexually, physically, and mentally. Abused him right up until the day he finally snapped, taking a kitchen knife upstairs while the family slept.

The Reynolds trial hadn't dealt with guilt, that was beyond question. Instead Douglas had fought to establish the level of culpability; arguing that a degree of blame must lie with the social services, to let it go on undetected for so long; with the teachers for not spotting the boy's moodiness; with knowing relatives who had turned a blind eye.

Douglas fully expected to lose the case. The people of Europe were achingly tired of psychopaths and terrorists and ideology warriors and street gangs. The death penalty had been reintroduced six years previously, the Federal Assembly finally bowing to enormous pressure from the electorate. The jury found Adrian guilty on three charges of murder. He should have been given a painless lethal injection. But with providential coincidence Dr Elliot announced Softlight was ready, and Douglas had asked judge Hayward to consider Adrian as an appropriate subject for the treatment. Judge Hayward agreed.

Adrian Reynolds was standing by the window wall, a tall skinny young man with a weak chin, puffy cheeks, his dark mousy hair lying lank over his ears. One of the Institute's green overalls hung loosely from his body.

He turned when Douglas came in, then dropped his eyes. "They want me dead, don't they?"

Douglas realised the gate and the mob were just visible from the room. "They don't know what they want." It was true enough. TRUE JUSTICE thought Softlight was a liberal/scientific cop-out, allowing criminals to escape punishment once again. LIFE! denounced it as a living death, court sanctioned zombiism. The only thing they had in common was their opposition to it.

"Is my will sorted out?" Adrian asked.

"Yes, half to Barnardo's, half to the RSPCC."

"There's not very much."

"Every little helps." Douglas was having trouble keeping his voice level.

*If people could just see him like this, see that he cares. He doesn't deserve Softlight. Maybe I should be on the other side of the gate, join in the chanting. If only it wasn't so utterly futile.*

"They asked me if I wanted a priest," Adrian said. "Last rites and all that crap. I said no. I said if there was a God then he wouldn't have made my father."

Douglas half smiled. "You said that to the Institute chaplain?"

Adrian gave a fast wild grin. "No." The humour faded. "Shall we go now? I don't think there's much point in dragging it out any longer."

Officially it was laboratory complex seven. But Douglas knew the Institute staff had taken to calling it the Light Chamber; and the press had somehow got hold of that title. It resembled a dental surgery, with a bulky hydraulic chair in the middle of the floor, a glass-topped desk, several cabinets of electronic equipment, and two voice-activated computer terminals. The Softlight imprinter was a triple-segment metal arm standing next to the chair; it ended in a bulbous plastic strip moulded to fit over the eyes like an optometrist's lens mask.

Judge Theresa Hayward was sitting behind the desk when Douglas walked in. She was sixty years old, her oval sun-browned face heavily wrinkled, which was exacerbated by her frown. During the trial Douglas had found her to have an astute mind, in court she was scrupulously impartial, and very aware of the political undertones of the case.

Harvey Boden, the Court Prosecution Officer, was studying a plasma screen on one of the computer terminals. He greeted Douglas with a thin nod.

The third person in the laboratory was Dr Michael Elliot. He shared Barbara Johnson's air of sheepish eagerness, desperately trying to camouflage his feelings below a crust of professional detachment.

Adrian walked straight over to the chair, not looking round. The orderlies who were escorting him slipped the restraint straps around his wrists and legs.

The knot of tension in Douglas's stomach twisted sharply when Dr Elliot swung the Softlight imprinter up, manoeuvring the black mask over Adrian's eyes.

"Will I see anything?" Adrian asked suddenly.

"The laser operates predominantly in the green section of the spectrum," Dr Elliot explained. "It will be quite bright, but not painfully so."

"No lasting damage, eh?" there was a quaver in Adrian's voice.

Dr Elliot managed a sickly smile.

Barbara Johnson was voicelining one of the terminals, reeling off a string of security codes to access the data core which stored the Softlight sequence. Dr Elliot joined her, and added his authorisation code, then he glanced at Judge Hayward. Her face showed nothing but regret. She jerked her head down.

Douglas closed his eyes, secretly terrified that a flash of green light would spill out from around the black strip, boring its way down his own optical nerves, exploding in his brain. Somewhere in the distance he heard Dr Elliot's voiceline: "Expedite."

The imprinter arm retracted automatically. Adrian's face wore the look of docile imbecility, eyes unfocused, every muscle relaxed.

Barbara Johnson walked forward carrying a white plastic sensor crown which she settled around Adrian's head. "No brainwave activity above the autonomic level," she reported, oh-so-careful not to display any satisfaction.

Douglas watched a bead of saliva leak from the corner of Adrian's mouth, and turned away.

*It worked, punishment and redemption wrapped in one neat package. Taking away the threat and salvaging our conscience. I ought to be grateful. If only Adrian didn't look so pitiful, so... wasted. But at least I cannot be faulted for that, I did my best for him.*

"Abschaum!"

The vehement shout electrified Douglas. He jerked round to see Barbara Johnson stumbling back from Adrian in panic.

Adrian stared at them with a covetous birdlike expression, his nostrils flaring as he sucked down deep breaths. He shouted at them again, the words making no sense as he snarled and spat.

Douglas heard Harvey Boden saying, "That's German."

"What's happening?" Judge Hayward demanded.

Dr Elliot shook his head, staring at Adrian in numbed consternation.

"It didn't work," Douglas blurted.

"It did work," Barbara Johnson insisted. "The brainwave function was zero."

"Does this sound like he's empty-headed?" Douglas waved his hand angrily at Adrian.

She appealed to Dr Elliot. "Some kind of residual activity?"

"I don't know," he said in a shaken tone.

"What's Adrian saying?" Judge Hayward asked.

"I've no idea, I don't speak German," Douglas said. "My God, neither does Adrian."

Judge Hayward gave him a sharp look, then turned to Dr Elliot. "Find someone who does, and fast."

"Not necessary," Barbara Johnson told her. She took some headsets from the desk and handed them round. Douglas slipped his on as she voicelined the computer terminal for a translation program. The earplugs muted another of Adrian's invectives, then the translator cut in.

"...bastard Yankees. No better than fucking Jews. Queers and women, nothing more, we'll shit on you yet. Your President Roosevelt is dead, from shame, from the pox –"

Douglas voicelined the headset to stand-by mode, an unnerving chill blossoming inside his head.

"All right," Judge Hayward said. "I want best guesses, and I want them now."

"It's quite obvious Softlight doesn't work," Harvey Boden said. "It doesn't wipe memories, it simply jumbles them up."

"There was no primary brainwave activity for two minutes," Barbara Johnson said stubbornly.

Harvey Boden shrugged. "People recover from comas. Weeks and months spent like a vegetable, then they're up and talking as if nothing had happened."

Douglas knew what Boden was doing. The Prosecution Officer wanted Adrian dead. For real.

It's obviously not just my skull those two girls are haunting.

"I can't even pretend to understand what's happened," Douglas said as Barbara Johnson and Dr Elliot started whispering together. "And you're certainly not in a position to give qualified neurological opinions, Harvey. We'll need a complete assessment made before any decisions are taken. And we certainly shouldn't decide anything in haste."

Dr Elliot nodded in agreement with something Barbara Johnson said, and faced the judge. "I believe we should consider regression as a logical explanation for this situation."

"Regression?" Douglas asked in confusion.

Harvey Boden gave him a contemptuous look. "Past lives, Douglas. People thinking they used to be Napoleon or George Washington, that kind of thing."

"There have been documented cases," Dr Elliot said. "Under hypnosis, subjects have related a wealth of details concerning their previous existence, details they couldn't possibly have known without extensive research."

"Rubbish," Harvey Boden said.

Douglas was inclined to agree, but that would be offering Adrian up to TRUE JUSTICE. "Are you saying this German personality popped up out of nowhere to fill Adrian's empty brain?" he asked Dr Elliot.

"Yes. A German from the Second World War, judging by the reference to Roosevelt."

Adrian had fallen silent, glaring round at them, teeth bared.

Judge Hayward voicelined the terminal for a two way translation. "What is your name?" she asked Adrian.

The terminal repeated the question in German.

"Mentally defective bitch," he shouted.

She backed away, badly disturbed. "Whoever Adrian believes he is, he remains our problem. The three of us –" her red fingernail lined up first on Douglas then Harvey Boden, "– have to decide what to do next."

"Is this an official session?" Douglas asked.

"We'll call it an In Chambers consultation, if you and the Prosecution have no objection."

"After this failure of Softlight, Prosecution has no alternative but to apply for the death penalty," Harvey Boden said quickly.

"On who?" Douglas snapped back. "On Adrian Reynolds, or this German?"

"There is no German, Douglas, only a mind screwed about by a subliminal laser code. Face facts."

"You don't know that. At the very least I would appeal for an identity check first."

"Oh yes?" Harvey Boden was scathing. "What kind of check, genetic fingerprinting?"

"My client, Adrian Reynolds, was sentenced to personality erasure. That has been enacted; successfully, as far as we can tell. The emergence of this second personality is outside the court's jurisdiction."

They glared at each other.

"We could try a hypnogenic," Barbara Johnson suggested.

"Fair enough," Judge Hayward said. "Any objections? No. Good."

Adrian spat on Dr Elliot as he approached with the spray ampoule. Phlegm dripped down the doctor's collar as he applied the nozzle to Adrian's neck.

Dr Elliot waited until the young man dropped into a waking trance, eyelids heavy, head drooping. "Can you hear me?" he asked.

Adrian mumbled something. "Yes," the translator program said.

"What is your name?"

"Erich Breuer."

"What is your job, Erich?"

"I am a member of the garrison troop."

"Where?"

"Dachau."

Douglas heard a quick hiss of indrawn breath from Barbara Johnson. Harvey Boden's face turned blank, unreadable.

"What is the last thing you remember before you woke up in this room?"

The man's hands started to tremble slightly. "The Yankees have arrived, their tanks halting by the guard post. There were shots, our officers were killed. The Yankees, they cried and they vomited when they saw the inmates, the unburied corpses. I am lined up against a wall with my colleagues, some are bleeding from the beatings. I hear the machine gun firing. Louder. Louder." His eyes widened with shock, mouth hanging open.

Douglas turned away, unable to look at the shell of flesh which had once been Adrian Reynolds.

"That's enough," Judge Hayward said as Dr Elliot began another question.

Douglas walked over to the chair, and studied the now quiescent figure.

*If Elliot is right about regression, if you are who you now seem to be, then that would prove the existence of men's souls. That would be so hard for me to really believe in. It would mean there is a God, that Jesus was born and died for us. A long agonising death nailed to a cross of wood. And how could we ever be forgiven that? Better we believe in some shared consciousness theory; that will be the scientists' answer. The other is too much to bear. An afterlife. That you have been sent back from Heaven. Or Hell. That life on Earth is nothing more than a penitence to serve before we can enter God's Kingdom for all time.*

"Now what?" Harvey Boden asked.

Douglas left Erich Breuer, wearied by the Prosecution Officer's unceasing assault. "I maintain the case is closed. We have now proved beyond reasonable doubt that this is no longer Adrian Reynolds. The Institute should help Erich Breuer adapt to modern life, and let him go."

"I can't agree with that," Judge Hayward said. "Douglas, you haven't thought this through. Suppose this really is Erich Breuer?" She held up a hand to forestall Harvey Boden's protest. "The body contains Erich Breuer's memories, camp guard at Dachau. Then what?"

"Oh," Douglas saw what she was driving at, his mind racing after the implications. "War Crimes."

"Exactly. If you bring an appeal over the question of this body's identity, and prove your case that this is Erich Breuer, then he will have to face the consequences of his actions in World War Two. Do you want that to happen, Douglas? Do you want the public spectacle of a trial? Because that's what you'll get. The Israelis were chasing the original concentration camp guards up until the middle of the nineties; old men whose identities were extremely uncertain. Erich Breuer, who by his own admission was part of the holocaust, would never be allowed to walk out of the Institute a free man. That's what your appeal would bring."

*Oh God, she's telling me it's my decision. Me! Forced into the role of judge, and probably executioner by default.*

"I don't know," he said miserably.

"Let me see if I can clarify the situation," Judge Hayward said. "I sentenced all the memories to be wiped from Adrian Reynolds's brain. Now we find a deeper, hidden set of memories." She narrowed her eyes, and fixed Dr Elliot with a lance-like stare. "Can these Erich Breuer memories be wiped by Softlight?"

He looked startled. "Well, yes. I would suppose so. But I don't think it's advisable."

"Why not?"

"We don't understand how they originated. It opens up an entire new area of neurology to study. It is quite possible that each of us possesses a similar mental heritage, a window into the past. Think of the data that could be uncovered, the true history we could learn."

That was when Douglas witnessed the showing of the Judge's claws for the first time. "Dr Elliot," she said coolly. "Adrian Reynolds is not an experimental subject, he is a multiple murderer sentenced to personality erasure. A sentence which this Institute is legally obliged to enact. You will either fulfil this function, or tell me you are unable to. Do I make myself clear?"

Dr Elliot considered his options, and settled for a reluctant submission. "Very well, I accept that a penal institution is not the place for an academic study of this nature."

Judge Hayward glanced at Douglas then Harvey Boden. "Any objections to a further Softlight administration?"

"No," Douglas said, partly ashamed. It was the easy way out.

*The one I always take.*

This time he left his eyes open for the whole procedure. Erich Breuer stared placidly ahead as the Softlight imprinter's moulded strip went over his eyes.

"That's it," Dr Elliot announced.

The arm retracted, folding back onto its pedestal.

Barbara Johnson moved in with the white plastic sensor crown again. She settled it on the man's head. "No primary brainwave activity registering," she reported.

"We'll wait for a little while," Judge Hayward said. "See if there's any change."

"It's happening," Barbara Johnson called. She was hovering around the computer terminal which was displaying the sensor crown readings. "His brainwave activity is picking up."

When Douglas checked his watch he saw that barely four minutes had elapsed.

Adrian's head had been bowed limply ever since the arm had retracted. Now Douglas watched him lift his chin, his expression perfectly calm. Then he began to hunch in on himself, bending his shoulders round as far as the straps allowed.

"Why doesn't he say anything?" Douglas whispered to Barbara Johnson.

"Because we haven't told him to," she whispered back. "The hypnogenic lasts for about three hours, he's still well under."

"Can you hear me?" Judge Hayward asked. "What is your name?"

He blinked slowly. "I hear you, miss. Please, they call me Deaf Willy, miss."

It was an American accent, a slow rich twang, setting off an unwelcome train of thought in Douglas's mind. It was the servile manner which he couldn't ignore.

"Why Deaf Willy?" Barbara Johnson asked impulsively.

"Cos I ran when the sheriff shouted me to stop, miss. I didn't hear him, I swear. Boxed my ears when he caught me. Said I must've been born deaf."

"Are you black?" Douglas asked. He ignored the looks the others gave him.

Deaf Willy's mouth split into a wide grin. "Yes sir. I surely am."

"How old are you, Deaf Willy?"

"Sir, maybe sixteen, seventeen. Don't rightly know for sure."

"Do you know what year it is?"

"Year, sir? No sir, I don't know that, sir."

"Who is the president?" Harvey Boden asked.

"Why, it's Mr Harrison, sir. Mr Benjamin Harrison."

Barbara Johnson started to voiceline the terminal, calling up a list of American Presidents.

"Where do you live?" Judge Hayward asked.

"Mississippi state, miss."

"Benjamin Harrison served one term," Barbara Johnson said. "Eighteen-eighty-nine to ninety-three."

"What is the last thing you remember before you woke up here?" Dr Elliot asked.

"Sir, it's the horses, sir. They's riding all around the house, sir. Must be twenty or thirty of them. They's got torches, razing everything as they go. Flames is rising halfway to heaven." Beads of sweat began to prick his forehead. "Little Jose, she's inside. I can hear her. Lord, I can't see her. Oh Jesus almighty, I'm on fire. Jose's still screaming. I'll get her momma, I will." Thick chords of muscle rose on his throat. He began to gurgle, a thick liquid sound as if he was choking.

Dr Elliot rushed forward. "Forget! Forget that, go back, right back. When you were a little boy. Think of that. When you were little. What do you remember when you were little?"

Judge Hayward pumped her cheeks out as Dr Elliot soothed Deaf Willy down with calming words, encouraging murmurs. "At least we haven't got a zealot this time," she said.

"No," Harvey Boden said carefully. "But you did rule that Softlight should be used until it was successful."

Douglas couldn't believe what the Prosecution Officer had said. "Are you telling me you want this Deaf Willy personality wiped?"

"Prosecution does have a valid point," Judge Hayward said. She looked unhappy at what she was having to say. "If I order a halt now, then that judgement will have to be reviewed by an appeal court. And it wouldn't hold up, it's abysmally arbitrary; we didn't like Erich Breuer so he was wiped, but we felt sorry for a downtrodden cotton picker boy so he was allowed to stay. What kind of legal basis is that? No Douglas, we committed ourselves when we wiped Erich Breuer. Either this body is wiped clean of all its memories, or it is physically executed."

"But we have neither the moral nor legal authority to order the death of an innocent like Deaf Willy," Douglas insisted. "And that is what we are discussing here; Softlight is a death penalty for Deaf Willy. He is nothing like Erich Breuer, he doesn't deserve to be erased. I contend that what we've found in this instance is an eminently suitable replacement personality for Adrian Reynolds's body. As you originally ruled, Judge."

"Not quite," Barbara Johnson said. "Examine that idea from a practical standpoint, Douglas. You will have one hell of a problem trying to integrate an illiterate nineteenth century black boy into modern European society, not to mention acclimatising him to a white body. Without such conditioning he would be totally adrift in time, no family to love him, nothing he can understand, let alone relate to. In order to survive, his antique behaviour patterns would all have to be suppressed. The memories too, I imagine. Could you stay sane with the memory of your own death in your mind? In fact you would probably wind up having to junk about ninety per cent of his memories. Only the name would be left. You wouldn't be saving him at all." She appeared saddened by the prospect. "Our era would be as cruel to Deaf Willy as his own."

Douglas thought about it, and couldn't see an out. "Very well," he said. "I have no objection to clearing Adrian's brain entirely."

"You want me to wipe every past life?" Dr Elliot asked in astonishment. "But that will probably mean going back down to pre-sentience, Neanderthal man, that's the Palaeolithic age. And from what we've seen so far there are about two or three lives per century. If that holds constant, you are talking about four-hundred-plus incarnations. It'll take a week."

"Did you have anything else planned?" Judge Hayward asked icily.

The third personality was called Rosin, another slave from Mississippi. He died from a whipping while James Monroe was President. He was still uttering little dog-like whines when Dr Elliot lowered the Softlight imprinter over his eyes.

Number four was French, a peasant killed at the start of the revolution.

They had some trouble coaxing number five to speak, there was no response to any European language. Barbara Johnson solved it by accessing Cambridge University's linguistics department computer, and requesting a list of greetings in all the languages known to be in use around seventeen hundred.

"If we have to do this each time, the whole process is going to take a month," Dr Elliot said as the terminal droned through the catalogue. "And I doubt that the university's memory cores will be able to help us when we enter pre-Roman history."

The man sitting in the chair mumbled something in response to the terminal.

"African," Barbara Johnson said triumphantly.

His name was Ingombe, a member of the Fon tribe; they were migrants based in Abomey, prey to the coastal slavers. He remembered the Ardra war canoes coming upstream to attack his village, a fight.

Listening to him, and the ones that followed, it seemed to Douglas as though Adrian had turned the tables on them, condemning them to witness a seemingly endless litany of misery, a refined torment for the empathic.

They had lunch delivered to the laboratory, compartmentalised airline-style trays from the canteen. Douglas just ate the cheese and biscuits, staring out through the window. The mist which swirled through the woodland outside was thickening, it already obscured the yellow-brown carpet of dead bracken.

Incarnations ten to twenty were mainly European – Portuguese, English, Dutch, German. Two of them awoke screaming and pleading in Spanish, their anguish so deep set it was beyond even the hypnogenic's ability to quell.

Harvey Boden grimaced while Dr Elliot hurriedly manoeuvred the Softlight imprinter over the first. "Spanish Inquisition," he said softly. "The time fits."

"And LIFE! thinks Softlight is medieval," Barbara Johnson said grimly.

Douglas abandoned his cheese and biscuits. He walked over to the window wall, only half listening to a man called John Diker give an account of Cambridge in the thirteen-forties; his job as a freemason, how he lost his mother, wife, and five children to the Black Death before succumbing himself. The autumn frost seemed to reach in through the thick glass to frost Douglas's body to the core.

*Why are there no memories of what happens between his lives? God's censorship? Or is it simply that the afterlife cannot be interpreted through human senses, the brain cannot hold it? Maybe Dr Elliot will choose that as his next area of study. If he does, I'd like him to fail utterly. Even before this we regarded life too cheaply. Now Softlight will reduce its value still further. In that respect it has already been a tragic failure. Perhaps that is our punishment for meddling with the substance of our own souls. But what kind of God would that give us? One who shows little compassion, one who will hold us to account for each of our actions on this Earth, one who is prepared to turn us away from the gates of the Holy City. An Old Testament God. He cannot be like that. He cannot.*

The evening wore on without respite, one tale of woe following another as the incarnations came and went.

When Douglas stood beside the window wall he could see the tiny yellow flames of the candles the LIFE! women were using for their vigil, a small dim galaxy lost at the end of time. Their flames held an unknowing poignancy; if they had lit one for every mortal death Adrian's soul had undergone they would have the number about right.

Douglas strode over to the chair as Dr Elliot was lowering the Softlight imprinter over Decius Tactus, a Roman centurion, and Christian, condemned to death by a local magistrate. His family had been butchered by soldiers, blaming the bad harvest on their alien God.

The man's eyes gazed back at him through a hazy chemical veil.

"What did he do?" Douglas whispered hoarsely. He met the blank faces of the others.

"Christians were blamed for everything," Barbara Johnson said. "It was convenient."

"No, not Tactus. Originally. What sin could possibly be so bad, so brutal, to deserve this?"

"What do you mean 'originally' Douglas?" Judge Hayward asked, there was a degree of petulance in the question. It was midnight, they had been in the laboratory for a straight fourteen hours.

"This man's soul has been sent back from the afterlife forty times in two thousand years. And each time he has suffered the most appalling degradations, known nothing but war, pestilence, and slavery; seen his families murdered, his homes razed, whole cultures wiped out. Torment without end. This is Hell for him, not Dante's Inferno, Hell on Earth. Every single time. Why? What did he do that God would subject him to this?"

He saw Judge Hayward and Harvey Boden exchange a heavy glance.

"Look, Douglas –" Harvey Boden began.

"Don't," he said angrily. "Don't you tell me it's been a long day, don't tell me I need to go home and get some sleep."

"Probability," said Dr Elliot. "That's all it is, Douglas. So far we've seen less than ten per cent of his incarnations. Apart from the last couple of centuries the vast majority of the human race has lived short miserable lives in unhygienic squalor. In any given historical era the number of aristocrats is a minute fraction. It always has been."

"No. He did something. Something terrible." Douglas could sense the conviction growing inside him. It was one of the most frightening experiences he had ever known. A precognition that could look into the past.

"Genghis Khan?" Barbara Johnson suggested.

"He was late tenth century," Judge Hayward said thoughtfully. "We've regressed well past that now."

We have another half hour before this hypnogenic wears off," Dr Elliot said. "Do you want me to go on?"

"Yes," Judge Hayward said before Douglas could voice a protest.

*Should I object? I want to know who he was, what he did. And I don't want to know. That is the way my life goes, always unable to decide. Well it ends now. Taken out of my hands. I could have stopped it, right at the start, I could have said no, stood firm. But I did what appeared best at the time. I cannot be blamed for that. It is not I who is stained by guilt.*

They waited in restless silence while the forty-first incarnation flooded into the body of Adrian Reynolds. His eyes narrowed, the irises appearing to blacken, receding to some indefinable depth. For one supremely disconcerting moment Douglas thought he was looking directly into a distance beyond that of galactic night.

I know that man, that look; he holds a terror from which even insanity is no refuge. I have seen it once before, so long ago. But where?

Douglas heard the terminal start with a Hebrew greeting; the man answered straight away.

"What is your name?" Dr Elliot asked.

The man blinked, his lips quivering as he fought against the words the hypnogenic was tearing from his mind. "I am named Judas Iscariot." His wounded gaze swept round the five of them in a voiceless plea. Then he saw Douglas, and a confounded light of recognition flared. "Pilate," he cried. "Pontius Pilate."

Douglas stared back at him in mute horror while time quietly dissolved inside his brain.

# Erie Lackawanna Song

Justina Robson

Jackson arrived early at the Hoboken ferry terminal, as he liked to do on sunny days. The ferry before his was just leaving but he made no move although other people ran and trotted past him along the wooden jetty to reach the gate before the guard closed it.

Jackson's ten minutes gave him time alone to walk to the end of the rising and falling pontoon, stand in the shelter offered by the clear and blue plastic sheeting, and look through the chain link fence to the old ferry port next door. Ever since he had moved to New Jersey from the Village this building had been a source of compulsion. It was derelict, with a couple of empty ferry bays facing onto the river. From the outside they were fancy, constructed grandly in a neo-classical style with columns and curlicues now greened all over in a uniformly bright verdigris. Inside, where the boats used to go, it was dark and rotting. The huge timbers that supported the main structure rose dark and wet with the pawing of the waves and the creeping clutch of the water. They leaned in warped neglect where they had once supported a boardwalk out to the boats, the spaces echoing to the crisp sound of many shoes moving purposefully into their journey. He fancied the ghosts of those echoes sometimes struggled to come to life there, when the river slapped the wood or made a knocking sound with some part of the old foundation.

Jackson didn't know if the place had always been that green or if it was painted that way. There were bold decorations on its outsides which looked like they ought to have been some other colour, even gilded or brightly red and glossy copper. The place had a kind of poetry which spoke to Jackson's inarticulate heart directly. When he looked at it, its very emptiness was part of the charm. There, only a few metres from where he stood above the dirty Hudson, it held fast and patient, the lettering of its old destinations staunchly upright still (he assumed they were destinations, anyway) – Erie Lackawanna, it promised, one on the great lakes, the other he didn't know where, although it must be Pennsylvania. But Erie was a vast water, far distant in space, and Lackawanna sounded native to him, a shore that might even be hidden inside the earth and concealing another world altogether. Or maybe it was a star in another galaxy and the name was here to remind humankind that they really ought to do something about getting there. No, it was definitely the emptiness that charmed.

To his right the ferry and the short hop to Manhattan waited. But from the green docks! If only he could find a ticket and a way in one day, from there he could travel to adventures unknown, worlds undiscovered, into futures so bright and dazzling that he could not imagine them, although he heard them calling him with a song like birdsong, almost drowned in the rush of water falling, falling.

Behind him he heard someone give a familiar kind of cough. It was a smoker's cough and one that sparked a recognition to close his daydreaming mind. Automatically he turned around to look. Celia Glick was there, bolstered in her heavy camel coat, a red scarf and a thickly furred hat. She smiled briefly at him and he returned it, re-establishing their old acquaintance.

"Good morning," Jackson said.

She nodded. The ferry was coming in now, too fast it seemed, until the last moment when a rev of the engines in reverse made smoke puff grandly. The boat bumped on the jetty's buffer; two fat dancers knocking their hips together in a stately mamba.

Glick and Jackson waited until the other passengers had disembarked and the people waiting with them had boarded and stepped on last. If they met in the morning it was the habit of each of them to stand in the prow and face the island and the wind all the way.

They stood at the rail and Jackson was grateful that there wasn't going to be much conversation today. Glick was pleasant enough but he preferred to keep his own counsel on the journey. Sometimes she would engage him in small talk and he would have to think hard all the way over, responding thoughtfully and politely to her equally thoughtful and polite chat. He watched the old terminal's mouths slide away behind them, silent shouting, until distance made the place seem small and insignificant after all, and then turned away. Erie Lackawanna, he thought, hearing a melody in the syllables – someone should write a song about it.

Glick's voice startled him.

"Here, look at this."

Dr Glick dug into the pocket of her overcoat and lifted out a glass vial. She showed it to Jackson, holding it against the light with a strong finger on either end of the slim tube to be sure of not losing it in the wind.

Jackson peered.

His first thought was that it would have made a good addition to the Manhattan skyline, against which it now appeared – roughly as high as the Empire State but much wider. It would be a monument worthy of someone truly original: a great glossy column with some kind of internal coating which cut down on sunlight entering the tiny space and cast it back in soft sheens of gunmetal and bronze.

"What is it?" The vial appeared to be self-contained, with no stoppers or seals of any kind. Jackson, ever the practical mind, began to wonder more about how it was made than what was in it. He expected Glick to say something about neurotransmitter drugs or one-shot specific inhibitors; something to do with her work at the Cognitive Institute.

"The end of the world as we know it," she answered, partly smug, but partly with an awe she couldn't disguise.

Jackson, startled, looked down at her and felt a frisson of some archaic emotion race down his back. Her face was triumphant in the early morning sun. She radiated the fire of victory. He recognised his feeling as fear and shifted his feet on the deck, searching for a stronger foothold on the shifting surface.

Jackson knew Glick only vaguely. They met occasionally at the Mapping Technologies Centre in the World Trades, or at conferences on such subjects as fluid dynamics and complex systems modelling. More often they saw each other on working days when they both took the same ferry from Hoboken across to the Trades Centre stop.

Like many other people they both liked to stand in the adventurer's pose as it made its brief crossing; Manhattan and the day both ahead of them and small enough to encompass with a single sweeping glance of conquest. At least, Jackson assumed this was the reaction that Glick had to the view.

Now the last of his morning dreaminess vanished. Glick's statement was so over the top that it was difficult to know what reaction to have.

Scientists, especially those with reputations like hers, didn't make that kind of overweening pronouncement. They just didn't. Jackson cleared his throat unnecessarily and repeated his question, "What is it?"

"This is a sample of MM5," she said. She spoke quietly, so that only she and he could hear before the words were stripped away on the breeze.

MM5. The letters and number wound a tortured route through Jackson's brain. He knew he should know of it, but the meaning – wasn't it something to do with a news story of last year? Some British scientist being found in a government laboratory with a dead intelligence man, possibly a CIA agent? Their project had been MM-something. The Ms stood for Mappa Mundi, a kind of mind-map perhaps. Of course it was in Glick's field, not his. "Cognitive mapping software?" he suggested, instantly feeling out of his depth. He wondered why she was being so coy, and why she was telling him.

"No. This is the complete item," she said, and shook the vial. Inside it silvery clouds swirled, stately and slow as smoke winding up through the overheated air of a gentleman's club. "MM5 is a real-time, self-modulating, complete cognitive upgrading system."

'Uh-huh," the words meant little to him. He leant on the railing of the boat and looked towards Battery Park, where he could just make out the day's joggers moving up and down the walks, some slow and some fast, both being overtaken by rollerbladers and bikes. Glick had a tendency to get heated about her work. She was probably only trying to interest him because she was bursting to talk about it to anybody at all.

"And there's enough in here to fix the whole of New York," she added, leaning on the rail with him, holding the vial out over the heavy, turbid waves. The wind blew her short blonde hair back and forth, forming rosettes on her head and then slapping them away.

Jackson looked at her questioningly. Manhattan was closer than New Jersey now. Soon they'd have to go their separate ways. She would walk with him as far as the bank and then head for her uptown bus. He would pass the twin towers' memorial and wend onwards to the meteorological offices. They would say a hurried 'see you later' and only think of one another again as they approached the ferry stop for the evening ride home, wondering for a split second if the other would be there on the pontoon or would be taking the PATH instead. The routine was well-known and had few variations. Jackson had always assumed Glick had no further interest in him and he had never explored whether he might have any for her since the question was thus moot.

Now he was uncomfortably aware of her mental sharpness and his own sluggish responses to power games of any kind. He gave her a wary social smile to convey interest and inoffensiveness at once, hoping that she would close down the encounter. At the same time his eyes strayed again and again to the vial. He wished she would put it in her pocket where it might not fall and be lost, or else break and further contaminate the dirty water. He wanted to take it from her and put it somewhere out of harm's way.

A curl of soft, glowing light shone from the glass.

"What's the coating on that?" he asked.

Glick seemed surprised. She recovered quickly. "Smart-lead," she said. "Atomic containment."

A bluster of cold fall air shouldered its way around the deck. Everyone around them huddled into their coats and turned their collars up. Jackson did not move. Glick folded her hand around the vial and put the hand in her pocket. For a few moments Jackson watched the surface of the river, a mass of planes continually changing. He let the images fill his mind but they could not wash out the certain conviction that there was something wrong now. Such items as the vial should not be out of a secure laboratory, and whatever the vial held should never be placed in a container so vulnerable; safe at the atomic level but open to the slightest accident in the real world – he shuddered. Perhaps it was a kind of joke?

He looked at Glick's face as she contemplated their arrival. Thoughts ran through his head, wildly. Should he allow her from the boat? Was she dangerously deluded? Perhaps she was playing with him to amuse herself. Perhaps she was showing him because the vial was given her by another and she wanted a witness to it. Perhaps the vial was full of lead powder and nothing else. Perhaps... perhaps...

On the face of it he knew little about her. She had a good reputation among her peers. Her work was well-regarded. Certainly she was a part of projects relating to national security, but weren't they all these days? Nothing in her manner over the last two years had ever suggested derangement, nor a playful nature. Glick was always serious.

Even in her casual smile and greetings there was the sense of a slight lifting of what was an otherwise-occupied attention, inward turning, serious and intense. Sometimes, if they happened to talk on a topic of mutual interest, she would lighten and chat with good humour. Mostly she was simply polite and he gave their association little thought.

"What does it do?"

They were now close enough to see the masts of rich people's boats in the harbour above the park. Glick lit a cigarette behind a cupped hand. She always lit one just before they arrived. She'd been a quitter for three months now but somehow the idea of arriving at work without a single puff was something she couldn't yet stomach and so she grabbed a few drags in the 'healthy' air on the boat before it docked, when she would flick the half- finished cigarette into the water.

Jackson stood free of the rail as she turned her back against it and took a long, grateful drag. She closed her eyes to enjoy the smoke and a heavy whitish trail of it poured slowly out of her mouth. She opened her eyes and jetted the last of the lungful straight out. It blew around Jackson. He smelt the familiar tarry, poisonous odour as it was dragged away and something else a little like the almond sweetness of cyanide or the sickly perfume of Turkish delight. He sneezed. As he was getting out his packet of tissues Glick took another mighty pull and spun the burning stick out over the water where it vanished in the ferry's wash.

She waited until he had finished blowing and wiping and then answered his question of a couple of minutes ago, "On entry into the human brain, MM5 sets itself at all synaptic junctions, producing new inter-bodies until every gateway is monitored. It also creates chemical stations at key points so that the whole of the cognitive function can be controlled. If there are any pre-set programmes MM5 will execute them. If it is to re-train some area, for instance, to alleviate a problem such as dyslexia. Or if it is to act as an auxiliary memory cache. Whatever. It spends some time," she wiggled her fingers, "making accurate records of the normal state of cognitive function in whosever brain – so that if a rollback were required then the person could be returned to their Eve-state of origin."

Jackson wondered at the strange term 'Eve-state'. It was unusually politically correct, even for Glick, who could be annoyingly scrupulous in her terminology. Some of the other implications were going past too quickly for him to catch, like high cirrus clouds being forced along and destroyed in a big blow. He struggled to listen properly.

"And then," she said, "there's nothing you can't do. You can suppress the dominant hemisphere to access the repressed persona of the other side – left or right. You can experience every type of lunacy, from the chemically induced to the structurally dysfunctional. Be schizophrenic for a day. Try psychopathy out and discover the mind of the criminal and the killer. Have a manic phase to get some work done. Have a depressed phase… no, why would you do that? But anyway – upgrade your intelligence in any area. Stimulate the dull and atrophied areas of your brain. Become a composer. Become a writer. Give yourself confidence. Assume the social skills of a master agent. But above all, be rational. Govern your emotions, even in the extreme situation, and let them contribute their own primitive wisdom to your thoughts." She pushed away from the rail and adjusted her scarf, as the ferry wallowed around and began to come in towards the waiting gate of the pontoon.

"MM5 is the master balance. You can set yourself to become what you will, but only temporarily. Its final function is to awaken the dulled, to access the forgotten, to improve the communications between low-connected areas. It can't create what doesn't already exist – people with cell depletion and retardation won't become geniuses – but maximal function and capacity will be restored to everyone in every measure they are capable of. With one exception."

Jackson was concentrating so hard on what she said that he almost fell over as they were ushered backward by the guard towards the safety line on the deck. He looked at the sharp little lines of light which made up Glick's heavy eyebrows as she finished. The detail was so sharp, like the tips of the fur on her hat. It was almost miraculous and he couldn't help noticing it.

"In a normal brain emotion has the capacity to override reason via the amygdala. MM5 reverses that dominance. In an upgraded cognitive system reason can always subjugate emotion. Not remove it or change it. Certainly you would experience your feelings as completely as you are able to. But no emotion would cause those brief surges of action without thought, those murders, those fits of anger, those stupid decisions that cost lives and livings. MM5 gives you control of yourself."

With a muted shudder the boat touched the edge of the dock. The gates were swung aside and people began to pour off the boat, thundering down the stairs from the upper deck, emerging blinking from the shade of the covered seating like cross dormice. Jackson followed Glick onto the swaying wooden pontoon, past the ticket office, up the ramp and onto the stone pavement.

In a couple of strides he was abreast of her. They walked at their normal pace towards the coffee shop beside the yachts.

"What is it going to be used for?" he asked, as much to know as make conversation, which he felt must follow that kind of revelation.

"Nothing so advantageous," she said and there was undisguised bitterness, which he recognised easily in her voice and the hard line of her shoulders. "It's a beneficent precursor to something much more specialised."

Jackson waited. They walked another twenty metres and came to the tables and chairs near the water. It was chilly and the few patrons were all well wrapped. The waiter huddled across the sidewalk, sheltering beside his stand of cups. He just couldn't decide if he believed her or not. His mind felt scattered, blown away. It seemed so ridiculous on this ordinary morning.

"D'you want a coffee?" Jackson found himself saying without intending to. There was a kind of urgency which even he could not help reacting to in Glick's manner and within a couple of minutes their journey would be over.

"Yes," she said quickly, moving towards a free table without a backward glance.

They sat beneath the red umbrella as it was buffeted this way and that. He watched Glick take out and put back her pack of cigarettes twice, from the same pocket as the vial. She put her lighter on the table and toyed with it for a moment.

"Stupid law this," she said. "Outside. Why would anybody care?" And she kicked at an old, stamped on butt near one of her boots.

"What are you doing with that vial, carrying it around like that?" Jackson asked her. He guessed that she wanted to be asked, or had to, before she could say whatever was on her mind. To their right a steady stream of people passed by singly and in groups, their steps quick or heavy in their different anticipations of what the work day held. Jackson longed for his warm patch of office, his orthopaedic chair, his weather maps, but he folded his hands between his knees and waited for Glick to unburden herself.

"I borrowed it," she said, taking her cup up and warming her hands with it. "I shouldn't have. I feel strange, having it. Like having some kind of dynamite. I even carried out tests before l left with it. MM5 is ready to roll. One crack in the glass and poof!"

"What are you going to do?" Jackson took a sip of coffee and wondered if Glick were crazy enough to do something silly, and if she were, what he was going to do about it.

"MM6 is underway," she announced, sighing. The wrinkles around her mouth deepened. "It's similar, but responds to an external operator instead of only the host. In fact, it may end up being engineered not to have the rollback function or the original process where the current personality..." she tailed off. "I think that MM6 is a bad idea."

Jackson pieced together what she meant. External operator? it took only a very little leap of the imagination to see where that kind of thing would lead, but Glick was already talking again, relentless as a machine.

"The original goal for MM5 was to restore criminals, the brain-damaged and the unbalanced, to states where they could return safely into society, able to live productive and happy lives – at least, as able as most of us are. But the scope of it was more powerful than we first thought. It can even improve people who, theoretically, don't need improvement and probably don't want it. That's the thing. There's no choice. It's like a disease. You catch it and you don't know you've got it. It changes you and you can't even notice it, because the old you doesn't exist any more. You can spread it in the water, in the air, in food… skin contact even. It has goals of its own. To replicate and find hosts. To adapt what it finds. To spread. Even after a long time at the Mapping Centre, I couldn't see very far into scenarios of what would happen if it were released." She stopped herself suddenly and took a drink of the hot coffee.

Jackson thought for a moment. He was cold. The wind was gentle here, but relentless, beating through his layers. A gust caught the waiter's apron and sent it flapping up, smacking at his face as he struggled self-consciously to tame it.

"What did you see?" The role of questioner was easy. The role of listener was harder. The more she said, the more he was implicated, the more he knew that when they left the table there would be something in motion from which there was no going back. It would demand that he act and he did not like any of the actions so far suggested.

"In farcasts, where the scenarios have played out for decades, I saw us under MM6," she said. "In all the situations tested, with and without MM5 undergoing organised release, I saw a prediction of the escalating rise of MM6. The controllers had mastery over their small nations of influence. The slaves were happy in their bondage. The old classes emerged; the ruling elite with their immunity and freedom from the technology; the intellectual bourgeoisie, using it to better themselves and produce art, theories, science and of course facilitating the elite's designs; the working drones, directed whichever way they were needed, with the minimal requirements of intelligence or reactivity, as happy as sandboys in all manner of disgusting degradation. MM6 is the immoral moral leveller. Nobody suffered, because where there was suffering there was no one conscious enough to understand their own plight. They were happy," she pushed the coffee cup, still half-full, away from her. "Happy, in their way." The lighter tapped on the table reproachfully.

Jackson did not know what to say. He was not sure what to think. It sounded too far-fetched. And yet he knew they already used the most basic forms of the cognitive technology to help the severely depressed and those injured or born with defects of the neural system. In a badly timed attempt at levity he said, "But maybe it is already out and we don't know it, because we are content in our jobs."

Glick shot him a look of loathing which was not meant for him personally. "Yes," she nodded. "I've thought of that. But look around you," and she gestured briefly to Manhattan and the boroughs beyond. Jackson had to admit she had a point.

She brought out the vial again and toyed with it, watching its strange contents flow and mingle within their minute prison.

"So," he said, "maybe even the reasoned use of this technology isn't the answer. If reason brings us MM6 every time." And he was still not sure he believed her, he told himself. He was just listening to a troubled soul. Helping out. Organising someone else's thinking, someone important and probably someone he ought to make a call about, though he didn't know who to, or how.

"It isn't reason that's the problem," Glick said, watching him add more sugar to his cup and stir it in. "It's that reasoning led to the ability to amass power and wealth for the most quickly adapted – those who were fastest to see and take opportunities for themselves. Humans cannot create any social order that doesn't require a hierarchy, overtly or not. Some rise and others must fall. MM5 and MM6 could not make us equals, that is the problem." She turned the vial over. "We aren't born it and we couldn't be made it. Only in our ideals and allocation of resources. But then, I tried a new version of MM5. One which weakened the hierarchical drive, with an embedded map of reality, which recalibrates meaning structure so that two individuals with different perceptions become able to perceive the same information in identical ways. It uses the first contact as a model and then passes on the adjustments to all the individuals it later encounters."

Jackson stared at her from his position of discomfort, frowning with the effort, "Wouldn't that make them the same person? If they thought everything in the same way?"

"No," she said firmly. "Their different experiences every day would constantly be leading them away from similarity of that kind. The brain is very fluid, even in adults. It would be changing rapidly from the moment of conversion along a different path in every individual. But every now and again, a tweak here and there could produce an effectiveness of communication that would really mean we did all speak the same language. We would be individuals, but ones made up of identical modular components which we all understood. And when I ran that scenario through the map systems – no MM6."

"The mapping technologies are very good," Jackson admitted hesitantly, recalling the pleasure of his accurate predictions of typhoons, even short and localised spells of weather, to the hour. "But they're not absolute."

She absorbed his words of caution slowly and then nodded.

"The thing is," she got a cigarette out and lit it as the waiter went inside. "I know," she touched her nose briefly, "that the military has plans for MM6, if not 5." She breathed in a deep draw of smoke and let it out in a single exhale. "Ah well," she said. "Last one. Must enjoy it."

"You always say that." Jackson was not really watching as she took what he presumed to be a mobile phone out of her pocket.

Glick smiled, a ghostly smile, and carefully stubbed out the cigarette, folding it in half. "Here," she handed the vial to him and picked up the phone unit.

He looked at the vial in his hand, not sure what she meant him to do with it, and looked up.

There was a beep as she depressed a button.

Jackson saw that he must have forgotten to return the vial of cloud tracking crystals to the canister before leaving work. Quickly he returned it to his pocket – must have that for the field testing – he'd put it with the rest of the equipment as soon as he got in.

"Better get going," he said, draining the last of his coffee.

"Yes," Glick said. She was pale with the cold wind. "See you for the evening boat?"

The weather balloon tugged hard against its moorings as Jackson fixed the equipment onto it. He was quick, but not rushed. He loved a field trip, and between the launch of the balloon and the assessment of the data there was a long afternoon's fishing ahead.

Once the rig was secured to the line he tested each piece of machinery to make sure it was still functioning and that no batteries had gone flat. Then he fixed the small dispersal unit underneath, set to release the wind-seed trackers once the balloon had reached the specified height. There was a storm system coming up over the panhandle which, if the mapping system was correct, ought to ride out all the way to the east coast, taking in Philadelphia, New York, even Washington on the way. When the survey was done he could post the severe weather warnings to the TV stations.

Finally he took the vial of trackers out of his pocket and fitted it into the dispersal clamp. Its contents surged up into clouds of distant and tiny turbulence through the dark glass.

He slipped the anchor and watched the balloon rise. Quickly it became a white blob, diminishing all the time, until, shielding his eyes against the glare of the noon sky, he could see first a thing the size of a dinner plate, then a dot and then nothing at all.

He packed up his equipment into the back of the van and began to drive north, towards the cabin where his fishing gear was waiting next to a picnic basket and a bottle of Merlot.

October. A calm day. The walkway out onto the dock was hardly moving as Jackson took a covered cup of coffee with him to wait for the ferry. He was late this morning – had taken time off to do some redecorating at his apartment – and there was almost no one about. Only a young woman in a leather jacket and jeans, who stood by the empty gateway, looking through the chain fence towards the old terminal buildings.

Jackson looked past her. The verdigris colour was the brilliant green of living plants in the low- angled light and the glancing waves shed enough of their glare inside to give a good view of the rotting stanchions. The red lettering was still defiant.

As she heard him approach the young woman turned around briefly to check him out and, seeing him looking at the same thing she was, said shyly, "It's kinda tragic. A gateway to nowhere like that, everybody gone. Someone should write a song about it or something."

Jackson smiled back, "l heard that someone's bought it and has plans to do it up."

"No kidding?"

"Probably just be a different service to the North points on Manhattan. Maybe trips to Staten Island."

"Yeah," she said, nodding, and looking back at the empty building. "But then it'll go somewhere. Now it could go anywhere you want to."

"Yeah," Jackson said. He could see her yearn towards that unknown journey with her whole body. And when a man in a suit joined them, briefcase in hand, he too looked at the empty bays with wistful longing for an instant before his lapel-phone rang and he had to tum away and answer.

Jackson turned from the fence. He hummed a tune beneath his breath, some old folk tune variation, and glanced at the sky with its load of overcast cloud. In his mind's eye he saw a great white liner, sleek as a seal and smoothed for space, emerge from the silent, dead bays of Erie Lackawanna and take to the air, her tail fins catching the low light and shooting it around like diamond spars.

He felt a strange certainty now that they were all going somewhere, and that the journey had started there, in that dark, deserted place. Even under grey skies it was unmistakable – that sense of brimming promise.

Smiling, he took a deep breath and turned to face the river where his boat was coming to fetch him.

# Through the Veil

Juliet E. McKenna

Ortel lowered her viewing glasses. She looked at the man seated to her left. 'Well?'

Her companion studied the stage for a moment longer, gazing over the heads of the crowd standing on the theatre's floor. Lacking the cushioned comfort of these gallery benches, roofed against sun and rain, didn't appear to diminish their enthusiasm. They whistled and applauded as the lithe dancers twirled away to the back of the stage.

As a swiftly drawn curtain hid them from view, the hero of the piece returned through the doorway on the right hand side. Advancing to the platform thrust forward into the crowd, he confided suspicions of his brother's treachery to the avid audience.

'Ferin?' Ortel prompted. 'Seventeen?'

'I believe you're right.' He lowered his voice seemingly out of consideration for the other men and women sharing this bay of the gallery. 'But first we have to identify her.'

Ortel nodded. 'We need more eyes.'

'I should be able to spare a couple of acolytes.' Ferin gazed around the theatre, his eyes apparently unfocused. 'This will be quite some test.'

'Every learning experience should be valued,' Ortel said wryly.

Ferin ran a hand over his balding head. 'How many can you muster?'

She wrinkled her nose. 'One, unless –'

A green satin and lace-clad woman behind them rattled her fan with pointed irritation. Ortel and Ferin shared a rueful glance and returned their attention to the stage. Both raised their viewing glasses when the dancers returned to the forefront of the stage. Seductive in their gauzy draperies, the young women entertained the crowd while the curtains to the rear closed to conceal the corpses of the Baron and his tragically innocent brother.

As the dancers struck their final, decorative poses, the curtains re-opened. The dancers withdrew to either side to allow the actors forward to take their bows. The crowd below cheered, deafening. Up in the galleries more prosperous folk forgot their dignity and stamped enthusiastic feet on the floorboards.

Ortel sat motionless, peering through brass-rimmed lenses raised on a long handle. Ferin was similarly intent, lips moving silently as he counted and counted again. Their eyes met.

'Sixteen,' Ortel said quietly.

'Sixteen,' Ferin agreed.

The noise ensured that no one could overhear them, to wonder what they might mean. Even the merchant's wife with the fan was too busy exclaiming to her friend to glare as they rose to join those keen to beat the rush and made their way to the stairs.

They halted on the second flight down. Ferin leaned over the rail to make sure no one below might hear him. 'Tomorrow evening, at the sixth bell?'

Ortel nodded. 'I'll see you then.'

Before they departed, Ferin took a moment to duck into the shadows beneath the staircase. As they emerged from the theatre amid a handful of others, he wore the black hooded cloak and silvered mask of his calling. Startled passersby made sure not to jostle the priest, though no one spared Ortel a second glance. Why would they? Nothing identified her as one of the Sun Goddess's servants.

They went their separate ways. The crowds enjoying the late afternoon sun parted to let the long-striding priest through unhindered. Ortel picked her own path around those to whom a grey-haired woman was apparently invisible.

Wysa fussed with her blue broadcloth skirts. She rose to her feet twice and then a third time, petticoats rustling as she settled herself on the bench. Ortel resisted the urge to rebuke the girl.

Wysa had barely been sworn to the Goddess long enough to have grown accustomed to her novice's unbleached linen robe. Today she had been startled to learn that sometimes the Golden Mother was best served when her handmaids went unrecognised. Now she was wearing a gown more costly than any she could ever have hoped for. She'd most likely never had a new dress in a tradesman's household with too many children and too little income. Hand-me-downs were all she would have known.

That wasn't all. Wysa was now called on to use her new-found magical skills under strictest seal of secrecy. Some nervousness was only natural. Ortel folded her hands patiently in her lap.

Finally seated, Wysa looked at the stage where the play's handful of musicians were arranging their stools in their alcove. She glanced at Ortel. The older priestess wore a prosperous matron's maroon velvet with the ease of familiarity.

'What do you want to know?' Ortel prompted.

Wysa leaned her chestnut head close to whisper even though they had arrived so early they were alone in this gallery. A gallery looking across the circle of the theatre to the seats where Ortel and Ferin had sat yesterday.

'If sixteen of these dancers are mortal flesh and blood, and only one is unreal, why is she not immediately obvious when you look into the unseen realm, sister?'

'Call me "aunt",' Ortel reminded her. She was easily old enough to be Wysa's mother but that title was reserved for priestesses who ruled over the Goddess's shrines. 'Tell me what you see,' she invited.

Wysa clenched her fists, sitting rigid. Her expression grew so unnaturally fixed that Ortel prepared to explain that her poor niece was prone to such seizures, if some other playgoer expressed concern. It's not as though Wysa would hear her, with all the girl's attention fixed on seeing into the unreal realm.

Ortel spared a moment to wish that Jashil was here. But she was fifty leagues away, near enough, newly installed as Mother in Erepen's shrine. For now, Wysa was all the help Ortel could call on. So few had any ability to see into the hidden world. Fewer still had the mental strength to tackle creatures spawned there from the fusion of emotion, imagination and still unknown mysteries.

Wysa shuddered as she turned to Ortel. 'I can't see anything clearly. It's like a fog –'

The older woman silenced her with a gesture as a handful of prosperous merchants and their wives arrived. Or perhaps these were their mistresses. Respectable women only wore such low-cut gowns for evening parties and private dances.

'A theatre is a place where highest to lowest escape the everyday world,' Ortel explained to Wysa. It wasn't as though these newcomers would understand the deeper significance in her words. 'They set aside their cares, entertained by the follies and antics of characters who can never exist outside some playwright's fancy. Truly, it's a magical place.'

She held the younger woman's gaze and Wysa nodded. Though Ortel wasn't convinced she entirely understood. Well, that was to be expected. Explanations could wait until later.

The floor of the theatre was filling up fast, leaving latecomers with the choice of missing the performance or paying for whatever view of the stage they could afford.

Ortel discreetly tallied how fast the galleries were filling, as well as assessing the clothing and the other adornments worn by those handing over coin for cushions under their buttocks. She pursed her lips, uneasy. This play's audience was growing by the day and not only with those who toiled in the city's workshops and warehouses. Word must be spreading through those taverns and salons where the moneyed classes mingled.

The more talk, the more folk would come to see what this excitement was about. More of them would glimpse this unreal dancer, never suspecting she was a phantasm from the unseen realm. After all, ghosts and fetches and all such things were merely stories for children and cautionary tales at that. Mythical creatures in such fables were invariably malevolent and best shunned. Everybody knew that; from those who merely learned their letters and numbers from retired priestesses in neighbourhood schools, to those who advanced to further study under the Moon God's priests.

Ortel shifted her gaze from the tangible world to the unseen realm. With her experience, doing so required no more than blinking. The theatre itself looked no different. Inanimate things were exactly the same in form and substance. The stage was just as empty though the mists which Wysa had mentioned were swirling all around.

Here and there, the vapours coalesced into half-glimpsed forms. Some appeared on the stage, others up in the balconies behind. Those upper levels served as everything from a tragic hero's prison to a valiant heroine's escape route, depending on the play.

Ortel identified the shadowy figures easily enough from their poses and gestures. A pining lover. A laughing seductress. A betrayed spouse.

A comic bumbler. A vengeful murderer. A pompous buffoon. A dogged nemesis.

These phantasms were playwrights' creations which had enthralled audiences more than any rivals' creations. Somehow that thinned the mysterious veil between the tangible and the unreal sufficiently for these lingering manifestations to appear to those able to see them.

The priestess glanced around the galleries and down to the theatre floor where other figures were visible for a fleeting moment. These were the playgoers who stood close enough to the veil to manifest in the unreal world without ever realising. Only being present in this theatre with their eager imaginations so deeply engaged, stirred whatever meagre magical talent these people possessed.

In their everyday lives, if an eerie shadow snagged the corner of their eye, as they woke from a dream or some daytime reverie, such things were readily explained away. Every shrine had somebody trusted keeping such perilous secrets from the unsuspecting populace.

Ortel was satisfied that she and Wysa were the only solidly visible figures in the theatre, thanks to their conscious engagement with the intangible realm. No one with untrained talents was deliberately creating this wraith of a dancer. That was both useful and unhelpful.

She blinked and was immediately surrounded by the noisy throng filling the theatre. People shuffled along between the gallery benches with whatever dignity they could muster. Down below, the crowd swirled and shifted as friends greeted each other with shouts and waves, edging past strangers to stand in companionable groups.

The galleries were perfumed with herbs that preserved merchants' fine clothes from moths or staleness. Earthier scents rose from below. The city's many trades demanded sweaty toil; weaving, tanning, foundry work to name but a few. As the outer doors opened to admit a last rush, the breeze carried tantalizing hints of sausage-sellers and ale-vendors outside.

The senior piper's warning trill prompted gallery latecomers to hurry to their seats. He glanced around the musicians' alcove. At his nod, a resounding chord from both pipes, fiddle, lute and viol was answered by the crash of the theatre's closing doors. The curtains at the rear of the stage opened. The dancers pirouetted out in their gossamer gowns. Sixteen of them, eight to either side.

'You need only look at what you see in the here and now,' the older priestess instructed Wysa. 'We must fix all seventeen faces in our minds. Concentrate on that and that alone.'

Though she took a moment to glance into the unseen realm, just in case. But the mists had thickened to impenetrability. As a single lithe shape twirled across the stage, the unnatural dancer's face was a blur.

Ortel took what encouragement she could from that. Creatures in the unseen realm were customarily precise in every detail by the time they grew strong enough to escape into the everyday world. Customarily, she reminded herself. How much scope that word allowed for the unexpected.

The play proceeded. During each of the dancers' interludes, Ortel committed their faces to memory. Every priestess was taught to hone her skills of observation as she served the Goddess by supporting families through life's trials from cradle to grave.

She noted that the additional figure appeared when all the dancers were skipping around each other with their arms swept gracefully up, stockinged legs elegantly extended with satin-slippered pointing toes. If a pair or a foursome advanced to show off especially intricate skills, the phantasm shimmered into invisibility.

Wysa was enthralled by the actors. Ortel had to stifle a smile at the girl's intake of breath when she realised the noble matriarch's conniving would set brother against noble brother. But the girl's back stiffened and her eyes focused intently whenever the dancers returned. She was doing her duty to the Goddess.

The drama wound to its tragic conclusion. Ortel frowned. As the actors advanced to enjoy their applause, the phantasm was clearly visible at the back of the stage, behind the line of dancers flanking the right hand side. That was a worrisome development since yesterday. Worse, if any actor or musician addressed the phantasm directly, to ask who she was or what she thought she was doing, this manifestation would gain a firmer foothold in the tangible world.

As the dancers followed the actors off stage, she grabbed Wysa's hand. 'Come on.' Ignoring affronted muttering, she pushed past other playgoers towards the stairs. The brawny theatre doormen had barely unbarred the exit as they reached the bottom-most step.

'My – aunt.' Wysa pulled her hand free with a grimace. 'Where –?'

'The players' door.' Ortel led the way around the whitewashed curve of the brick and timber building.

Quick as they were, a small crowd of men and women, young and old, had already gathered outside this entrance to the storehouse behind the stage and its balconies. These rooms were given over to the mundane necessities of dressmaking, rehearsals and fashioning props.

As the actors emerged, admirers stepped forward to offer flowers and small tokens such as kerchiefs or ribbons. By the time the dancers appeared, a significant number of eager young men had joined this avid throng. Several of the theatre's burly henchmen emerged to flank the door, glowering at any youths who might be overwhelmed by ardour.

The dancers had swapped satin slippers for sensible leather shoes. Plain cloaks hid whatever dresses they now wore, but most still wore their hair loosely dressed with ribbons and curls and few had bothered to wipe off their greasepaint. They still passed for the elegant, marriageable beauties of the tragic Baron's court, epitomising the rewards of love and family which the brothers squandered through their folly.

Wysa counted the girls departing in groups of three and four, or escorted by a brother or lover approved with a curt nod from the theatre's guardians. 'Sixteen,' she murmured.

'Quite so.' Ortel was watching the youths now drifting away. Some had a spring in their step thanks to a dancer who had graciously accepted their posy of late-spring flowers, an enamelled hairpin or a string of beads. Others walked more slowly, shoulders slumped after failing to catch the object of their devotion's eye. However there wasn't a shimmer in the unseen realm to hint that any of them had inadvertently conjured the phantasm of some unattainable desire.

She turned to Wysa. 'Come on.'

The closest of the Sun Goddess's shrines wasn't the one Ortel and Wysa were sworn to but that didn't matter. The priority was recording the phantasm's face before it faded from their memories. That such manifestations were infuriatingly prone to do so was merely another of the intangible world's mysteries.

As they curtseyed to the Golden Mother's statue in front of the pale stone building's door, a linen-clad novice appeared. 'Good day to you. How may I help you?'

Ortel drew out the sunburst pendant she wore concealed beneath her gown's high neckline. 'We require privacy, paper, pens and ink.'

The pendant shone bright as the sun to prove she spoke the truth in the Goddess's service. The novice nodded as Ortel tucked the pendant away. With the Sun Temple's magic endorsing their request, further discussion was unnecessary.

The girl led them through the entrance hall where suppliants of all ages waited patiently. Ortel noted a few curious glances as the young novice ushered them into a side room. No matter. No one would ask impertinent questions. Everyone knew that a shrine's discretion was inviolable.

'Sisters.' The novice opened a cupboard beneath the high, barred window. 'Ring if you need anything further.'

'Thank you.' Ortel took the closest chair beside the plain table.

As the novice closed the door, Wysa fetched drawing materials and pulled up a stool.

Ortel reached for a sheet of paper. 'We need to draw the dancer who we didn't see leaving the theatre.'

Wysa looked thoughtfully at the blank page for a long moment. She flipped the inkwell's lid, dipped a fine-nibbed pen and began sketching. Ortel envied her swift, fluid strokes. The girl's artistic talents were truly a gift from the Mother of all. Because the Golden Goddess knew that Wysa would serve her lifelong? Ortel guessed she would.

She could tell the Sun Goddess's true daughters after seeing countless devotees come and go. Some sisters spent a handful of years in a shrine, even a decade, before handing back their pendant and leaving to marry, to run a business, or both. Others offered a mere handful of months as novices who never took a sister's vows and no one thought the worse of any them for however long they stayed. The Goddess valued all service.

Her own drawing was cramped and hesitant. Ortel threw it away before it was half completed, screwed into a frustrated ball. Her next attempt went the same way, bouncing across the tiled floor. And a third. Why couldn't her uncooperative fingers convey the image she held so clearly in her mind's eye?

As she reached for another sheet of paper, Ortel realised that Wysa's pen had stilled. The girl's head tilted as she considered her portrayal of the phantasm.

'Well?'

'I think –' Wysa caught her lower lip between her teeth.

'Show me,' Ortel commanded.

Wysa slid the paper across the table.

Ortel spun it around. Truly, this was a lesson in humility from the Goddess. With a tenth of the effort and ink which she had wasted, Wysa had captured the elusive dancer's likeness, at least on paper. The phantasm was a delicate, limber beauty, barely old enough to take to the stage had it been a mortal girl.

'Goddess bless you, sister,' she said fervently. 'Now we know what we're looking for.' She stood up. 'Come on.'

Ferin didn't bother with the brass knocker in the shape of a heron. He simply opened the terraced house's red-painted door. As he turned on the step, he saw his two companions exchange a glance of mutual curiosity. He smiled, not that they would see him do so behind his silver mask. With their own faces still covered they doubtless had no idea he could tell what they were thinking. True enough, no one whom they encountered doing their usual duties could have guessed it. But Ferin had spent more than twice either youth's lifetime reading his fellow priests' unspoken thoughts through their stance and gestures.

He entered and beckoned to them to follow.

'This place is...?' Gremase removed his unpainted wooden mask as Ferin closed the door.

'A haven for the use of those trusted with magic's secrets.' Ferin noted that Dewald was waiting for permission before uncovering his face. He nodded to the lad as he shed his own mask and threw back his cloak's black hood. Dewald did the same.

Gremase was staring around the modest dwelling. Son of a wealthy moneylender, he'd probably never been in a home with so few rooms. Son of a man whose business depended on swiftly assessing likely risks and rewards, he had been taught from the cradle to take in every detail of a situation.

There was little enough to see. A settle softened with painstakingly embroidered cushions stood in front of an empty hearth. The only ornament on the mantel shelf was a spray of painted wooden flowers. A scrubbed deal table was flanked by four upright chairs between the three of them and an inner door. A kitchen presumably lay beyond that and stairs to the upper floor.

Dewald's attention was fixed on Ferin. His ability to ignore distractions was admirable and augured well for his future progress in the study of magic's mysteries. He also refused to become a distraction. As far as Ferin knew, no one else in their shrine, and barely a handful of those in the upper ranks of the Moon God's priests, had any suspicion that this particular novice was the Landgrave of Pryne's eldest son.

He wondered if either youth had yet realised that their magical talent now tied them to the Moon God for life, not merely for the handful of years' service which families customarily offered by way of devout offspring, or which the less devout were persuaded to offer to reflect well on their families.

An ebony clock with a gilt and ivory face hung on the chimney breast. It struck the first of six soft chimes. Gremase waved a hand at the dangling weights. 'Who winds that? Who keeps this place dusted?'

The inner door opened. 'Good evening, brother.' Ortel looked past him to the novices. 'Good evening to you, brothers, and may the Mother bless you.'

'Good evening, sisters.' Ferin bowed to Ortel and to the girl who followed her.

'Sisters.' Gremase and Dewald bowed hastily. Ortel's novice curtseyed and mumbled a greeting.

Ortel laid a sheet of paper on the table. 'Well?'

Ferin studied the portrait. 'That's our dancer.' Looking up he saw the novice blush with pleasure. 'Very well done, my young sister.'

Ortel favoured the girl with a smile of her own before returning to the business at hand. 'There was no sign of the phantasm outside the theatre when the other dancers left. During the play though, the manifestation was notably more established than yesterday.'

'Already?' Ferin frowned.

'Indeed.' Ortel explained what she had seen.

Ferin considered this. 'We had better visit the theatre this evening.'

Ortel nodded. 'We'll visit the closest shrines and see if anyone recognises our copy of this likeness.'

'But if –' Gremase bit back his question.

Ortel answered him regardless. 'She may be the figment of some imagining but every desire, every fear, every jealousy is provoked by something tangible, by some person or some event. If this picture prompts a recollection from a neighbourhood priestess or priest, that may lead us to a house or a family where we may find some useful clue.'

'Of course.' Gremase ducked his head. 'Thank you, sister.'

'We'll meet here tomorrow at noon?' Ferin looked at Ortel. 'To share what we've learned? If needs be, we can go to the next performance together?'

She nodded, laying a ring of keys on the table to weigh down the sheet of paper. 'Goddess go with you, brother.'

'May the Moon God light your path.' Ferin opened the front door. He bowed to the departing women and then made sure the latch clicked securely. He saw the two novices looking at him, wide-eyed.

'Who –?' Gremase ventured.

'They are our sisters who serve the Goddess. That's all you need know.' Ferin looked at Dewald. 'What is your question?'

The novice gestured towards the pen and ink portrait. 'How dangerous could she be? Someone so slightly built and ignorant of this world besides?'

He was asking honestly, not sceptically as Gremase might have done. The Moon God's lore decreed that all phantasms were dangerous so Dewald accepted it. He simply wanted to know what he might be facing.

It was time that the pair of them learned that the intangible realm was far more complex than fireside stories.

'*It* –' Ferin stressed the word ' –is unlikely to pose a direct threat, not to us at least. Though we should always remember the emotion that's created it colours the nature of such a *thing*.'

Once again, his emphasis reminded the novices how often they had been warned not to grant a phantasm some foothold in reality by thinking of it as a living person. Ferin was pleased to see them both look abashed.

'If it's been spawned by hatred or envy or some dream of revenge, it may well be malicious from the outset, and we'd be fools to assume anything about its strength based on its outward appearance.

'Then again.' He shrugged. 'It may just as easily be as frail and unassuming as it seems. That doesn't mean we can leave it be.' He looked from Gremase to Dewald as the novices stared at him, confused.

'Let us suppose this creature is harmless. Let us suppose it grows real enough to step through the veil and enter the tangible world. Let us suppose it summons up the courage to leave the theatre one day. What happens to it then?'

He gazed at the novices, unblinking. The silence lengthened. Ferin waited. One element of this particular lesson was these boys realising he wasn't going to spoon-feed them the answers.

Gremase glanced at Dewald but didn't speak.

'Where would it go?' the young nobleman wondered. 'It could know nothing of the city. It would have no idea who to turn to. So it would be easy prey for those who hunt such innocents. Whoremasters and rapists and such.' He scowled.

Ferin wondered what tales he'd heard of foolish youngsters from Pryne who'd left that peaceful downland town? How many such hopefuls were seduced by tales of fame and fortune to be found in Hurat under the aegis of the Paramount King? How many were returned to their grieving families degraded or dead? How many vanished utterly, their fates known only to the Moon God?

'Not necessarily,' Gremase protested. 'One of the theatre company might befriend her. She might just as easily find an open hand on the streets instead of a fist.'

He wanted to think the best of his city and truth be told, travellers had every chance of being greeted with goodwill. After all, you never knew when a priest might be watching. That's what children tempted into mischief were warned; a lesson most folk remembered lifelong.

'True enough.' That surprised both novices. 'But what happens then, if some kindly soul offers shelter or help to *it*.'

He looked pointedly at Gremase and the youth coloured. Once again, Ferin waited. After another long moment, Dewald replied.

'They will want to know where it came from. They will ask questions about its family, its home, what's befallen it before they met. It won't have any answers, will it?'

'And then?' the priest prompted.

The novices looked at each other, considering this.

'Sooner or later, someone will bring her – it –' Gremase quickly corrected himself '–to a Crescent Moon Gate, thinking that it must be ill or injured, to have lost all such memory. It surely couldn't be long before someone realised its true nature.' He looked hopefully for Ferin's confirmation.

The priest nodded. 'But by then it will have been present in this tangible world long enough to become flesh and blood. A living creature still confused by a world it doesn't understand and with no place to belong. A creature whose very existence could prompt curiosity about the magic which we are sworn to keep secret.'

He picked up the drawing on the table. 'Would you be prepared to kill it, to keep the innocent and powerless safe from such perilous knowledge?' He turned the picture towards them. 'Could you look into this face and cut such a beauty's throat?'

'I –' Gremase's inarticulate protest died away.

Dewald shook his head, looking at the floor.

The steady tick of the clock on the chimney breast filled the silence in the room. Ferin waited and finally nodded. The pair would take his words to heart. Of course, in all his years wearing the silver mask, he'd encountered a good few situations far less straight-forward than this, but that was a lesson for another day.

'So you agree it is simpler for us to make certain that such a creature doesn't cross over from the intangible realm in the first place?'

'Yes, brother.' Dewald was convinced.

'Indeed.' Gremase looked troubled but resigned.

'Very well.' Ferin rolled up the portrait and stowed it in one of the many useful pockets inside his hooded black robe. 'Let's do our duty.'

He picked the keys off the table and donned his silver mask. The novices replaced their wooden ones and all three raised their hoods. As they left the house, Ferin locked the door and stowed the keys safely away.

The modest street was conveniently close to the theatre. This district where the highways from the west met the king's road running from north to south between the city's great bridges was thronged with people. The working day was done and the sun sank slowly at this time of year. Those who toiled in workshops and warehouses were as likely to linger over a drink in a tavern as they were to head home. Those whose families could spare them, or those who didn't care what their families thought.

Crowds were no hindrance to Ferin. Men and women stepped aside to let him pass. Dewald and Gremase hurried after in his wake. They soon arrived at the theatre. It stood alone in an irregular cobbled expanse left empty by some long-ago fire.

Two constables appeared around the curve of the building, each with his iron-shod ash stave casually sloped over one shoulder. They stopped and one turned to the other who promptly reversed direction to circle back around the theatre.

The remaining constable advanced, carrying his stave in a ready grip. 'Brothers? Do you need some assistance?'

Ferin offered a hand. 'Badre, good evening to you.'

'Brother.' Recognising his voice, the constable looked past him to the novices. 'Training some new pups to the whistle?'

Ferin smiled behind his mask as he heard indignant feet shuffle to his rear. His reply was wholly serious though. 'Teaching them to hunt a particular scent.'

'What's on the loose?' Now the constable was just as intent.

Ferin reached inside his cloak for the phantasm's portrait. 'Have you seen this?'

The constable studied it then shook his head. 'No.' He glanced in the direction where his partner would soon reappear. 'Inside?'

'Please,' Ferin confirmed.

'Quickly.' Badre produced a ring of keys and unlocked the theatre's closest entrance. He handed the keys to the priest.

'Move.' Ferin ushered the novices through and locked the door behind them. 'Come on.'

Stairs on either side offered access to the gallery. An aisle between them led to the rush-strewn, beaten-earth floor in front of the stage. Ferin walked out there and looked up. The blue circle of sky overhead was shading towards lavender as twilight approached.

'Brother?' Gremase still lingered by the doorway. 'That constable knows something of what we're seeking?'

'You don't imagine we're the kingdom's only guardians against the unseen realm?' Ferin removed his mask and tucked it away in its pocket inside his robe. 'We have allies in many walks of life. Badre's responsible for guarding this theatre in both the tangible world and the unseen realm.'

Dewald looked thoughtful, one hand on the rail separating the lowest gallery from the open floor. 'In case some thief who breaks in stumbles across a phantasm?'

Ferin wondered when the temple elders would decide that the boy could best serve the Moon God's purposes by returning to take up his inheritance? Well, it wasn't his place to ask. His duty was teaching this pair whatever they needed to know as soon as they needed to know it.

Gremase followed him to stand by the stage. He had stowed his own mask away and his unfocused gaze told Ferin the youth was already gazing into the intangible world.

'In case something dangerous breaks out.' The priest pinched Gremase's ear, not cruelly but forcefully enough to get the novice's attention.

Gremase spun around. 'What –?'

'Follow my lead,' Ferin said sternly. 'Get ahead of yourself and you may get into trouble I cannot get you out of.'

'What must we do first, Brother?' Still by the stairs, Dewald looked around, apprehensive.

'First? Listen and learn.' Ferin waved towards the outthrust platform. 'It's still some while until nightfall but people will already be dreaming of plays they have seen here. Others will be enjoying their leisure at some fireside or with a glass in hand, imagining stories they've loved being acted out on this stage. Such things thin the veil and all the more so when all those dreams focus on one place.'

Gremase frowned. 'Then why –?'

Ferin anticipated his question. 'Why permit theatres in the city? Because it's easier to keep watch for such things when you know where they'll most likely manifest. Now, both of you, concentrate on the unseen realm. You need not fear tripping over any other mortal presence. We're the only ones with business in this place and Badre will see that all the doors are secured.'

He waited a moment to satisfy himself that both novices were concentrating on the intangible. Then he drew his broadsword out from beneath his robe.

'Brother!' Gremase stepped back, startled.

Dewald blinked and Ferin knew that he had shifted his gaze back to reality to confirm that no such blade existed. He grinned as Dewald shook his head, focusing on the unreal once more.

'Now you see it, now you don't and now you see it again.' He shifted the weapon from hand to hand, luminous as a shaft of moonlight. 'Can you arm yourselves?'

Radiance flickered in Gremase's hand, only to gutter like the light of a burned-out candle. Dewald had more success. The smallsword he gripped was dull as pot-metal but the magic held steady enough.

Was that because a nobleman's son was drilled in swordplay, if only for formality's sake? That was a question for another time. Ferin had more immediate concerns. 'Gremase, stay behind me and keep watch to all sides. Dewald, guard the rear.'

He led them up the steps to the lowest level of the gallery, where the tiered seats were raised just high enough for those spectators to see over the standing crowd's heads. The shadows were thickening here. Thankfully his phantasmal sword shone bright enough to show them all that nothing lurked here. Ferin strode quickly to the door that led to the maze of rooms behind the stage. A key on Badres' bunch unlocked it.

The darkness within was complete. The silence was not. Something scuttled across the floor. Ferin brandished his moon blade and the light showed them a rat's fleshy tail vanishing beneath a chair.

Gremase turned his gasp of relief into a laugh. 'If that's all –'

A shadow by the opposite door coalesced into a looming figure. Taking a step forward it threw up gloved hands in a dramatic gesture. The sword's pallid light showed them a bearded man wearing the furs and leathers of a high plateau wanderer. He raised a fearsome, double-headed axe and snarled as Ferin brandished his blade.

The priest took another step forward. The edge of the moonbeam glinted like sharpened steel. The wanderer shimmered into nothingness.

Ferin chuckled. 'The Hound Master really made an impression, didn't he?'

Neither novice managed a coherent answer.

'We must find out where that play's being revived, to set people dreaming of that villain again. It may not even be in the city,' Ferin continued as he unlocked the far door. 'Some players may be staging it in a town up or downstream. A traveller may have brought his memories of it home.'

Gremase cleared his throat. 'What could such a phantasm do to us? To anyone who encounters such a thing?'

Ferin halted on the threshold. 'That depends how much you fear it. Dread feeds a manifestation's strength.'

'We need not fear something that does not exist.' Dewald spoke up from the rear and the unreal blade in his hand shone brighter.

Ferin nodded and went on through the door that opened into the gallery on the far side of the stage. There was nothing to be seen. Ferin walked swiftly towards the steps rising to the floor above. 'Gremase, watch the other stairs. It may try to escape us by heading down while we're on our way up.'

The priest caught a faint gleam in the corner of his eye as they reached the next gallery. Now Gremase grasped a streetfighter's knife, or at least, the intangible form of one. Ferin noted the ease with which the novice held it and the way his balance shifted as he walked, ready for any assault. Gremase's father hadn't forgotten his own lowly origins, when it came to teaching his son what he thought he should know.

'Brother!' Dewald hurried forward to the gallery's rail. 'Down there! Do you see?'

A pale figure stood centre stage. The mists solidified into a woman wearing a bloodstained gown.

'Horseshit.' Rather than take the stairs back down, Ferin ran round to the balcony behind the stage. He heard the hurrying novices behind him but there was no time to explain. He cursed under his breath as he fumbled for the key to unlock this door leading from this gallery. 'Is it still there?' he demanded.

'Yes.' Gremase didn't waste time on questions.

'Stay here and keep watch. We mustn't lose sight of it.' Ferin hurried into the room behind the balcony and found the ladder he knew was kept there. Hauling up the trapdoor in the floor, he thrust the ladder through. As soon as it hit the floor, he began climbing down. With no one to hold it, the ladder skidded on the boards. Barely halfway down, Ferin jumped rather than risk a fall. He landed at the rear of the stage with a thud that echoed around the empty theatre.

As he ripped the curtain aside there was no sign that the phantasm had heard him. The woman had collapsed to her knees, her hands tangled in her hair. She swayed from side to side, racked with grief. On the edge of hearing, her eerie keening sent shivers down Ferin's spine.

The sword in his hand blazed bright. He thrust it between the figure's shoulder blades and the phantasm vanished in a blinding flash. Ferin pressed the back of one hand to his eyes, waiting for the dazzling smears across his vision to subside.

'Brother?'

Ferin squinted to see Dewald and Gremase still up in the gallery. Following his orders or too afraid to come down?

'I don't suppose either of you were old enough to see The Widow of Cormir performed here?' He knuckled his eyes. 'We had better warn the good sisters as soon as we're done here. This news cannot wait until morning.'

'What does it signify?' Alarm sharpened Gremase's tone.

Ferin blinked a few more times. 'According to the play, and the ballad that it was drawn from, the Widow of Cormir was persuaded into a second marriage to advance her family's interests. Alas, she was tormented by her new husband but always in private and in ways that left no bruises. He betrayed her with other women but always in secret and taking lovers with their own reasons for discretion. No one believed her pleas for help, since he convinced all their friends and family that she was feeble-minded. Ultimately she was truly driven mad and killed herself to escape him, but only after killing her children to save them from life at his mercy.'

'But now you've dispelled that phantasm, where's the threat?' Dewald was searching for understanding.

Ferin walked around the lower gallery and used the stairs to rejoin them. 'Correct, there's no immediate threat of violence, now that the phantasm is gone. No unfaithful husband slinking home from his mistress's bed will meet that horror in some alleyway.'

He turned to Gremase. 'But you are right to ask what has prompted that manifestation. Its appearance tells us that somewhere and none too far distant, a woman is being abused. A woman who believes herself friendless and helpless. A woman so without hope that she sees herself reflected in this old, tragic story. We must ask our good sisters to enlist all their shrines to find out who she is. Then they can remedy her situation before she slits her own throat or stabs her husband in his sleep.'

He gave the novices a moment to share a glance of mutual horror. Ferin was pleased to think they had both been raised to find such abhorrent behaviour unthinkable. Though that did mean the youths had all the more to learn. Well, their service to the Moon God would teach them how truly vile some people could be.

'Now, let's see if we can find this elusive dancer,' he said briskly.

They continued the search, all three now holding blades that illuminated every corner of the theatre, but alas, to no avail.

The unexpected news of the Widow's reappearance kept Ortel and Wysa busy all morning. Rather than gathering at the little house with the red door, they met the priest and his novices at the corner of Raparee and Menson's Street.

Ferin offered his arm and Ortel smiled graciously as she slid her hand through his elbow. She gestured to Wysa and as the girl preceded them, the novices fell into step to either side of her.

Ortel amused herself by imagining passersby's assumptions. Did they suppose that she and Ferin were this amiable young lady's parents, supervising a noonday stroll with her rival suitors? Why not? Both youths were passably handsome and dressed like the sons of prosperous merchants today.

'Mother Bresline at the Beggar's Bush shrine already has cause for concern about one family,' she remarked quietly as they walked on towards the theatre and the afternoon's performance. 'She will investigate further, to see if that's the source of the Widow's tears.'

Ferin nodded. 'Please, thank her on my behalf. I have already sent word to Constable Badre to alert me to any more sightings. I will let Mother Bresline know what he reports.'

They rounded the corner, skirting an ale-seller's wagon offering horn beakers topped with foam to those who'd abandoned their counters and workbenches for this afternoon's entertainment. Where the lane widened into the cobbles surrounding the theatre, a trestle table draped with a red-checked cloth enticed a more select clientele. A winsome girl offered fruit ices and wine-cordials in small, sturdy glasses. Her sharp-eyed mother was refilling them as fast as her son could wash them clean in a barrel behind their cart.

A knot of early arrivals lingering by the table broke apart in loud confusion. An elderly man sank to his knees, supporting a white-haired woman who appeared to have fainted. Her face was ashen and her eyes were closed.

'You.' Ortel plucked at the closest novice priest's sleeve. 'The nearest Crescent Moon gate is at the shrine on Hind Lane. Run and fetch a healer!'

'Quickly!' Ferin confirmed her order with a jerk of his head.

'Brother, take these two into the theatre. I'll stay here until help arrives.' Now it was Ortel's turn to urge her novice on with a nod. 'Go on. I'll see you after the performance.'

'Quite so.' Ferin offered his arm to Wysa instead. 'My dear.'

Ortel knelt beside the distraught man, heedless of the dirt on the cobbles. 'Has she been under the Moon God's care?'

The husband nodded. 'She suffers from palpitations.'

Ortel felt for the pulse in the stricken woman's neck. It was faint, fast and erratic. 'Mistress, can you hear me?' Seeing no sign of any response, she turned to the refreshment sellers who were looking on aghast. 'If you please, a glass of cold water?'

'Of course!' The son swiftly filled a beaker from a jug standing in their ice chest.

Ortel threw the cold liquid into the old woman's face. The crowd of onlookers exclaimed, startled. Their protests subsided somewhat when the old woman's mouth opened and her eyes flickered.

'Suese,' the old man exclaimed, relieved.

Ortel didn't share his optimism. 'Mistress, can you hear me? No, don't try to raise her.' She laid a quelling hand on his arm.

'Madam, may I ask, who are you to give such orders?' A man of middle years with a strong resemblance to the stricken woman challenged her.

'A nurse of many years' experience.' That was true enough, if not all of the truth. Ortel kept her gaze fixed on the old woman. 'Mistress, can you take a deep breath?'

The woman's eyes fluttered again but that was all her response.

'We should never have come,' the middle-aged man insisted to no one in particular. 'How many times does anyone need to see the same play?'

'How far away is your home?' Ortel asked the husband.

'We came here in a hireling carriage.' He looked up at the middle-aged man.

Just occasionally, Ortel reflected, it would be helpful if people answered the question they had been asked. She studied the old woman. Her colour was still ghastly, her withered lips bloodless. Goddess grant that the Moon God's servants would be able to get her into comfort and privacy before she died. She clasped the woman's cold, limp hand between her own and prayed fervently.

Sooner than she expected, a bustle stirred the crowd behind. The priests had arrived. She released the old woman's hand, rose to her feet and withdrew. No one paid her any attention now that black-robed, silver-masked healers clustered around their patient and her distressed family.

Ortel looked around for the novice whom Ferin had sent to fetch help. The youth was hesitating by the wine-seller's table, not wanting to add to the crowd but close enough for a healer to summon him.

She walked over to join the boy. 'Find out where they are taking her, then come and tell me. I'll be at the shrine on Isod Lane.'

'Yes, sister.' He ducked his head obediently.

Ortel went on her way, satisfied. Ferin was doing a good job with his current charges.

Her home shrine wasn't far. She curtseyed to the Goddess and entered like any other suppliant before passing through the inner sanctuary and the door that led to the stairs. Once in the dormitory, she shed the day's disguise and donned her linen robes with relief. She laid her hand upon her sunburst pendant, now gleaming on her chest, and breathed a prayer to the Golden Mother for the stricken woman's sake.

'Sister.' Tanise poked her head around the door. 'A messenger for you.'

'Thank you.' Ortel hurried back down.

As she'd hoped, Ferin's novice was waiting in the entrance hall. He wore his hooded cloak and mask but she recognised his hands and the set of his shoulders.

'Sister, Mistress Suese has rallied. The brothers of the Crescent Gate have permitted her to be taken home. The family name is Anlen and their house is on Heron Street.'

'Thank you, brother.' Ortel walked outside with him. 'Come with me, keep your mouth shut and your eyes open.'

She snapped her fingers to get the attention of a passing hireling gig. The driver halted his horse without question and nodded as Ortel told him where to go. Only a fool declined to help the Goddess's servants going about their sacred business.

He drove them westwards into a leafy district of spacious houses surrounded by generous gardens. An anxious cluster of friends and neighbours indicated the Anlen household's gate in Heron Street.

Ortel assessed their mood and the tone of their conversation. Unless she was very much mistaken the old woman wasn't dead yet, or if she was, that grievous news hadn't been shared with these well-wishers.

She leaned forward to tap the gig driver's shoulder. He drew to a stop and she handed him a silver crown. 'Thank you.' The goddess rewarded those who helped her servants.

'Sister.' The novice jumped down and held out his hand.

'Thank you.' Ortel accepted his assistance from the vehicle. 'You go on ahead. I'll follow.'

'Of course, sister.' The youth squared his impressive shoulders and advanced towards the crowd at the gate.

The throng parted, as Ortel had known they would. Women whispered behind their fans and men regarded the novice priest with a mix of awe and apprehension. What was he doing here? Not that anyone would ask him, even the lackey guarding the gate.

Few gave her a second glance and Ortel knew they would scarcely remember her face. Good. If she'd come here alone, she'd have faced far greater scrutiny and there was always the possibility that one of these people had been in the party going to the theatre. Being recognised as the woman who'd come to Mistress Anlen's aid was a complication she would rather avoid.

A harassed maid with reddened eyes opened the house's door at the novice's knock. She dropped a hasty curtsey.

'The Horned God's grace to you,' the novice said smoothly.

'Together with the Goddess's blessings.' Ortel slipped past him into the entrance hall. 'Has the household gathered to pray, my child?'

'Not yet.' The girl choked back fresh tears.

'May I?' Ortel headed for the closest door, not waiting for permission to open it. She found a withdrawing room furnished with comfortable seats and side tables holding flowers and ornaments. A suitable place for the house's sons and daughters to entertain their friends, with family portraits hung on the walls to remind them of the duty they owed to their parents.

She turned to the maidservant with a kindly smile. 'I will beseech the Mother's kindness in here. Those who wish to join me will be most welcome. Please let the household know.'

'Of course.' The girl curtseyed again and hurried away.

Ortel looked at the novice. His stance betrayed indecision. She took matters out of his hands. 'Go and see if you can be of use to the healers. If not, go to the theatre and tell Brother Ferin what's happened.'

The novice scratched the back of his hood. 'Forgive me, sister, but what has happened?'

Ortel reached into a pocket. She unrolled a copy of the portrait which Wysa had drawn. 'Take a good look.' Once he'd done so, she gestured around the room, 'Now, do you recognise anyone?'

The youth made a circuit of the portraits, studying each one intently. Finally he halted and turned to Ortel. 'It's her, isn't it?'

Ortel joined him and pointed to faint writing in the bottom corner of the picture. 'Suese Feroud on the occasion of her marriage to Heyte Anlen.'

'How did you know?' The novice gazed at the girl in the portrait. 'How does this explain the phantasm?'

'I saw the beauty she had once been in the old woman's face.' Ortel contemplated the long-ago bride's expression of dutiful obedience as well as the hint of some longing that the artist had captured. 'When the household comes to share their memories as they mourn her loss, they will tell us how much she loved the theatre. Some will know she had a particular fondness for the dancers. She may even have confided in some favourite daughter, sharing girlish dreams of taking to the stage if she had been born to a life where that was possible.'

A heartbroken wail echoed through the house. Ortel briskly tucked the portrait away. 'Our business now is with the living. Go and ask your brothers how you can be of use to the family while I see to those who grieve below stairs.'

In the theatre, Rediker watched Walvin intently. The ensemble's lead piper made certain all the musicians were looking at him and ended the music with a final flourish. The curtain's rings rattled one final time as the dancers followed the actors off the stage.

The audience headed for the exits, loud in their appreciation for the play. Rediker wondered idly if one of them might ever remark on the music.

Walvin looked at Shabber, Aidel and Grest. 'The Basket of Grain?'

The viol, lute and fiddle players nodded. That particular tavern's landlady always agreed to them playing in her taproom for whatever coin other drinkers might spare.

Walvin nodded at Rediker as the others rose from their seats. 'See you there, lad.'

'As soon as I can.' Though he was in no great hurry to gather up the stools as they left. He listened for the actors' voices in the room behind the stage. They would be the first to leave then the dancers would follow.

Pick the right moment and he could catch that new girl on her own, ask her name and let her know she had a friend in him. She always left after the other dancers, for no reason that Rediker could see. He would never understand girls.

Gathering his courage along with the stools, he headed for the back room. A lone dancer sat on the floor, knotting her bootlaces. She looked up and Rediker stifled his disappointment. She wasn't the mysterious, entrancing stranger.

Jahel held out a hand. 'Help a girl up.'

He set down the stools and did so. No need to be rude.

Jahel groaned. 'You have no idea how my blistered toes hurt.'

'I can guess.' Playing every afternoon, Rediker had ample opportunity to see the demands each performance made on the dancers. He could see sweat beading her forehead. Beneath her greasepaint, she looked exhausted.

'Shall we go and find something to eat? I'll walk you to your lodging after.'

Jahel looked at him, surprised. Then she smiled. 'That would be nice.'

Rediker realised how attractive her smoky blue eyes were. He abandoned all thoughts of that ethereal beauty, whoever she might be. She was always so keen to leave without talking to anyone anyway. Whereas Jahel had been his friend since his first days here.

As the priestesses always said, contentment is cherishing what you have here and now, not longing for what you lack.

# The Coming Of Enkidu

## Geoff Ryman

North along the edge of the mountains something happened that had happened once before. The dust stirred.

The dust felt warmth at first, sunlight and moisture and something seeping up from itself. It wanted to be part of it. It wanted to stand up and walk through the sun and air. Life impelled it. It was a patch of dust that yearned.

The dust saw sunlight through itself and that awoke memories of flesh, light through flesh, warm and orange. It wanted to be flesh. It felt the wind caress it and felt some of its substance rise up, blown away. The dust hoped then that it might be lifted up whole, and carried, be blown away as dust through life, the world of life about it.

At night when the sun was withdrawn, the dust saw things move within it, like shadows on a closed eyelid. The patch of dust dreamed. Half-formed shapes of light played about the individual grains of its being. Muffled voices in faraway conversation came out of it, out of the ground. One voice was paramount. It was the voice of the one who had called it. The dust could hear this voice, and it struggled to tear itself up out of the earth. The voice was like the cry of a lamb whose true mother is lost. The very earth had answered it. It tried to stand and succeeded in rising and falling as if with breath. Dust escaped in small puffs, like smoke.

The dust began to grow fur, like grass. It was rich black fur, streaked with human white. If there had been people near, they would have heard a faint sizzling sound come out of it, like water draining from bogsoil after a rain. Under the fur, the dust was going red and moist. It could have been pulled up then, like mould, and the dirt underneath it would have been flecked with blood, and there would have been white roots.

The worms brought it sustenance in the moonlight. They felt the love in the ground. They felt it in the dust through which they laboured and which passed through them, feeding them too. They lightly kissed the new tender flesh and left behind the rich things they had collected from the earth, minerals and organic matter. In the moonlight, a lioness settled there, because it was warm. She groomed the new fur with her serrated tongue that swept away the tiny insects that could have devoured it. The lioness felt the dust shiver at her touch, and gather, trying to soothe itself against her warmth. She settled and slept. Sheltered by her, the new life grew. In cells that traced themselves through the new flesh like the mycelium of mushrooms, the dust began to be aware of itself, to feel its own existence.

The next day, the dust had a mouth. It opened in the morning with a sickly peeling sound. The mouth gaped and smacked, toothless and drying in the air. The dust had no breath with which to speak and it needed to speak or call, but it could only smack its lips. It had no tongue. The lioness suckled it. Her own cubs had been lost. The mouth pulled in animal protein until it was full. Then it waited untiI the milk was absorbed, and would click and smack again for more. Fur began to sprout elsewhere, through the grass. Where the head would be, fur began to grow down, curl around to enclose and define. Precipitated like crystals, bone began to form from the salts of the ground.

A perfume arose from it, a scent that was both milky and herbal, sweet as rosemary and as pungent. The scent made the lioness excited. She circled round and round the dust, and growled when others of her pride approached, warning them off. Her tail lashed. Finally, quivering and desperate, worried, she left the dust, and came back trotting and anxious, with a mouthful of field mice that she had already chewed into paste. This she deposited into the mouth of the ground.

Night came again and was an agony for the dust. The pictures were so clear and the voices almost made sense. It knew exactly where the thing that had called it lived. It was as if there was a cord between them that would hoist it to its feet, and haul it across the desert. It ached with growth.

In the morning, with a pop, its lungs inflated. The dust had grown firm and lumpy, and it writhed to be free. It opened its mouth and wheedled for milk and mice and love. The lioness whimpered for it, and licked it. A furred hand emerged from the grass, and flapped, rooted to the earth. The lioness nestled her head against it, hoping to comfort and to still it. With sudden inspiration, the hand began to scratch her behind the ears and the lioness purred, and the vibration of her ribs made the carpet of new flesh under her buzz and go numb. The new thing coming to the surface was suddenly sure: tomorrow it would move. Tomorrow it would rise.

It felt the cooler breeze of night on its feet and saw blue instead of orange through its skin. For the first time, it felt a respite. For the first time the pain, and the leaning toward the south were eased, and comfort did come to it. For the first time, it slept.

In the morning, its blind unformed head was free. Its hands worried flaps of flesh on it, until its ears were unfolded, like petals. It mumbled the tips of its fingers, to learn exactly where they were, and the tips of its fingers spidered their way over its face. It tugged and tugged until it tore open its nostrils. It breathed through them, burbling with blood that trickled into its mouth. It grabbed onto its lioness for purchase and pulled until its arms above the elbows were ripped out of the earth. The thing howled in pain. There were raw wounds along the back of its arms. The lioness moaned, and began to lick them, and the new thing sobbed. Then it began to rock back and forth, back and forth against what held it, snarling with impatience and pain as the boundary between itself and the ground gave gradually away.

Suddenly it sat up. It gasped, and squealed for the lioness, who prowled round behind it. Two great swathes of open flesh marred the fur covering of its back. White roots wriggled in the ground behind it; blood seeped up out of the earth in small puddles. The thing tried to kick its legs. It pushed with its arms. Its legs came free, and it drew its knees up toward its chest, and then it lunged. It lunged, and fell forward on all fours. It hung its head, and a tongue separated from the roof of its mouth. The tongue curled like a dog's to form a channel for cooling sweat.

The new creature stood on its hind legs and walked. It had no eyes, and it staggered with exhaustion, but it could smell, and what it smelt as it moved in and out of cool shadow was water. It smacked its dry lips, and stumbled, and it righted itself against the back of the lioness who was beside it. It held onto the loose skin of her neck and let itself be led. The air was dry and seemed to make its sore back shrivel and tighten. The Beast slipped on a rock and fell. It snapped in frustration, and sat up, and pushed upwards on its forehead until its eyes opened. But its eyes were unformed, white with only a ghost of an iris, as if covered by a cataract, and it still could not see, and the air parched its eyes as well, and it wept blood.

So it limped on until it found the spring that was the Source. It could smell the water shifting, like a living thing.

Then, like a door opening, words came to it. 'Drink,' said a voice. The voice was bated, gentle. 'Drink. That's water. It's good.' The half-formed Beast understood the words; they seemed to carry meaning like an arrow. It leant forward over the water, unbalanced itself, and fell into it.

Delicious and cool, and the Beast swallowed it, and then breathed it in, and the water seared the tender new chambers inside its head.

'No! No!' said the voice. 'Get your head out. Get out! You'll drown.'

The word carried terror. In a panic, the Beast pushed itself out of the water, and scuttled back onto the sandy bank.

'Ow!' moaned the Beast, repeating what the voice had said, trying to bring it back. 'Ow! I hurt.' The Beast could hear the lioness lapping the water. It felt her warm back, and her legs folded under her, and the arch of her neck that throbbed as she swallowed. The Beast learned how to drink.

It drank, and lay back on the warm bank, and slept. The lioness watched over it for some time. But she herself was hungry now after several days' care. Finally she gave the new Beast a lick inside his cupped and pointed, blooded ears, and left to find a kill.

When the Beast awoke again in the night, he had become male. He could also see. The first thing he saw, dimly emerging through tears, was the moon. Then he rolled over and saw his second thing: a face.

The Beast started with recognition. He knew that face. It was the face he had struggled to become. He leaned over the water and extended a warm, padded hand, flesh in segments like beans, to touch this face. The image shook and disappeared, and the Beast made a mournful mewing sound. The water settled again like jelly, and the Beast touched it, and the image swelled and shrank and broke apart, and something like understanding came to him. He was looking at himself.

He had a fine, fierce face, with a small black chin. He pulled back his lips to see tiny white fangs. His eyes were round and large and green. They seemed to glow back at him from the water, with vertical slits. The face was black, except for the upper lip, which seemed to be puffed out with indignation. There the fur vas white. This white fur ran along the upper edge of the mouth in both directions, and turned upwards in a permanent, beaming grin. The Beast saw it and grinned, a needle-toothed smile within a smile, and it purred with pleasure. Then he knew. The one who called him also had a large white grin in black.

The Beast had a tiny, multi-nostrilled snout, very neat and delicate, with a fan of whiskers underneath it. The whiskers caught the silver moonlight, and broke it apart into an arch of turquoise light across his face. The white fur concentrated again on his high-domed forehead. Above and between the luminous eyes was a streak of white that looked like a lick of flame. He had white eyebrows too, but they were not human. His eyebrows were made of isolated long white filaments - more whiskers, from his head.

His own face pleased the Beast. He turned from side to side, to admire himself. He was especially pleased with his white eyebrows.

'Clown,' said the voice in his head, suddenly, very warm and close, like breath in the middle of his head.

He spun around on his haunches. 'Clown?' croaked the Beast, hoping the one who called him would be there. 'Clown? Clown?' But the voice was not there.

The Beast stood. Love impelled him. Love gathered into a point somewhere south of the horizon, but it flowed there from everywhere else. He loved the grass that brushed his ankles and felt nice on his soles as it crunched underfoot. The thorny scrub combed his fur as he walked through it, and clung to him after he had passed.

The Beast walked up and out of the depression in which he had been born, a grassy hollow with a spring. He climbed up and out of it, and made a noise like a dove in astonishment. He saw the world. The world rose up in two high walls on either side of him, and it swooped gently down to where the walls opened out, and there was a plain of rock and scrub and slender river.

And over it, as white and soundless as the moon, a large white bird soared. It seemed so beautiful that the Beast called for it. 'Oh!' he said. He wanted it to come nearer and he held out his arms. 'Aw?'

Silently the bird rose up and over the canyon walls, out of sight. Then just as silently, it landed from behind on the shoulder of the Beast.

The two of them looked at each other, heads cocked first this way and then that. Then, its wide eyes stately blinking, the owl popped a mouse into the mouth of the Beast. And then it rose away.

'Ghost,' said the voice in the head of the Beast.

'Ghost,' croaked the Beast, and made a loud, trilling sound of pleasure.

'Bllllllrrrrrrr!'

'Whooooooo,' said the owl, softly over the plain.

The Beast walked on down the slope, through strands of scent from all about him, from purple-bitter thorns and from sage and from once-hot earth and droppings. For him, the desert was a garden, safe and fruitful.

For him, the slope, which was made of dust and basalt and wispy grass was flooded, flooded with something soft and kindly, which seemed to come with the moonlight, but was not part of it. It trickled slowly down the slope, glinting. It gathered in pools and shimmered, and turned on Itself, and rose up again in funnels that wound across the wilderness, twisting and turning, and settling again in sudden flurries. The voice in his head had no word for these.

By these pools of light were pools od shadow and these tried to speak. The Beast could feel them straining to speak, as he had once strained to move and see. The voices of the dark pools seemed to scratch the inside of his ears, but had no meaning.

Looking up, the Beast saw not only stars. He saw the distance between them, and he knew how far away they were. He saw the lines or force that held them, force that did not emanate from them, but were like wrinkles in space between them, folds of tension in something elastic. The sky for him was a coalescence, as coherent as a face. Overhead the owl circled, protecting. Ripples of air about his wings supported him.

The dust and grit underfoot were to the Beast like eyes and mouths that had not opened. They might at any moment, and see or speak. For him, the dust might at any torment begin to sing in chorus. The Beast wanted to hold all of it to him, the desert and the sky.

Then a new smell was drawn across his face, like a knife. The smell was sour and sick and metallic and it made all his fur bristle. He could feel his skin rise up in protest.

He dropped low to the ground. His ears flicked and began to move independently of each other, straining for sound. His many nostrils fanned open and shut, and he could feel the pupils of his eyes yawning open. He saw it then, a good walking distance away. There was a blemish on the earth. It had a spider shape, dark and many-limbed, by the river.

The Beast darted between low bushes. He moved from shadow to shadow, thinking like the earth, smelling like the earth, moving like the earth moves, unnoticed.

He came near without the think knowing he was there. When he was near, he groaned. Oh for pity.

It was a young animal on the ground. It reeked of panic and exhaustion. It lay still, but its back legs trembled and its eyes were stretched wide in terror, showing white. It was bound. Its hind legs were wrapped round by something that smelled of the sour, musty thing, and of the animal itself. It had a thick body and long delicate legs. All about it in the dust were deep gouges that its forelegs had made struggling to escape.

'Waw! Waw!' lowed the Beast.

The young gazelle tried to lift its head. The Beast approached it. Its forelegs arched and feebly tried to move, but its strength was gone. It did not know that the Beast loved. It had lived in a world without love.

'Ssssh,' said the Beast, and laid his hand on it, and the gazelle went still, but in a bad way, its flesh was taut.

There was a dry prickling in the nostrils of the Beast. The thing that held the gazelle was made of gazelle, made from skin that had been pulled off and sliced into strips. The gazelle knew it. It knew that one of its own kind had been caught and torn apart to make the thing that held it. The trap was pulled back tight like a smile. The trap grinned.

The Beast snarled and tore it apart, his sharp claws plucking at the thongs until they broke. The gazelle did not move. The Beast saw life leaking out of it. For him, it seemed to deflate. It lost potential. It seemed to him to go flat, to shed all its possibilities for one dead stillness. Its tongue, swollen and grey, slipped out of its mouth.

The Beast snatched up the gazelle, hugged it, ran with it to the river, its legs joggling loosely. The Beast dropped to his knees on the riverbank and held the gazelle's head over the water. The legs bent like slender grass with its weight, and the head lolled and the tongue lapped, too weak to pick up water.

The Beast laid the animal out on the damp sand, and remembered how to drink, and took a surge of water into his mouth. He kissed the gazelle and passed the water over to it. He did this several times. Finally the gazelle twitched its ears and lifted its own head again, and the Beast helped it to drink, holding its neck as it managed to splash water into itself. Then it rested, and the Beast shot more water from out of his bulging cheeks into its gullet.

The Beast sat with the gazelle and murmured to it, and put handfuls of grass in front of it, but it was water it needed above all else. He watched it swell with life. For him it seemed to extend more deeply into space again. For the Beast, there were many kinds of space.

'You run,' the Beast told the gazelle as it slept. 'You run. Run in life. Run in dream.' It answered him with a deep intake of breath, and a tremor.

The Beast saw it run, whole, across the plain, with new long horns. That was its future now.

The Beast sniffed his claws. They still stank of the thing, the leather grin. They smelled of salt, salt that had been filtered through poison flesh. They smelled of rot and decay and fruity enzymes that had sweltered for too long. The Beast gagged, and snatched his hand away, and shook it in the river.

'A snare,' said the voice in his head. 'We set them by rivers.' The voice was sorrowful. The word snare carried a picture with it, of hidden lines and bent sapling trees, and the Beast shook his head to get rid of the picture. You, voice, you know this? You?

The voice was silent

Voice? Did you do this?

'No,' said the voice, but there was an echo, very faint. 'But I have done.'

The Beast thought of the trap and saw how blunt and clever it was, twisting round the river and the innocent tree to its own ends. The trap was made of lines, lines that were like a mockery of many things, a sour joke on spider webs or the pattern or a leaf.

What was foul about it was its simplicity. The world was a garden of tangled shapes. Here was something that hated the world, that wanted to reduce it to crippled patterns. The trap had grinned. The Beast knew its smile was like the smile on the face of the one who had called him. Like the smile blasted into the whiteness of the fur around his mouth. Like the smell on his hands.

Voice, oh Voice, it's you.

He felt the tug, towards the south. The Beast stood up, and looked over the bank. He looked towards the one who called him.

On the horizon, as if something new was about to rise in the sky, there was a disturbance. It was like a fire in space. Space, like flame, rose and fell and fragmented, flickered. Prismatic, it bent the light, broke it into silver-shapes. Something had hold of the world and was shaking it.

And there were little bonfires of it, all about the plain.

His fur bristled again.

'That is the City,' said the voice. 'That is where the City is.'

The word carried meaning like an arrow, and the Beast saw it, saw the City.

What he saw was the earth itself in cages. Boxed, held, and piled up into false hills with steep stark sides on which no bushes grew. From the heat of the day, they still smelled as if the earth had died. The bricks were the corpses of the earth.

And the ground between the buildings had been scraped bare of any living thing and milled into dust. The wind would blow it away, leaving only stone.

The ditches were dug in straight lines and were poisoning the ground with salt. In the fields the plants had been made to march in lines, all the same height, all the same plant. The animals were crowded in pens together and made to stand in their own shit, bleating, miserable.

'Clown,' said the City on the horizon.

And the Beast felt himself pulled, felt his mind move, and the world seemed to yawn open, and he fell. He fell towards the one who called him, fell into a rank chamber in the captured earth, fell towards something that smiled and smiled. The one who had called him.

With a wrench of terror, the Beast pulled himself free.

The King awoke. His heart was pounding and there was sweat on his upper lip. The dream had seemed so real that he still felt the Beast's terror. The King's heart was pounding with fear of himself.

And he wanted to be back in the garden.

'You won't come here,' the King said. 'So, Clown, I will go to you.'

# Red Sky in the Morning

Adrian Tchaikovsky

That morning, as he took his flock to graze, Rhys ap Owain saw red skies in the east and knew them for a warning. Inigo Bower's camp at Beachey had fallen to Decameron's Army of the M4 Corridor,

Rhys had liked Bower. True, the man styled himself a defender of freedom while being mighty free with others' goods, but Decameron's attack had little to do with a desire for justice and more to secure his supply lines over the Severn Bridge.

Decameron's forces would be marching back for Chepstow, and Rhys knew he would need to see what had befallen, or the lack of knowledge would gnaw him to madness.

He whistled until the boy came. Rhys had many whistles: some set his dogs after the sheep, some signalled other shepherds. And there were whistles taught to Rhys by his dying father in the dark house of the night, which he had carried in his head all the long years since and never dared to use.

Now he whistled until the boy came running from the farm. No doubt he had been lying on his belly looking at the faded images of Rhys' picture books: dinosaurs, King Arthur, Neil Armstrong on the moon, all as mythical as each other now.

Rhys told the dogs to listen to him, then strode off towards Chepstow to see what trouble was brewing.

Nobody had set fire to the houses or turned over the market stalls, but Decameron's soldiers were about and the buying and selling was hurried, people wanting to be gone as quickly as possible. Most market days, they had entertainment in the centre of the square: a musician plucking out a Tom Jones ballad, a poet reciting Thomas or a girl's pure voice rising to one of the Church Canon, '*Pie Jesu*' perhaps, or 'Just Wave Hello.' Today there was a gallows under construction, and the trebled lions and Union Jacks of the soldiers' heraldry. Rhys reckoned Decameron had brought maybe forty men into Chepstow. The remaining two-hundred-odd of his expeditionary force was camped outside the town..

They had a half-dozen bound and held at gunpoint: Inigo Bowers and his lieutenants. The Chepstow Assembly had often talked about bringing the man to heel and some of his people had been hung when their thieving had turned nasty. *But that was* our *justice. We had the right.*

Rhys saw Bethan Meridy there, a solitary representative of the Assembly. No doubt Decameron had beaten on doors with a rifle butt until someone came to legitimise the execution. Nobody could have believed that a counter-order from the Assembly would have stopped him. Bethan herself looked pale and drawn, hands clenching and unclenching.

Rhys should have left then, but his eyes met Inigo's and he knew he had a duty. He shuffled and elbowed through the gathering crowd until he was close to the man, under the gaze of the guns.

"God keep you, Inigo," he murmured.

The brigand chief gave him a defiant smile, but Rhys could see the sheen of sweat there. "He will, will he?"

"Or else the Devil has a love for stories, and you could always tell one."

Bowers swallowed. "We missed you at our fire last night, old man. I told a rare one. Vortigern's castle and the dragons fighting, only like you never heard."

"I'm sorry I missed it," Rhys said, then a soldier had a hand on the brigand's shoulder and the prisoners were fitted with new collars. Rhys turned to go and found himself staring at a chestful of shiny medals. He looked up into the face of Gleaming George Decameron, neat as a pin from his pressed uniform to his slick hair to the white of his teeth.

"The people of Chepstow can sleep safely, eh?" Decameron's accent was a Surrey drawl. "With such a ne'r-do-well out of the way." When Rhys made to leave, the man's hand barred his way. "I know you, old man," Decameron said wonderingly. "You're that Owen chap. To hear these yokels, you're some sort of wizard."

"I'm Rhys ap Owain." Keenly aware of the soldiers' presence.

"Well then, in celebration of the liberation of Chepstow, you'll take tea with me, surely?" There was something other than the expected derision in the man's voice, though Rhys couldn't place it. He was aware of Bethan Meridy close by and anxious. Rhys was known in these parts; he had been old before most of the current population was born, as much a part of the landscape as a standing stone or a mound. Which meant someone might do something foolish and get themselves killed if he got into a scuffle with the soldiers.

"White, no sugar," he growled. Behind him the first box was kicked away and he heard a sound like a brittle gunshot.

Decameron's men had commandeered a house overlooking the market, and the soldiers cheered each brigand's end in between propositioning the local women. A word from their commander had the front room cleared, while a girl brought in a tray of tea, her trembling hands making the pot lid rattle.

"The people around here tell all sorts of stories about you, old man," Decameron noted.

"Stories." Rhys waved a dismissive hand.

"And can you call spirits from the vasty deep?" Decameron grinned boyishly.

"Perhaps," said Rhys, knowing what came next.

"Why so can I," the officer trotted out, "or so can any man. But will they come when you do call for them?" His pride at recalling the play made him almost likeable. "It's what you claim, is it not? The Owen of your name."

"I am the last of the line of Owain Glyndwr." Rhys wished he had been less free with the knowledge after the collapse, but it had been the only way to get people to listen to him.

He had to hear more schoolboy reciting after that, whole slices of *Henry Fourth* lampooning his mystic ancestor, and he ground his teeth and let the Englishman prattle. He understood what was not being said. Decameron knew the locals would heed Rhys. The old man was on display here so the people of Chepstow would see him in the company of the conquerors, and he had this prime view of the nooses in case he was thinking of causing trouble.

Afterwards, the Assemblywoman Bethan Meridy found him.

"Tonight," she said.

"I'm done with politics."

"Please, Rhys." She was an honest woman; he had known her grandmother. "Don't you care?"

"You think this land cares whose boots march over it?"

"I think before they came we just wore shoes." Before her sincerity he could only mutter, "No promises." He knew he'd be there, if only to see her fall.

The Assembly chambers had once been the castle gift shop, and perhaps the dragon flag that hung on the wall had been made in China for sale to American tourists. *Ah, Wales…* He shuffled in and saw the usual faces: Bethan and fourteen other Assemblers. Across from them was Decameron, a pair of soldiers flanking his chair and noting faces.

One of Bethan's colleagues began a dry address intended to offend no one, but Decameron broke in almost immediately. "Your thanks for liberating you from the brigands are noted," he said, as though there had been any. "London values every corner of the kingdom. You've done wonders keeping civic authority together – believe me, the north's done far worse. I'm impressed with the level of prosperity you've maintained."

"Built," said Bethan. "This isn't something we just *found*, Mr Decameron. When the power went out, when the fuel ran dry, we got together and *built*."

"And jolly well you've done, too," Decameron condescended. "Your little market was charming. But now control of the M4 Corridor has been secured by His Majesty's forces, you don't have to just barter like savages. We bring the regained wonders of our ancestors. London is minting coin again, and is not short of buyers for your surplus."

"Coins that could only be spent with *you*," Bethan pointed out.

This time, Decameron just spoke over her to the men in the room, waxing lyrical on the benefits of becoming part of a greater state. Loud was the message of economic profit, louder still that of protection from unspecified threats.

When he was done, several Assemblers spontaneously stood to add their voices to his. Rhys wondered if their pockets were already heavy with London coin.

Bethan Meridy was not among them. "General," she began, "as you have observed, we found our feet after the collapse. Nobody here starves. We would happily trade our surplus for yours. Send your merchants and we will welcome them, just as we welcome those from Cardiff, just as we welcomed those from Bristol before it fell." The name dropped heavily into the room. Everyone remembered the bangs and flashes from across the Severn when Decameron's army broke up the fishermen's commune there. "Bring your merchants, but not your soldiers, and not your governors."

"You're turning your back on a great deal." Decameron leant back easily. "We'll be generating electricity soon enough. There are mines in Wales that can still yield coal. Think of the wealth when all that trade passes before your doors."

"That you would tax," Bethan noted, "to pay for your conquests."

"*Re*conquests," he snapped, and for a split second the chummy grinning act was gone. "The kingdom will be united once more."

A few other timorous voices rose to support Bethan. Most remained silent, plainly wishing they were not there to have their faces remembered.

Rhys thought about the collapse, how it had all come crashing down. Contrary to the old fictions, it hadn't been zombies or plague. Just bad harvests, flooding and storms, and those with the power to help profiting from each misfortune instead, until the system couldn't take it. The collapse had been economic: no food on the shelves, no emergency services, no jobs, no power. Nobody had realised how fragile it all was.

Londoners had starved in their thousands, he'd heard, and fought each other over the scraps. When enough had died, the old money had returned from its country estates to take over. Rhys had heard about the War of the Nine Prime Ministers, the siege of Slough and the Battle of Bristol, and now London was sending troops across the Severn for food and coal.

At last, Bethan invited him to speak, to support her. All heads turned, Decameron watching like a hawk. The man spoke of an age of unity and prosperity, but Rhys saw through him. It was not Decameron's *Englishness* – half Chepstow was no more Welsh than he, and many market traders up from Cardiff were descended from Yemeni or Somalian stock, from the Islamic enclave they were calling the Cardiphate. But Rhys heard Decameron's grand words and saw only caravans heading east across the Severn Bridge: food, coal, men for the war, women for service, and nothing coming west but trinkets and commands.

He said nothing.

When the meeting was done, he lingered to speak in Bethan's ear: "Get yourself and your family somewhere safe."

"It won't come to that," she said, and he knew she wouldn't run, and they'd make her disappear.

The sun had long set by then, but the moon was full. He set off walking towards the abandoned land at Chepstow's periphery. The Thornwell Farm estate was broken windows and collapsed roofs now; once, though, it had been holy. They had buried kings here whose names had been forgotten long before Rhys's day. And one day a Saxon lord had come to build a castle…

And that had been in Gwynned, not Chepstow, surely, but if King Arthur was buried in a hundred different places, why not this?

*We build and build, and it keeps getting pulled down*, that was how the story went. Vortigern had gone to Merlin because his castle walls collapsed each night, and Merlin had looked into the earth and seen a white dragon striving with a red. What might Rhys see now, with Merlin's eyes? The red dragon beset by three lions?

The housing estate seemed like the ruins of an elder age that had come and gone in the blink of an eye while the mounds remained. He felt their deep time stretching back to prehistory. The earth trembled, or perhaps it was his old legs.

"I know you're there," he said into the silence, thinking of that bold red dragon on the gift shop flag. "You were there for Merlin. You can be there for me. My father couldn't call you from the earth, and all the years since then just laid more weight on you, but the collapse has stripped that all away, if anything can. It's your time now. Will you come when I call, or else slumber forever?"

The earth trembled. He heard falling bricks and the tinkle of glass from across the estate. Rhys began to whistle.

The next day he hobbled the slow road home. He had been awake for too long and his mind was full of what the night had brought. Noon had come and gone before he reached his front door.

Five soldiers were at his house. They had shot his dogs and the boy was trembling in a corner with a bruise across his face. Half a sheep was charring over the fire.

"Mister Owen, I have a sense you weren't convinced by my words," said Gleaming George Decameron, the flames dancing over his medals.

They manhandled Rhys inside and sat him down in his own chair. Decameron leant on the mantle like he owned everything he saw.

"Mister Owen, I need you to go to the Chepstow Assembly and talk them into bowing the knee."

Rhys was exhausted, emptied out by the walk and by the night's work before it. "I'm just an old man," he wheezed.

"And yet they listen to you," Decameron countered. "Last son of Owen Glendower, the wizard of Wales. But he was a rebel fighting against his true king, Mister Owen, and you're going to the Chepstow Assembly to take on a different role. Do you know *Henry V?* There's a nice Welshman in that, Fluellen, you know him? A good and honest soldier, fond of leeks and loyal to the English crown."

The dogs, the boy, the lynching, none of these had stung him past his self control, but somehow the theatrical reference was the last straw. "*Owain Glyndwr* does not belong to your bloody Shakespeare," Rhys spat. "He was real, and his blood is mine. And why is it always Shakespeare, eh? When someone writes about what comes after the end of the world, everyone goes about crammed full of Shakespeare and not one quoting the *Mabinogion.*"

The firelight showed just how shallow Decameron's smile was. "Well that just shows the superior culture, doesn't it? The only thing your lauded ancestor is known for is failing to call up spirits."

Rhys made a hacking noise that sounded like a cough. "You're right, he never did, though he studied all his life. But on his deathbed he gifted that lore to his son, all the magic that was left to his conquered age."

"And what use did his son make of it, or any of his line?" Decameron scoffed.

"His son lived many years through that lore, to do what his father could not," Rhys said, and that was when the soldiers outside began shouting for their leader.

Decameron and his men rushed out, leaving one standing guard. When the old man levered himself out of the chair, the soldier tried to plant him back down, but Rhys knocked him aside as easily as a straw. That was when he realised it had all been real, and not some desperate dream.

Outside, smoke rose in a black column from Decameron's main camp outside Chepstow. Rhys imagined Bethan Meridy and Chepstow's stoutest running between the tents with burning torches, and perhaps that was true, but it was not the only truth. That strength of certainty was in him, that he remembered from his distant youth before learning the lore at his father's deathbed.

"I am the last son of Owain Glyndwr," he shouted at Decameron. "I can call spirits from the vasty deep and you had better fucking believe that they will answer when I call. So go gather your men and leave this land with your demands and your threats, while there is still a road for you to travel on."

Decameron had his pistol out but he could not look at Rhys, as though the fire in the distance was blazing from the old man's face. The shadow of a great red form passed over them, keening in triumph. Perhaps it was just smoke and embers blown by the wind, but Decameron looked up into the dark sky and screamed, and then he was staggering away, his soldiers dropping their rifles to flee alongside him.

Rhys sank down and put his back to the farmhouse, knowing they would tell stories of this. Some of them might even be true. Later the boy crept out and Rhys clapped a hand on his shoulder and called him Wart.

They watched together as the survivors of Decameron's forces took the bridge across the Severn.

"Will they be back?" the boy asked, and Rhys had no answer. He was wondering, still, whether it had been a Chepstow uprising that had driven the Londoners off, or something else. Wonder had been absent from his life for a long time. He could not just believe in it, even when he had brought it about.

After sunset, something vast and bellowing flew over the house and the Severn Bridge bloomed with flame so that half of it fell into the river, glowing like coals, and Rhys looked out at that red sky and knew delight.

# The God of Nothing

## Ian R. MacLeod

Then came a day when the king of all the known lands summoned his Chief Administrator to his presence. Surprised and fearful, for his was the least of all the senior callings, the Chief Administrator hurried from his cell in the bowels of the palace. Sentries raised their spears as the great bronze doors of the throne room boomed open and he prostrated himself before the royal throne.

"Who are you?"

"I am your Chief Administrator and you summoned me, Highness."

"Oh, yes..." The king scratched his beard. "I suppose you are aware of my glorious reign's many successes?"

"I rejoice in them as all, Highness."

"But even with success and glory, problems can arise."

Still prostrate, the Chief Administrator felt a ripple of fear. To have the king speak of problems after summoning you to his presence did not auger well for the prospects of your head remaining attached to your neck, or your torso keeping its most treasured appendages. "So I have heard said, Highness."

"And, this being the season of harvest, I have received reports from across the known lands that the vineyards and the grain fields, and the groves of fruit and olive, are all overflowing with bounty."

"As indeed they should under the blessing of your sovereignty," the Chief Administrator agreed, although he was struggling to understand how this state of affairs might be seen as a problem, or have anything to do with him.

"And, as you know, it is the time-honoured custom for my royal guards to go out from this city and take tribute as and when they see fit."

"Which is a great honour to us all."

"But I have recently had a visitation from the gods. They came to me in a dream," the king added airily, "as they often do. And they told me that from this season forward, there should be a more proper reckoning."

"A more *proper* reckoning, Highness?"

"Yes." The king leaned forward. "Do you not understand my words?"

"Well, perhaps not, Highness, as well as you do yourself. In my humble fashion –"

"From now on all of my subjects shall pay the tribute in this proportion..." The king held up the spread bejewelled fingers and thumbs of both his hands. Then he closed them, leaving just his right index finger pointing up. "Is that clear to you?"

"Yes, Highness."

As he bowed and retreated, the Chief Administrator reflected that a system in which every subject gave exactly one finger's worth of every double handful of their wealth as royal tribute had a simplicity and fairness to it that the current one lacked. If he hadn't held the post he did, he would have been entirely in favour of it. But now, and with harvest already underway and the royal guards doubtless itching in their barracks, it would fall to him to somehow implement this innovation. Which was clearly impossible.

It was one thing for the king's guards to head out from the city with their swords and wagons to grab whatever they could find. It was something else entirely to somehow actually *count* the vast produce of all the known lands, and to then take away exactly one finger's worth in every double handful as tribute. Not, of course, that he and his assistants didn't do their best to record the contents of the royal cellars, coffers and granaries, but they did so by scratching a notch on the thigh-bone of a goat for every handful they counted; a cumbersome system that often resulted in confusion, especially in the seasons of bountiful harvest and with the bones varying in size.

The Chief Administrator returned to his cell in the bowels of the place and sat staring bleakly at nothing even as his assistants went merrily on with the business of bone-stripping and knife sharpening in preparation for the tally-work ahead. He could, he supposed, somehow pretend to extract this season's tribute as the king had stipulated without actually doing so. After all, the king could be forgetful, but this whole business of being visited in a dream by the gods was exactly the kind of thing he'd share with his High Priest, with whom the Chief

Administrator had always had a difficult relationship, and who wouldn't hesitate to use the situation to his advantage. At the day's end the Chief Administrator returned to his modest home through the busy streets of the city sunk in deep gloom. His whole life, his lovely wife, his boisterous children, his carefully nurtured lowly position at court, even his head and other precious appendages, already seemed lost.

After spurning dinner, and ignoring his wife's anxious enquiries, he went out again into the flame-lit bustle. The people all seemed so happy, and he didn't doubt that they would be happier still if they knew that their king proposed to take only a precise amount of their livelihood as tribute instead of the usual random pillage. That dream of his – the dammed gods…! He glared up over the rooftops at the moonlit bulk of the holy mountain glowering above the city, and the mountain seemed to glower back. Then he was struck by a thought, or at least by a despairing notion. For if the gods really had visited the king with this vision, was it not also possible that they might be able to help him…?

The mountain wasn't particularly high or large as mountains went, but scattered across its flanks and ridges were temples devoted to every imaginable god. There were the gods of travel and there were the gods of the home. There were the gods of the sea, and the gods of the seasons, and the gods of maternity, love and procreation. The temples devoted to these last gods, the Chief Administrator thought as he heard raucous music and laughter, bore more than a passing resemblance to the bars and brothels in the city below. He certainly didn't expect them to provide the enlightenment he was seeking. But what kind of god would be able to help him? The god of hopeless causes?

He wandered on, lost both in his thoughts and the rambling silvered pathways. Here were the fallen pillars and ivied ruins of temples to gods forgotten, or at least neglected, and he really should turn back. After all, he had his life, his family, his faithful assistants and his duty to his king to consider. But still he climbed where now there was no pathway, scrambling over boulders and beside dizzy precipices.

Then, suddenly, in a narrow gap between two rocks which might once have been pillars, he reached another temple, or at least a rough platform. There was an entrance into the rock face framed by more suggestions of pillars – although it could have been a natural cave; it was hard up here to distinguish the works of man from those of the gods – and its mouth was blacker than even the deepest spaces between the stars above. So black, in fact, that the darkness seemed to seep out like smoke into the grey moonlight, and he was staring into it, both fascinated and appalled, when he heard an everyday sound – the swish of a broom – at his back.

He turned. The broom was being wielded by a bare-footed young woman in grey robes.

"Excuse me… I was wondering what kind of god this temple serves."

"Oh, that's simple," she said, still swishing her broom. "It doesn't serve any god."

"But surely…" He gestured at the rocky platform, the cave's black-breathing mouth. "...you are here for some purpose? And what purpose is there, up here on this holy mountain, other than that of the gods?"

"Well, if you put it that way, let's just say I serve the god of nothing."

"Nothing?"

"Yes," she said, now leaning her hands and her chin on the handle of her broom. "Nothing at all."

The Chief Administrator nodded. After all, she was far too plainly dressed to be a proper priestess. Yet her eyes… They were large, and the pupils were dark wells, and who else did he have left to turn to?

"If I told you what my problem is, would you listen?"

She shrugged. "I don't see why not."

So the Chief Administrator began to speak, describing the endless travails his work, and sheer impossibility of keeping a full record of the royal stores, let alone the entire kingdom's output. Although if, the gods forbid, there should not be enough wine and grain set aside to see them through the winter, he would be the one who would be held to account. And now the king had had this idea or vision – or the gods had had it for him – and was demanding a new level of reckoning which went entirely beyond his skills.

"So that's it?"

"Yes, it is."

"Well…" She gave a few more sweeps with her broom. "I'm sure something will turn up. Or perhaps nothing."

Despite what she had said about serving no god, he had still expected something resembling the kind of cryptic utterances most priests and priestess seemed to specialise in. Still, he supposed, turning to leave this crumbling ruin from which even the thin glamour of the moonlight was now fading, if you sought help from the so-called God of Nothing, what else could you expect?

Knowing sleep would be impossible, the Chief Administrator spent the rest of the long night prowling the city, and found himself standing at the riverside docks in the bloom of dawn, where a few urchins sat listlessly prodding sticks into the mud. Yet now he envied even them, for they marked their days with simple thievery and begging, and making these pointless marks in wet clay. Whereas he…

Then, he was struck by a thought. In fact, it was more than a single thought, rather a whole chain of the things, one leading on to the next without break or pause, and the Chief Administrator was laughing as he returned home and shook his wife awake and assured her that, no, no, he wasn't possessed by some new madness, but by a better way of serving his king.

Predictably, his assistants were deeply suspicious to begin with, and many still stuck to stubbornly notching their tally-bones, even though the harvest was as vast and bountiful as any in living memory. There was also little the Chief Administrator could do at first to stop the royal guards acting in their usual plundering fashion. But when people saw just how easily the tablets of wet river clay could be tallied, and then kept dry as a permanent and indisputable record of their tribute, they started to change their ways – especially once he ensured that every line counted exactly a double handful of marks, and was thus readable at a glance. All of this took much more than a mere season to accomplish, and of course there were many setbacks, but once the idea of all the king's subjects making the same contribution toward the royal purse in exact proportion to their wealth – be it in salt, jewels or sacks of grain – took hold, the old habits began to fade. The unwanted tally-bones, meanwhile, proved popular with the city's large population of feral dogs.

The kingdom prospered, and so did its subjects, and the granaries and the wine stores were filled, and filled again, and there had never been more produce in the markets, or more trade. Every morning, the farmers with their pigs and goats, and the chicken-keepers with their eggs, and the milkmaids with their pails, and all the wagons groaning with apples and grain, and the merchants with their rolls of rare fabrics, and peddlers with their trinkets, and the jewellers with their gems, all poured into the city to bicker and bargain – and also to complain. Such was the noise and the stench of all this prosperity, with the streets as full as farmyards and often sounding and smelling much the same, that some even dared to mutter that the old days of unfairness and confusion might not have been quite so bad after all.

When the Chief Administrator was summoned to the throne room this time, he was somewhat rounder in girth, and also slightly less terrified. He had, after all, played his own largely unacknowledged role in the abundant seasons following his previous audience. Not only that, but he'd developed a series of distinctive markers to distinguish the different tablets, so that one which recorded the number of sacks of grain in the royal coffers had a small image of a wheat ear in one corner, while that for pigs was decorated with a tiny pig, and so forth. Some these symbols could even be strung together to praise the king's wisdom and bounty, which was always a good thing to do.

"You are...?"

"I'm your Chief Administrator, Highness."

"Oh yes..." For a while, the king gazed into space. Then he scratched his beard. "I suppose you're aware of the problem."

"Problem, Highness?"

"Yes – don't you know what a problem is?"

"Indeed, Highness. But, with the great bounty of your reign, and the blessings of all the gods –"

"The gods might be bountiful in many ways, but they seem to know little of street cleaning. Or how long it takes my favourite concubine to arrive from her villa with the entire city crammed with wagons and carts, not to mention the stench she brings with her on her robes."

"Indeed, Highness. It has been noted that the city is as prosperous and busy as it has ever been."

The king leaned forward from his throne. "Are you mocking me?"

"Mocking?" The Chief Administrator felt his most treasured appendages shrivel. "Absolutely not, Highness. If only –"

"Then put an end this chaos, or I will put an end to you!"

The Chief Administrator's spirits were as low as they had ever been as he returned home that evening through the press of bodies, handcarts, sheep, oxen and goats. He couldn't eat. Nor could he explain to his wife, whose figure was now as ample as his own, what his sudden preoccupation was about. He went out again straight afterwards, thinking of going nowhere at all, although his steps through the crowded streets unconsciously retraced those he had taken many seasons before. But that problem had been effortlessly simple – a mere matter of better record keeping – whereas this... For no better reason than knowing he wouldn't sleep, he began to ascend the paths leading toward the holy mountain.

Just like everything else in the kingdom, the temples had prospered. There were new priests, new engravings – even new gods. But none of them spoke of whatever it was the Chief Administrator was seeking, and he found himself climbing toward a place where two rocks which might once have been pillars framed a gap leading to a platform, even though the route seemed even harder and higher than before.

There was no sign of the priestess, who he decided had probably been just some beggar who'd briefly made this peculiar spot her home, and cursed his own stupidity in coming here. Then he heard the swish of a broom at his back.

"You *are* still here!"

"Where else would I be?"

She still looked remarkably young; life up here clearly agreed with her, away from all the shit and mud and noise below.

"I'm not here to seek your help."

"That's good." She smiled and leaned on her broom. "Because I have none to offer."

"Neither am I seeking false illusions."

"That is also good." She tilted her head. "Although aren't all illusions a little bit false?"

The Chief Administrator had no time for this kind of sophistry, and was about to turn and head back down the mountain when it occurred to him that explaining his previous difficulties had perhaps helped him come up with the idea of the clay tablets. So, once again, he began to talk. About the noise and the congestion, the sheep coming from the hills in one direction and the wagons full of wine and olive oil from another. And the geese, and the chickens, and the merchants selling their bolts of cloth… How were he and his assistants, who now called themselves scribes, supposed to deal with *that*...?

He trailed off. The eyes of the priestess were twin, dark, wells.

"You don't have an answer, do you?"

"Did you really think I would?"

He shook his head and stumbled his way back down the holy mountain. For once, the city seemed quiet as the glow of dawn rose over the holy mountain, and he stood again at the banks of the river, where most of the clay, which was now a valuable resource, had been removed, and picked up some of the smooth, round stones that now lay there, and was about to toss it into the water when he was struck by a thought.

In a way, this idea was even simpler, or at least could be more simply explained. Instead of all the merchants and farmers in the entire kingdom bringing their entire produce to market so that it might be bartered for other produce, which then often had to be bartered again, why not have a thing – a *something* – representing the produce instead? The king's subjects could then sell their wares without everything always having to be physically exchanged, with a stone or perhaps a small brass token representing the value of a sheep or a bag of grain.

The king frowned and fretted when the idea was explained, as did the Chief Administrator's family and his scribes. For how was wealth and prosperity and status to be reckoned, if it could be reduced to mere handfuls of metal? But by now the Chief Administrator was a man of some reputation, and if this odd idea stood even a chance of reducing the mess and congestion it was surely worth trying.

So the edict was issued, and each bronze token was affixed with a royal crown as a symbol of its provenance, and their use began to clear the streets of the worst of its gaggles and herds. Not that there weren't problems. Some people started hoarding these tokens instead of using them, whilst others attempted to fabricate their own. But soon there were less wagons, and the markets were no longer impossibly overcrowded, which would have been a sure sign of the kingdom's imminent collapse in any other era, but now people found that their lives were not only a little easier but more prosperous as well. There was even a reduction in disease, although of course the High Priest, who was never backward in coming forward, took the entire credit for that.

All the known lands grew in their tribute and bounty, and the temples across the holy mountain were expanded and enlarged, and merchants started using pieces of slate, which be easily wiped and re-used, to keep their daily tallies, and the king had never been more venerated in his glory. Yet there was a growing problem of which even the Chief Administrator, who now enjoyed an extremely comfortable life, was aware. The sacred festivals and rituals which the entire kingdom followed had somehow moved from the seasons they were supposed to honour.

It wasn't that the seasons didn't arrive, and the birds and all the other wild things behaved as they had always done, but all the holy days and celebrations were dreadfully awry. The god of the cornfields now found that the day which had always been devoted to his power and worth took place in the middle of what was unmistakably winter. Whereas the god of what used to be spring was now required to gaze down from on high at his prostrate worshippers though the blazing heat of full summer. Not, of course, that a record of the passing seasons hadn't been kept in the highest temples using sacred tally bones since time immemorial. But something had gone wrong, and it was all most unsatisfactory, as the king explained after his usual terse fashion when he finally summoned the Chief Administrator.

"But, Highness, surely this is a matter for the High Priest?"

"D'you think I haven't spoken with him about this?"

"Of course, Highness."

"But he assures me that this disarrangement is a matter of administration rather than theology, which you must deal with," the king waved a bejewelled hand, "or the gods themselves will punish us all."

Despite this dire threat, the Chief Administrator was less concerned than he might once have been as he sat at the family table beside his ample wife and grown-up children that evening. The seasons, after all, had unquestionably been kind to the kingdom's subjects, and he had already dealt with many problems which would have foiled a lesser bearer of his office – or a High Priest, come to that.

So he set out into the city, noting the many ships moored along the river, and the cleanliness of the streets, and the surprisingly good health of the beggars, who were now happy to accept the bronze tokens he tossed into their begging bowls, and began to climb the holy mountain past the many grand temples, most of which were equally happy to accept these tokens in lieu of penance or prayer.

The climb proved even steeper than he remembered, and he was close to turning back. After all, why should a man of his substance have to visit a temple that honoured no god at all? He also had a sense that he was being followed, and by a more cumbersome personage than a mere barefoot girl. He even thought he glimpsed the edge of a bejewelled priestly robe. Still, though, he climbed, and here was the surprisingly narrow gap between what might once have been pillars, and here was the platform, and that yawning cave mouth.

"I didn't expect to see you again," a voice said at his back.

"Well…" He turned. "That's good, because I wasn't expecting to come."

"Yet here you are. And, doubtless, you have a problem, and you somehow expect me to help solve it."

"What makes you think you've ever solved anything? I'm the king's Chief Administrator, and everything I have achieved is down to my own wisdom and hard work."

"Well," she shrugged and swiped her broom, "not *everything*, perhaps... Or even *anything*… But when it comes to *nothing* –"

"And that," still angered, the Chief Administrator stabbed a finger toward the mouth of the cave, "that is just an empty hole."

"Then why don't you go inside and take a look..." Again, she swished her broom, although the sound now was harsh and cold, as empty as the growl of the winter wind. "...if you're so sure there's nothing there?"

For moment, and if only to prove this young woman's arrogant folly, the Chief Administrator really was prepared to step inside the cave. But it looked very dark in there, even in the blaze of this moon, and of course you never knew what kind of creature you might encounter in such a place, be it snakes, bears or spiders, or just an endless, empty drop. He shook his head and waved an admonitory finger. "You're not going to catch me out that easily."

And with that he left the ruined temple, still somewhat angered, and still unable to shake the feeling of being followed by a much larger personage than the girl. Yet he was still less concerned than he might once have been by the enormity of the challenge he still had to surmount. He didn't fear the gods now, or even believe in most of them that strongly. Nor did he believe in the prospect of another life after this one that the priests of many temples now promised in exchange for a suitably large donation. What he did believe in were the simple pleasures of the life he was actually living. The smiles of his family and the taste of good wine and the beauty of this silvered moon and the first glow of the rising sun as it shifted, season to season, along the flanks of this very mountain...

The Chief Administrator smiled to himself, and no longer cared whether he was being followed as he made his brisk way back toward the city below.

It was all very well the High Priest and his acolytes choosing to celebrate the festivals and holy days according to the sacred tally-bones they still insisted on venerating in their temples, some of which they even claimed were the remains of the gods themselves. But what if the bones were wrong? Not greatly so perhaps, but over enough seasons, and with even a small amount of error… Not that it was wise to use such words as *wrong* or *error* when it came to matters of holy writ. But it was important that the proper passage of the seasons was followed, which could surely be achieved by making observations of the sun's rising using marker posts, or perhaps small stone cairns, along the flanks of the holy mountain.

In many ways, the task was simple and repetitive, but to the Chief Administrator it was thrilling as well. It was good that the records on the slates and clay tablets he and his scribes used were now more sophisticated, with different symbols representing different quantities, thus saving a great deal of unnecessary counting up. Standing beneath the hot noonday sun, or watching the moon and the stars wheel through the frosty darkness, he felt as if he was close to finding the hidden weave which bound the heavens to the earth.

Then came the day when he was ready to present his findings to the king. He bore with him several finely ornamented clay tablets. They were beautiful things in themselves, set not only with a precise tally of the sun's rising and falling throughout every season both past and future, but also with the appropriate symbols of many birds, beasts and flowers – along with, as was now always necessary, a great deal of praise for the king himself.

The Chief Administrator was not entirely surprised to find the High Priest also in attendance, for despite his claims, these matters clearly concerned him as well. He felt confident the evidence of his tablets was entirely correct, which was surely all that mattered, and when the king raised a hand to still his words he imagined it was to raise some minor query, or simply to praise his hard work.

"No!"

"No what, Highness?"

"This defames the gods themselves! The very *idea* that the days and seasons can be controlled by these slabs of dried mud –"

"Not controlled, Highness, but –"

"Enough! You are right…" Now he spoke toward the High Priest. "...this is worse than wizardry."

"Indeed, your highness," the High Priest bowed smugly. "And, just as you willed, I have ordered the destruction of all the crude shrines this man has erected to his nameless gods across the holy mountain, along with the greater one to some dark monstrosity I, personally, have observed him frequenting, although we are still searching for the harpy who serves there."

"They're not shrines, they're markers – and the temple is barely a ruin. And as for that girl, she's not really a priestess and she serves no god."

"You see, Highness," the High Priest gestured. "Even now he is filled with disrespect and lies."

The Chief Administrator was at a loss to come up with a defence to the charges of necromancy, blasphemy and trafficking with demons other than to insist that he had simply shown how the sun and the moon travelled across the heavens not according to the whims of the gods, or a scratched pile of bones in some temple, but to the precise tallies he and his scribes had diligently recorded –

At which point the Chief Administrator was advised that it was only because of his evident madness that he would be allowed to keep hold of his head and his other precious appendages. He would be imprisoned for the rest of his days instead, whilst his family would be banished to the furthest reaches of the known lands.

The ex-Chief Administrator had heard a great many stories about the royal dungeons, and none of them were particularly pleasant. But although the cell into which he was thrown was damp and dark, it proved little worse than the place where he had long laboured in service of the king in the bowels of the palace, and the food was surprisingly decent.

So his life continued, at least in the sense that he wasn't dead, and he heard through the warders that his tablets had been taken to a secure shrine, and the High Priest was quietly re-ordering the holy days according to their writ. His family, meanwhile, sent word through various intermediaries to let him know that life at the far edge of the known world was very much like life in the better known parts, and that they were enjoying the fresh air and the absence of courtly intrigue. All in all, he supposed he could count himself lucky, even if the passage of the days and the seasons was abominably slow.

He was grateful for his cell's barred window, which not only granted him some light, but also allowed him to watch the sun's passage across the walls and floor shift from season to season. And there was also the silvering moon, with whom he felt a special affinity. He even asked his warders for some slates and a sharp flint so that he might better record their movements.

It began as a whim, but the slates soon mounted up and it became an obsession. He still didn't believe that merely keeping track of the heavens was an act of blasphemy – for if there really were gods, then surely it was only right to have a proper understanding of their works? Neither did he believe in their capricious wrath, or a life after death, although he did certainly believe in the wrath of the High Priest. The anger of the gods – ha! – that was ridiculous. Why, back in distant memory it was even said that they had shown their displeasure by darkening the noonday sky…!

The ex-Administrator paused in his scratchings. Struck, as he had often been before, by an intriguing thought. After all, if the sun and the moon revolved across the heavens according solely to the courses he was recording, that meant there would come a point when positions coincided in the sky. Which would certainly explain those stories of the midday sun slowly being consumed by a dark circle, which he'd always imagined were old wives' tales.

Now, even more than before, he was a man driven. It was all simply a matter of mirroring the movements of the sun and the moon through the marks on his slates to determine when the next daytime darkness would arise. But his markings grew ever-longer, and the slates grew ever larger, and figures were stubborn and intractable as mules. Something was missing, he was certain of it – some last insight which would allow him to see things as they truly were. And then, perhaps, another thought whispered in his head, he might even get back his job, his family and his reputation.

He barely slept, and when he did sleep his dreams were of slates and the marks he made upon them, piling up into a vast mountain which he somehow had to ascend. In his fitful night-time wanderings he sometimes even glimpsed temples and pathways with the gleaming city spread below. But still he scratched and still he worked and still he climbed until he found himself confronted by two familiar rocks that might once have been pillars, and passed between them into a familiar rocky platform where cave mouth yawned.

"I didn't expect to see you again," he said to the girl.

"Nor I you."

"But this is only a dream. In the real world, you and your temple have been destroyed on the orders of the High Priest."

She shrugged and leaned on her broom. "Have it as you will. Although how can anyone destroy nothing at all?"

The ex-Chief Administrator laughed. Whatever kind of oblivion had befallen this girl had not, it seemed, changed her fondness for speaking in riddles.

"Have you come again to ask a question?"

He shook his head: the problem he was wrestling with was so vast he couldn't even express it through the symbols on his slates, let alone using mere words. But perhaps the symbols themselves were the obstacle, for otherwise the problem would lie within the workings of the universe itself, which was surely impossible… And so he rambled on, and she listened and smiled as she leaned on her broom.

"And I already know what you're going to tell me..." he muttered as he stumbled without conclusion.

"Which," she said, gazing at him with eyes blacker than the cave itself, "is nothing?"

"Exactly," he replied, or thought he did, for the dream or vision was already starting to fade, and once again he was back amid the heaped slates of his cell, and as ever he was fumbling in darkness. There had to be something, some way of solving this problem, yet the solution seemed as blank and black as the circles of that girl's eyes, or the cave itself – or even the darkness, come to that, which lay between the wheeling stars.

There was a great deal of nothing to be found in all the known lands and the heavens, the ex-Chief Administrator supposed, if you thought about it in a certain way. There was the nothing of death, at least if you didn't believe the stories the priests now told, along with the nothing that came before life itself, not to mention the nothing that was left in your pockets when you had spent all your tokens, or when one amount was taken from another; a problem of record keeping some of his scribes had occasionally complained about when doing their seasonal tallies. But it was the nothing of that cave mouth and the nothing of the girl's eyes that kept returning to his thoughts, around and around like a serpent consuming its tail. He even made that mark, a mere empty circle, on one of his slates as dawn began to illuminate his cell. Then, in a fever, he began to make it again and again.

He'd never felt so wise, yet so foolish, for surely he should have thought of this long ago! The space, the gap, the absence, was exactly what all his intricate tallies and symbols lacked if he truly was to use them to track the movement of the heavens. This blank circle allowed, simply and easily, for amounts to be increased by neat graduations which reached up as far as the sky itself, and beyond, in endless progression. There was beauty here and there was elegance, and at last he was able to render the passage of the moon and the sun as they truly were. He was even able to determine the precise moment when the moon would once again block out the sun. Which – and this really was something close to divine destiny – lay not far ahead.

The warders, understandably, were suspicious, but they listened warily, and agreed that such a strange augury should be brought to the attention of the king. And if it were true, well, at least he would have some fore-knowledge. And if it were false – well, what, apart from his most precious appendages and his life, did the ex-Chief Administrator have left to lose?

Then came the day of the prophecy, although the ex-Chief Administrator would have preferred to call it a mere reckoning, as he paced and followed the sun's passage across the walls of his cell. Something which had only recently occurred to him was that the display might be ruined by a heavy covering of cloud, but the sky was blue and clear, and he watched the birds dart, and he heard the sounds of life across the city, until, with no preliminary at all, he heard cries of alarm and wailing prayers as everything began to darken.

The moment of absolute blackness lasted barely an instant, and soon the cocks were crowing as full daylight returned, and it was almost as if nothing had occurred. The ex-Chief Administrator was relieved and thankful, and even muttered a small prayer of thanks to the God of Nothing, although as a proud man of some substance he was mainly looking forward to bowing once again before his king, and hearing him concede that he'd been right all along, and would he like to return to his family, and his home, and his old job? It was thus a disappointment when the High Priest, of all people, came to stand before the bars of his cell, although of course he was owed an abject apology from him as well.

"So now you see!"

"All I see is a condemned man..." The High Priest smiled. "Although you should thank whatever gods you believe in that your death will not take very long."

If any last words were spoken by the ex-Chief Administrator as he fell toward what he truly believed to be the absolute emptiness of death, they are not recorded, although they would probably have consisted of little more than a few groans. Most reputable scholars are also of the opinion that there never was a ruinous temple tended by a young priestess high up on the holy mountain, although a few still insist that this non-existence is the sacred purpose she served.

When it comes to the High Priest, however, all are agreed that, having inspected the scrawled slates piled in the ex-Chief Administrator's cell, he instructed the warders that they should be kept for further study, even though they probably amounted to nothing at all.

# The Ships of Aleph

Jaine Fenn

Every day, I ask myself the same question: would I be happier now if I had never sailed off the edge of the world?

As a child, I wondered what lay beyond the sea. One of my earliest memories is of asking my father that very question as he sat by the fire after a hard day hauling the nets. He said simply, 'Such matters are for God to know, Lachin,' and drew on his pipe. I may have pestered him further; I remember mother telling me to let him rest.

But for me, God was not the answer. God was real, of course. He looked down on us every day; sometimes he answered our prayers. And sometimes – rare, terrible times – he sent punishment.

I saw that for myself once. I was eight years old and had recently experienced a small injustice of my own. I was playing in the woods with my brother and his friends. The boys shook the tree I was climbing and I fell and broke my leg. They claimed it was an accident, of course. The injury healed slowly, and left me with a permanent limp. During my recovery I was housebound, and overheard the women gossiping. Our neighbour's brother believed his wife had been with a peddler who had passed through the village not long before. The talk went to and fro, as such things do, until one stormy spring night he took her up to the cliff and pushed her over. He claimed she'd wandered out alone after an argument and must have fallen. The priest said the truth was for God to decide. So, the next time a storm rolled in, the man was pegged out on the cliff top above where his wife's body had been found. Sure enough the lightning came, and the next morning he was reduced to a burnt and lifeless corpse.

He was guilty of killing his wife, and God had judged him. But what of the wife? Had she wronged him, or was that purely gossip? We would never know now, and though the incident was talked of for years afterwards no one other than me cared that the full facts would never be known. I did not want gristle to chew over with my fellow villagers: I wanted reasons, explanations. I wanted the truth.

Because the sea is the heart of life on the coast, it was only natural that my questioning mind kept coming back to that. I wondered at the tides: they came and went with the seasons, so something in the heavens must cause them – but what? I wondered at the fish: do they venture beyond the bay out into the Current? Perhaps, my father said, but we cannot go there. Why, I asked? Because our small boats would be destroyed in the open sea; besides, he added, we have no need: God provides.

Though I loved to go out on my father's boat, my lameness and my tendency to day-dream made me a liability. I was apprenticed to the priest, who taught me my letters and what wisdom he had. I used that knowledge to record my observations on the few scraps of precious paper I was allowed. I even created a table of tides, which some of the fishermen said was of use, though perhaps they were humouring me. Most people preferred knowledge passed down by word of mouth or won by hard experience.

When I reached my sixteenth year, I persuaded the priest to write to his superiors in the hope of finding me a rich sponsor in one of the inland burghs. I began to dream of travelling to places where knowledge was prized, maybe even to Omphalos itself with its University and Cathedral.

No reply came. But next spring, the Duke arrived.

He came without warning, accompanied by fifty men and supplies sufficient to last the summer. He told us to gather by the well and explained that he had come to our 'modest hamlet' because our bay was the most suitable for his project. Before explaining what this project was, he went on to say that he had heard this place was home to a fisherman's son with a keen and enquiring mind, and he hoped to enlist this young man's help.

Around me, people drew back. My voice shaking, I asked what he planned to do.

He told me he wanted to discover what lay beyond the Current. He would build a boat – no, a *ship* – such as the world had never seen, and sail it further than any man had ever gone. He said that he would welcome anyone who wished to work with his engineers or improve his men's scanty knowledge of sea-craft.

Naturally, I was the first to volunteer.

Though I was not alone in lending a hand, some thought the Duke's obsession ungodly. My father was one such, although he did not forbid me to answer the Duke's call. Perhaps he was even glad, in his own quiet way; certainly he was relieved I had found something to divert me. The way I saw it, there was nothing in the Scriptures forbidding exploration, and if God disapproved then he could easily have destroyed the great wooden skeleton taking shape on the beach.

Our priest, after too much honey ale on Midsummer Eve, suggested the Duke might be an exile who had come here to escape the intrigues of his home burgh.

Accommodating the Duke's men caused some disruption in the village, although they were well-disciplined, and the Duke paid the council more coin than we'd see for five years of sending salt fish inland. He was also liberal with his gifts of fine cloth and metal goods. At first I did not question this generosity, but then I began to wonder if the priest was right, if this was a man who did not expect to need earthly goods for much longer. My suspicions grew as the date of departure neared and several of the Duke's men deserted.

By now the ship was afloat, and had been out on short proving voyages into the bay. It would leave for good before the winter storms arrived.

I was not surprised when the Duke offered me a place on board. He asked others too, but although my fellow villagers were happy enough to pass on their expertise for the right price, all the electrum in Omphalos would not have persuaded them to sail with him. What fool would venture into unknown waters on a ship crewed by inexperienced sailors and captained by a man who appeared to have a death-wish? Yet if I did not go on this voyage I'd spend the rest of my life wishing I had. I held off giving the Duke my final decision for as long as I could.

In the end the choice was made for me. The day before the departure, the girl I had set my heart on told me she would never marry me, and our dalliance had come about only due to my association with the Duke. So in the end I left my home not in the spirit of discovery, but to spite a feckless wench.

On the morning of the launch I was scared beyond reason, but determined not to show it. I waved goodbye to everyone I had ever known with a smile fixed hard upon my face.

The ship was fast, and within half a day we were free of the encircling arms of the bay. It was another day before the Current began to tell, forcing us rightwise, even though we tacked into the wind which came, as usual, from outwards. 'God's constant breath' the villagers called the breeze that blew ceaselessly inwards from the edge of the world, though out here it was not so much a breath as a scream. The great rudder strained, and my advice was constantly called on in minding the sails. It did not matter to the Duke that we were being swept around the circumference of the world, provided we also progressed away from land, but I found myself wondering if we would fetch up on the far side of creation.

For three days and two nights we continued fighting the sea and making what we could of the wind. The Duke used his optic glass (an instrument I eyed up with envy) to observe the way ahead, hoping to glimpse the edge of the world. As the Scriptures had little to say on the matter, theories abounded as to what it might look like: according to the Duke, some scholars said it was a great wall, others a void that men's eyes could not bear to look upon, others still that the sea arched up to meet the sky and there was no edge at all. We saw no change in the horizon, and if the Duke's optic glass revealed more, he did not say.

On the third night, a storm blew up. As the sun set, cloud piled on cloud, racing to meet us. The more superstitious men made the sign of the Eye, seeing the oncoming storm as God's judgement. The sails were reefed. Against my advice, the Duke ordered the oars deployed; he would not give up the headway he had made, even in the face of God's wrath.

Then the storm was upon us.

I remember an indeterminate time of soaking panic, of seeing men washed overboard and hearing the masts groan like the unquiet dead. Some of the oars splintered – killing one rower and injuring several more – before the Duke saw sense and shipped them. Finally, the aft mast snapped.

When the storm finally spent its fury he ordered those men still able to row to go back below. I saw the futility of this command, for we had no idea whether we were still heading for the edge, but the Duke had a powerful presence, and I felt the need to do something, if only to stave off fear.

So I rowed, along with every man still capable of doing so, even the Duke himself. I think I slept as I pulled on my oar, for I remember jerking awake at a shout. Then I heard the low rumble filling the ship, and saw the rowers abandoning their posts and running up the ladders. I followed them, too dazed to be afraid, to find that the Duke's quest had been successful.

Behind us, the sky was lightening towards dawn; ahead it remained clouded and dark. But I could see enough to make out a great lip over which the sea disappeared. The spray coming up from the drop shrouded the whole scene in mist, giving it a deceptive tranquillity. Without landmarks to provide a sense of scale I had no idea how far away we were. Then I looked down, and saw the speed of the frothing sea that carried us towards the edge, and knew that we were lost.

The Duke shouted something about ropes and holding fast, which I barely heard above the now-constant thunder, but when a ship goes down the last thing you want is to be attached to it. Instead I fetched one of the float-bladders we used to rescue sailors who fell overboard. As the Duke lashed himself to the remaining mast, I tied the bladder to myself.

I both felt and heard the impact that destroyed the ship, and just had time to be surprised – we hadn't fallen yet, so how could we strike anything? – when everything turned to chaos. Wood split, men fell, and I tumbled down the rising deck and over the side. In my last sight of the Duke I saw the cross-spar fall from the remaining mast. It crushed him instantly.

Then I was in the roiling sea, unsure which way was up. My head came out into air, and I gulped a breath before a wave broke over me and I was turned around. I clung to my float, eyes closed, battered by water and occasionally wood – and softer things. One of these clawed briefly at my arm before being whirled away.

The sound of rushing water changed and deepened. I opened my eyes to see the world tilting, a crazy view of black lightning-laced clouds filling the sky. Sky meant breath – I breathed again, though the effort was almost too much.

I was going faster than any man ever had. Though I knew I should try and observe the process, terror and exhaustion got the better of me and I screwed my eyes shut.

The next time my head broke the surface I took a breath. Nothing happened. I opened my eyes to darkness and a strange sensation. I felt as though I were floating, not falling, yet I was no longer in the water. Eerie silence had replaced the roar of the sea.

How interesting, I mused. No one ever predicted *this* about the edge of the world: there is no air, and yet you float!

However, because there is no air, you also drown.

I woke up in my bedroom.

At least, so I thought when I opened my eyes; that I lay in my bed in the room where I had slept all my life. But the bed was against the wall, not under the window as it should be and when I looked around I discovered other out-of-place details. I recognised the wooden puzzle my father had fashioned from different colours of driftwood, but it was next to my bed, not on the high shelf I had relegated it to when I grew tired of it. And the clothes chest my brother and I shared lacked the large splotch on the lid where father had spilt limewash on it while he was recoating the walls.

I sat up. I ached, but not badly, which was unexpected because… ah, because *I had died*! In which case, this had to be Heaven. Or Hell, although I saw no sign of the expected fiery rivers and cruel imps.

When I stood I found another argument in favour of this being a place of celestial reward. I went to adjust my stance to allow for my shortened leg and discovered that both legs were the same length. I sat down again and felt my shin: there was no lump, no bend.

A miracle to be sure, but Heaven was said to be perfection, so why was the room not as it should be? And why was the scar on my wrist, a burn from a foolish accident one midwinter, still there? And, if Heaven was where I should find my heart's desire, why was I still in the village I had died trying to escape?

I stood again, and opened the shutters. The view outside was as expected, save for a faint mistiness.

I went downstairs, almost stumbling as I adjusted to my restored leg. The kitchen and parlour were the same as upstairs, familiar yet subtly wrong, not least for being empty: my mother or sister should be here. I called out, not expecting an answer, and not getting one. For the first time I felt a flutter of fear: if this was not Heaven it must be Hell, and that implied things were likely to become a lot less pleasant soon. I decided to face my fear. I opened the door.

On the threshold stood an angel.

I recognised the description from Scripture – *a bronze being in the form of a perfect, shining man* – even as I felt immense relief that I was not, in fact, damned. Having never expected to meet such a being, I had no idea how to react. The Scriptures told of those lucky enough to receive angelic visitations prostrating themselves in awe, but although I was both impressed and disconcerted, I felt no inclination towards abject worship. Instead I stepped back to let it in, as though I were receiving a normal caller into my home.

It showed no offence at my lack of piety, and merely walked across the threshold. As it passed me it said, in a clear but not particularly angelic voice, 'I expect you have some questions.'

*Some questions*? Where to start?

I thought for a moment, then raised my most immediate query: 'Am I dead?'

'You are not,' it said. 'You were saved, though the others on your ship perished.'

I wanted to ask why I alone had not died, but that seemed impertinent. Instead I said, 'So this is not Heaven, then?'

'No.'

'I see,' I said, though I did not.

'You do not sound surprised or disappointed to find that you have not reached the reward the Scriptures promised.'

The angel's voice showed no emotion and its perfectly proportioned face was as immobile as a mask. I had no idea if my unexpected behaviour was angering or pleasing it. 'I did wonder if this were Heaven,' I said carefully, 'but I have found small differences from my expectations, and so concluded it was not. May I ask where I am?'

'You are beyond the world. However, there is nothing to be afraid of. You will find this a pleasant place to live.'

I had no idea whether to be grateful for the reassurance or concerned I was not being given the option to refuse. I reminded myself that I was lucky to be alive, and said, 'Thank you.'

'Food will be provided for you, though you may also wish to cultivate a garden. I suspect the contents of the other cottages will be of more interest to you, though.'

Did I imagine amusement in the angel's tone? 'I assume I am alone here,' I said.

'You assume correctly. And you are advised not to stray more than a thousand steps from this house. I will return.' With that it turned and left.

I watched through the open door as the angel walked out of the village on the path down to the sea. It was soon swallowed by the mist.

I stayed where I was for some while, thoughts running through my mind in time to my racing heart.

Finally I resolved to follow the angel. It had not forbidden me to do so, and I would stop before I went beyond the limit it had set.

Though I had never counted the number of steps from the village to the sea, I knew it to be far less than a thousand; yet, once clear of the village, the path merely continued as it had, a narrow track through the low grass. The further I went, the thicker the mist became, though in truth it was more like smoke, being not at all damp. By the time my count reached eight hundred I could barely see the path. I carried on for fifty more steps before unease forced me to turn around.

Back in the village I examined the re-creation more closely. The detail was perfect, right down to the newly mended rope on the well-bucket and the yellow foxtails and late-blooming purse flowers nodding in the verges. I decided to investigate the other cottages, as the angel had suggested. I started at the modest home of the widow whose daughter was betrothed to my brother.

I was not sure what I'd expected, but what I found certainly surprised me. The place was full of books.

The village priest had kept a handful of religious works on a shelf in his study – Morius' *Lives of the Saints*, Campur's *On the Transience of Souls* and suchlike – but here every wall of every room was covered with shelves, and every shelf was full! I scanned titles until I found one I had heard of: *The Travels of Alban the Tall.* Alban was said to have visited every burgh in the world, and seen the sun both rise and set above the sea. I pulled the book out carefully, placed it on the table in the centre of the room, and began to read.

Some time later I was distracted by the rumbling of my stomach. I closed the book and went back to my cottage. In the larder I found black bread and pale, bland cheese. The meagre fare was enough to stop the hunger. I drew water from the well – it tasted odd, but quenched my thirst – then went back to my book.

When darkness fell I reluctantly left off my reading; although the recreation of my family kitchen had lamps on the shelves the angel had said nothing about providing oil, only food.

That night I slept fitfully, and dreamt of drowning.

The next morning more bread and cheese had appeared, along with a pot like the one my mother kept honey in; this contained a thick gloop which tasted as sweet as honey, though it held hints of other, unidentifiable flavours.

I waited a while in case the angel returned. When it did not, I examined the other cottages and found every one packed with books. I had not known there were so many books in the world! I also found, lying on their sides rather than upright, books with empty pages, and beside them, a quill.

All my life I had sought learning, and here it was.

I resolved to approach this bounty with an ordered mind. I would record my reading, and my conclusions, a job made easier by the strange quill, which wrote flawlessly without ink. I set to my task with joy.

I also took time to explore my environment, as much to rest my eyes as because I thought I would find any new information out there. As expected, I soon encountered the thickening mist in every direction, and I experienced a disquiet that grew the further I walked from the village.

The angel returned after ten days. I found it standing beside the table in my kitchen when I came back to my cottage for my evening meal.

'Are you happy?' it asked, as though we had left off our conversation mere moments ago.

'Yes,' I said, 'I believe I am.'

'Good. Do you have all you need?'

'I… Yes, I think I do. Actually… could I have some oil? For the lamps.'

'Light can be provided,' it said. Then it added, 'You have no wish to return, then?'

'Return where?'

'To your village.'

It had not occurred to me that this was even possible. I thought about it, though not for long, balancing my old life as a misfit who dreamed against my new one, living in my dream. 'No. I have no desire to go back.'

'Good. Then I will leave you for now.' It made to go.

'Wait… You said when I first came here that I could ask questions. Is that still true?' I should have thought about this before, maybe considered what I wanted to ask.

'It is.'

'Then…' I searched my whirling thoughts and hit upon the book I had been studying most recently, a treatise on the disposition of the heavens, '… I want to know about stars.' Some scholars thought them eternal fires; others, holes showing a glimpse of the light of Heaven beyond. 'What are they made of?'

'That is not a question I can answer.'

I wondered if I had misheard it. 'But you are an angel! You know the mind of God.' My words were thoughtless, insolent. Who did I think I was to talking to?

But the angel merely said again, 'That is not a question I can answer.' Then it left.

The next morning, along with my food, I found a white hemisphere the size of my palm. It was featureless save for a slider on the bottom. When I moved this along its track, the object lit up with a cold white light, like starlight. Presumably I had not angered the angel with my presumption, for it had granted my request. I wondered if I were being tested; perhaps it had refused to answer my question because I needed to find out the truth for myself. Maybe the answer was in the books.

I began to keep a note of questions to ask the angel when it returned, which it did, every ten days. I noted its answers with equal care and as the sun grew smaller and winter – or a re-creation of it – arrived, I found a pattern emerging.

The angel would answer any question I posed, save those that dealt with God, or with the sky, such as queries on the nature of the sun or stars. It would even provide answers I could have found in my books: for example, the writer of a treatise on the fauna of the Inner Spine mountains suggested that perhaps the snow-hares did not hibernate, and instead changed form. The angel confirmed the truth of this. Sixty-seven days later, in a different book, written some years after the first one, I found this written down as a solid observation. Had the angel known I would discover the answer for myself, yet chosen to tell me anyway? I asked that, but this was another question it would not answer, presumably because it strayed into matters of the spirit.

It also told me some things no man had recorded, such as why the Duke's ship had finally foundered. There was, it said, a ring of rock just inside the lip of the world that helped control the flow of water over the edge. When I asked what was beyond that, and where I was in relation to it, the angel was predictably uninformative.

I asked about myself. It told me that I could choose to live out my allotted span of days – however long that might be – either here or back in the village. I was becoming emboldened so I asked, 'What if I were to ask to be returned, not to my village, but to Omphalos, to the halls of the University?'

'If you wished. But what would you do then?'

'Why, tell people what has happened to me!'

'Are you sure? You would go back to the world exactly as you left it, save for the time that has passed and your remembered experiences of being here. Why should the words of a rootless stranger be heard in the halls of great scholars?'

It was right, of course. 'But why am I here at all?' I asked.

Again I thought I detected faint amusement. 'That is a question every thinking being must answer for themselves.'

'No, I mean why am I *here*, in this constructed place, with all these books.'

'To learn and think and question,' it said. 'Such is your talent.'

'But *why*?'

'That is not a question I can answer.'

Repressing a flash of irritation, I tried another. 'Is this solely my fate? You have told me this is not Heaven but I have read of another place, which some theologians believe must exist though the Scriptures do not mention it, a place where those who are taken from the world before their potential is fulfilled live out their lives to determine whether Heaven or Hell is their eventual destination. Is that where I am?'

'To answer your questions in reverse order: this is not such a place; and you are alone here.'

'But am I *unique*?'

'You are alone,' it repeated.

In truth, I did not greatly miss human company. However, I did miss the sea. I asked the angel whether it might be possible, now I had been here for nearly two hundred days, for the re-creation to be expanded, perhaps to include the sea. It refused, giving no explanation.

It did accede to other requests, such as one for seeds and tools. I planted out the garden behind the cottage with my favourite vegetables, consulting various books to ascertain how best to cultivate my small patch of ground. I enjoyed the contrast to my life in the libraries, and took joy in the physical exertion, the chance to replace the smell of musty paper with that of newly turned earth. When summer came, the fruits of my labours were a welcome addition to my diet.

I also asked for chickens, but was told that chickens, like the sea, were not permitted. I was not surprised, for I had seen no animal larger than an insect here. I asked the angel why insects were permitted while chickens were not. It said that the insects were necessary for the cycle of life, a theory I had come across before. For a few weeks I made a practical study of the interaction of these small creatures with the plants they lived among. But I found such experimentation less rewarding than the pursuit of pure knowledge already gained by others' observations. I went back to my books.

I often went days without considering my situation, lost as I was in investigations into the categorisation of flightless birds, or the history and genealogy of the great families of Omphalos, or the construction and operation of the complex devices used to thresh wheat on the outer plains. I had a routine, involving regular meals, time in my garden and, odd though it might seem, small but regular religious observances. I found they gave me comfort. I also felt compelled to continue my devotions because if I were truly outside the world then by implication I was closer to God, even if the one servant of His I had encountered was careful to steer clear of divine matters. I often wondered if the angel's refusal to answer certain questions was due to my mind not yet being ready to comprehend the answers. This possibility encouraged me to further improve myself with study.

Yet I was also aware that I was a prisoner. Sometimes I felt compelled to test the bounds of my prison. I never got more than nine hundred steps from the village before giving up, driven back by an apprehension that came in part from piety.

As time passed I found my conversations with the angel changing. I began to spend less time asking questions and more time explaining my own thoughts and conclusions. Insofar as I could tell from such a bland countenance, the angel was not bored by my observations, and our one-sided conversations often went on for some time. One day, when I had been here for just over a year, my heavenly visitor waited until I had finished speaking, then asked, 'Do you dream?'

Momentarily thrown I answered that I thought so, but had never been good at remembering my dreams. It suggested I keep a book by my bed, to record them.

I did as the angel said, and my recall quickly improved. However my mind's nightly musings provided few new insights, being usually a reflection of my day's study, sometimes mixed with recollections of my old life, and occasionally infected by the nightly passions normal in any young man of solitary habits.

I decided, as my second winter approached, that I was going to attempt a small act of rebellion. Remembering childhood tales of heroes and magic I chose to make my stand when I had been in my comfortable prison for five hundred days – the magic period of time for spells and enchantments.

I spent some of that day asleep. When I retired for the night I attempted to stay awake, with the help of a tracklebur I had picked earlier; whenever I felt my eyelids getting heavy I ran it along the tender skin on the inside of my wrist.

At the same time, I listened. I may have fallen towards sleep, but I jerked awake at a tiny sound from below. Heart hammering, I slid out of bed. I crept across the bedroom floor, taking care to avoid the creaky board. On the landing I crouched low, then lay flat in order to peer down the stairs.

In the minimal starlight that came through the open shutters it was hard to make out much detail, but I could see a figure, paler than its surroundings, walking across the room. It gave no sign of knowing I was there and simply carried on to the door, opened it, then left, closing the door gently behind itself.

I counted to fifty then went downstairs. In the pantry I found the usual provisions. Perhaps my sustenance did not manifest through God's bounty after all but was brought to me by a physical messenger, who appeared unaware of being watched.

The next night I repeated my experiment. This time, however, I did not attempt to hide myself. Instead I rushed downstairs as soon as I heard the door open. The angel carried a shallow box under its arm, and was heading for the pantry as I stumbled into the kitchen. Before fear could get the better of me, I blurted, 'Are you the same one?'

'I do not understand the question,' it said, in the calm, even tone I knew so well.

'Are you the same one, the same angel who comes to talk to me?'

It said, 'We are all the same one.' Then it opened the pantry door.

Its words made me feel cold inside; I had begun to think of the angel who visited me as a particular friend but that was no more than a comforting self-deception.

The angel did not mention the night-time encounter on its next visit, and nor did I. I resolved to remember that my visitor was a manifestation of God and as such it should not matter whether the same individual came to me each time. It was not as though I could tell them apart anyway.

As time passed I became convinced that the angel – or angels – did indeed have an interest in my musings. This motivated me in my research. Yet the angel's restrictions and refusals continued to chafe.

In my third spring I decided to directly disobey the angel. I resolved to walk a thousand steps from my cottage. To prepare, I fortified myself using a technique of purifying and focusing the mind I had found in an obscure text on the less well-known teachings of Saint Aperion of the Lake. It involved fasting for three days, which also meant hiding the food brought each night. I half expected the angel to question this. It did not, which was illuminating in itself. On the third morning I carried out the exercises of the mind and breath that the Saint recommended. Then I headed out of the village, towards where the sea should be.

I forced myself to employ a casual saunter. As my steps approached nine hundred, I felt increasingly light-headed, disconnected from the task I was undertaking. At the same time my guts felt heavy, as though my gross mortality was slowing me down. I observed these reactions, categorising them as being due to a mixture of spiritual unease and the physical after-effects of my fast. However, as the Saint had instructed, I did not let such transient feelings affect my actions.

Nine hundred and fifty steps. In truth it was probably less: I had lost sight of my own feet in the mist and was reduced to sliding them along, hoping there was solid ground ahead. I had considered bringing a stick to deal with this problem, but had decided against it in case it made my intent too obvious. Though of course God should know what I was up to anyway.

If He did, He made no move to stop me. Nine hundred and eighty steps, albeit the last dozen more of a shuffle. I found myself quaking, the urge to turn around growing stronger by the moment. I told myself it was a passing desire and I had risen above such feelings.

Nine hundred and ninety. I imagined it was getting dark, then discarded the illusion. My body felt like wet clay. I visualised it as a vessel that was wholly subject to my will.

One thousand. The darkness was complete and I could neither see nor hear anything. But I could still feel the ground beneath my feet. I forced myself to take another step, though my limbs shook and sweat oozed from me.

One thousand and one. My breath deafened me, yet I carried on.

One thousand and ten. What if there was no end, and I would just continue forever. *What if I could never go back?*

On the one thousand and twenty seventh step, I stumbled. I do not know if the path was gone, or uneven, or whether my body had finally betrayed me. I do know that I did not feel myself hit the ground.

I woke up in bed. It was only when my stomach contracted and rumbled that I remembered this was no ordinary morning. Memory returned in a rush that made me want to grasp my head. But, aside from hunger, I felt no ill effects from my attempted disobedience and subsequent punishment. On venturing downstairs, I found only the usual fare, which I devoured eagerly.

I had timed my expedition mid-way between visits from the angel, but that evening I found it waiting for me in my cottage. It sat, as usual, at the table. I sat, as was my wont, opposite it. For once, I was unsure what to say.

It saved me the effort. 'If you are so unhappy, does that mean you wish to return now?'

'Return to the world, you mean?'

'Yes.'

'I'm not sure. I'm not unhappy. I have been given access to the wisdom of ages, a treasure beyond any material wealth. It's just… sometimes I find it hard to bear, every day being the same, just me and my books, in a place I cannot leave.'

The angel said, 'You have an enquiring mind; it is only natural that you explore and question. But no matter how keen your mind, your body resents its captivity. This is understandable. Yet your choices remain as they were: stay here, or return to the world.'

'I will stay.'

Perhaps my foolish disobedience had relieved some hidden pressure, or perhaps my assertion to the angel made me see sense. Whatever the cause, I found myself accepting my situation, at least for a while.

Then, on the first day of summer, I woke up knowing something had changed.

It was no more than an intuition, formless and irritating as an unreachable itch. I went down to the kitchen muttering to myself. I was just breaking my fast when I heard noises from above: what sounded like a gasp, then the creak of a floorboard. I rushed to the bottom of the stairs just as a figure emerged from the room that, in the original cottage, my parents had slept in. Seeing me, the intruder recoiled, and I saw her head – it was a woman! – turn from side to side as though searching for an escape route.

Without thinking I called out, 'It's all right – I'll not hurt you!'

She gasped again, and fled back into the room. Thinking she might try and jump from the window, I ran upstairs. But she had not jumped. Instead she had drawn herself into a tight ball in the far corner of the bed, from where she watched me with fearful eyes. Her clothes were tattered and torn, barely covering her in some places. She was my age, or perhaps a little younger.

'It's all right,' I said again. 'You're in no danger here.' When she neither moved nor spoke I said, 'My name's Lachin. What is yours?'

For a moment I thought she had not understood me. Then she whispered, 'Merel'.

I wanted to ask where she came from and how she had got here, but first I wanted to put her at her ease. 'Are you hungry, Merel?' I asked. She looked like she would benefit from a decent meal.

She nodded.

'I have food. You can share it with me.'

She relaxed a little, then asked, 'What is this place?' She had a strange accent, with longer vowels and a downward intonation even when asking a question.

'It's where I live,' I replied, not untruthfully, then added, 'But you are welcome to share what I have.'

My answer appeared to satisfy her, but my mind raced as I led her downstairs. I made myself stay silent, and gestured for her to sit. I got down utensils for the two of us, and we broke bread and ate. She held the bread close to her mouth and tore lumps off with her teeth.

Finally I could resist no longer. 'Where are you from, Merel?'

'My village is on the Coast of Shoals, but…' she looked down for a moment, long dark eyelashes dipping over pale cheeks, '… I was taken by sea-raiders. How long ago, I cannot tell.'

The Coast of Shoals is a fascinating place; many writers have investigated its mysteries. I said, 'I would love to hear tales of your homeland, Merel.'

Again the downcast eyes. 'If you wish.'

Something in the way she spoke pricked at me. Carefully I asked, 'Did the sea-raiders… keep you on their ship?'

She nodded, and the flush of colour to her cheeks confirmed my suspicions. I felt my own face grow hot. I stood up. 'I will find you something to wear. Wait here.'

I knew the other rooms had items similar to those I would expect to find, so I looked in my sister's clothes-chest. I came back with a tunic and skirt to find Merel sitting where I had left her. She appeared more relaxed. I decided it was not unreasonable to ask one more question.

'Do you know how you got here?'

She frowned. 'I'm not sure. They kept me below-decks most of the time. I think the ship got caught in the Current, and there was a storm. I heard them shouting, and the ship was tossed around. One of the water-barrels came loose. The last thing I remember was seeing the barrel heading towards me. I closed my eyes… and woke up here.' She turned to me, and I tried not to look at the curve of her throat, the warm, soft skin leading lower. 'Can I really stay?'

'Of course. You can have the room you woke up in if you like.'

She smiled, which made her look even younger. 'Thank you,' she said.

*

I got little study done that day. I told Merel we were alone here, and she would be safe provided she stayed near the village, information she accepted without question. When I mentioned I had work to do she said she would be content by herself. As far as I could tell she meant it, so I returned to my books. But my mind kept coming back to my visitor, both to the many questions her unexpected appearance raised and to the simple presence of a living, breathing woman.

When I returned to the cottage she asked, shyly, whether she might get clean. She had seen the tin bath hanging in the outhouse and wished to use it. I saw no reason why not, and we heated water on the stove. When the bath was full I muttered an excuse about unfinished work and went out. I paced the bounds of the village as night came on, trying not to think of Merel, naked in the warm water.

I returned to find her already abed, for which I was grateful. She had even managed to empty the bath by herself.

I slept badly that night, and once thought I heard Merel cry out. I nearly went to her, but remembered the sting of tracklebures on my skin, and disciplined myself to remain in my room.

As dawn lightened behind the shutters, I resolved to consider my visitor as a source of information, a living book, though also to treat her gently, for she had obviously suffered at the hands of men. Having categorised her to my satisfaction, I could safely talk with her at length, rationalising the pleasure this gave me as a worthy one. Although knowledgeable about those parts of the world she had seen she was, I soon realised, a little simple. I also thought her remarkably incurious, but then I thought that about most people.

I slept better that night, until I woke in the darkness, confused. Then the sound came again: a woman's incoherent cry.

I leapt from my bed and ran to Merel's room. I found her tangled in the bedding, her mind caught in some nightmare. 'Wake up,' I called. When she did not respond I called again, louder. Still she moaned and thrashed.

I caught her hand. Suddenly she stopped and opened her eyes, looking at me first with fear, then with slow recognition. Her wrist was warm and frail in my grasp.

Her face creased and she began to cry. Without thought I gathered her to me, holding her while she wept. When the tears passed, I did not let go, and she did not pull away. Instead she nestled into my arms. My world was filled with her intoxicating presence, so intense I could barely breathe.

I knew I should let her go, but she was more real than my books, more real than this place. Trying to break the spell, I murmured, 'I will leave you to rest.'

I felt her shake her head. 'Don't go. Stay with me.'

I wasn't sure she was asking what I thought she was. Then she lifted a hand and stroked my face.

The next morning I was torn between elation and guilt. But as I looked down on Merel's sleeping form, I decided I had no reason to feel guilty. She was happy, and that made me happy. I had found something I hadn't even known I was missing.

My next angelic visit occurred two days later. I had told Merel about the angel, and the workings of my – our – strange home, though I did not mention my previous small rebellions. They were in the past now, irrelevant.

Merel was apprehensive about meeting the angel, so I said she didn't have to. I was secretly glad of her reticence, for I had questions she might be happier not hearing. I started with the obvious one:

'Why is she here?'

It replied with a question of its own: 'Are you not happy?'

'Yes, yes I am. But… why her? And why now? Will there be others?'

'Those are questions I cannot answer.'

I knew better than to pursue the matter. Instead I told myself that even if, as I suspected, Merel had been plucked from her doom merely to provide company for me, I had done one good thing in my life by inadvertently saving hers.

Merel and I settled into life together as summer waxed. She took on the cultivation of the garden, a task I missed a little at first, though I was glad she had found something to occupy her. She also cooked and cleaned; not that I hadn't done these things before but she applied herself to them fully. Our house became her pride; she started to mend clothes, and sew new ones, even though such tasks were not necessary when the angel would bring whatever was requested within the bounds of its remit.

It occurred to me that, things being what they were, one day it might be more than the two of us in our house. I asked her about this one summer evening as we sat outside the cottage, my arm around her while she sewed in the golden light. She dipped her head. 'I'm sorry, Lachin, but the raiders gave their bondswomen a certain herb. I only took it for a season but the effects are permanent. There can never be children.'

I could have asked the angel whether it was possible to reverse the effects of the drug – God had cured my lameness, after all – but I was still unsure how I felt about the idea of a child. It had not been something I'd given much thought to in my old life, and none at all here. I decided that unless Merel wished otherwise, I would leave things as they were.

We had plenty to fill our time without the need for anyone else. Merel displayed a skill and enthusiasm in the ways of physical love that made me discount my earlier brief experiences of sex. Outside of our bed, she was always happy to talk about her life on the Coast of Shoals, and beyond in the company of her captors. She told me of the shallow coral seas with their low islands and the great whirlpools off the headlands of some of the bays. For my part, I taught her to read. She showed little enthusiasm at first, then took to it with a surprising aptitude. She remained shy around the angel, while it generally ignored her. It visited with the same regularity, once every ten days, but our conversations tended to be shorter now that I was spending more time living life rather than analysing it.

All through that summer and autumn, we were happy.

The first cracks appeared after we argued about the wine. Merel wanted to brew with some of this year's crop of berries. I have no taste for drink, and I felt it was not something we needed. In the end I conceded to please her.

Our argument, though not long or fractious, got me thinking about the future. Would we always want to live together? If not, what then? The angel's offer to return me to the world still stood, but how about Merel? As far as I knew it had never spoken to her directly. If I tired of her, or she of me, what would it do?

Such questions never concerned her, an attitude I initially envied but which came to trouble me. The first flush of love was past and I began to return to my old routines and regain some of my objectivity. As I gave the matter more thought a terrible, unthinkable possibility started to dawn on me. I found myself considering questions I dared not voice, either to her or to the angel. Small things at first: why had my research never uncovered the herb she said the raiders had given her? Why had she taken to reading so quickly? Why would one as misused as she be so eager to press herself upon a man? Even the way she'd recognised the bath when she first came to me: I only knew of such things from my reading, and had asked for it when I found no sea or river to bathe in; she, like me, came from a coastal village, and was unlikely to have encountered such an object.

Yet I loved her, and loved our nights of pleasure and our days of contentment. So I hid my fears, even from myself.

In the end it was the wine that did it. We drank the first batch at midwinter. The young, fruity brew went straight to my head and I became playful and silly, though in the back of my mind I was annoyed at myself for such frivolity. She seemed as intoxicated as I. But I had a growing conviction that she was not actually drunk, that she was playing with me. Pretending. We rowed about nothing, then made up in the usual way. But afterwards I found myself unable to sleep and, still mildly intoxicated, went downstairs and waited for the angel's nightly visit.

It paused on the threshold when it saw me sitting at the table.

'Is something wrong, Lachin?' it asked.

The drink made me speak harshly when I asked, 'Is she real?'

The angel never played games but neither would it hazard guesses when my meaning was unclear. 'That would depend on your definition of real,' it said.

'Is she a person, an actual person? Is what she told me true, or just a story?'

The angel said nothing.

When I heard a step on the stair I stood up and turned around. It was too dark to see Merel's face, but her voice was the same voice that had whispered endearments in the night, that had laughed with me, that had declared its love. 'You once asked one of us if it was the same as your usual visitor, and it said we are all the same. That is not entirely true. We can take any form.'

'No.' The word dropped from me like a stone.

'Yes. I am sorry, Lachin.'

'You're sorry? There is no *you*! You're just… There's just…' speech left me.

She – it – knew better than to approach. Instead it simply said, 'Goodbye,' then walked out, followed by the more obvious construct.

I stood there, silent and shaking, my chest too tight for breath. Then the nausea came, and I rushed over to the sink, barely reaching it before I vomited.

My memories of the following days are unclear. I remember screaming myself hoarse and later, crying myself dry. I remember shouting at God, cursing him for a bastard, daring him to destroy me.

I drank more of the wine, then threw the rest away. I think I may, under the wine's influence, have tried to walk the thousand steps again; certainly I stumbled around in the mist for some time, raging and swearing.

Despite my desire to do so, I did not die. Or perhaps I did, and was resurrected. I cannot be sure.

Food continued to be brought. I ignored it. I wanted nothing from those who kept me here. Eventually hunger overcame revulsion. Aside from the unseen angel who brought my food, I had no visitors. Presumably they knew I had nothing to say to them.

My dreams, which I'd trained myself so carefully to remember, were haunted by Merel. In them, she would transform from the woman I had loved into a featureless bronze automaton. Sometimes this happened during the very act of our lovemaking.

Days passed, and the pretence of winter gave way to the pretence of spring. I went back to my books because there was nothing else. Slowly, the dreams of Merel grew less frequent.

Eventually it came to me that I could, if I wished, be left alone for the rest of my life. Did I want that? Or did I want to go back to what had once been my home, to try and forget all that had happened here?

I went out into the square and called up to the sky, 'I'm ready to talk.'

An angel arrived that evening, at the usual time.

When it walked in I felt a sudden blinding fury. I hefted my chair, thinking to strike the angel. But there was no point. I put the chair down and said, 'Why did you do it?'

'To make you happy. It was hoped having a partner might provide some of the normality and stability of an ordinary life.'

'But I don't have an ordinary life!'

'No, you do not. But you still can, if such is your desire. Do you want to return to the world now?'

I wished, not for the first time, that the angel's toneless voice didn't make it so hard to know its thoughts. After all, I thought bitterly, it was not that it couldn't speak as a human did, only that it chose not to.

God and His servants had perpetrated an obscene joke upon me. But I felt sure it hadn't been done with malice, and the only real harm was to my heart and dignity, my frail human emotions. To let such hurts continue to wound me would be small-minded. 'No,' I said. 'But I do want answers. I need to know what you want from me.'

'The same as always: your insight, your observations.'

'But why does God need that? What are the musings of one lone mortal to Him?

The angel said, 'Would you like to see this place as it really is?'

I stared at it, unsure I had heard correctly. 'You mean… travel beyond the village?'

'Yes.'

'Why now, finally?'

'You were not ready before.'

'And I am now?'

'If not now, then never.'

'Then yes, of course!'

'From tomorrow morning, the path that should lead to the sea will lead you out.'

'Out where?'

'Follow it and see.'

I managed to sleep, but I awoke early, as the illusory dawn was burning off the chill dew of the artificial night.

I wondered whether I should take provisions on my expedition before dismissing the notion as absurd. But I did take one of my books: a new, blank one, ready for my notes and observations.

The path disappeared into the mist, the same as it always had, but when I followed it this time I found the mist no longer thickened, but remained constant. The sense of foreboding that had driven me back before was also absent. I forced myself not to count my steps. After a while I made out a wall ahead. It was as featureless and grey as the mist itself, save for a rectangle drawn on its surface.

And then, between one step and the next, the shape changed – no, opened! It was a *door*. I went up to the doorway and peered through. It gave onto a passage, plain-walled and constructed of a smooth off-white material. Light came from the glowing ceiling. The passage curved away gently in both directions. It appeared I was entering some sort of structure, a building far larger than any I had ever been in.

I stepped into the passage – no, *corridor* was a better description – and started to walk. My eye caught movement behind me. I whirled around to find the door back in place. Heart hammering, I ran back. The door opened; tendrils of mist curled out into the corridor, disturbed by the abrupt motions of this strange device. I resisted the temptation to retrace my steps and check if the village was still there. Instead I turned away from the door – trying not to flinch when I heard it swish shut – and carried on down the passage.

Now I did count my steps, and I found, some fifty-three steps further on, another door, this one on the opposite wall. It did not open as I passed it. Seventy-eight steps in, I found a further door on the same side. This one did open, and led into a cavernous hall, unlit and filled with structures whose function I could not begin to guess. The air was dry, and filled with a faint hum. I decided to carry on along the corridor.

I had gone just over a hundred steps when the revelation hit me: I was not in a building. Instead, the structure, with its strange gleaming surfaces *enclosed the entire reconstructed village*. Whatever this place was, it was huge!

I will not detail here all the wonders I found on that day, nor on the many days since that I have spent exploring my unimaginably vast home. I have mapped and recorded and postulated about my findings in other books, which can be found in my library back at the ersatz village.

I agree with the angel's assertion that my mind as it was when I arrived would have been unable to encompass the true scale and complexity of this place. Consider the door that opens into a space whose walls are almost invisible, due both to their great distance and to the clouds that form and dissipate within the chamber. Or the long door-less section of corridor where I hear a faint but thunderous rush of waters behind the walls. Then there is the huge cylindrical room I have glimpsed through a window, actually a contained hurricane whose true nature is only revealed when some unidentifiable scrap of matter flies past.

I can move freely about and not come to harm here; in places where I have inadvertently walked into danger, such as the cloud chamber, I was held back from the lethal drop by an invisible force. More than once I have chosen a direction and walked for days, carefully mapping my route. Even so, I can only have explored a fraction of this place.

It has occurred to me that if a complete re-creation of my village is enclosed by this endless expanse of corridors and rooms, then perhaps the entire world I once knew also exists within the same, vast space. Could the roaring waters I heard at a distance be the sound of the very sea I once sailed, cascading over what I once thought of as the edge of the world? When I asked the angel this question it said, in its unhelpful way, that such a possibility was 'quite feasible'.

Though I continue to explore, there is one place I keep returning to: the starry window.

I found the window two years and sixteen days after my first foray from the village. I call it a window, but that is merely a theory, formulated after much observation. It is to be found in a stretch of straight corridor located approximately ten thousand paces from my home. The corridor has a patch of wall forty-five paces long which is not like any other wall I have seen: it shows darkness relieved by scattered lights. This view bears a passing resemblance to the night sky I remember from my old life, but it is a night never relieved by dawn and many of the 'stars' do not rotate around the zenith but wander in a random fashion. Or not entirely random: many leave and return periodically, and some of these have a most unusual motion, and a hint of colour. Other stars come and go quickly enough that a patient observer can map, if not understand, their chaotic path.

I return to the village to rest, as it is still my home and the changes it undergoes, whilst illusory, are a comfort to me. I still study too; these days, I spend more time with my books than I do exploring. I have seen enough to know that this place is too big for me to chart, and too incomprehensible for me to understand. The only location beyond the bounds of my home that I return to regularly is the starry window. I confess I have become a little obsessed with it.

Every ten days the angel – an angel – still comes to me, and we talk. Sometimes in my wanderings I encounter other angels; they ignore me unless I question them, in which case they usually provide an explanation full of words I have never encountered, despite my wide reading.

If I ask about the starry window they give the usual frustrating response: 'That is not a question I can answer'.

I have now lived here for almost seventeen years – as long as I lived in the real village before I sailed with the Duke. It has been a good life in many ways, but the approaching anniversary of my arrival has made me restless. I keep coming back to that foolish question I can never know the answer to: whether I would have been more content had I chosen to remain in ignorance in my village.

So, when the angel last visited nine days ago, I asked it two difficult questions, both of which I had given up enquiring about some years ago. The first related to my obsession: 'What is the starry window?'

To my surprise it replied with a question of its own: 'What do you think it is?'

That threw me for a moment. Then I said, 'I believe it may show the truth of the world, though I cannot prove it. Am I right in this?'

The angel said nothing. I remembered the only other time it had answered me with silence, when I had voiced my suspicions about 'Merel'. The memory made me uneasy.

Finally I could bear the silence no longer. 'I will take that as assent, then,' I snapped. Propelled by my frustration, I voiced my second, more dangerous question. 'In my years here I have seen many angels, but not felt any closer to God than I did in my life before. Does God actually exist?'

'That would depend,' said the angel, 'on your definition of God.'

The strange response sounded almost frivolous. I thought of the arguments for and against the existence of a truly divine power. I had certainly experienced miracles: that I lived after falling off the world was one, my healed leg another, this whole place arguably a third. Yet the re-creation of my village was not perfect, and more than once I had acted in ways that – as far as I could tell – surprised the angel.

I chose my next words with care. 'I sometimes wonder if everything I have seen and experienced in my life is some great machine, running faultlessly, but mindlessly.'

Though I had not asked a question, the angel responded as though I had. 'Be assured that there is a mind at work here.'

'But not an omnipotent being?'

Once more, silence.

Which I broke, again. 'I'm not the first, am I? There have been others who have been plucked from the world to live in this place.' I did not say *like some pet* – if God truly knew my mind He would know what I was thinking. And if He chose to punish such blasphemy I would at least have my answer.

'You are correct,' said the angel. 'There have been other rare enquiring souls who have lived for a while beyond the world of men.'

'And they have not satisfied this mind you speak of either, have they?'

'All have come upon insights of interest.'

'Have any returned to the world with these insights?'

'Some, though they had little success in passing on their wisdom. Others have lived out their lives here.'

I had no taste for further discussion, and told the angel so. It left without a word.

I considered for a full day before reaching my decision. In my musings I concluded that God – or rather, the mind behind the world – might know more answers then I, but he – or it – had far more questions too. It also occurred to me that this mind might be lonely, with only the cold, logical angels for company, and that this, as much as anything, could be why frail, transitory beings such as I were sometimes brought here.

In the end it comes down to a simple choice: to live alone in a machine I can never understand or with others of my kind who will never understand me.

When the angel returns tomorrow I will ask to be put back in the world, though not in the village. I would like to see Omphalos, the city I have read so much about. I do not know how I will fare there: all I can do is try.

Before that I will leave this account at the starry window. Call it an odd indulgence, of significance only to myself.

Perhaps the angels will find this book, and I will not have to state my decision boldly. Or perhaps they, or God, really do see my every act, and know already that I have failed to find whatever answers they brought me here to provide.

When I went to the starry window, clutching the book containing my story to my chest, I found the window had disappeared. The wall was blank.

My first reaction was fear; I have tested God more than once these last seventeen years, but he has never punished me. (Merel was not a punishment but an experiment.) Now I have made an irrevocable decision: have I finally damned myself in the process?

Yet no angel came to me, no clarion sounded, no force struck me down. I felt, if anything, rather foolish. I left the book anyway, and headed back to my cottage to sleep.

As I made my way through the mist I thought there was something odd about the village square. I hurried forward, straining to see. A figure stood by the well, a woman dressed in peculiar clothes that managed to be both tight and modest. Her skin was unusually dark, almost reddish in hue. She stood casually, arms crossed, a friendly smile on her face.

I was in no mood for games. I strode past her, waving a hand. 'I see you did work out my intent after all,' I said.

'I'm sorry?' Her accent was odd, though her voice was perfectly understandable. I wondered where 'she' would claim to be from – the Sunrise Veldt perhaps, or the Parsan Traps? Some writers had recorded strange skin tones in those high places.

I stopped. 'I'm not sure what you think to achieve by adopting this form; we may as well just get on with it. Yes, I wish to go home – to Omphalos actually. Tonight would be fine, thank-you.' A sudden, awful realisation began to grow. What if I had missed my chance to return to the world? Perhaps the option had been revoked. Perhaps instead I was being given a real person from the world to keep me company. I looked at her more closely. She was a little younger than me, not physically attractive but with the look of intellect about her. This was no construct.

Her smile changed, becoming something more complex. 'Ah, I see. The avatars didn't tell you, then?'

Now it was my turn to be confused. 'The avatars?'

'You call them angels.'

'You know of the angels?'

'Yes.' She sounded uncertain. 'I assumed they'd discussed this with you. Obviously not.' Then, almost to herself, she added, 'Well, your patron is a little eccentric.'

'Madam, I have no idea what you are talking about.' I found it hard to maintain my tone of hurt pride given how fascinating this all was.

'Of course not, there's no reason you should. Let me start by introducing myself: I'm Captain Estrides.'

Interest gave way to confusion. Some of the corsair schooners in the Blood Sea had female captains, but somehow I didn't think my visitor was a corsair. 'My name is Lachin,' I murmured.

From her expression, this was not news to her. 'I'm here with a proposition, Lachin. Before I put it to you I need to ask you something.'

'Please do.' What else was there to say? I had no idea what was going on.

'Do you know where you are? By that I mean not just the reconstruction of your village, but what this place you live in actually is?'

'I am aware that this village, and quite probably the entire world I knew in my youth, are contained in a machine too great for me – perhaps for any mortal mind – to fully comprehend, though I am told that there is a mind at the heart of it.'

'That's correct, as far as it goes.'

'You sound very certain for – forgive my presumption – another mere mortal. Assuming that's what you are.'

'I'm as mortal as you. I just have access to information you don't.' Her tone was sympathetic. Pitying, almost.

I laughed, a little bitterly, 'And here I was thinking I had been given all the knowledge in the world in order to… ' to what, though?

She completed my sentence gently, '… to give a unique perspective. Come up with unexpected insights. Your patron – the being you think of as God – is powerful and immortal. But he's not omnipotent. He seeks answers, and he uses his subjects to work towards them. He watches over you, but he also watches you.'

'So you are saying that I, no, everyone in the world, is an *experiment*?' It was preposterous, yet now she stated it, entirely logical.

'Not exactly. There is a word that would be closer – *computer* – but you won't know that term.'

'You're right. I don't. What does it mean?'

'It's… This is going to sound odd but I don't think I can tell you what a computer is, because I'm using one in order to talk to you. Some of the concepts simply won't translate.'

I couldn't decide whether to be incredulous, impressed or offended. All three, perhaps. 'And you're not part of this great *computer*?'

'No. I have a patron of my own and he runs his domain in a rather different way.'

'Ah. You come from beyond the starry window, don't you?'

'The starry window? Oh, I see. Yes, I do. Are you familiar with the concept of islands?'

'I am.'

'It might help to think of this place – your world, this village, the great machine enclosing them – as one massive island. Many of the lights you see from your starry window are other such islands.'

'Islands in a sea of darkness! How far do these islands extend?'

'Forever. Can you imagine an endless sea with numberless islands in it?'

I thought for a moment; it was a new concept, but until Captain Estrides corrected me I had assumed the machine containing the world must go on forever. 'I can,' I said.

'My island – my hab, as we call it – is still part of the same… archipelago as yours, though we use the word system. The name for this system is Aleph.'

My mind whirled, as question piled upon question.

'Are you all right?' asked Captain Estrides.

I realised I had staggered backwards. 'Yes, I just… this is a lot to take in.'

'Of course. And there's more, if you think you can handle it.'

'Yes! I want to know it all!'

'All right. Firstly, there's something I need to show you.'

I followed her out of the village and through the mist. A strange contraption awaited us in the corridor, like a low ox-cart with no oxen – and, I realised when I looked below it, no wheels. It floated just above the floor. She told me to get in and sit, which I did. The contraption moved, smoothly but with alarming speed. Thanks to this device – which the Captain called a 'flitter' – it did not take long to get to the starry window. I asked questions all the way, and she did her best to answer them. Some of her answers even made sense.

Back at the window, we dismounted from the machine. The view had returned, but now it was dominated by a construction beyond my wildest dreams, floating in the dark. I reached for comparisons to make sense of what I was seeing, and came up with a dragonfly, a thin silver body with wings at one end. But what wings! They spread wide, yet looked thin as gossamer, so much so that I could see the brighter lights beyond them. In colour they were reddish, save for flashes of iridescence in their slow unfurling, for these great wings were not yet fully extended. This dragonfly was newly hatched and feeling its way, yet even so its magnificence was awe-inspiring.

Captain Estrides gave me time to absorb the view before speaking.

'That's my ship. I'm the head of an expedition travelling from Aleph to another system, an unexplored one. Your patron is contributing materials to this expedition, which was why we've stopped off here. The mission will take many years though we'll be asleep for most of that time. My crew are all volunteers who know they may not return; even if they do, everyone they know will be dead long before we get back to Aleph. We have sufficient crew, but only just; people willing to leave everything behind are understandably rare. That's why I would like you to join us, if you will.'

I managed to look away from the great ship to see the expression on her face; the ship filled her with wonder too, even though it must be familiar to her. 'You want me to journey with you, on that?' I asked.

'If you want to. You're still free to go back to… Omphalos, wasn't it? If you prefer. Or stay in the reconstruction of your village. I must warn you: if you do come with us we'll have to speed-train you before you go into stasis, and you'll need to be prepared for hardship and danger.'

I thought of the Duke's expedition. That same formless fear I'd woken with on the day of departure had returned.

The Captain waited, then when I did not speak said, 'It won't take us long to conclude our main business here; we'll be taking the cutter back to the ship in about three hours. I'm afraid that doesn't leave you much time to decide.'

'*Hours*? I'm not sure how long…'

'That would be under half a day, for you. I'll come back here before we go: if you want to come with us, just be at the window when I return. I wish I could answer more of your questions or at least give you longer to consider, but I've got duties elsewhere and once a lightship gets going, you're just along for the ride.' She smiled at that thought, and I yearned to ask her to explain further.

Instead I just said, 'Thank you.'

She climbed back onto the flitter, and left.

It has been hard to make myself write. I want only to watch the ship as it sails imperceptibly slowly through the darkness, propelled by unimaginable winds. But Captain Estrides will be back soon and I must hurry to finish my account.

It fills me with fear, this idea of a dark and endless sea, of countless worlds beyond my comprehension. My hand shakes at the thought even as I write.

Of course, I knew my answer as soon as she asked the question. I will miss my books, but if I cannot take them all, then I will take none of them, not even this one.

There are other seas, and they extend farther than my mind can grasp. The time has come to continue my journey.

# BLOODBIRDS

Martin Sketchley

The clock tower at the University of Birmingham was Nikki's favourite post. Old Joe's sturdy brick construction minimised the impact of weather: some platforms swayed so much it was almost impossible to work. She assessed conditions as soon as she reached the top: gusting wind; fading light; rain imminent. She'd keep her wings safe and warm within her cape for now. As she swung the satchel from her back and laid it on the floor, the bloodbirds settled on the battlements around her.

She walked to the platform's telephone, lifted the receiver and dialled four-five-one. The metal disk spun.

Two rings, then a click.

'Vanguard control,' said the operator.

'Angel 602 in position.'

'Thank you, 602. Stand by.'

Nikki replaced the receiver, took her Zippo from her breast pocket and lit a cigar, then leaned on the wall and looked out across the city.

The tower gave a panoramic view, but she preferred to face north, looking across the once well-kept green space and paths, the canal and the railway tracks. The height also gave options: she could reach Edgbaston and Selly Oak any day of the week, but with favourable conditions, decent thermals and careful use of waypoints, she could get to Stirchley, Northfield, Harborne. At a push, she could reach the city centre; but all that concrete and glass? No thanks. Leave urban targets to urban cops.

She exhaled smoke and watched a patrol van making its way along the cracked and weed-riddled Bristol Road. The roof-mounted speakers were broadcasting the final warning on a loop:

THIS AREA IS ABOUT TO BE CLEANSED. OFFICERS ARE AUTHORISED TO DETAIN OR DESPATCH SUSPECTED

SURROGATES, COLLABORATORS AND SYMPATHISERS. GIVE YOURSELVES UP NOW AND YOU WILL BE TREATED FAIRLY. GIVE YOURSELVES UP NOW. THIS AREA IS ABOUT TO BE CLEANSED...

She'd requested an extended forty-eight hour warning when she'd submitted the ticket to Scheduling, but she had a hunch that no amount of time would be enough. Somehow Nikki suspected there was a certain inevitability to all of this.

Killing people wasn't something she did in her previous life. It wouldn't have gone down too well with the teachers at Thomas Aquinas. Back when everything was boring and she just wished something would happen. Then the Qall came, and everything turned upside down.

Instead of the benevolent civilisation we had always hoped for, they neutralised our technology and weaponised us to fight their battles on other, distant worlds. The transformative powers of their organic pods equipped us with all we'd need: enhanced perception; the ability to survive harsh environments; physiological upgrades and integrated weapons. They used and abused us in much the same way we had used and abused our fellow terrestrial species. What goes around comes around, some might say.

But when we proved too resistant and unpredictable to bend to their will, they gave up on us and departed. And when they left, those on Earth with power seized their abandoned technology and sold its capabilities to address distinctly human needs: just a few hours could imbue the user with mystical insight and wisdom; physical perfection and extended life were attainable; menstruation became elective, the menopause a banished curse; men of any age could acquire boundless virility and proportional egos.

Yet over time it became apparent this cornucopia of glorious gifts carried a price: many of those who used the Qall pods were impregnated with their alien cells. In time these divided and formed embryos, which eventually emerged from their unwilling, often unknowing human surrogates, releasing countless more to impregnate others in turn. So Vanguard's job was simple: to contain the spread by killing surrogates before the embryos reached term; get any live examples captured to the surgeons, whose butchery would increase our understanding. The difficulty was that no symptoms were evident until hours, sometimes minutes before embryos emerged, the appearance of dark smudges on the surrogate's skin signalling the approach of an excruciating death. Some people carried cells that never matured. It was a lottery. Frequent collateral damage, coupled with Vanguard's often questionable methods and officers' reputation for doing whatever was necessary to get a bonus, meant they were universally despised.

Nikki wasn't particularly bothered about being hated for what she did. She didn't particularly like herself. What she liked was being renowned. Feared. Notorious, if you really wanted to go for it. Because there lay power, and some level of control.

The teleprinter next to the phone chattered and produced a strip of paper. Nikki exhaled a cloud of smoke and tore off the message:

OFFICERS ADVISED FIVE MINUTES STOP

Still time for a coffee. She clenched the cigar between her teeth, took her flask from her satchel, unscrewed the cup and poured. The birds fluffed and fidgeted and ruffled their shiny black feathers.

'Settle down,' she said. 'You can go when it's time.'

The birds shrieked and squawked in protest. Nikki both loved and loathed them. Another legacy of the Qall, they were as loyal and true as they were ugly and stubborn, adopted by Vanguard because they could sense their creators' presence within human blood. Coupled with angels' intuition, they were essential tools for identifying surrogates.

As she sipped and smoked Nikki looked down on boarded up, looted and abandoned Selly Oak. She saw what remained of the pizza place where she'd once had a date. When she'd first started going out with boys her dad had told her she called the shots. She'd laughed. Good old Dad, giving advice from another age. It turned out the boy in question thought paying for the meal gave him other entitlements. So now she carried a gun and killed surrogates, collaborators and sympathisers, and a fair few innocent bystanders, all in the name of Vanguard. Shots duly called.

She looked at her watch; three minutes. She placed the cup on the platform, took her knife from its sheath, exposed her left forearm and drew red lines in the flesh. She felt pain and pleasure and self-loathing. She was, she reminded herself, slicing deep, the best officer this side of Nechells. Begrudgingly respected even by the meathead daemons.

Always asking what she'd done to get her rank because just being good wasn't enough for her or any other female officer, right? Right. And at the barracks they would visit her bunk, sometimes more than one, and tape her mouth and bind her wings and tell her this was all angels really deserved. And who was she to disagree?

The bloodbirds fluttered and squawked and shrieked as her wounds deepened. Gyre, the oldest and most experienced of her flight, cackled and hopped and flapped beside her.

After a few minutes she'd had enough of his protest. 'All right, I'll stop!' she said. 'You're so bloody judgemental. The pain I cause in others, it's only right I hurt myself.'

Nikki re-sheathed the knife and wiped away the blood. At least the sting was comforting. She rolled down her sleeve and looked at her watch again; not long now.

As she shed her cape, spread her wings and prepared, she reflected on recent times. So much had changed. She had changed. Not so long ago the thought of one last, glorious descent that brought it all to an end was more and more appealing.

Then Steve came out of nowhere and changed everything.

It was a day a few months earlier. A day of blue skies and sunshine and still air. Perfect for an angel to swoop and soar.

She'd sat on the edge of the platform and spread her tobacco leaf wings and basked in the warmth, struggling to stay awake on the slowest of slow days. She'd scanned and re-scanned with her binoculars, smoked and dozed and watched the reflections of the clouds on the canal's oily surface. She'd looked to the north and wondered.

As she settled into the final hour of her shift, the bloodbirds gathered like a thundercloud. She scanned the area beneath them and saw movement near the canal. The birds were never wrong.

She climbed on to the battlements, spread her wings, and jumped.

She'd plunged towards the location of the sighting, bloodbirds racing alongside and shrieking in excitement. Whether because she was unfocussed or tired or complacent, she didn't notice one of the younger, less experienced birds drift close until a collision was almost unavoidable; she banked hard away, but misjudged speed and height and clipped a power line.

There was no current, but the impact sent her spinning. The canal approached in a blur, then she hit the embankment and tumbled through weeds and nettles and abandoned detritus.

She lay still, the quiet and stillness a contrast to the speed and rushing air of a few moments earlier. She was aware of birds circling overhead, others hopping around her in concern.

Having established that she could still move her limbs, Nikki sat up and stretched her wings. They were bruised and scratched, but no serious damage. When she heard movement and saw a man approaching from the tunnel, she scrambled to her feet and drew her gun.

'Vanguard!' she said. 'Stop and identify yourself.'

He stopped. 'You okay?'

She assessed him. Late forties, maybe. Kind eyes, but wary of an officer with a gun. Crude street armour made from salvaged biker gear and scraps of leather.

'Hit that wire,' she said. 'Bloody birds can be a liability sometimes.'

'Even monkeys fall out of trees,' he said.

'You a comedian or philosopher?'

He shrugged. 'You tell me. Would you mind putting the gun away? I'm clean.'

'My birds are unhappy about something.'

'Probably that kid.' He glanced back towards the canal.

She looked beyond him and saw a corpse just inside the tunnel. A child, female, ravaged by the embryonic Qall that had erupted from her body. Nikki sometimes wondered about her baby. Where they had taken it. What they had done to it. What role it had been given. She felt a little dizzy.

'You okay?' he said.

'Fine.'

'You could be in shock.'

'I've crashed harder, believe me.'

'And you look half-starved.'

'You shouldn't have touched her.'

'She's long dead. No chance of contamination. I was trying to cover the body. Even a dead surrogate has a right to some dignity. Especially a kid.' He nodded towards Nikki's arm. 'Anyway, what about you? That looks nasty.'

She lifted her arm; among the other cuts, some healed, some fresh, all self-inflicted, was a gash on her wrist, blood dripping from her fingers.

'It's nothing,' she said.

'Here.' He produced a handkerchief and took a step towards her.

'Stop! Officers are authorised to detain or despatch suspected –'

'– surrogates, collaborators and sympathisers. I know, I've heard it all before. But you're hurt. Look –' He unzipped his jacket to reveal his neck, then pushed up each sleeve to show his forearms – the most common places the first dark smudges appeared on surrogates' skin. There was just a tattoo in script-style lettering: *Janet.* 'See?' he said. 'I'm no threat.'

'That's what they all say.' She adjusted her footing and winced.

'You in pain?'

'No.'

They looked at each other for a moment, then he offered his right hand.

'Name's Steve.'

She looked him in the eye. What was this guy playing at? Why wasn't he scared of her? Everyone was scared of her. 'Angel 602, Birmingham South.'

He raised his eyebrows.

What harm could it do? 'Nikki,' she said.

He withdrew his hand with a shrug. 'When did you last eat?'

She couldn't remember. 'This morning.'

'Can you walk?'

'I'm not a pensioner.'

'Okay, so how about you come back to mine –'

'Back to yours?'

'Come back to mine and I'll treat that cut and make you something to eat. I live right there.' He pointed to one of the blocks visible between the buildings. 'Then you just forget to file a report and no one knows any of this happened.'

'If I can get to a callbox a van will pick me up.'

'All the boxes round here have been trashed, so you're a Vanguard angel looking at a long walk at street level with a twisted ankle, bruised wings and a bloody arm. That would make you either really tough or really stupid.'

Really tough or really stupid. She'd have to think about that one.

She looked at him. The birds were still agitated, but his skin was clear.

Really tough or really stupid.

The young bird that had caused Nikki's crash landed nearby and hopped across the embankment towards her. She shot it without hesitation, leaving nothing but a cloud of black feathers. The other birds fell silent.

She holstered her gun. 'Okay, Steve,' she said. 'Your place it is. But try anything funny and you'll end up like that, got it?'

They emerged from the stairwell at the fifth floor, her birds circling alongside and watching through the windows.

'This used to be student accommodation,' he said. He was a little breathless.

'I know. I used to live round here. Bournville.'

'Ah, right. Up the posh end. Lift hasn't worked in years. First they took the metals, then the rubbers and the plastics. Even if there was power the bloody thing wouldn't run. It's a bit of a pain but I'd rather climb a few steps than be at street level. Here we are.'

They reached a door with sheets of metal mesh across the front, secured with three heavy-duty padlocks. Nikki watched as he took a bunch of keys from his pocket. The birds were still acting up, but there was something intriguing about him. He was a fair bit older, and certainly not brawny like the Vanguard daemons she usually ended up with, by choice or otherwise, but the tingle in her belly was real enough. Maybe it was his vulnerability. Or the apparent lack of fear. Or the fact that he was being nice to her. No one was ever nice to her. She wasn't sure what to do about it.

He removed the mesh from the frame and nodded for her to go inside.

'Ladies first,' he said.

'First time anyone's called me a lady.'

'I can't believe that.'

'It's the uniform,' she said. 'Scares 'em shitless.'

'So take it off.'

Nikki looked him in the eye.

'No, I just meant... Doesn't matter. I'll get these locks.'

She looked at him; was he actually blushing?

The apartment was small: combined cooking and living area, bathroom, tiny balcony; her birds were already lined up on the rail looking in.

There were sketches all over the place. Dark. Abstract. Some erotic. And in the kitchenette, a photo of Steve with a woman and two kids.

'Want a drink?' he said as he took off his jacket. 'I've got a bit of whiskey but no ice. Or if you'd rather just eat –'

'Love a drink. But just a small one. Another crash I can do without.'

He poured a whiskey and gave her the glass. 'I'll get something for that cut.'

As he went into the bathroom she sat on the small sofa and folded her wings and cape around her. She lit a cigar and sipped the drink. Steve returned a moment later with a bandage and antiseptic cream.

'Don't smoke that in here, please,' he said. 'It stinks.' He fetched a saucer and held it in front of her.

She stared at him for a moment, then stubbed it out.

'You draw all these?' she asked as he knelt in front of her.

'Just a form of self-expression and escapism.'

She nodded towards an image that seemed to be two women engaged in an erotic act. 'And what are you expressing there exactly?'

He didn't look up. 'Suppose it's open to interpretation. Hold out your arm.'

She hesitated, then reached out.

He glanced up at her as he applied cream.

'What's the matter?' she said.

'You're a Vanguard Angel.'

'And?'

'And you've got a reputation for cruelty and brutality. Rounding people up and carting them off to those so-called observation camps.'

'Is that what you see in me? Cruelty and brutality?'

'You're different to most Vanguard I've encountered, I must admit. Must be tough.'

'Because I'm a petite female?'

'Your assumption of my prejudice is prejudicial.'

She shrugged.

'Why do you do it?' he said.

She'd had no desire to become an angel. But as they sharpened their knives the surgeons pointed out that they'd repaired her injuries and saved her life; wasn't she grateful for the opportunity to give something back? Didn't she want to make her family proud?

Truth was, Mum and Dad never got on. She presumed they must have loved each other at some point in some way, otherwise she wouldn't exist. But when Dad wasn't pissed up and punchy, Mum was out being generous with her charms. Six of one and half a dozen of the other. Then Nikki went home one day and found her dad with a suitcase on wheels. 'I'm off to Edinburgh,' he'd said, just as if he was popping to the shop for a few bits. 'The one with the castle? Still work up there apparently. Want to come?'

Scotland was cold and wet and everyone walked around in those stupid wax jackets. Besides, if he was at the other end of the country he couldn't visit her room when he'd had a few.

When she'd said no thanks he'd just shrugged and left. Looking back, he was all packed up and ready to go, so she probably wasn't part of the picture anyway. Mum never did come home.

'Revenge,' she said.

'And these marks.' He nodded at the cuts on her forearm as he bandaged the wound. 'Are they revenge too?'

'Mind your own business and be a decent host.' She held out her empty glass. 'Make it a big one.'

'I thought you didn't want much.'

'A girl can't smoke, she might as well drink.'

He secured the bandage with a safety pin, poured some more whiskey, then took his own glass and sat beside her.

'You want to talk about it?'

'Now you're a psychotherapist?' She drank.

'You're too delicate for that sort of thing.'

'I kill people for money.'

'So the uniform's for protection.'

'You can talk. You look like a prospect for some middle-aged saddos motorcycle club in all that leather. Those trousers – please.'

He glanced down. 'Made them myself,' he said.

'No shit.'

'Must admit they're pretty uncomfortable.'

She leaned in close and gazed into his eyes.

'So take them off,' she said.

The fact that he simply finished his drink then insisted on walking with her to the nearest working callbox was confusing. For once the choice was hers and he didn't want to. Why didn't he want to? They always wanted to.

But a couple of days later she found him waiting outside the Vanguard building at the end of her shift. She hurried over, grabbed him by one arm and dragged him into a side street. Her birds swarmed around them, flapping and diving and pecking.

'What the hell are you doing here?' she said, glancing back.

'I bought you some flowers.' He smiled and presented a thin bouquet of weeds gathered from patches of wasteland and the cracked walls of ruined buildings.

'I'm a Vanguard angel, Steve. If they find out I've been with a surry they'll cut off my wings, lynch me and then come looking for you.'

'I'm not a surrogate.'

'You're a lunatic is what you are.'

'I'd prefer romantic. Although I admit that as flowers go they are a bit shit.'

She batted them to the floor with one hand then kissed him with a fevered passion.

He pushed her back. 'Take it easy.'

She gripped his wrists. 'Don't tell me what to do,' she said. 'And stop being nice to me. I don't deserve it.' Then she shed her cape and wrapped her wings around him.

There followed an emotional storm that carried them both into uncharted territory. He felt new confidence, his fragile masculinity reaffirmed as this young, powerful, beautiful creature showed interest in him; she felt able to be herself in a way she'd never before experienced.

He didn't seem to want from her the things everyone else did. There was no pressure to be or do anything. They'd sit in his apartment and talk books and music and make each other laugh. He'd make feasts from whatever scraps he could find. Sometimes he would sketch her. His old-school romancing amused her; the fact that it amused her amused him in turn. Their physical relationship was tentative and warm. Nikki struggled to process these feelings. Pre-invasion there would have been judgements about the difference in their ages, but in this new world few had time for such trivialities.

When on watch, she wondered what he was doing, would long to be with him and talk to him. But with her birds constantly agitated and emotions she could not control, as time passed it became clear that issues and loyalties would have to be addressed.

She suggested they climb a tower: a repurposed electricity pylon outside the city with an observation platform at the second level.

'We might get caught,' he said as she unlocked the security gate.

'If that wasn't a possibility it wouldn't be naughty, would it. And then what would be the point?' She opened the gate. 'Ladies first.'

He looked up. The structure looked pretty solid, but even though it wasn't as high as a lot of the others, it was still a long way.

'What if I fall?'

'Jesus Christ, Steve. If you fall you'll probably die. Now do you want to climb a tower with me or not?'

Nikki was swift and agile. She seemed to barely touch the ladder's metal rungs as she climbed, her cape and wings drifting like banners behind her. Steve found things more taxing. She laughed as she helped him through the gate on to the platform. 'Good job I didn't pick a higher one,' she said. 'You'd never have made it.'

He caught his breath. 'If your aim was to make me feel my age you've certainly succeeded.'

'My aim was to get you away from the city for a while.'

He smiled. 'It's a lovely idea. Thank you.' He kissed her cheek then walked to the rail. 'Great view.'

'One of the perks.'

'Don't you get lonely?'

'It can be the most peaceful job in the world. The purest solitude. For now we're the best option, but I suppose the tech will come back and replace us eventually. Not sure what I'll do then.'

He looked up. 'Those clouds,' he said. 'Proper cotton wool jobs. You could almost touch them.' The birds circled and shrieked and cawed above them. 'Don't those things ever shut up?'

'They're jealous.'

'Of me?'

'Of everybody. But especially you. Because they know that when I'm with you I don't need them.' She reached out, turned his face towards hers and kissed him.

She responded to Steve's caress as he ran his hands down her back, across her flying muscles and her soft, sensitive wings. He had by now learned the things that made her shiver. But she knew this could not happen. Not this time. She stepped away from him, turned and looked across the fields.

'What's the matter?' he said.

'Your area's going to be cleansed. Day after tomorrow.'

'How do you know?'

'I just know. But it means you've got time to leave.'

'Why would I leave?'

'Because you're a surrogate.'

'I'm not a surrogate, Nikki.'

'The birds never lie. I'm on that squad, Steve. If you're arrested –'

'I won't be arrested.'

'If you're arrested they'll cart you off and turn you inside out.'

'Why don't you believe me? Because of these stupid birds?'

'The birds are never wrong.'

'Well that's obviously not true.'

She started walking backwards away from him. There were tears in her eyes. 'You don't want those surgeons getting their hands on you. You know what they do, Steve? They need cells for their experiments, so they take them from captured surrogates. When they've removed cells new ones form, so they'll keep you alive, milking you until there's nothing left. It's a living hell. If you're not a surrogate, fine. Go somewhere and live a life.'

'What about us?'

'What about us, Steve?'

'If you leave Vanguard we can be together. Properly together. We could go somewhere far away. Scotland, maybe; how about that?'

Nikki laughed. 'Scotland. What, like Edinburgh? The one with the castle?'

He looked puzzled. 'Yeah. Sure. If that's what you want.' There was a long silence. 'Nikki?'

'You don't leave Vanguard, Steve. You don't even try. So you'd better go. Because if you don't, you might just get some unexpected visitors.'

'What do you mean?'

'Just go, Steve. For both our sakes.'

She looked at him for a moment, then turned and sprinted across the platform and dived into the sky.

Nikki swept low across the countryside, bloodbirds shrieking and cavorting all around her, the wings she'd never wanted spread wide.

The teleprinter chattered. Nikki flicked away the cigar stub, screwed the cup back on her flask, then tore off the strip of paper.

BIRDS AUTHORISED FOR RELEASE STOP

She looked across at her flight; they were watching her, all beady eyes, beak and claws. To the east, Vanguard helicopters were on their way to drop the rest of the angels and daemons assigned to the sweep. She had a few minutes tops.

'Right, you ugly sods,' she said. 'Go and do your work.'

The birds launched themselves into the air, then flew around the clock tower as if reluctant to hunt.

'What's the matter?' she said. 'Shoo! Scram! Go and find him.'

The birds gradually began to disperse, but their confusion was evident in the lack of formation. Could she dare to hope that he'd gone after all?

The birds were circling aimlessly; some in the vicinity of Steve's block, but still lacking intent.

'Okay,' she said to herself. 'If you want something done...'

She put down the binoculars and stood on the battlements. She was not much higher than his apartment. In perfect conditions this wouldn't be a problem, but conditions were far from perfect. She flexed her wings, encouraging blood into their thin surfaces, and took several deep breaths.

'Here I come,' she said. 'Ready or not.'

As she landed elegantly outside his building, thundering helicopters swept cones of light across the streets, patrol vans broadcast warnings, and Vanguard's finest hunted prey. She entered quickly and ran up the stairs, accompanied by a dozen or so unquiet birds.

The screens on his door were locked from the inside. The mesh rattled as she banged upon it.

'Steve! *Steve!*'

The door opened. 'Nikki.'

'Why are you still here?'

'Keeping my head down. It'll be fine. Come inside.'

He removed the screens and she strode past him into the apartment, accompanied by her birds.

'Do these things really have to be here?'

She turned to face him. 'Why didn't you go?'

'Because I'm clean and not on Vanguard's radar.'

'Everybody is on Vanguard's radar, Steve. Especially the surry who's consorting with an angel.' She looked at him. 'Do you trust me?' she said.

'Trust?' He took her hands in his. 'You don't get it, do you, Nikki. I've only ever been in love twice. One of them I married – the other one is you.'

Tears welled. She turned and walked away from him. 'This can't happen, Steve. Even if you were clean –'

'I am clean.'

'Even if you were clean and I could leave Vanguard and we could run off into the sunset together – what then? You get bored? I get bored? It all goes tits up and we're far away and alone?'

'Or we live happily and grow old together.'

'You really believe that sort of thing happens?'

'Don't you?'

There was a bang on the door and a barked warning.

'What's that?'

'Sorry, Steve,' she said. 'Guess it's a case of better the devil you know.'

'Nikki?'

She took a step back, her eyes full of tears, as a squad of daemons burst into the room, all testosterone, guns and shielding. The birds shrieked and squawked and were booted aside as officers slammed Steve to the floor and bound him tight.

'I'm clean! Nikki. Tell them, Nikki!'

'Shut it, surry!' An officer pistol-whipped Steve into silence, then he was hefted to his feet and manhandled away.

The senior officer looked down at her; his armoured physique seemed to fill the room. 'You raise this ticket?'

She nodded.

'Then you better call it in.'

'And the bonus?'

'Got enough on my plate. Take it.'

He turned and left, and suddenly it was just Nikki and the birds. They continued to flutter and flap and squawk. 'Calm down,' she said as she walked to the phone and dialled. 'It's all over.'

'Vanguard control,' said the operator.

'Angel 602,' Nikki said quietly. 'IC1 male confirmed in custody. Aston Webb Boulevard, Selly Oak.'

'IC1 male in custody. Thank you, 602. Well done.' The operator rang off and Nikki put down the receiver. She looked around the room. They had laughed here. They had loved here. She had felt loved here. But in the end she had no choice. Such was her life.

As she looked around the room she saw a new sketch: a winged female hovering above a pleading man. She knelt. As she reached out to the picture her sleeve rose up her arm; and there on her wrist, a patch of dark, oily skin, like an old bruise – spreading fast.

The clock tower at the University of Birmingham was Nikki's favourite post. As she stood on the battlements she looked across the city to the north and wondered.

The kid who had strapped her wings together with a belt had looked fearfully at the marks spreading across her body. She'd told him not to be scared. He was reluctant, but even at eight or nine years old knew better than to disobey an angel – especially one as beautiful as this.

According to Processing there was no sign of alien cells in Steve's body. The birds were reacting to their presence in her all along. So much for an angel's intuition. So much for the wings she never wanted.

She looked down and prepared for one last, glorious descent. At least this time the choice would be hers.

# About the Authors

**Iain M. Banks** (1954 – 2013) was a Scottish author, critically acclaimed for both his mainstream fiction and science fiction. His first book, *The Wasp Factory* (1984), drew instant praise and censure, and established Banks as one of the most important voices of his generation. In 2013 *The Times* included him in a list of "The 50 greatest British writers since 1945". His first SF novel *Consider Phlebas* (for which his middle initial M was introduced) was published in 1987, and became the first of his seminal Culture series. Iain Banks' work has been adapted for TV, radio, and the theatre, and has won numerous awards.

**Stephen Baxter** was born in Liverpool, and now lives in Northumberland. He sold his first short stories in 1987. *His* fondly remembered Novacon was just a few years later – and his story contribution was set in his ongoing 'Xeelee Sequence' universe.

Born in Haworth, West Yorkshire, **Eric Brown** has lived in Australia, India and Greece. He has won the British Science Fiction Award twice for his short stories, and his novel *Helix Wars* was shortlisted for the 2012 Philip K. Dick Award. He's published over seventy books and his latest are the SF novella *On Arcturus VII*, and the novel *Murder at Standing Stone Manor,* eighth in the Langham and Dupré mystery series set in the 1950s. He lives near Dunbar in Scotland, and his website is at: ericbrown.co.uk

**Jaine Fenn** writes fiction, video-games and endless lists. After having been banned from Novacon in its, and her, teens for a gronk-related incident, she was the Guest of Honour at Novacon 42. She is the author of the Hidden Empire space opera series and the Shadowlands science fantasy duology. This story is located in one of those universes.

**Peter F. Hamilton** was born in Rutland, but now lives in Somerset with his wife and two children, along with a not-terribly-well-trained labradoodle dog. He began writing short stories in 1987, and three years later sold his first novel, *Mindstar Rising*, to Macmillan. Since then he's written several series, including the Night's Dawn trilogy, the seven books in the Commonwealth Universe, and the Salvation Sequence, as well as two stand-alone novels *Fallen Dragon* and *Great North Road.* He has just finished writing the final book of The Arkship trilogy.

**Paul McAuley** is the author of a score of novels and more than a hundred short stories, as well as a Doctor Who novella and a BFI Film Classic monograph on Terry Gilliam's film *Brazil.* His first novel, *Four Hundred Billion Stars*, won the Philip K. Dick Memorial Award; his fifth, *Fairyland*, won the Arthur C. Clarke and John W. Campbell Awards. Other works have won the Sidewise Award, the British Fantasy Award, and the Theodore Sturgeon Memorial Award. His latest novel is *War of the Maps.*

**Juliet E McKenna** is a British fantasy author living in the Cotswolds, UK. Loving history, myth and other worlds since she first learned to read, she has written fifteen epic fantasy novels so far, starting with *The Thief's Gamble* (1999). *The Green Man's Heir* (2018), wass her first modern fantasy rooted in British folklore, followed by *The Green Man's Foe, The Green Man's Silence*, and *The Green Man's Challenge.* Her short stories and novellas venture into darker fantasy, steampunk and SF. She has also written murder mysteries set in ancient Greece as J M Alvey.

**Ian R MacLeod** is the author of seven critically acclaimed novels and five short story collections, plus two large new 'greatest hits' e-book collections, *Everywhere* and *Nowhere.* His work has won the Arthur C Clarke Award for the Year's Best Novel, along with Sidewise Award (twice) for Alternative-World Fiction and (again twice) the World Fantasy Award, and the John W Campbell Memorial award. He lives in the riverside town of Bewdley in England. He maintains a website at www.ianrmacleod.com and his Twitter feed is @IanRMacleod1

**Anne Nicholls**' published works include the acclaimed novels *Mindsail* and *The Brooch of Azure Midnight.* Her short story "Roman Games" was reprinted in the year's best fantasy. Having been the editor of the *SciFi Zone*, one of the earliest online magazines, she moved into the role of agony aunt for both Tiscali and the Department for Children, Schools and Families. Her collection of short stories, *Music from the Fifth Planet,* was published by Alchemy Press. She is currently having fun writing the Fortyfied trilogy, a humorous urban fantasy.

**Justina Robson** is an award-winning author of novels, novellas and short stories. Most of her books and stories are Science Fiction, dealing in particular with transhumanism, genetic engineering, nanotech and human evolution. A graduate of "Clarion West" (1996) she has gone on to teach at the Arvon Foundation in the UK and in 2005 she was a judge for the Arthur C Clarke. In addition to her all-original work she also wrote *Transformers: The Covenant of Primus*, the official history of the Transformers in the Prime Continuum, in 2013. She lives in Yorkshire with her husband, children and pets.

**Geoff Ryman**'s work has won numerous awards including the John W. Campbell Memorial Award, the Arthur C. Clarke Award (twice for *The Child Garden* and for *Air*), the James W Tiptree Memorial Award (for *Air)*, the Philip K. Dick Memorial Award (for *253)*, the British Science Fiction Association Award (three times, once for the series of interviews with African writers) and the Canadian Sunburst Award (twice for *Air* a volume of short stories, *Paradise Tales*). In 2012 he won a Nebula Award for his Nigeria-set novelette "What We Found". He is currently the administrator of the Nommo Awards for Speculative Fiction by Africans.

**Martin Sketchley** is a writer, editor, Royal Literary Fund Fellow and creative coach. "Bloodbirds" is a sequel to his 2010 story "Songbirds". Visit www.martinsketchley.com.

**Kari Sperring** is the author of novels *Living with Ghosts* (2009) and *The Grass King's Concubine* (2012), both via DAW, novellas *Serpent* Rose (2019) and *Rose Knot* (2021), both via NewCon Press, and an assortment of short stories. As Kari Maund, she has written and published five books and many articles on Celtic and Viking history and co-authored with Phil nanson a book on the history and real people behind her favourite novel, *The Three Musketeers.* She is British and lives in Cambridge, with her partner Phil and three very determined cats.

**Adrian Tchaikovsky** is the author of the acclaimed ten-book Shadows of the Apt series, the Echoes of the Fall series, and other novels, novellas and short stories including *Children of Time* (which won the Arthur C. Clarke award in 2016), and its sequel, *Children of Ruin* (which won the British Science Fiction Award in 2020). He lives in Leeds in the UK and his hobbies include entomology and board and role-playing games.

**Ian Whates** is the author of eight published novels, plus two co-authored, and some eighty short stories. In 2019 he received the Karl Edward Wagner Award from the British Fantasy Society, while he has also been shortlisted for the Philip K. Dick Award and on three occasions for BSFA Awards. In 2006 he founded NewCon Press by accident and has now edited some forty anthologies for NewCon and other publishers. In 2004 he attended Novacon 34, his first convention, and they have failed to get rid of him ever since.

Novacon Guests and Chairs

| | Guests(s) | Chair(s) |
|---|---|---|
| Novacon 1971 | James White | Vernon Brown |
| Novacon 2 | Doreen Rogers | Pauline Dungate |
| Novacon 3 | Ken Bulmer | Hazel Reynolds |
| Novacon 4 | Ken Slater | Jack Cohen |
| Novacon 5 | Dan Morgan | Rog Peyton |
| Novacon 6 | Dave Kyle | Stan Eling |
| Novacon 7 | John Brunner | Stan Eling |
| Novacon 8 | Anne McCaffrey | Laurence Miller |
| Novacon 9 | Christopher Priest | Rog Peyron |
| Novacon 10 | Brian W. Aldiss | Rog Peyton |
| Novacon 11 | Bob Shaw | Paul Oldroyd |
| Novacon 12 | Harry Harrison | Rog Peyton |
| Novacon 13 | Lisa Tuttle | Phil Probert |
| Novacon 14 | Rob Holdstock | Steve Green |
| Novacon 15 | James White | Phil Probert |
| | Dave Langford | |
| Novacon 16 | E.C. Tubb | Tony Berry |
| | Chris Evans | |
| Novacon 17 | Iain Banks | Bernie Evans |
| Novacon 18 | Gary Kilworth | Tony Berry |
| Novacon 19 | Geoff Ryman | Martin Tudor |
| Novacon 20 | Jack Cohen | Bernie Evans |
| Novacon 21 | Colin Greenland | Nick Mills |
| Novacon 22 | Storm Constantine | Helena Bowles |
| Novacon 23 | Stephen Baxter | Carol Morton |
| Novacon 24 | Graham Joyce | Richard Standage |
| Novacon 25 | Brian Aldiss | Tony Morton |
| | Harry Harrison | |
| | Bob Shaw | |
| | Iain Banks | |
| Novacon 26 | David Gemmell | Carol Morton |
| Novacon 27 | Peter F. Hamilton | Martin Tudor |
| Novacon 28 | Paul J. McAuley | Martin Tudor |
| Novacon 29 | Ian Stewart | Carol Morton |
| Novacon 30 | Christopher Priest | Tony Berry |
| | Rog Peyton | |
| | David A. Hardy | |
| Novacon 31 | Gwyneth Jones | Tony Berry |
| Novacon 32 | Ian McDonald | Martin Tudor |
| Novacon 33 | Jon Courtenay Grimwood | Martin Tudor |
| Novacon 34 | Ian Watson | Martin Tudor |
| Novacon 35 | Alastair Reynolds | Tony Berry |
| Novacon 36 | Ken MacLeod | Tony Berry |
| Novacon 37 | Charles Stross | Steve Green |
| Novacon 38 | Ian R. MacLeod | Helena Bowles |
| Novacon 39 | Justina Robson | Alice Lawson |

Novacon Guests and Chairs

| | Guests(s) | Chair(s) |
|---|---|---|
| Novacon 40 | Iain Banks<br>Brian W. Aldiss | Vernon Brown |
| Novacon 41 | John Meaney | Steve Lawson |
| Novacon 42 | Jaine Fenn | Tony Berry |
| Novacon 43 | Jo Walton | Yvonne Rowse |
| Novacon 44 | Kari Sperring | Steve Green |
| Novacon 45 | Stan & Anne Nicholls | Tony Berry |
| Novacon 46 | Juliet McKenna | Douglas Spencer |
| Novacon 47 | Adrian Tchaikovsky | Helena Bowles<br>Alice Lawson |
| Novacon 48 | Chris Beckett | Dave Hicks |
| Novacon 49 | Mike Carey | Steve Lawson |
| Novacon 50 | Christopher Priest<br>Chris (Fangorn) Baker<br>Claire North<br>Emma Newman | Tony Berry<br>Alice Lawson |

Below is a list of Committee, Staff and Volunteers who have made the many Novacons possible. We would also like to thank the many Gophers not mentioned here; we couldn't have done it without you!

Chris Baker
Doug Bell
Ray Bradbury
Claire Brialey
Tim Broadribb
Chris Chivers
Kevin Clarke
Cat Coast
Noel Collyer
Vicky Cook
David Cooper
Dave Cox
Serena Culfeather
Julia Daly
A. Denham
Theresa Derwin
Chris Donaldson
A. Donnelly
Helen Eling
Mick Evans
Nic Farey
Sarah Freakley
Nigel Furlong
Jenny Glover
Steve Glover
Carol Goodwin
Ann Green
Dave Haden
John Harrold
Eve Harvey
John Harvey
Liese Hoare
Martin Hoare
Robert Hoffman
Dave Holmes
Alan Hunter
Jan Huxley
Tim Illingworth
Al Johnston
Marsha Jones
Steve Jones
Paul Kincaid
Linda Krawecki
Christina Lake
Dave Lally
Erhard Leder
Ian Maule
Janice Maule
William McCabe
Pat McMurray
Chris Murphy
Joseph Nicholas
Keith Oborn
Krystyna Oborn
Anne Page
Darroll Pardoe
Rosemary Pardoe
Carol Pearson
Eunice Pearson
Arline Peyton
Catherine Pickersgill
Greg Pickersgill
Mark Plummer
Graham Poole
Stephen Rogers
Mike Scott
Mike Siddall
Maureen Spellar
Maggie Standage-Bowles
Gary Starr
Alex Storer
Stephen Tudor
Paul Vincent
Chris Walton
Pam Wells
Pete Weston
John Wilkes
Geoff Williams
John Wilson

## Also from NewCon Press

**Paper Hearts – Justina Robson**
Are humans to be trusted with the important things, or would an AI be better suited to the job? If an AI truly cared about humanity, would it sit back and watch us bumble along, making a mess of things, or would it step in to guide us? Despite the best of intentions, could such intervention ever work? At the end of the day, are any of us – human or AI – truly free?

**On Arcturus VII – Eric Brown**
Former pilot and planetary pioneer Jonathan James is tempted out of retirement by an offer he can't refuse. It means going back to the one place he vowed never to return to: Arcturus Seven. A Closed Planet; a hothouse world where every plant and animal is hell-bent on killing and consuming you; the place that cost him the life of the only woman he has ever truly loved.

**Rose Knot – Kari Sperring**
When Gaheris is tasked with escorting his brother's wife, Llinos, home from court, neither suspect the tragic consequences that will result, as they lose their way and become stranded within a beguiling forest. A gripping tale of love, infidelity, loyalty, misguided intentions and the price of nobility, featuring some of the lesser known members of King Arthur's court.

**Spoils of War – Adrian Tchaikovsky (Tales of the Apt: 1)**
Tales of the Apt gathers together short stories from disparate places and supplements them with a wealth of new material. Together, they combine to provide a different perspective, an alternative history that parallels the *Shadows of the Apt* books, where epic fantasy meets steampunk, filling in gaps and revealing intriguing backstories along the way.

**Pelquin's Comet – Ian Whates (Dark Angels: 1)**
A group of misfits, ex-soldiers and adventurers set out to find a cache of alien technology, intent on making their fortune. They are not the only interested party and find themselves in a race against corporate agents, hunted by the authorities, and facing enemies without and within, all under the watchful eye of Drake, agent of the bank financing them, who has his own dark secrets.